# FATE CONQUERED

## BOOK THREE

### TARA LYTLE

SCRIBBLED READS

Published by Scribbled Reads

E-Book ISBN: 9781960319012

Paperback ISBN: 978-1-960319-03-6

Hardcover ISBN: 978-1-960319-05-0

# DEDICATION

For Seth who conquered my heart.

ABERRON
PORTS END
JAYDORIA
DRAMERA
FRESTAN
HAYLORE
STRELL
BERUND
ORINDALER
N
W
E
S
M

KORRUN
CARASMILLE
LAND
THIMBLETON
TRIVAIL FOREST
ABERRON CLIFFS
PRASTIS
LOCHENLOCK
KISTER
SAREN
MANARIA
CAILEN
PENDRA
CALLAN OUTPOST
NEDRA
...... Isabelle's Journey

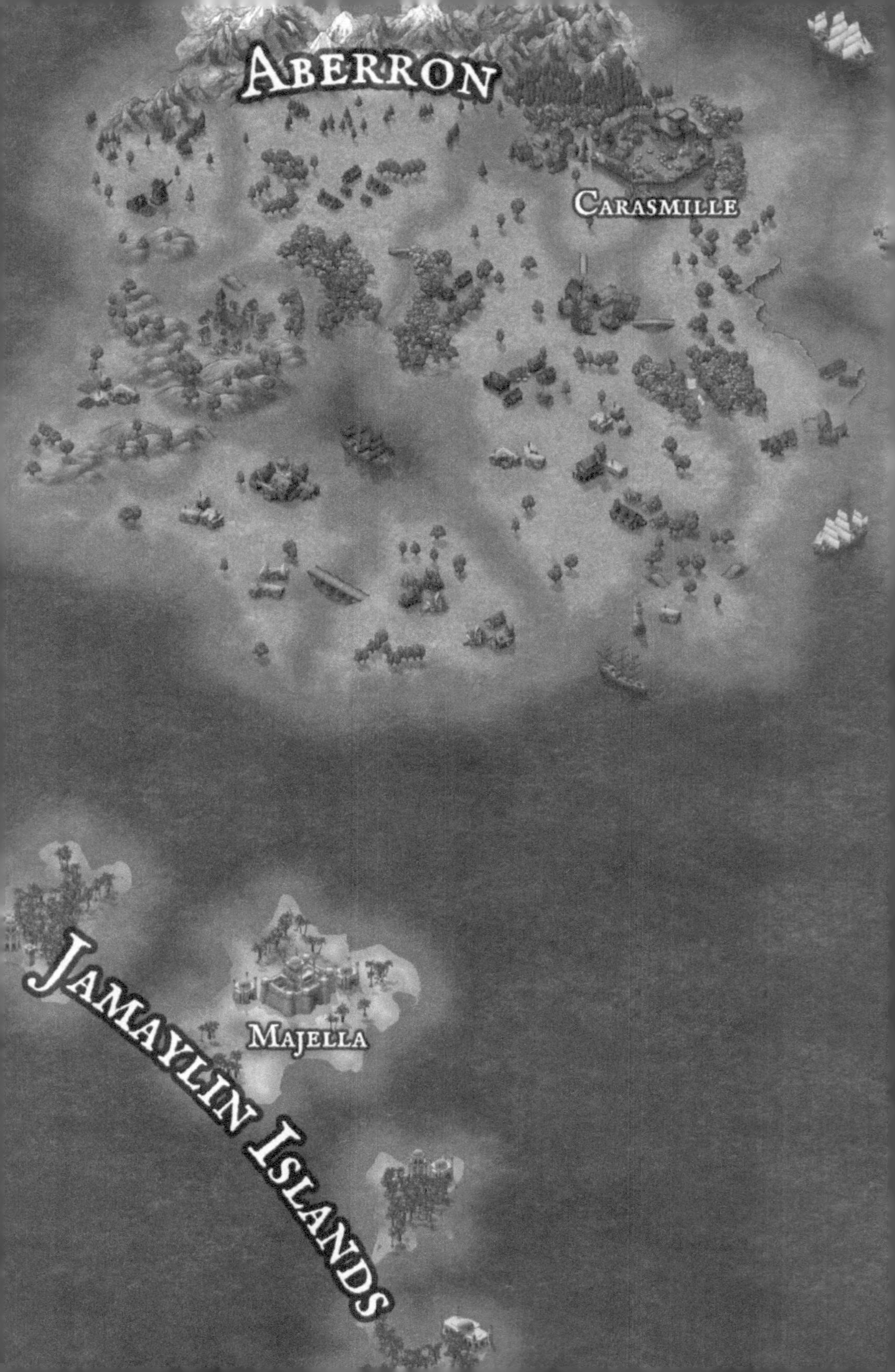

Aberron
Carasmille
Majella
Jamaylin Islands

NISTIER
LA
WEYUT
KASHTINE
DREGAITIA
RAYLORE
MACHRA
RAYNORA
HESTAS
SARZE
REECHI

# PROLOGUE

WALKED HAND IN HAND with Nathan and Adel, my new adoptive parents, to Saren's fall harvest picnic, my excitement bubbling over. Adel told me they had this party every year, and she'd even outfitted me in a new dress—yellow with sunflowers and white lace—just for the occasion. I loved it.

Nathan told me everyone always brought their best dishes. I eagerly anticipated the pies, especially the berry one Adel and I made. When we got to the picnic, I saw a number of tables overloaded with food, my mouth watering as I stared at the desserts.

Many families had spread their blankets under the shade of the apple and peach trees. Nathan chose a spot for us and laid out a quilt while Adel unloaded the basket of food we had prepared.

"Go play and have fun." Nathan smiled as he made a shooing motion. "We'll come get you when we're ready to eat."

Adel's eyes twinkled. "Stefan should be around here somewhere."

With the mention of my new friend, I dashed off to search for him, darting around the blankets and families, my gaze bouncing from one face to the next. Just when I was about to give up, I spotted him with a group of other children close to our age. I hurried over.

Stefan waved. "Hi, Iz!" He'd taken to shortening my name from Isabelle to Iz, but I didn't mind. I kind of liked it, even.

I waved back.

His eyes widened as he looked at my clothing. "Wow, that's a fancy dress!"

I smiled shyly and nodded.

"We were about to play a game of chase," he said. "Want to play with us?"

Another boy named Ned stepped forward. "She can't play."

I stiffened at the anger I saw on his face.

"Why not?" Stefan asked, his face hardening.

Ned pointed to the Mark of the Gods on the back of my hand. "She's cursed by the Gods! That's why she can't talk. She will maim us like her."

Hurt blossomed. I wouldn't do anything of the sort.

"That's not true!" Stefan's hands curled into fists at his sides.

Another boy, Josiah, spoke in a singsong voice. "Isabelle is cursed. Isabelle is cursed. Get too close and you'll catch your death!"

Ned and a few others joined in the cruel chanting.

My lower lip trembled as tears formed in earnest. They would never want to be friends with me. I turned and ran, needing to get away. Stefan called after me, but I didn't stop. I would go home, where the bullies couldn't taunt me. My legs pumping, I raced out of the orchard and into the neighboring cornfield, wincing as a few of the leaves on the stalks slapped me as I hurried past.

The back door slammed against the wall as I raced into the kitchen. I wiped at my tears, then brought my left hand up to look at my birthmark. I hated it! I was never going to be liked as long as it was there. It needed to go. If I could make it disappear, maybe other people wouldn't hate me.

I dragged a step stool over to the kitchen sink. Turning on the water, I let it fill while I reached for a washcloth. Then I dumped it and half a bag of soap shavings into the sink along with the washcloth. Soon, bubbles rose to the edge. I quickly deactivated the water and felt around for the washcloth. Once I had it in my grasp, I scrubbed at the birthmark. When it didn't budge, I scrubbed harder, not caring that it was starting to hurt. I didn't want this birthmark anymore. It had to go.

"Isabelle!" Nathan and Adel burst through the back door.

I watched their expressions switch from panic to relief to confusion and finally concern.

Adel gently pulled me away from the sink. She gasped as she saw my bloody hand. "Oh, my darling girl." She held my hand up. "Were you trying to get rid of your birthmark?"

Tears streamed down my cheeks as I nodded.

Adel picked me up and sat in a kitchen chair, pulling me onto her lap. Nathan sat next to us.

"I happen to like your birthmark very much." Adel smiled at me. "It makes you special."

"You're perfect just the way you are," Nathan said. "Anybody who says differently will answer to me." He made a show of muscles.

I liked that they wanted to comfort me, but I knew the truth. My birthmark wasn't normal. One day it would tell my fate. My gut said it would be a curse.

# CHAPTER ONE

 WOKE TO THE DARKNESS of night, snuggled against Andrew, my mind racing despite the ache in my bones and muscles. I felt too agitated to sleep any longer.

My family and I, plus the First and Second Waves, were resting for the night in the Trivail forest with plans to continue to Carasmille when morning came. We had successfully beaten the Dregans and ended the war between us. It was time to rejoice and return to our normal lives.

Only, I didn't feel much like celebrating—not after the war had cost me two precious lives, Stefan, my best friend, and Nathan, my adoptive father. I recalled how they looked in the Realm of Souls just moments ago when Isaac, a Fate over Fates, had shown them to me. They were happy and safe, and the grieving in my heart turned bittersweet.

I gently extracted myself from Andrew, trying not to wake him. Sitting up, all I could hear was soft breathing and snoring. The smallness of the shack we rested in forced us to sleep close. I waited a few heartbeats before I stood, then, using the light from the embers of the fire, hopped over my family members and away from the shack.

Head down, I walked aimlessly along a narrow path between the two-person tents outside the shack. My mind bounced between seeing Nathan and Stefan in the Realm of Souls and Isaac revealing that Haldren, a God over Gods, had created the dual bond I shared with the princes. Confusion and doubt dominated me. Haldren told me not to listen to Isaac, who said the same thing about Haldren. In reality, I couldn't trust either of them, nor could I escape their powerful grasp. The most powerful mage alive, powerless. I hated being subjected to the whims of the Gods. I craved a solitude that would never be mine.

I walked into a group of soldiers standing watch at the end of my red heat dome. I stopped short before their fire.

"Lady Isabelle," they said in surprise.

I backed up a few steps. "Sorry, didn't mean to disturb."

A soldier with long dark hair that rivaled Braidus's silky locks set himself in front of the others, his silver earring flashing in the light of the flames. "You should be resting."

I shrugged, a corner of my lips curving in a wistful smile. "Can't sleep." I turned to go, but he stopped me with a gentle hand on my shoulder.

"It is not safe for you to walk alone among us at night," he insisted. "Not all men can be trusted."

Another soldier commented with concern, "The commander will have our heads if we knowingly let her wander."

"We should escort her back before we get flayed alive," a third soldier said worriedly.

I wanted to laugh at how they feared my brother. I also admired how he instilled a healthy respect in his men. Joshua never threatened idly, always following through.

"Please don't trouble yourselves," I said as I dashed around the men and exited the heat dome I had created into the heavy snow. I needed a moment to myself, and I wouldn't get it inside the campground. Within minutes, the instant cold had me shivering, and my teeth began to chatter. Wrapping my arms around my chest, I trudged into the woods, ignoring the calls of the soldiers.

I again pictured Nathan's and Stefan's smiles in the Realm of Souls. Haldren had said they were safe, and he appeared to be right. They were not truly gone, just in another realm. I tucked the thought close to my heart.

The bond thrummed with sudden fear. Andrew and Braidus had woken and discovered my escape. I sighed. So much for my solitude. Knowing they'd turn the camp inside out to find me, I turned around and headed back. The two princes stepped through the dome as I approached.

Andrew cursed and shivered. "It's freezing out here!"

Braidus spotted me before his brother did. "Isabelle." In two strides, he took me by the hand and pulled me out of the storm, the heat in the dome melting the snow off me and soaking my clothes.

The soldiers on watch looked relieved when they saw me. "You found her," the long-haired one said, relaxing.

"Yes, thank you," Braidus said to him.

I suspected he had alerted my family. I should've made myself invisible and then snuck out.

Andrew rounded on me. "What in the Gods were you doing out there?" I acutely felt his anger, worry, and lack of sleep.

I bristled. "I needed a moment to myself. I wasn't planning on being gone long."

"I put you in a deep sleep. You shouldn't even be awake right now." His eyes accused me of circumventing him.

Braidus wrapped his arms around me, pulling my back against his chest. "She's soaked to the bone. Let's get her back to our camp, warm her up, and get some answers." His eyes darted to the listening soldiers.

Andrew raked a hand through his hair. "Fine." He turned to the men on watch and thanked them for their service and for alerting him to my absence.

Braidus tucked me into his side as we returned to our shack. Andrew threaded his fingers through mine on the other side. Joshua, King Brian, Malsin, Henry, Dominic, and Falden sat around a roaring fire. I felt a flash of guilt for waking them all and then annoyance and frustration that I had to be watched.

Braidus guided me close to the fire. "Warm up." He and Andrew sat on either side of me and squished me into their sides.

From across the fire, Joshua scowled at me. "You know you're not to go out on your own at night. Why did you disobey me?"

I took a breath, then exhaled, trying for patience when I felt anything but. "I'm suffocating with all this attention on me. I just needed an hour to myself. I left the camp so I wouldn't be near any of the soldiers. It's a blizzard out there, so I didn't think anyone would follow me. I'm sorry to have bothered everyone."

"This prolonged snowy weather is unnatural." King Brian frowned, looking upward. "I pray to the Gods that Aberron doesn't suffer from it."

Joshua scrubbed a hand down his face and sighed. "I know you hate having all these eyes on you, but it can't be helped. Trouble clings to you more than to the princes. Even a short walk to the edge of your heat dome on your own is dangerous. My men have just battled for their lives and won. They're ready to celebrate, and you might be too hard to resist."

"Yes," the other men agreed.

I gestured to the tents behind me. "Everyone here saw me defeat the Dregans by myself. You think they'd have the guts to try something with me?"

"The unthinkable always happens to you," Joshua said, undeterred. "It's been proven over and over."

I couldn't argue.

Andrew reiterated his earlier thoughts. "I put you in a deep sleep. You weren't even supposed to be dreaming—"

I interrupted him. "I didn't circumvent you. Isaac pulled me from sleep to talk to me."

"You could've started with that!" Henry exclaimed.

Andrew's green magic flared the second I'd mentioned the Fate. "Did he injure you?"

My heart clenched as my mage mate's concern increased.

I shook my head. "No. He tried to sway me away from Haldren by giving me a gift. I saw Nathan and Stefan in the Realm of Souls." My eyes misted and my throat thickened at the memory.

I read the surprise in the men.

"Is that all?" King Brian asked, his blazing-blue eyes searching mine.

I glanced at my mage mates. "I'm told Haldren created the Amora bonds I share with Andrew and Braidus and nearly killed himself to do it. I did not get an answer as to why."

I stiffened as a double sense of unease reached me through the bond. Like me, they didn't enjoy being subject to the whims of the Gods.

Malsin's eyebrows rose. "If your bond has the strength of the God over Gods, it explains why Amora couldn't break it."

"It also explains his insistence on me courting them," I said offhandedly.

"For what purpose?" Dominic asked, rubbing the stubble on his chin.

"And to risk death to create it?" Henry asked, sounding astonished.

Everyone shrugged.

The guilt that now came through the bond hit me hard. Then it was abruptly pulled back. It happened so quickly I couldn't tell which prince it had come from. Andrew and Braidus wore matching expressions. Both had been rather silent on Isaac's revelation concerning our bond. Perhaps one of them knew something and didn't feel inclined to share.

King Brian spoke, his eyes on the darkened sky again. "Well, now that Isabelle's been found, I'm going to get some rest." He went back to his bedroll and lay down. This prompted the others to return to theirs.

My mage mates turned to me, clearly expecting me to settle in beside them.

I shook my head. "You two rest. I'm staying here."

My heart tugged as they explored the bond to read the whisperings of my heart. I made no point of disguising my feelings. I was tired of divulging all I knew when they wouldn't return the favor. Andrew hadn't even told me he had a brother. I'd only found out after Braidus had kidnapped me. No one had told me Haldren was behind Braidus playing the villain. I'd had to learn that from Isaac. Finally, how many Gods-forbidden times had I asked them why Haldren and the Gods had taken an interest in me and they'd refused to tell me when they knew the answer? I was done ignoring the fact that the princes, Joshua, King Brian, and the Gods kept secrets about me. I needed to know the truth concerning my importance.

I felt another stab of guilt that was quickly swallowed up with irritation from both.

Andrew gathered me into his arms. "You're exhausted and making problems out of nothing." He pressed his lips against mine in a soft, searing kiss. My eyes shut. I didn't catch the glow of green magic putting me to sleep.

I woke to the rustling of my family members. Dawn had come.

Andrew held out a mug to me. Taking it, I leveled my eyes at him. "Your distraction kiss was clever, but I won't fall for it again."

A corner of his lips curved up. "You feel better, though, don't you?"

I did, but I didn't care to admit it. "Still, it won't happen again."

Andrew chuckled, reading my unspoken truth. "As long as you quit getting up in the middle of the night."

"I make no promises." Nights had turned unfriendly, and I'd gladly avoid them if I could.

Andrew frowned and turned to Malsin. "We have got to get Isabelle's nightmares under control."

Malsin nodded over the rim of his mug. "Oh, I know it. As soon as we're back in Carasmille, I plan on doing a full health assessment with all my books, tools, and medicines at my disposal."

I shrugged. "Fine."

Andrew smiled. "Excellent."

I sipped my drink, but inside, my silent quest simmered. It was time for the secrets to end. One way or another, I was going to find out why I was so important to the Gods. Since my family repeatedly thwarted me on this, I would start by going to the temple in Carasmille. Hopefully, the priests could give me a little more insight.

Braidus sat down beside me. He bent his head until it touched mine and spoke quietly. "You're awfully tense. What are you conspiring?"

"Nothing." No way would I tell him my plans. He and the rest of my family would try to stop me. I forced my mind to go blank, chasing away all thoughts of visiting the temple so Braidus or Andrew would not know.

"Liar." He pressed a kiss to my temple.

I looked up into his eyes. "Don't think you can charm your way into my thoughts. They are mine and mine alone." I spoke lightly, but the conviction behind my words rang loudly.

He backed off. "Duly noted."

I sighed inwardly at the concern I felt emanating from him. Perhaps I shouldn't have been so firm, but I didn't want to be circumvented this time.

Finished with my drink, I helped disassemble camp and prepare for departure. We planned to ride to Thimbleton, rest there for the night, and make the last leg to Carasmille the following day. With Thimbleton in mind, my thoughts turned to Adel. She and the other residents of Saren had been sent there to wait out the war. Had she gotten word of Nathan's passing?

While our family collected our horses, I sought out King Brian. "Has Adel been told about Nathan?"

"No," he said, his expression grim. "I felt it was best I tell her in person. Should I have sent word to her already?"

I shook my head. "No. I think Adel will take it best if she hears it from a friend—or me." I felt a weight on my shoulders at the prospect, but she had to know. I had promised her that Nathan would be safe. Would she resent me for breaking that promise—for not being strong enough or smart enough to save him? I had a strong urge to run in the opposite direction so I wouldn't have to face her.

King Brian surveyed me. "I won't put that burden on you, Isabelle. You carried us through this war and have suffered enough."

My chest warmed with gratitude. "I appreciate that. Thank you."

He nodded. "I plan to address the Aberronians from Prastis, the Aberron Cliffs, and Saren when we arrive at the Thimbleton outpost. They need to know what they're coming back to."

"Of course," I said.

Once everyone was mounted and ready to go, King Brian gave the order to march out. With a flick of my fingers, I removed the heat dome over the campground. In seconds, a dusting of snow coated us. The sky had dumped a good amount during the night, on top of what we already had, and it continued to fall in blizzard-like conditions.

With limited visibility, we couldn't see the road to keep us on track as we moved out of the forest. The horses and wagons struggled. I read the worry on many faces and did my best to protect everyone by creating a ribbon of heat above their heads to keep them dry. Joshua enlisted the help of the soldiers who knew the trail well. Everyone couldn't help but remark that this winter had been the harshest one they'd seen. The trees around us groaned from the weight of snow and ice. Branches littered the ground, and the sound of cracking limbs reverberated throughout the forest. The first two hours into our ride felt like five.

*"The snow is too deep. I tire quickly,"* Nisha complained.

I relayed this to King Brian. "We cannot continue like this."

"Agreed."

He called for a halt. We hopped down, giving our mounts a rest. My family gathered.

"Options?" King Brian asked.

"We need a large shovel," Henry said.

"Very funny," Falden remarked dryly.

"I'm not kidding!" Henry exclaimed. "Why can't we create one with blue magic and Isabelle use her yellow magic to push it? Something like this."

He opened his palm and a syrupy blue substance appeared, then morphed itself into an upright rectangle. Then the edges began to curve, the middle bowing in response. He set it on the ground, keeping his fingers on it to prevent it from falling over.

"Give it a little wind, Isabelle."

I did as he asked, and Henry let go as the shovel surged forward, pushing the snow aside and creating a little path.

His face brightened at his success. "See? Now we just make it on a larger scale."

King Brian grinned proudly at Henry. "You have your mother's inventive mind. Let's try it."

Using Henry's model as a guide, I created a shovel large enough to make a path for us. Then I gathered a strong wind to push it forward. Snow billowed out and piled on the sides of the road.

Nisha whinnied in approval as we got going again. *"Much better."*

Soldiers yelled not far behind me. "Watch out! Out of the way! It's coming down!"

I turned in the saddle to see a mature fir tree fall toward the men on the road, the top half crashing into another fir. The ground shuddered as the force pulled its roots out of the ground, dirt and snow flying all about. Horses screamed and men shouted as they fought for control. An agonized yell rang out.

Gods forbid. I jumped into the air to help. A soldier lay in the snow, his leg at an odd angle. He clutched his shoulder, his face tight with pain. Beside him, a horse reared up and whinnied, kicking its front hooves out.

*Calm the horse,* I told Boomer, wanting to prevent the animal from injuring herself or those around her. Ribbons of green magic shot from my hands, penetrating the mare. She stilled, her breath coming in heavy pants. A soldier rushed to grab the reins.

I dropped to the ground and placed my hands on the injured soldier. *Heal.* Boomer barked, his tail wagging.

"Thank the Gods for you," the soldier said, his voice thick with pain.

I smiled into his eyes, doing my best to infuse him with tranquility. "You'll be good as new in a moment."

The ground rumbled, and I heard another tree come down. Curses rang through the forest. The winter storm had turned the trees into frail twigs. We had to get out before it got worse.

A red mage cut through the fallen tree to clear the path. Once I finished mending the soldier, I helped move the rest of the trunk out of the way.

Joshua appeared on the other side of it. "Everyone all right?"

A chorus of yeses answered him.

"Good." His eyes found mine. "Braidus went on ahead to clear the path. The wind is picking up. We need to hurry."

"I'll see what I can do to help him."

Jumping back into the sky and passing my family, I followed Braidus's tracks, blinking furiously to see through the snow. Around a curve, I caught sight of him. He hovered in the air, his hands directing the shovel.

"Is everyone all right?" he asked.

"Yes." A stronger wind pressed into our backs. Branches still cracked and fell from all directions. Just as I threw a rainbow shield over our heads, a thick limb came down with a heavy thud and slid off onto the ground.

Braidus frowned. "We should have remained at the campground until the storm abated."

"Nothing we can do about it now," I said. "Better we keep moving than try to turn back."

"Indeed."

Together, we worked to remove the debris and shovel the snow. The wind blew the snow sideways, lessening our visibility and coating the road with another layer. The air crackled and snapped, and the ground shuddered as trees toppled. My heart tugged as Braidus drew from my stores to keep his yellow magic fueled. We recharged while in the air, one after another, to keep going.

Sometime later, when we reached the end of the forest, Braidus and I looked at each other in dismay. We could not see even a pace in front of us and now had no trees lining our path.

"If memory serves me right, I think we just go straight," I said, thinking of my first ride to Thimbleton with Andrew. "It's not too far."

"Straight isn't as easy as it seems in these conditions," Braidus said. "We could end up going in circles."

"The road turns into cobblestone the closer we get to the city," I said. "We just need to find that."

Braidus gestured to the shovel. "We cannot reach the ground with this. We will never see the stone."

I frowned, knowing he had the right of it. "What if I torched what the shovel isn't reaching? We could do patches after so many paces to see if we break through to cobblestone."

"It's that or we make camp here until the worst passes," Braidus said.

We turned when we heard our family and the First and Second Waves approaching. Half the men trudged on foot and led their horses, some stumbling and slipping. There was more cursing. Everyone looked bedraggled and defeated. My heart went out to them.

Falden's gray gelding collapsed as Falden walked alongside him.

"Rhys!" Falden cried.

I rushed forward to help. Putting my hands on the horse, I activated my green magic to search for the problem. Thankfully, I saw no major issues. "He's all right. Just tired." I gave him a boost of energy.

"Thanks, Isabelle." Falden coaxed the horse into a standing position once more.

Nisha snorted at the gray gelding. "*Weakling.*"

Falden heard him as well. "Hey! Rhys is a great horse."

Nisha shook his head vigorously, the snow in his mane flying in all directions. "*He is a pompous prancing pony.*"

Falden gasped with indignation. "How dare you."

I put my hand on Nisha. "Be nice, please."

Nisha only snorted at me and turned away.

I apologized to Falden. "I'm sorry. Nisha has hated your horse since he laid eyes on him at the Sorrenian and saw he had a better stall." I lowered my voice so Nisha couldn't overhear. "I think it's jealousy."

Falden scowled. "He better not try anything on Rhys."

"He won't," I said. "I'll make sure of it." Turning to the others, I said, "I'm going to give everyone a little bit of energy. I'll be right back."

I rose above everyone's heads and went down the line, sending smoky green ribbons of energy to the men and their mounts.

The men cheered. "Lady Champion!"

When I returned, Braidus said, "Father has decided to continue."

I nodded in grim determination. "Let's do it."

We pushed forward, praying to the Gods that we were headed in the right direction. Along the way, I torched patches of ice, searching for the ground underneath. Sometimes, I found the dirt and wagon-wheel ruts of the road. Other times, I found grass, prompting us to correct our course as best we could. I figured Thimbleton was big enough that we'd find it sooner or later.

"Aha!" I shouted in excitement when I found cobblestone.

Braidus flew over and gave me a quick hug. "Good job." His relief enveloped me like a warm blanket.

"We're close enough now that I think I can torch the rest of the way," I said. I didn't want to lose sight of the stone for nothing.

I read the same feelings in him as he nodded. "Just be careful with your levels."

With renewed energy, we cleared the path, our arduous journey ending quicker than expected when Thimbleton came within sight. Every building was blanketed in snow, and the heavy, darkening clouds cast the city in shadow, giving it a gloomy, uninviting appearance. Braidus and I waited near the closed portcullis for no more than ten minutes as the rest of my family and the First and Second Waves arrived. We mounted our horses as the gate was raised to allow us passage inside.

We'd made it. Finally.

# CHAPTER TWO

A S WE MADE OUR way through the silent city and to the Thimbleton outpost, the heavy snow let up. I hoped it would continue to decrease. Today had not been fun. Other than a couple guards stationed at the gate, I didn't see another soul. I prayed everyone had a warm place to lay their heads.

King Brian spoke as we entered the outpost gates. "I'll need you to make another heat dome for our men in the fields. The people of Saren, Prastis, and Aberron Cliffs are staying in the barracks. After I address them, we'll settle in for the night."

I saw a few heads poke out of the mess hall as I followed King Brian's orders. No one I recognized. It must be dinnertime, or maybe they all gathered for entertainment.

The soldiers whooped and hollered when I finished making a space for them to sleep. "Lady Isabelle!"

"Rest well!" I replied.

We next settled our horses in, Falden making sure to keep his horse as far away from Nisha as possible. Joshua threw out orders to the men, but I didn't pay attention since it didn't apply to me. My family then made its way to the mess hall, my stomach tied in knots and dread hanging heavily on my shoulders. Adel and Stefan's family would be there. I didn't want to watch them shatter as I had when they heard the news of Stefan's and Nathan's deaths. Terror held me in its grip at the prospect of facing Adel. I had broken my promise. She was going to hate me.

"Come here." Andrew tucked me against him, offering silent comfort.

Families gathered around the mess-hall tables with bowls and cups. I smelled baked bread and spices like pepper, thyme, and rosemary. Little children chased each other around the benches with peals of laughter. I envied their obliviousness to the stress I read in the adults as they chatted quietly amongst themselves. I could not immediately pinpoint Adel or Stefan's family.

King Brian grabbed a wooden chair from against the wall and positioned it in front of the rows of tables. He climbed onto it so all could see him, then amplified his voice with magic. "May I have your attention, please?"

Parents gathered their children and shushed them.

He smiled as the room quieted. "Thank you." He took a breath. "I believe you've heard we have successfully dealt with Dregaitia."

A few people answered. "Yes."

King Brian smiled. "Excellent. I wish to confirm that your homes are, once again, safe."

A cheer went up. A few people hugged each other, relief on their faces.

King Brian smiled and then held up his hand to speak again. "Supplies will be sent to sustain your families for the winter and to make repairs to any homes that may have been damaged during our battles."

"Thank the Gods!" a few cried out.

"Saren residents, we used all of your emergency provisions," King Brian said. "Your underground safe haven aided us greatly." He put a hand on his heart. "I am extremely grateful for your forward thinking in providing protection for your town, and I will personally replace everything we used. I'll also set aside tax money to put into a fund for you to maintain it. You'll never have to worry about using your money or materials to expand or repair your safe haven again."

Another cheer went up.

"I suggest you wait to return until this storm has passed. The snow is deep and difficult to navigate. I urge extreme caution through the Trivail forest. Many trees have fallen, and many more will come down. Our journey through it today was fraught with peril. I do not wish to see any harm come to you."

The people nodded, seeming to accept his counsel. Mothers held their children tightly. I could almost see them envisioning the danger of journeying right now.

King Brian's expression turned solemn. "I regret to inform the residents of Saren that your orate judge Stefan Ashter and also Nathan Whysten of Saren perished during our battles with the Dregans."

My heart tightened with anguish, and my breath faltered. Somewhere in the back, wailing could be heard. Andrew tightened his grip around my waist. Braidus took my hand and squeezed lightly.

King Brian continued as if nothing were amiss. "You will need to elect a new judge for your town. Also, a regiment of soldiers will be staying in Saren for an undetermined amount of time. They will be in charge of ensuring you receive the supplies you need to sustain yourselves. If you have any questions, please report to them. That is all."

Stefan's father weaved his way through the tables to reach us. He bowed, clutching his leather hat. "Highness, I'm Patrick Ashter. How did my son die?"

"He was impaled by a formidable Dregan mage during our final battle in Saren," King Brian explained. "He bled out before we could heal him."

Stefan's father flinched.

King Brian put his hand on Mr. Ashter's shoulder. "Stefan was an example of true courage in the face of adversity and one of the most honorable men I ever had the pleasure of meeting. His efforts helped save many lives. He will be remembered as a valiant hero of Aberron."

Mr. Ashter nodded, face grim. "Thank you, Highness."

King Brian stepped back.

Mr. Ashter's pale-blue eyes flicked to mine, and his expression softened. "Stefan was in love with you, Isabelle. I hope you know that."

Tears flowed down my cheeks now. My throat closed up with emotion, and I couldn't speak. I nodded, conveying as best I could that I knew. Mr. Ashter looked at me with sympathy, his lower lip trembling before he retreated, moving to comfort his wailing wife and daughters.

In shock, Adel moved slowly forward, her face pale. In quick strides, King Brian gathered her into his arms. He spoke quietly, words I could not hear. She collapsed into him, sobbing, my own grief and guilt intensifying. I buried my face in Andrew's chest, unable to face Adel and own up to my broken promise. I was a coward.

Time moved fluidly. Andrew kept me tucked into his side while Joshua procured rooms for us at the barracks in the king's quarters.

"You can thank King Elan for the rooms," Joshua said. "He hated bunking down like a common soldier. It's Aberronian law that every outpost have rooms for the king or queen and a small entourage. Soldiers are required to clean them weekly, so they're always prepared."

"Lucky for us," Henry said, seeming happy at the prospect of a real bed.

Joshua led our family to the king's quarters. Once there, I sat between my mage mates on a brown couch in a large circular sitting area that had doors leading to the separate bedrooms. A fire roared in a stone fireplace, giving light and heat to the room. I turned my thoughts to the vision of the Realm of Souls Isaac had given me. Picturing Nathan's and Stefan's faces and reminding myself that their souls lived on eased my grief. Andrew and Braidus sighed in relief as they felt the difference in the bond.

Adel needed to know what I'd seen. I rose, mustering the courage to face her. King Brian and Malsin approached from one of the rooms; I didn't catch which.

Malsin shook his head at me, no doubt reading my intentions. "She is resting. I suggest you wait until morning."

I nodded, trusting his judgment.

Henry, Dominic, and Falden had acquired food—some sort of stew that smelled like what the people in the mess hall had eaten and two loaves of bread. I didn't have much of an appetite and ended up going to sleep earlier than the men.

During the night, I dreamed I battled the Mazika. Ice bolts impaled my shoulders, fastening me to the ground. My terror ratcheted. I was pinned!

The Mazika converged and morphed into Joshua, Andrew, Henry, and Braidus. I cried out in surprise. They approached with maniacal expressions. I looked down to see I'd changed too. My hands had grown and sprouted dark hair. I wore a white fur coat with spiked metal. Horror engulfed me. *I'm a Dregan.* They attacked swiftly, their blades cutting into my skin. Hot blood poured from my wounds, turning the snow a crimson red. I screamed but could not break free.

I woke to the darkness and slapped a hand over my mouth to stop my cry. I shivered, my body clammy with cold sweat. I created a blue orb for light. Terrified of going back to sleep, I rose. I couldn't wait to face Adel any longer. I prayed we could find comfort in each other.

I opened the door and stepped out into the darkened sitting room, then looked around, not knowing which door to go to. I switched to purple magic and sent Boomer a command to listen for Adel. He whined, and my blood ran cold. Find her! He lay on his belly, his head low in a distinctive no.

I frantically pounded on the door closest to mine. Braidus answered, blinking back sleep, his eyes squinting against the light from my orb. "What is it?"

Panic laced my voice. "Which room is Adel's?"

My heart tugged as he read the bond. "That one." He pointed to a door across the room.

I spun on my heels and sprinted past the couches and tables. I grabbed the handle on the door Braidus had indicated. *Locked.* I blasted at it, then pushed it open.

"Adel?" I called out, my voice hoarse with my escalating emotions. I stepped inside.

She slept on the bed, a hand over her heart. I went to her and touched the hand. *Cold.* "Adel?" I shook her slightly.

Nothing happened. I activated my green magic. Boomer whined once more.

"Adel!" I screamed.

Braidus came with Andrew and Malsin. Andrew pulled me out of the room as I shrieked. The doors in the quarters opened, my family pouring forth in various states of dress.

"What's happened?" Joshua asked Andrew, eyeing me with concern.

"Adel." Andrew struggled to speak as he got caught up in my emotions. He shook his head.

"Dead?" Joshua asked.

Andrew nodded.

Joshua paled. "Gods forbid."

I shook. I cried. I screamed. I pushed at Andrew, but he held me in a viselike grip. I punched and kicked. I wanted to run, to escape this pain. He took the abuse without complaint. I had gone to Saren to save my family. Instead, I'd lost them all. Stefan, Nathan, and now Adel—dead.

Suddenly, the fight in me was gone. I shuddered in Andrew's arms. He pressed me against his chest, his hand smoothing my hair. How many more loved ones would I lose? How many lives had I tainted by my association? I froze, barely breathing.

Andrew slid to the floor and held me in his lap. I watched Adel's closed door, unable to look away even if I wanted to. Someone brushed against me, and out of the corner of my eye, I saw that Henry, Dominic, and Falden had sat down beside us. Someone knocked on the door to the king's quarters, and an indecipherable conversation came from nearby.

Andrew's voice trembled. "Dominic, Isabelle feels like ice."

Dominic took my hand and warmed me up. It did nothing for my heart, though. And it took only moments for the heat to dissipate, leaving me as cold as I was before.

The door to Adel's room opened, and King Brian, Braidus, and Malsin stepped out. What had they done with Adel?

Andrew called out to my brother. "Isabelle needs you."

The others moved out of the way, and Joshua sat beside us. Andrew moved me to Joshua's lap. "I can't keep her warm."

Joshua held me against him and used his red magic to keep a steady flow of heat around me.

"Were you able to determine the cause?" Henry asked Malsin.

"I saw no evidence of foul play. She was obviously upset, but nothing terribly concerning, when I left her to rest," he said, rubbing his forehead.

"I believe her heart stopped from stress and trauma—a broken heart, if you will."

"What are we going to do about Isabelle?" Falden asked, his brown eyes flitting between me and Malsin. "She's as good as a statue."

"The Gods have been especially cruel to her," Joshua growled. "Two sets of parents and her first love. I don't need a bond to know it's fear that paralyzes her. No doubt she's wondering who's next."

"I suggest everyone get another few hours of sleep," Malsin said, glancing at the clock, now striking 3 a.m. "We're still planning on getting to Carasmille when dawn breaks—if the weather allows."

What was going to happen to Adel?

Braidus spoke quietly to me. "Haldren has taken her to rest beside Nathan."

Together in death.

I easily imagined Adel standing at the back door, wiping her hands on her apron as she watched Nathan fencing with Stefan. She'd call them to breakfast, and their swords would drop to their sides. Nathan would clap Stefan on the back, joking with him about his progress. Laughter would ring out as they walked to the house. Nathan would stop on the steps to press a kiss to Adel's lips. Concerns would vanish, and joy would blossom.

"I take it you'll stay with Isabelle?" Malsin asked my brother.

"Yes," Joshua answered.

Malsin touched his arm. "Here's a bit of energy for you."

"Thanks." Joshua turned to my mage mates. "You two get some rest. Your strength will be needed."

Braidus pressed a light kiss to my cheek, then spoke to Joshua in a knowing voice. "Keep her close tonight. She is entertaining thoughts of death."

Joshua stood, pulling me up with him, and cradled me in his arms.

Andrew spoke to his brother. "Let me put you to sleep."

Andrew turned and kissed my forehead, then followed Braidus to his sleeping quarters.

Joshua took me to his room and set me on his bed, where I leaned against the headboard with a pillow propped behind my back. I wrapped my arms around my stomach as he created a mini heat shield around my body. He then moved to a chair and watched me with concern. I remained awake, silent and motionless, for the rest of the night.

Would Joshua be next? He was my only living kin. Or maybe Andrew, since he owned the majority of my heart. Anyone I associated with could be a target.

Were the deaths of my loved ones some sort of test from the Gods to see how much tragedy I could take? Haldren said the tests he gave me were to make me strong enough to survive this world. Well, he was wrong if he thought taking my loved ones would strengthen me. How in the world was I to survive this? I couldn't.

As Joshua worked on filling out several reports by the small fireplace, his eyes darted to me often, but he didn't try to engage me in conversation. I couldn't tell if it was because he didn't know what to say or if he was trying to give me space while making sure I didn't do something stupid. Regardless, he wasn't much of a talker.

When morning came, Malsin came in and sat on the bed beside me. Joshua removed the heat shield. Malsin touched my knee, using green magic to check me out. Then he pried my fingers away from my stomach and pulled me into a standing position, wincing at the popping sounds my bones made.

His green eyes studied mine. "I know you're hurting, but I need you to be here." He put his hands on my shoulders. "Don't make us any more worried than we already are. Can you do that for me, please?"

I wanted to say no, but I also didn't want to disappoint Malsin. He worked so hard to look after me. I shut my eyes, took a breath, and exhaled slowly, trying to find my footing in the present. Malsin removed his hands. I repeated the breathing exercise until the tightness in my chest let up. When I opened my eyes, I noticed Andrew and Braidus had also come in. They sighed, grateful for the respite. A profound sense of sadness lingered, but I could function.

Malsin smiled. "There's a bit of light in there."

I managed a weak smile.

He grinned. "Let's get you ready for the day. It's stopped snowing. We've got a journey to Carasmille to make."

Andrew kissed my temple. "We'll meet you in the mess hall for breakfast."

Malsin helped me find the bathroom, where I quickly washed and dressed. I then followed him to the mess hall.

People from Aberron Cliffs, Prastis, and Saren filled the space with their chatter. Bowls of oatmeal and jugs of milk and honey were spread across the tables. A hush fell over the room and I felt every eye on me as I walked to King Brian's table at the very back near the Saren residents. Someone had talked.

Millie, Saren's herbal healer, quickly shuffled over. She hugged me, then took my hands in hers, her gaze soft but direct. "You have suffered so much, my girl. I am sorry for it."

"Me too," I whispered.

"I presume you'll be returning to Carasmille?" she queried. At my nod, she asked, "What would you have us do with your house and livestock?"

"I would like to keep the house as it is, but if you could find good homes for the livestock, I would appreciate it." Joshua told me he'd had soldiers tending to the animals until everyone returned home. "Take the food in the cellar, too, lest it go to waste."

Millie nodded. "That can be arranged."

"Thank you," I said, grateful for her thoughtful and pragmatic nature.

She smiled. "Thank you for saving our homes. It will not be forgotten."

We parted ways. Others from Saren offered their condolences as I passed their tables, but no one engaged me in conversation. I murmured my thanks, appreciating their consideration.

King Brian stood at the head of the table and held out his hands to me. When I put mine in his, he pulled me into a hug. "Adel and Nathan were never meant to be apart. They are together now and at peace in the Realm of Souls. I cannot think otherwise."

Tears pricked my eyes. "Yes."

"They loved you very much," he said.

"They did." I blinked rapidly to hold back the tears.

"You have every right to grieve, but don't let it consume you," King Brian said gently. "You are young, with many years ahead of you. Don't let despair close your eyes to the love and friendship around you."

"I'll try," I promised.

"Good." He released me.

Braidus stood so I could sit between him and Andrew. Our eyes met, and a flicker of warmth passed between Braidus and I.

"Thank you," I murmured as I slid in, grateful for his desire to be a comfort to me.

He leaned down and kissed me sweetly. "You're welcome."

Andrew held out a steaming mug. "Hot chocolate." He pressed his forehead against mine. "Whatever you need, we're here."

"Stay close," I whispered, needing an anchor.

Andrew captured my lips with his. "Always."

A chorus of gasps hit my ears. People I'd known since childhood stared at me with scandalized expressions. Great. There went my respect in the community. I'd just been reduced to a harlot for the prince's enjoyment.

Mava caught my eye. She sat at the table adjacent to ours beside her husband, Carl, her parents, her younger brother, and Mr. and Mrs. Bryder. With raised eyebrows, she mouthed, *Two to one?*

I lifted my left hand with my birthmark and dropped it. "The Gods like to fiddle around with me for who knows what reason. They tied me to the princes with a magical bond. I am courting them both to decide who to marry."

"Everyone knew the Gods would have a hand in your life," Mava said, not sounding surprised. Her tone lightened to awe. "You're going to be queen."

"Gods, I hope not," I answered without thinking.

Braidus turned to me with a mischievous grin. "Does that mean you're choosing me?"

"Absolutely not," Andrew answered for me. "She's choosing me, and she'll put up with being queen because she loves me."

A chuckle escaped my lips, surprising me. "We shall see."

After a breakfast that felt like sludge, I followed my family out to our horses to prepare for the ride to Carasmille. I longed to get away from Thimbleton—to escape the place where Adel died. It didn't matter where I ended up.

For the first time in ages, a blue sky and sunshine greeted us. Every soldier I passed looked at me with compassion. A few offered their condolences, for which I murmured my thanks. My name passed through many lips.

"My heart goes out to Lady Champion."

"The Gods sure know how to be cruel, don't they?"

"She's a fierce little thing. She'll survive it and come out a conqueror, just like she did with the Dregans."

Nisha lipped my face, giving me horse kisses. I rubbed his neck.

To Nisha, Andrew said, "Isabelle's not quite herself today. Don't let her try to convince you to run off."

Nisha whickered and rocked his head. *"I have orders from Haldren to make sure she stays in sight of family."*

Andrew's face filled with relief. "Good." He patted Nisha's neck. "Thank you."

I touched Andrew's arm. "I'm not going to run off."

He smiled. "Just taking the extra precaution."

We took a side road onto Capitol Road to avoid going through the city. For the first part of the journey, Braidus created a shovel and used the wind to push it while remaining on his horse. The farther north we went, the more the snowfall lightened up, giving our horses less trouble. A few hours later, he did away with the shovel.

I found the ride to Carasmille long and stifling. King Brian spent most of it speaking business with his sons and Malsin, their conversation quite uninteresting to me. Henry, Dominic, and Falden amused themselves with old tales of the Sorrenian and their impressions of the professors. They also spoke of their eagerness to return to the comforts of home, to have servants to do their cooking and cleaning for them. I didn't exactly feel like I belonged in that discussion either. No one tried to engage me in conversation. Occasionally, I received a glance as if to make sure I hadn't run off. I tried to remain present by lending a listening ear, but I found myself slipping. I doubted anyone noticed when I slid into oblivion.

Close to sunset, we arrived at the gates of Carasmille. King Brian turned his mount around and stood tall in the stirrups. He then used his magic to magnify his voice and shouted to the thousands of soldiers trailing behind us. "Welcome home, heroes of Aberron!"

A cheer rent the air.

"Celebrate with your friends and loved ones. You deserve it!" King Brian placed his hand on his heart, emotion in his voice. "From the depths of my soul, thank you for protecting Aberron." He bowed.

I might have seen tears glistening in some of the soldiers' eyes closest to us. As one, they drew their swords and shouted, "For Aberron! For our king!"

King Brian rode off to the side and gestured for the soldiers to enter Carasmille, the men inclining their heads as they passed King Brian on their way into the city. When the last entered, we made our way to the castle. In front of us, the soldiers' laughter overflowed the cobblestone streets. I suspected the pubs in Carasmille would have a profitable night. When we passed groups of them, they shouted, "Cheers for our champion, Lady Isabelle!" I forced a smile until we reached the castle.

It wasn't until I was getting Nisha happily tucked into his stall that my mage mates bestowed their attention on me. Together, they waited while I gave Nisha a treat and plenty of hay and water. By then, however, I was exhausted and annoyed. I had no wish to be around anyone.

I closed Nisha's stall and then patted his neck. "Rest well. I love you, Nisha."

He lipped my face. "*I love you.*"

When Andrew and Braidus reached for me, I purposely shoved my hands into my pockets. My heart tugged. I detected a bit of guilt as they read where a portion of my frustration lay. Not once had they reached out to me during our ride. I hadn't needed to take them away from their father, but I would have appreciated a few simple gestures, a quick word or touch, to help me stay on the right path. Hadn't they promised to stay close?

"Welcome home, Highness," a guard said as he opened the door.

"Thank you," King Brian said briskly.

Queen Averly met her husband at a run from the bottom of the stairs. They hugged fiercely before King Brian kissed her soundly.

"I'm so happy you're safe," she cried, tears running down her face. She reached out and snatched Andrew by the arm, then Braidus, and then Joshua, pulling them all into a family hug. "All my boys—home."

The sight made my heart ache. I wrapped my arms around my chest, trying to stave it off. When they broke apart, Queen Averly said, "You must all be hungry. I'll have something prepared for you."

I spoke up. "Please, may I be excused to go to my quarters? I'm tired."

"Of course, Isabelle," Queen Averly said good-naturedly. Then she opened her arms and pulled me into a warm hug. Quietly, she said, "Thank you for keeping my boys safe. Words cannot express my gratitude."

"It was nothing," I told her.

"No, it was much more," she disagreed as she stepped back.

I managed a wobbly smile, then glanced at my family members, seeing concern on many faces. I got the impression my mage mates were trying to figure out how to get back into my good graces.

"Good night." I hurried up the stairs, ignoring the eyes I felt on my back.

# CHAPTER THREE

STOOD IN THE WHEAT field as Haldren surveyed me with his cold blue eyes, his mouth curled into a hint of a frown. I had the sense he was displeased with me, but I was too tired to be worried about it.

"Losing another loved one has taken a toll on your heart." He put his hand on my shoulder. "I am sorry for it."

"Thank you," I said, surprised by his compassion.

He stepped back.

Now that I had him in front of me, I had to ask. "Why did you bond me to the princes?"

He grinned. "To see you happy."

I raised an eyebrow. I wasn't stupid enough to fall for that. "The truth, please."

His blue eyes penetrated mine with an intensity that caught my breath. "Love is powerful. I need you to experience it. Do not shut the princes out. Allow them to comfort you and soothe your pain." His head tilted as if listening to something. "I must go. Good night, Isabelle." He waved his hand, and the field dissolved.

I woke to darkness. Haldren had moved me to my bed from the chair in the sitting room where I had fallen asleep by the fire. Pulling the covers up over my shoulders, I rolled onto my side and fell back asleep.

Again, I dreamed of the white stone courtyard and the black sludge climbing up the opal trunk of the multicolored tree. It saddened me to see the destruction of something so beautiful. I walked over to the glass ball with the Creator frozen inside, eyes closed, a soft smile gracing his lips, his chest softly rising and falling. Not dead but asleep. Perhaps someone should wake him. I went to put my hand on the glass, and the scene dissolved.

I regained consciousness to pale morning light streaming through the curtains. Resolved to get some answers concerning this recurrent dream, I got out of bed. As soon as I could, I was going to the temple to talk with a priest.

As I brushed my hair, a knock came at my door. Setting the brush down, I answered it to find Braidus and Andrew standing there with soft smiles. My eyes dropped to the vase of yellow tulips Andrew held. He handed them to me.

Braidus spoke. "We're sorry you felt ignored yesterday. I wish to assure you that you were in my thoughts. I should have been better at expressing them to you."

"Same here," Andrew said, mirroring Braidus's apology.

"Thank you," I whispered, warmed by their gesture. I set the flowers on a small table in the sitting room.

"Would you like to fence with us before breakfast?" Braidus asked.

"I'd love to."

Grabbing my sword, I followed them through the maze of hallways and stairs to a large training room at the base of the castle. I was grateful they knew the way. I needed more time to familiarize myself with the castle and its comings and goings.

In the training room, roughly fifty soldiers sparred with various weapons or engaged in hand-to-hand combat. I felt their eyes on me as we walked into the room. I spotted King Brian and Joshua working together with staffs. They nodded in welcome, and we chose an open spot near them for our sparring. I turned to face my mage mates.

Unsheathing my blade, I gave them a teasing grin. "Come at me."

"With pleasure." Braidus lunged, sword in hand.

Andrew quickly followed suit.

Excitement surged through me as the three of us fought, my grief and stress melting away with every block and thrust of my sword. I relished every second. An hour passed without me realizing it. Sweat dripped off our brows, and our chests rose and fell with heavy breaths when we finished the session to go to breakfast.

After breakfast with the family, Henry left for the Sorrenian to visit his parents and Aliyah, whom he courted. Dominic and Falden went home to their families. They planned to officially move into the castle in a couple of days. And Malsin was taking a day trip to the Healer's Guild to stock up on supplies. King Brian planned on sending out a formal notice informing Aberron of Braidus's reinstatement as a prince of Aberron.

"What do you plan to say?" Queen Averly asked.

"That the Gods returned Braidus to me with new information concerning his crimes," King Brian answered smoothly. "They deemed him innocent, and, therefore, I have happily reinstated my much-beloved son to the rank of a prince of Aberron." He turned to Braidus. "What do you think?"

"It sounds acceptable to me." Braidus pushed his hair out of his face. "I will appreciate the ability to walk around without worrying about a guard trying to arrest me."

"No guard will touch you," King Brian said. "I promise."

Braidus smiled warmly, his love for his father flaring bright through the bond. It made me happy to see their relationship growing and mending.

I spent some time with Queen Averly while she went over a basket of correspondence delivered to her—one of the many duties of a queen. I was nervous that she had asked me to visit with her until I learned her intentions.

"Tell me about Braidus," she said while opening a note with a letter opener. "He's changed greatly. I don't see the young man I once knew."

I couldn't help but smile. "Besides his strength and intelligence, he is kind, loving, and considerate. He has a huge desire to please his father and make up for his shortcomings as a youth. I think he will be a strong asset to Aberron and the healing of your family."

Queen Averly wore a thoughtful expression. "Indeed. I have already noticed a change in Brian since Braidus's return. There is more energy in his step. A light in his eyes I haven't seen in years." The corners of her lips tugged down. "Braidus never truly accepted me as a mother. I came into his life too late, and his nursemaid, Greta, had doted on him enough to be the parent he sought. Still, I have always considered him my son and tried to love him as a real mother would."

I had the stark impression she thought she had gone wrong somewhere. I reached over and put my hand on hers. "I think you will like the man he has become."

At dinner that night, a frazzled King Brian raked a hand through his hair. "My kingdom is a disaster. It will be weeks before everything is sorted. I think I need to remove half the staff for their incompetence."

"Many of the lords have grown lax in your absence," Queen Averly agreed while dabbing her face with a napkin. "In fact, several have not been coming in at all."

"Perhaps it is time I threaten their stations." King Brian smiled.

Andrew spoke dryly. "There are several I wouldn't mind letting go. Lord Kalder, for one."

Joshua, King Brian, and Queen Averly laughed. Andrew shuddered.

"What am I missing?" I asked.

Joshua explained. "Every time Andrew and Lord Kalder meet, the man is insistent his nearly forty-year-old daughter is the perfect match for him. Despite her age, he believes she can bear him the greatest child Aberron has ever seen." He laughed once again.

"Age isn't the main issue," Andrew added. "Lady Kalder remains unmarried because every man is a treat she can't resist. I've been informed by reliable sources that she prefers a large variety and pays sundals to get them."

I grimaced. "Definitely not your match."

"Not in the slightest." He went on to say, "Everyone thinks their lady is the perfect match of the crown prince regardless of my personality or interests."

I frowned. "That's not how it should be. Your royal birth is not the basis for my love."

"That is why I love you. You choose character over circumstance." He pressed a light kiss to my lips.

"Always," I promised.

The following morning, Joshua took me to his office near King Brian's study. Having never been inside, I found myself a little curious. Upon entering, we came face-to-face with five soldiers standing at attention.

Joshua gestured to the men. "Isabelle, I'd like you to meet your guards for outside excursions." He then introduced them. "This is Zachary, Oliver, Eric, Weston, and Micah."

They all wore the traditional dark-blue uniform with black boots, weapon belt, and light-blue king's crest patch on the chest and upper arm. Upon further inspection, I discovered their insignias were outlined in gold. That must make them important.

When the men smiled with open friendliness, I returned the gesture. I had to crane my neck to look up at Zachary. He had to be as tall as a Dregan.

Joshua went to his desk and opened a chest from which he retrieved a gold-and-ruby necklace with the Mirran crest. He fastened it around my neck, then faced me. "You are to wear this at all times. It will alert your guards every time you step outside. Gods know you'll not seek them out first."

Returning to the chest, he withdrew five pins also displaying the Mirran crest and handed one to each guard. They secured the pins to their chests with care.

I rolled my eyes. "I saved Aberron against the Dregans. I think I can keep myself safe."

My brother's expression hardened. "Do I need to list the number of times you've broken a bone, been bruised, sliced, shot, poisoned, burned, stabbed, kidnapped—"

Beside us, the soldiers' eyebrows rose in surprise.

I held up a hand, cutting him off. "I get it. I have a penchant for trouble and bodily harm."

Joshua relaxed. "Your magic *will* make you a target. I believe Dominic and Falden will do well enough for your outings *inside* the castle, but *outside* requires an entirely different stratagem. There are more opportunities for harm."

I sighed, feeling like I'd been reduced to a baby. "Fine."

He pulled me into a hug. "Don't stay mad at me forever. You know I'm doing this because I love you."

His affection warmed my heart. "I'll put up with it because I love you too."

"Oh, I almost forgot. All of your guards are trained mages." My brother stepped back, gesturing to the men. "Micah and Eric are both yellow, so your invisibility tricks won't work. They'll see right through them."

I cursed, Joshua grinned, and the men snickered.

"I know Malsin is your preferred healer," Joshua said, "but Oliver is a trained green, so let him help if you find yourself in a bind."

I nodded, then turned to Zachary and Weston. "And you two?"

"Red," Weston said.

"Blue," Zachary answered.

"You're not leaving anything to chance," I said to my brother.

"No," he answered, seeming pleased with himself. "Now, go see Malsin for that health assessment so you can get those nightmares under control. He's waiting for you in the study." He ushered me out the door.

I spent a good portion of the day in Malsin's care. He smiled, his mossy-green eyes bright as he surveyed his healing room. "It's so good to be back in Carasmille with all my supplies. By the time we're through, you'll be in perfect health."

"I am in perfect health," I told him.

"We'll see about that," he answered.

After a physical assessment, he delved into my mental and emotional health. I left his office with a small chest of vials for various ailments—one for sleeping, another for emotions, another for vitamins, and so on. My mage mates, my brother, and Malsin had me covered. Trouble would have a harder time finding me.

# CHAPTER FOUR

ATE THAT AFTERNOON, I got my chance to sneak out of the castle and visit the temple. A helpful guard opened one of the doors for me, and I murmured my thanks as I walked out. As I headed to the stables to see if Nisha would take me, my locket with the Mirran crest suddenly glowed blue. It must have alerted my guards that I'd stepped outside, but I continued walking, figuring the men would find me sooner or later. I wouldn't put it past Joshua to have put some sort of tracking on it to ensure they could find me wherever I went.

I'd not gone more than eight paces when the guards appeared out of nowhere, their pins glowing as well. Stopping, I raised an eyebrow, impressed at their speed. "How did you get to me so fast?"

"We often patrol the front entryway when we're not guarding you," Zachary said.

"But I didn't see you." I definitely would have noticed walking past all five of my guards on my way out.

Micah grinned. "That's because we were invisible. King Brian implemented this new security measure right before he left for the Dregan War. We have caught many thieves and ne'er-do-wells this way."

Eric snorted. "Too many people thought they could get away with stuff while the king was gone."

"I see." I wondered if King Brian had made this rule after he learned that I'd easily walked in and out of his castle with two bags of gold from the royal treasury, having made myself invisible.

I resumed my journey to the stables, my guards following. Reaching Nisha's stall, I pulled an apple from my pocket and fed it to him.

"Are you up for a ride to the temple?" I asked.

He whinnied. "*Yes.*"

I opened his stall door. I didn't bother with a saddle, instead jumping on his back and grabbing a handful of his black mane. Upon realizing my intentions, the guards quickly procured mounts of their own. Attempting to be a dutiful sister, I waited.

It occurred to me as we trotted through the castle gates that I didn't exactly know how to get to the temple. It was late at night when I had gone with my family for Braidus's trial by fire.

"You guys wouldn't happen to know how to get to the temple, would you?"

"Yes, follow me." Zachary spurred his horse forward so that he rode in front of us.

Passing carriages, carts, and people, we navigated through the streets at a steady pace. A scruffy black dog weaved its way through our mounts, earning a stern command from Micah to get out of the street.

Zachary led us to a hitching post on the side of the temple, out of view of the main street, and we walked around to the front. An elderly priestess sat in a chair by the door, a large basket of rolls in her lap. A few people in well-worn clothes surrounded her, eating. She offered us some of the bread.

"Don't mind if I do." Zachary took a roll and bit into it.

Oliver laughed. "You're always hungry."

"There's so much of me to fill!" Zachary said as he referenced his height.

Micah and Weston also grabbed a roll as we entered.

A priest who looked to be in his thirties rose from a seat next to the donation table, his eyes scanning our group with interest. "May I help you?"

"Yes," I said. "Might there be a priest or priestess available? I have a few questions about the Gods."

The man's eyes zeroed in on my birthmark. "Your name, please?"

"Isabelle Mirran," I supplied.

"Ah," he said as though familiar with my name. "Excuse me a moment while I see if our high priest is available." He scurried off down the hall.

My eyebrows furrowed. Did I warrant the high priest? Any priest or priestess would likely do.

I must have unknowingly spoken out loud because Weston said, "You're Lady Champion. You deserve it."

I shook my head. "I'm just Isabelle, nothing more. I don't require or deserve anything better than anyone else."

My guards smiled.

My shoulders slumped. I hated that I'd never again be treated like a normal individual. Wherever I went, I would be viewed as the champion who'd won us the war against Dregaitia. It was as good as having the title of queen for all the attention it brought me. It wasn't the life I wanted.

I turned when I heard multiple footsteps. A man with shocking white hair and bright-blue eyes approached with the other priest. He held out his hand in welcome, a warm smile on his face. "Lady Champion. I'm High Priest Jorrun."

I took his hand. "Just Isabelle, please."

He smiled. "Isabelle. I'm told you have questions about the Gods." He glanced briefly at the other priest, who nodded.

"Yes." I pointed to the artwork on the wall depicting the Creator and the tree. "Specifically, I have questions about this painting."

"Ah, King Aberron's painting." Jorrun walked over to it. "Magnificent, isn't it?"

We all followed.

"It is," I agreed, gazing at the swirls of color, so many different hues of black and blue making up the night sky. "I wish to know if this tree and the Creator are real."

"I believe so," Jorrun replied. "It has been written that the Creator started our world with this tree. It is Earth's beating heart, its roots encompassing the whole world. King Aberron was a great prophet in his time, his words always accurate, his prophesies always fulfilled."

"Gods come and go freely here, right?" At his nod, I questioned, "Have you ever met the Creator?"

The high priest shook his head. "I have not, but that does not mean he doesn't exist. If I may, why do you ask?"

"I dream often of him and this tree." I gestured to the painting.

Jorrun's eyebrows rose with interest.

"What have you seen?" he questioned, eyes alight with curiosity.

I explained the first dream of the Creator imparting his magic into the tree, followed by the second, where the black sludge crept up the trunk and limbs and the Creator was trapped in the glass ball. "His chest rose and fell with breath like he was asleep. Meanwhile, the tree seemed to be dying."

"Hmm." Jorrun frowned. "We are taught that the Creator feeds the tree with his magic. In turn, the tree keeps our world in good working order. If what you've seen in your dream is actually happening, the world may be in danger. Would you like to consult with the Gods on this matter?"

I shook my head quickly, throwing my hands up in avoidance. "Oh no, I'd rather not. Every time we meet, they meddle with me. I desire peace."

The high priest nodded, his expression impassive. "As you wish."

"I appreciate you seeing me."

He smiled. "Feel free to come back should you have more questions."

Impulsively, I lifted my hand, showing my birthmark. "You wouldn't happen to have any ideas on why I was born with the Mark of the Gods, would you?"

Jorrun briefly glanced at my birthmark. "The Gods would never lightly bestow their mark on someone. Every person seeking to be a priest or priestess must be interviewed by a God or Goddess before they are granted the position and allowed to wear the mark."

He lifted his sleeve to show me his mark. Unlike mine, which was bright red, his was black and outlined in gold, the gold probably marking him as the high priest.

"I would wager that you are of some importance," he said. "Though, for what purpose, I cannot say. The Gods are extremely secretive."

"Indeed." I tried not to show my disappointment that he didn't have an answer. "Thank you again for seeing me."

My guards and I took our leave. As we collected our horses, I spoke to the men. "I would like to ask a favor."

"Yes?" they all said at once.

"Promise me you won't repeat my conversation with the high priest to anyone, not even my brother or the royal family." I did not need them to stop me from learning why I was important to the Gods.

The men looked at me with hesitant expressions.

"We are required to report to Commander Mirran," Zachary said. "We cannot lie if he asks us, lest we lose our jobs."

I would not budge, but I also didn't want any of these men to lose their jobs. "If Joshua asks, tell him I ordered you not to say a word. If he presses you or threatens your jobs in any way, let me know, and he'll answer to me—or, better yet, tell him he'll *have* to answer to me. I abide by my brother's guidance and rules out of love, but my magic is powerful enough to afford me the right to do as I please."

"Yes, my lady," the men chorused.

"Thank you," I said in gratitude.

The road back to the castle went through the heart of Carasmille. Nisha trotted leisurely, allowing my guards to keep pace. The evening sun tinted the clouds pink, and the wind whipped through my hair, chilling me to the bone. I welcomed the numbness, though. I gazed at the mass of people going about their daily lives. Men with long poles lit lanterns in preparation for the night. Businesses began closing shop, switching their signs to closed, securing shutters, and locking doors. The sidewalks and streets bustled with people, livestock, carts, and carriages, all moving with purpose. I seemed to have caught Carasmille in the height of activity.

As I rode past the crowds, I received a significant amount of stares. I'd probably asked for it as a lady riding bareback on a huge black horse with five high-ranking guards trailing me.

I took in the chatter, clattering hooves, and rattle of wheels against cobblestone. I drank in the cold air, catching the scent of manure and then the aroma of freshly baked bread from a nearby bakery. *This is what I saved.* These people would never know Dregaitian tyranny. They would crawl into their beds this night protected. The knowledge brought peace to my heart.

Four men in military attire exited a dining establishment called Worth Your Thyme. They waved in good cheer. "Lady Champion!"

I smiled and waved in acknowledgment.

Word of my importance appeared to have raced through the streets. Carriages and carts pulled up short, blocking the way. People halted on the sidewalks, some in the middle of the road. Hundreds turned to me with studying gazes. My guards positioned themselves beside me.

A plump, middle-aged gentleman about to enter a gleaming black carriage spoke loudly. "This is the champion everyone is talking about? Why, she's a little sparrow." He wore a black fur jacket and a gold waistcoat. A noble or a wealthy merchant, to be sure.

Then, like wildfire, suspicion engulfed the people. "Is it really her?"

A man called out, "I heard Lady Champion subdued thousands of Dregans with blade and magic. Does this pretty little lady look capable of that?"

*Always my size and appearance.* Many shook their heads.

"Maybe it's not her," a middle-aged woman said.

"Those guards with her carry the protection of the king. She's got to be important." Another lady gestured to my entourage.

"Show us!" the rich gentleman shouted at me. "Show us you're the champion!"

The crowd began to chant. "Show us! Show us!"

"You don't have to do anything, my lady," Zachary said.

"If she doesn't, she might incite a riot," Micah said from my other side.

Indeed, the air felt volatile.

"More people are coming," Oliver said. "We're surrounded."

I didn't feel comfortable putting on a show, nor did I like the ordering tone the rich gentleman had used on me.

I raised my voice to the people. "I do not wish for attention or to show my powers to satisfy curiosity. Please let us through," But my words seemed only to enrage the crowd.

The wealthy gentleman shouted, "She doesn't have any magic! It's not her!"

The soldiers who originally called out to me argued, "It is! We were there! She saved our lives!"

"Don't harry her, please," one soldier said, his hands out. "Let her go on her way." To me, he said, "We apologize for drawing attention to you."

"Thank you," I kindly said to the soldiers.

"Stop this!" an Aberronian male yelled and threw a rock the size of a man's fist toward Nisha and me.

Nisha reared up, whinnying. I lost my grip on his mane and fell onto the icy cobblestones in a tangled heap. As he dropped back onto all fours, he stepped on my boot, and I felt the bones in my foot break, a pain-filled cry escaping my lips.

"Lady Isabelle!" My guards scrambled off their mounts to assist me.

Additional stones flew at us, startling their horses. I dodged kicks and tail whips. I tried to get up, but couldn't put pressure on my right foot. My heart thrummed with my mage mates' anxiety. Zachary dragged me out of harm's way, cursing as a small rock struck his cheek and blood welled.

Then I saw red, and Boomer burst from his cage with a growl. All colors shone as I combined them, wrapping rainbow shields around Nisha, my guards, and their mounts. Then the wind carried me into the air, where I hovered, giving the crowd a good view of me.

I spoke with deadly intention. "Continue to accost me and my guards, and you'll get more than you bargained for." For added measure, I ignited my hands with rainbow fire.

People rapidly retreated in silence, the rich gentleman jumping into his carriage and drawing the curtains. No more rocks flew, and a path rapidly appeared for my entourage. I extinguished the flames and removed the shields. I couldn't believe the Aberronians had accosted me and my guards for refusing to reveal my powers. Their brutality astonished and angered me. Perhaps they hadn't deserved to be saved if this was how they treated people.

Oliver healed the cut on Zachary's face, then wiped the blood off his cheek with his shirtsleeve. I lowered myself onto Nisha, who now stood quietly.

"Is everyone all right?" I asked my guards.

Zachary spoke quietly into a locket, probably informing my brother of our problems.

"Fine, my lady," they chorused.

"Isabelle," I corrected. "I'm no better than anyone else." I would repeat it until it sunk in.

The men chuckled good-naturedly.

Oliver moved to my side. "Do you have any injuries that need attending?"

I waved my hand airily. "Nothing of consequence." I knew my foot was broken, but I wasn't ready to do anything about it. A sick part of me relished the pain, just like I loved the cold. It was real and tangible in a way my emotions weren't.

Hurrying to exit the business district, we urged our horses into a trot. I saw nothing but terror in people's faces as we passed. My ire dissipated, and I felt sick. My stomach churned, my chest tightened, and my fists clenched. I'd made things worse with my ride to the temple. The bond heightened with Andrew's and Braidus's increasing concern.

At the stables, I used magic to dismount, hovering an inch above the ground since I couldn't walk.

Nisha snuffled my face, giving me horse kisses. "*Sorry.*"

I rubbed his neck. "It's fine. Don't worry. I'm sorry for putting you in that situation. Perhaps I'll take a carriage if I ever need to go into the city again, and we'll limit our rides to the castle."

He whinnied in approval. I pressed a kiss to his nose, then allowed a hostler to attend to him.

My guards then cornered me, concern on their faces.

Oliver eyed me shrewdly, gesturing to the magic that kept me aloft. "Nothing of consequence?"

I met his gaze with a hard one of my own. "That's right." I glided past, still unwilling to do anything about my condition. I ignored the murmurs of disapproval behind me.

"Lady Isabelle—" Oliver started in as he joined me.

I sighed. "Do not fret. I will be taken care of inside." I had made Andrew and Braidus anxious enough and would not be allowed to suffer long.

The princes and Joshua stood in the entrance hall, conversing quietly. Just inside, I paused to allow three young maids to pass with a cart of linens. The round woman pushing the cart looked at me with wide eyes and open mouth, fear written across her features. The other two focused on my mage mates and brother. They curtsied while batting their eyelashes and grinning impishly. My heart spiked hot. Braidus and Andrew soaked up my emotion with smirks and grins. The two maids blushed and giggled, obviously thinking the attention was on them. The frightened maid prodded them forward and out of sight.

Joshua, Andrew, and Braidus closed the distance between us. Anticipating a reprimand, I spoke before they could. "I'm not going out again."

I started to move past them, but Braidus caught my arm. "Not so fast, my darling." Gently, he swooped me into his arms, cradling me like he would a small child. "You're hurt. You're not in trouble with us."

Andrew nodded in agreement.

Since Braidus had me, I deactivated my magic. He carried me to my room. Andrew followed, leaving Joshua to converse with my guards. Hopefully, my brother wouldn't push them for why I had gone to the temple. He could focus on the rock-throwing incident all he wanted.

Braidus laid me on the couch, and Andrew gently pulled off my boots and socks. I winced as it pulled at my broken foot.

"Gods, Isabelle," Andrew whispered when he saw the swollen, black-and-blue skin.

"It's not so bad." I'd suffered worse.

"Your foot is literally crushed," Braidus said, his tone one of disagreement.

Andrew quickly activated his magic and healed the damage. I sighed in relief as the pain abated. Braidus handed me a glass of water. I smiled as I accepted the drink.

A knock came at the door. Braidus answered it, and Joshua strode in.

His green eyes zeroed in on me. "What have you done to my guards?"

His guards? Since when did Joshua need personal guards? "Nothing."

Joshua crossed his arms. "All of them refused to tell me what you were doing at the temple. They said if I pestered them, I'd have to answer to you."

Ah, my guards. I couldn't help but grin. "Excellent."

All three men looked at me sharply.

"What were you doing at the temple?" Joshua spoke in low, precise tones.

He couldn't scare me. "That's my business."

"Isabelle," all three men entreated.

I stood my ground. "No. If you're allowed to keep secrets, then so am I."

The bond heightened with guilt. I whipped my head to see which prince it came from, but it vanished as abruptly as it had come. I bit back a sigh. Figured.

"I'm trying to keep you safe," Joshua countered, his tone softening. He sat down on the couch opposite me. "How am I supposed to do that if you're not being honest with me concerning your activities?"

I softened my tone as well. "You are doing a fine job of protecting me, Joshua. The guards you hired are top-notch, and not once have I tried to hide my activities. I'm simply keeping my conversation at the temple private."

Andrew and Braidus shared a concerned look. Joshua scowled. They could be mad at me all they wanted, but it was time I ceased giving in to them—time I stop telling them every meddling thing the Gods had done to me when they refused to be honest with what they knew of the Gods. I was done letting things go and giving them the upper hand. I was going to learn of my importance to the Gods, and no one was going to stop me.

Braidus broke the tension. "Isabelle, are you hungry? You missed dinner."

"A little," I admitted.

"I'll have food delivered," he said, and stepped out of the room.

Joshua leaned back and rubbed his eyes. Andrew tipped his head back against the couch, his eyes opening and closing slowly.

My heart went out to them. "You both look exhausted."

"We're overwhelmed with work right now," Andrew said. "We have stacks of reports to go through, and we're trying to get trade reopened with Nistier and the Jamaylin Islands as well as prepare for trade with Dregaitia. Royals from all three countries will be coming here to discuss business."

"King Brian and I signed way too many death notices today for the families who lost family members in the war." Joshua sighed, his expression grim. "After that, I started the process of reorganizing the First and Second Waves. I have to replace the men we lost, promote those who had level heads, and demote those who showed poor leadership. I'm also trying to replenish our supplies so we're prepared to go at a moment's notice should we fall into war again. I'm having a hard time getting everything I need because the market is a mess right now. On top of all that, it's also the commander's job to present our king with a detailed history of our entire Dregan War."

I gave them both a look of sympathy. "Sounds extremely stressful and busy."

"Mm-hmm." Andrew and Joshua nodded.

Andrew pushed his hair out of his eyes. "Father brought in a bunch of lords who haven't been fulfilling all their duties, and he threatened their jobs and court status. He was exceptionally harsh, but they needed it. Aberron is close to shambles due to the lack of trade and poor management during this crisis. For example, we have the lords overseeing the market, ensuring people aren't getting cheated when they buy products or receive services. These lords hardly did anything and allowed numerous counterfeit products and services to show up on the market."

"Like what?" I asked.

Andrew reached into his pocket and pulled out a thin hemp-string necklace with a circular copper charm. "More than half of Carasmille bought these little necklaces supposedly enchanted to ward off a Dregan. Of course, they do nothing of the sort. There's not even a drop of magic in the copper." He jangled the necklace. "People paid as much as twenty sundals for this worthless thing." He shoved the piece of jewelry back into his pocket. "The lords should have put a stop to it. Instead, they let the merchants run wild, and all they did was collect the taxes so Father would have enough to pay them."

"That's ridiculous," I said, outraged on Aberron's behalf.

"It is," Andrew said. "We also had some nasty business this afternoon with stripping a noble of his land and titles and sentencing him to the Carasmille prison. While we were off fighting the Dregans, he created a counterfeit seller agreement for a small section of property we own just outside Carasmille. He forged Father's signature so it appeared we had sold it to him."

My eyes widened. "How could someone be so bold and stupid?"

Andrew made a sound of disgust. "Well, Father has had some mining teams combing the land for gold deposits. Last summer, Mother found a sizable gold nugget, and this noble bribed some of the miners to report to him if they found anything. Apparently, they found several areas that had gold. He thought he could quietly take a section of the property and add it to his land, which bordered ours, and we wouldn't notice."

"How did you find out?" I asked, curious.

Andrew smiled. "Our caretaker informed us when he went to check on that portion of our land and found himself banned from entering."

Braidus returned with a cart of food and drink. Joshua had fallen asleep on the other couch. I contemplated waking him but chose not to. He looked like he needed sleep more than food.

"Did I miss anything important?" Braidus asked quietly. He handed me a plate with fruit and slices of meat, cheese, and bread.

"No," I said. "Andrew was just telling me about his day—about the nobles shirking their duties and the one who tried to steal your property."

Braidus made a face as he sat on the other side of me. "Most of the ruling court in Aberron are greedy and lazy. No noble in Dregaitia would dare behave as these have. Cekaiden would have had them all executed."

I popped a grape into my mouth. "Why doesn't that surprise me? It seems Cekaiden's answer to everything is death."

Braidus smiled without humor. "It is a good deterrent, for sure. Father's lords should count themselves lucky he gave them two days to have everything in order before he terminates their positions and standing in court."

"We could use some new blood to shake up the courts," Andrew said. "Promote people who actually have a passion for Aberron and what they're doing."

"I agree," Braidus said.

My eyes darted between the princes. "I don't envy the two of you at all." Just the thought of having their jobs made me feel stressed.

They chuckled.

Andrew grinned. "Don't let our difficult day deter you. You're still going to be my queen."

"No, she'll be mine." Braidus pressed a light kiss to my cheek.

I laughed. "You two are going to be the death of me. I don't know why I agreed to this dual courtship."

"Because we want an honest chance to see who makes you happiest." Andrew shrugged.

"Yes," Braidus said.

I smiled, not disagreeing, as I picked up an apple slice. "You know the court isn't going to take to this dual courtship well." I looked at Andrew. "I had enough trouble at the Sorrenian when you kissed me in front of all the students. Two princes will be even worse."

"What do you want to do about it?" Andrew asked.

"Whatever is to be done must be done equally," Braidus said, his tone firm. "I will not be hidden."

"Hidden?" I gave him a strange look. "Why in the Gods would—"

Braidus cut me off. "I am illegitimate and therefore not considered as desirable as Andrew."

Anger filled my veins. "Braidus, you have just as much a right to be seen and loved as Andrew. I would never even think"—my throat choked with my fury—"to conceal you."

Andrew's ire swirled with mine. "Neither would I. Isabelle is right."

The bond swelled with Braidus's affection. "Thank you. That means a great deal to me."

I set my plate down on the cart. "Then it's settled. We're not going to do anything different. If we shock or anger people with this dual courtship, who cares." I threw up my hands, then dropped them.

"Fine with me." Andrew grinned, giving off the impression that scandalizing the court amused him.

"And me." Braidus's attitude matched his brother's.

I looked over at Joshua as he rested. He hadn't stirred once. Reading the tiredness in Braidus and Andrew, I sent them off to their rooms and to bed. I left Joshua in the sitting room as I retired to my sleeping quarters.

When I woke the following morning and stepped out into my sitting room, I discovered Joshua had gone. I hoped he had gotten enough rest. I hurried through the motions of washing and dressing for the day. A knock came at my door as I put in the last pin in my hair. Braidus and Andrew stood there. Together, we walked to the family dining room for breakfast.

I looked for Joshua when I arrived. He sat between Queen Averly and Malsin.

Reaching him, I put my hand on his shoulder. "Sleep well?"

He gave me a smile. "I did, thanks."

"Good."

Breakfast was a hurried affair as everyone, save me, had a busy day planned. I contemplated seeking out a library to see if I could find any information on the Gods.

As breakfast ended, King Brian sought me out. "Isabelle, would you mind accompanying me to the study? I wish to talk to you about some plans I have."

My interest was piqued. "Of course."

I walked with him into the study, my mage mates, brother, and Malsin following. Once we were all seated, King Brian shifted in his seat to face me.

He clasped his hands together. "Now—" A knock at the door interrupted him. He sighed. "Enter."

James appeared, holding a folder. "Forgive me for intruding." He strode forward. "I bring reports that require immediate attention." He paused at King Brian's raised eyebrows. "No, it's not war-related. It's merchant."

"What happened to Earl?" King Brian asked, taking the folder. "He's in charge of bringing me these reports."

"There has been a revolt with your staff, Highness," James said, straight-faced.

Queen Averly came in, her skirt swishing as she hurried to her husband. "Brian, we have a problem."

"So I heard," he said dryly.

Joshua moved over so Queen Averly could sit beside her husband.

"What have you learned?" she asked.

"Nothing. James was about to tell me." King Brian looked pointedly at him.

"The revolt is in response to what happened near the town square with Lady Isabelle last evening." James spoke in an even voice.

Anger flared in my chest, and Braidus and Andrew tightened their grip on me. Joshua scowled.

King Brian frowned. "I am aware of it."

James spoke frankly. "The people are afraid. They took Lady Isabelle's actions as a personal threat. They believe you are housing a dangerous, irrational woman. They call for her removal. Most of your staff has refused to work because they are afraid to cross paths with her. They believe she will strike them dead with a look."

I couldn't hold my tongue. "That is absurd! I don't want to kill anyone. They threw rocks bigger than my hand at me!" I balled my hand and lifted it. "I got trampled, and they drew blood on Zachary. What was I supposed to do, sit there and take it?"

Joshua said grimly, "The reports from her guards all say they used violence to incite her into showing her magic."

"Isabelle normally has the temperament of a fluffy kitten." Andrew spoke knowingly. "Loving and perfectly harmless unless provoked."

Braidus, Joshua, Malsin, and King Brian chuckled.

"Her claws would not have come out unless she truly believed herself or someone else in danger," Braidus said. "Andrew and I can attest to feeling such emotions within her during the event. As such, she hurt no one physically. I suggest we turn this on their heads. Is it not an offense to stone people?"

Joshua agreed. "We should consider it an attack on our champion, make a show of going after those who threw the rocks and then see where the people lie."

"Let's take a ride to the town square and address the people," King Brian said. He turned to his wife. "I will address my staff after. Gather the names of those who did not report."

She nodded, her lips pressed tight.

King Brian rose, prompting us to rise as well.

Henry walked in just as we made it to the entry hall. "I got here as soon as I heard. Carasmille is up in arms. The Abominators are out in full force."

The men cursed.

I frowned. *Great.*

A host of royal guards escorted us, my five among them. The snow fell lightly, dusting the street. At least it wasn't a blizzard. A town crier had been sent ahead, announcing King Brian's visit. Aware that I had ridden in a business district during the time most people were closing shops, King Brian demanded that all shop owners in the area present themselves.

I cringed as people flat-out ran in terror as I rode by on Nisha. Mothers gathered their children close. Men grabbed their wives protectively.

On the corners, men and women stood on wooden crates. They cupped their hands around their mouths and shouted, "Magic is a great evil! It is a curse that will ruin your families! Stay away!"

*Abominators.*

We stopped by the marble statue of Aberron. At least a thousand Aberronians gathered, trepidation and confusion evident on their faces. By then, my gut twisted with horror and shame. I wished I had made myself invisible traveling through Carasmille to reach the temple.

Dominic and Falden showed up on horses, their mounts pushing through the crowd. When Henry motioned for them to join us, the guards moved to let them through.

"Glad you got my notes," Henry said to them.

"It's crazy out there," Falden said, eyes wide.

Dominic nodded vigorously. "I haven't seen Carasmille this riled in a long time."

Henry gave me a teasing grin. "Leave it to Isabelle to stir things up."

"Ha, ha, very funny," I said, my tone light.

The boys chuckled.

King Brian magnified his voice with magic, his eyes blazing. "I am here to discuss the altercation that took place near here last evening."

I read the unease on many faces.

"Would those who witnessed my champion's display of power please come forward?"

About a hundred people, men and women, slowly stepped forward. There had been more last night. I didn't see the rich gentlemen anywhere. He probably had the power to vanish.

King Brian interrogated them. "In your own words, please tell me what you saw my champion do."

Several kept to the facts. Most embellished.

"She had it out for us, hovering in the air on fire, ready to strike us down," they said.

"She's a terror for us common folk," a bold-faced lady ventured. "We have no way to defend ourselves against her."

King Brian raised his hand for silence. "I require an accounting of what happened moments *before* Lady Isabelle revealed her magic."

Silence.

An older matron stepped forward, chin high. "Many shouted for the champion to reveal her magic to prove she was the one who saved Aberron from Dregaitia."

"And what else?" King Brian asked her.

Her expression showed she knew King Brian already had the answers, but she proceeded anyway. "Stones were thrown at her and her guards."

King Brian let anger filter into his voice. "*Stones* were thrown at *my champion*?"

"Yes, Highness," the older lady said in a clear voice.

King Brian thanked her and then asked the crowd, "At what point did you decide it was a good idea to assault a young lady to determine her worth?"

"I didn't throw a rock at her!" a man cried, prompting others to shout the same thing.

"Did any of you try to stop those who did?" King Brian asked, leaning forward.

Guilty silence.

King Brian straightened. "You allowed it to happen by doing nothing. You demanded a demonstration and incited it with violence. Your actions forced Lady Isabelle to show her magic to protect herself and the guards accompanying her. You received exactly what you asked for. I consider this incident an attack on my champion. A full investigation will be conducted, and those in attendance will be legally reprimanded."

The crowd gasped in dismay.

King Brian gestured to me. "As for believing my champion is a menace, tell me what you would have done differently had you been assaulted in her place. My champion came to me with broken bones."

A few people gulped. Others paled as if they hadn't realized the severity of the assault.

"Frankly, I am appalled by the lot of you. To treat Lady Isabelle so poorly after she saved us from Dregaitia—at great personal cost." He shook his head. "As your king, I am ashamed of my fellow Aberronians." He turned to me and said, "On behalf of Aberron, I would like to formally apologize to you. As Aberronians, we should be better."

"Thank you," I said, touched.

"What if Lady Champion decides to attack us for this, Highness?" The bold-faced woman asked, eyes darting nervously to me.

I stiffened as I felt a fresh wave of anxiety sweep through the people. I doubted King Brian's words could fully heal the damage done.

King Brian said, "I am fully confident in Lady Isabelle's ability to handle herself with decorum—in *any* situation. In the time I have known her, she's proven to have a forgiving heart even in the face of numerous wrongs bestowed upon her. To be blunt, I fear more for her safety than I do yours." King Brian turned to me. "Isabelle, is there anything you'd like to say?"

My stomach lurched at the thought of addressing all these people. And yet I didn't want my harsh words from last evening to be the only thing they remembered. I wanted to show them I wasn't malicious. So, taking a breath of courage and feeling the support of my mage mates, I summoned my magic and amplified my voice.

"I regret causing the amount of fear I see today. My only intention last night was to stop the assault on my guards and myself. Perhaps I should have gone about it in a better way, but it is harder to think straight while in intense pain." Though I read understanding on a few faces, most still wore wary expressions. "I do not wish to be a cause of discord among Aberronians. My agenda has been and always will be peace among all. I desire to be a help to Aberron and its citizens wherever I can." I looked to King Brian, hoping I had said enough.

He nodded appreciatively and faced the people again. Gesturing to me, he said, "There you have it. You have nothing to fear."

Shutting off my magic, I let out a breath of relief.

A young man in rich dark velvet called out. "Highness, is Lady Champion available for hire?"

I raised my eyebrows, surprised. My heart sensed possessiveness, giving me the impression Andrew and Braidus did not want me accessible.

King Brian spoke firmly. "Not at this time. I have a need for Lady Isabelle as I work to reopen trade with Nistier and the Jamaylin Islands and begin business talks with Dregaitia in our new agenda of peace. News of her feats on the battlefield has traveled far and wide, and our neighboring kingdoms are exceptionally interested in what she can do for them. Her presence in our upcoming talks will be key to Aberron's success."

I wondered how many directions I would get pulled in once the royals arrived. My need to ensure Aberron's survival still outweighed mine, but I hoped they wouldn't ask anything too hard of me.

King Brian took a breath. "If you have a request for Lady Isabelle, put it in writing and send it to the castle addressed as an employment inquiry for Lady Champion. I will store invitations for her services should Lady Isabelle wish to take on various tasks when I do not need her."

Another man shouted from somewhere in the back. "Dregaitia tried to conquer us again. Why should we open trade with those greedy giants?"

King Brian answered. "A full account of our battles with Dregaitia will be made available by the end of the week. In the report, you will learn that Aberron *and* Dregaitia were victims of a plot to overthrow *both* monarchies. They are *not* the enemy."

A woman questioned, "How soon will trade be reopened with Nistier?"

"And the islands?" another added.

"Yes!" multiple people shouted, sounding eager for an answer.

"I cannot give you an exact date, but I assure you I am doing everything in my power to make it happen." King Brian then ended the gathering.

On the ride back to the castle, I saw varying expressions of fear and interest in those we passed. I hated it and fought against the urge to make myself invisible.

When we stepped inside, King Brian ordered his staff to assemble in the throne room. My family stood on the dais, Andrew and Braidus hovering around me protectively, their hands intertwined with mine. We watched the people trickle in until there had to be at least two hundred, with soldiers lining the doors.

"I believe this is everyone," Queen Averly said.

King Brian spoke in a clear, no-nonsense voice. "I cannot have a staff ruled by fear and intolerance, especially while I host the royals from Dregaitia, Nistier, and the Jamaylin Islands for trade talks. Those who refused to work due to my champion are dismissed immediately."

The workers cried out in alarm. I flinched at some of the glares sent in my direction.

"This is not your fault, Isabelle," Braidus said. "You've done nothing wrong."

I couldn't help but feel it was. They'd lost their jobs over me.

King Brian read a list of those who did not report, which numbered close to seventy. They were given their last bit of pay and ordered to be out by the evening.

Several pleaded for mercy. "I've nowhere else, Highness. Please."

But King Brian was unswayed. "Actions have consequences. You made yours when you chose to revolt against the champion staying in my castle."

When they vacated, King Brian addressed his remaining staff. "I do not tolerate discrimination in my home. Should I hear or see the slightest bit of it, I will terminate you."

The subdued workers watched their king in silence.

King Brian clasped his hands together. "Since I have dismissed so many, there will be numerous positions available. If you wish to be promoted or know of someone who would be a good addition to my staff, please take time over the coming week to prove your worth. That will be all." He strode into the study.

My family and I followed.

As the door closed behind Dominic, I apologized to King Brian. "I'm so sorry." I felt awful about everything.

King Brian's eyes softened. "You have nothing to be sorry about. In fact, I'm sort of relieved this happened. I've let little discrepancies with my staff slide for far too long—enough for them to believe they could get away with this. With all these royals arriving, I need people to attend them respectfully. As king, my home is bound to have all sorts of interesting people visiting or living here. There is no room for fear or discrimination." He surprised me with a hug. "Just try to be on your best behavior in public, please."

"I will." I leaned into the hug, feeling better about what had happened.

# CHAPTER FIVE

OMINIC'S AND FALDEN'S THINGS arrived that afternoon. Henry and I helped them settle into the rooms next to ours. While they unpacked, I listened to the three boys tell me about their home life.

"Leavesden got Professor Morel's sister, Healer Marjorie Morel, to replace Malsin as the Sorrenian's healer," Henry explained. "Aliyah told me she's been tossing foul-tasting tonics into everyone's mouths to combat Aubrellianger fever."

"What is that?" I asked.

Henry shrugged. "No one knows, but Healer Morel insists it's dangerous and extremely contagious. Most of the students think she's making it up just so she can test different concoctions on people. She's like a substandard version of Malsin. There have been some strange reactions. Ryan, Cole, and Marie broke out in boils, but Rodger's skin completely cleared up, and he literally smelled like wildflowers five paces away from me." His eyes widened. "Three girls were hanging on his arm!"

I couldn't forget Rodger, the boy who'd tried to coach me on how to get bullied. "I think it's lovely he's finally getting some friendly attention."

The boys rolled their eyes.

"Anyway, spending time with Aliyah was *amazing* as always." Henry grinned dreamily. "Seriously, I think I'm in love."

Dominic and Falden laughed. I smiled.

"That's not news," Dominic said, hanging up the last of his clothes. "You've been in love with her forever. Just took you a while to see it."

Falden crowed, "I've finally gained some respect in the family. My brothers were jealous of me for once. Mother was so happy to see me safe that she couldn't stop sobbing."

Dominic rolled his eyes. "All our mothers did that."

"Father let me sit at the head of the table," Falden said, unperturbed.

"That's a big deal for his family," Henry explained to me. "Means he's finally a man."

Falden grinned. "Best family time ever." He turned to me. "Oh, Isabelle, my parents would like to thank you in person for saving my arm."

"Sure," I agreed.

Finished with Dominic's room, we moved to Falden's.

"My parents want to meet you too," Dominic said, his silver eyes meeting mine. "Once Mother heard about the invitation for me to stay and about your power, she pointedly told my father and me how important it was that I make myself indispensable to you. Since I can't change into a girl and marry Prince Andrew, she's willing to settle for the most powerful mage. She even gave me a book called *Romancing the Nobility of Aberron*." He wrinkled his nose in disgust. "I told her the princes had claimed you, but it didn't matter to her."

My eyes widened. "Are you serious?"

"My mother thrives on flaunting her wealth and nobility. She's a calculating vixen." Dominic shuddered.

"My family's rank is lesser than Dominic's, so my parents know not to push their luck with convincing you to join us. However, your power would greatly improve our standing. I'm sure they wish it too," Falden said, opening a red chest.

"They and every other noble in an Aberron family with magic or one seeking to acquire it," Henry said, undoing the latch on another chest. "The school's talking about it too. Their opinion of you has greatly changed. You're famous—and not in a bad way this time."

"Gods forbid. Does no one marry for love?" I asked.

The boys chuckled and shook their heads.

"What's love when you can have power?" Dominic said mockingly as he leaned against Falden's bedpost.

Henry slung his arm around my shoulder. "So, anything new with you?"

I shrugged. "For once, I don't think so."

"Enjoy that while it lasts," Henry replied.

I smiled up at him. "I will."

"Well, we have a few hours before dinner," Falden said, glancing at the clock. "What does everyone want to do?"

I spoke up. "I'd like to go to the library. Could one of you point me in the right direction?" Andrew, Braidus, and Joshua were tied up with King Brian in the study, and Malsin had heaps of correspondence from different healers around Aberron to reply to. Now was the perfect time to continue my quest.

"What do you want to go to the library for?" Dominic asked.

"If I tell, you'll have to swear to secrecy." I put a finger to my lips.

The boys' expressions instantly lit up.

"Now we have to know," Henry said.

"Promise you won't say anything?" I arched a brow.

"Promise," the three of them said in turn, their tones firm.

I believed them. "I'm researching the Gods to find out my importance to them." I raised the hand with my birthmark. "It's time I learn the truth about this, and I'm tired of being thwarted by those who know—which is why I'm not telling them what I'm doing."

"So that's why you went to the temple and ended up attacked in the business district," Falden said, his eyes brightening.

"It is," I said.

"Did you learn anything?" Dominic asked.

I frowned. "No, not really. They asked if I wanted to consult the Gods, but I declined. I don't want them meddling with me any more than they already have."

"Definitely," the boys agreed.

"We'll help you as much as we can, Isabelle," Henry said. "I think it's wrong that your importance is being kept from you."

"Especially after all you've done to help Aberron," Falden said.

"Yes, you deserve to know," Dominic said.

I smiled. "Thanks, guys, I appreciate it."

Henry led us to the library, where rows upon rows of shelves crammed with books lined the massive room. It also had a second level with a wrap-around balcony and spiral staircases at either end. My heart leaped at the sight of so many books. So much knowledge contained in one room, just waiting for me to discover it. I couldn't wait to delve into it.

Henry pointed to a door on the second level that bore the king's crest. A small square fence and gate had been built around it. "That is Uncle Brian's personal library and record room. It's got a crazy amount of enchantments on it. I'd wager it's more protected than the royal treasury. He's the only one allowed to enter—no other person has ever been inside, not even Aunt Averly or my mother."

"Seriously?" I said, surprised.

"Seriously," Henry said, his tone grave. "I touched the door once and got a ghastly burn on the palm of my hand. I didn't want anyone to know what I'd done, so I said I had accidentally burned myself in the kitchens when I was sneaking dessert—but Uncle Brian knew. He took me aside and said to never, ever, touch that door and that if I did it again, the consequences would be worse. I've steered clear of it since."

"Wow," the three of us said.

"What do you think is in there?" Falden asked.

Henry shook his head. "No clue. It's not spoken of." He lightened his tone. "Come on, let's see what we can find on the Gods." He led us in the opposite direction.

I glanced over my shoulder at King Brian's door. Could the answers I sought be found there?

Turned out the library had a decent-sized section on the Gods. The four of us spent several hours searching through the writings. Most of the books were accounts of the Gods' dealings with Aberronians. I read of their benevolence, like when natural disasters occurred and how they helped to ensure crops could still be sowed and harvested. Other stories spoke of their harshness when people had sworn upon them and didn't follow through with their oath or committed a crime. They were swift to send people to the Realm of Souls. I didn't read anything about someone claiming the Gods had deemed them important, nor did I see another account of someone with a birthmark like mine. The boys didn't either.

We gave up when it came time for dinner, the disappointment of our fruitless search weighing heavily upon me.

It must have shown on my face because Henry put his hand on my shoulder, his expression compassionate. "I'm sorry we didn't find anything, Isabelle. It would appear your case is truly unique."

I nodded. "It must be." I cast my eyes at the boys. "Thank you for your help, anyway. I really appreciate it."

"Maybe we can come back tomorrow and search some more," Falden suggested.

I smiled. "Maybe."

As we entered the dining hall, I shoved all thoughts of my quest aside. I'd do more research when I could, though I was starting to think I needed to become more aggressive and demand answers from those who knew.

During our meal, King Brian spoke to me. "I meant to speak to you this morning, but the day got away from me. Would you be willing to sit with me in the study regularly?" A corner of his lips curved into a sly grin. "I think you're just the thing I need to give me an edge against the opposition. And as you're to marry one of my sons, I believe a front-row seat to what it takes to rule Aberron would be beneficial."

I saw no reason to object. "As you wish."

King Brian grinned. "Excellent."

"If Isabelle's going to be in the study, where does that put me?" Henry asked.

"With us," King Brian said. "Falden and Dominic also, since they are helping us keep an eye on Isabelle. The four of you will get a firsthand education on how to run Aberron."

"We could use help with the simple reports," Andrew said.

"Indeed," King Brian said with a satisfied smile.

Much to his delight, Malsin was given more time to tinker with his healing experiments. The following morning, I walked hand in hand with my mage mates to the study, King Brian and the boys accompanying us. Settling into the room, I learned King Brian usually went over reports in the morning and reserved afternoons for speaking with people. The morning passed rather quietly as everyone scanned page after page on anything and everything, from hot springs, to business ventures, to farming operations, to plumbing, and so much more.

Queen Averly had lunch delivered. After we ate, we turned our attention to the door where guards escorted people in and out.

Fashionably dressed men and women proudly walked into the study, then shrank with fear at my presence. I tried to keep a pleasant expression on my face, but it didn't seem to help. Eyes darted nervously to me throughout every interview on subjects such as taxes, land management, and employment. I felt many were more agreeable than they had previously planned to be with King Brian's responses. Throughout the meetings, King Brian's sly smile seemed to grow. Gradually, my mood worsened. What I saw in the eyes of those who came and went said I was a ruthless killer. I had not become a champion but an enforcer for King Brian's views. No wonder he wanted me in the study.

When a plump, middle-aged man in purple-and-gold attire stepped into the room and saw me, he let out a yelp and fell to his knees, groveling. "All the taxes I owe will be paid. I promise. Please, I beg of you, don't use Lady Champion on me."

I choked. "Please excuse me."

Sick to my stomach, I shot out of my seat and through the door, passing the man, who threw his hands over his head in terror. I ran through the maze of hallways and down the stairs, pushing myself faster and faster. I needed space and figured the best place I would get it was in the sky. Workers, guards, and nobles alike jumped out of my way, some pressed against the walls in alarm. Stepping outside, I activated my magic and, like a loosed arrow, flew into the sky. I found relief in the fact that not many had the power to fly.

I rose until the air began to thin, then hovered in the damp clouds, hugging myself to stave off the chill. My heart pounded with anxiety. Taking slow, even breaths, I willed my tumultuous stomach to settle.

A few minutes later, Eric flew into the clouds and found me. "Lady Isabelle, are you all right?"

"I just need a minute to collect myself," I told him. "I'll be down shortly."

"As you wish," he said, then descended.

I reflected on my situation. *I have a crazy amount of magic. Of course, people are going to fear me.* Just like they did at the Sorrenian. But it wasn't what I wanted. I'd done what was necessary during the Dregan battles to keep Aberron free. I'd exposed my power in the Carasmille streets because I was assaulted. I couldn't change the past or get rid of my magic, but could I reinvent my image into something good? How could I show them I wasn't a beast?

"You're going to catch your death." Suddenly, Braidus hovered behind me. He wrapped his arms around me.

"I'm fine," I said despite leaning into him.

"You're like ice. It's time to come down."

He tugged a little, and I allowed him to bring me to the ground.

My five guards waited. "Is she all right?" Oliver asked Braidus.

"She will be," Braidus said as he guided me inside.

My body stiff with cold, I buried my face in his chest to avoid the stares as he led us wherever.

"Warm up." He kissed my forehead.

I sent a wave of heat through my body and sighed as I thawed out.

"That's better."

When we arrived at the dining room for dinner, my family was seated and waiting for me. I felt a twinge of embarrassment for my abrupt exit. "I'm sorry for running out. I needed a moment to . . . refocus."

King Brian spoke. "You get used to it—the groveling and cowering. I learned from a very young age that people choose what they want to see, especially when power is involved. I learned to trust in my self-worth. Despite what others say, I know I'm not inherently cruel, nor do I take pleasure in every justice carried out." He reached over and took Queen Averly's hand. "Gratefully, I have loved ones like my dear Averly to rely on for support and strength."

She leaned over and kissed him on the cheek.

He smiled, then turned his attention back to me. "As I recall, when we first met, you trembled with fright."

A soft chuckle went around the room.

I met his blazing-blue eyes. "You are the king and Andrew and Braidus's father. Plus, I was coming to you from the execution block because I stole from your treasury and nearly murdered Braidus. I think a large dose of terror was warranted."

He chuckled. "Granted."

Braidus took my hand. "Thank you for not killing me."

I grinned. "I'm very glad I didn't."

Andrew spoke from the other side of me. "You shouldn't care so much about what other people think. You will meet many as Lady Champion and hopefully my queen. Their presence and opinions will be fleeting." He gestured to everyone at the table. "Your family knows your true worth. We are permanent. We'll love and cherish you for the rest of our days."

"Hear, hear!" Henry said, tapping his glass with a spoon.

Unexpected tears welled in my eyes. "Thank you," I whispered.

Andrew leaned over and pressed a light kiss to my cheek.

"Do you really think I'd make a good queen?" I asked him quietly.

Andrew didn't hesitate. "Absolutely. You're intelligent and kind, and you have much passion for Aberron. I think you'll be our greatest queen yet."

Hearing the conviction in his voice made me smile. I prayed that one day I would have as much confidence in myself as he did.

Soon, the talk turned to the expected arrival of King Cekaiden of Dregaitia, King Nickoli of Nistier, and Crown Prince Jakobe of the Jamaylin Islands, acting on behalf of his mother, Queen Vianca. A ball would be held to welcome them.

Queen Averly said, "The invitations were sent out today. Major preparations start tomorrow."

I offered my assistance. Because King Brian wanted a display of my power, we planned to have the ball outside on one of the training fields near the castle.

Around dessert, Henry announced, "I want to see if Aliyah and I are mage mates. Can I bring her around tomorrow?"

His request caught me off guard. Considering how poorly checking for a bond had gone with me, I hoped he fared better. I wanted him to be happy.

"Are you that serious about her?" King Brian asked, eyeing Henry speculatively.

He nodded. "I've wanted her for years but was afraid to make a move and lose her. Turns out she felt the same. I'm hoping if we are mage mates, it'll look favorably for her father. Lord Amdor is confident Aliyah will catch Andrew's eye. He disapproves our courtship."

Displeasure coursed through the bond. "I'm taken," Andrew said.

"No one will believe that until you have recited your wedding vows in front of the high priest," Henry said bitterly. "Until then, I'm only second best."

"You are not second best," I said hotly. "Aliyah's father is an idiot if he thinks that."

Henry grinned at me. "You're a treasure."

King Brian asked, "Have you spoken to your mother and Lyle about this?"

Henry shook his head. "No, but I don't foresee any objections. You know Mother advocates for love over status."

King Brian smiled over the rim of his cup. "Yes, she infuriated your grandfather when she married your father, a man with no title who'd snuck into a ball and stole her heart."

"I don't want to invite Lord Amdor while Aliyah and I check to see if we're mage mates," Henry said, his tone firm. "If we're not, he'll tell me I'm not good for her and try to foist her on Andrew."

"And if you're not, then no one has to know she ever came over," Andrew said.

Henry grinned. "Right."

"What are you going to do if you are?" King Brian asked. "You won't be eighteen and eligible to marry until the last month of spring."

Henry rubbed his chin, seeming thoughtful. "It's near the end of the first month of winter. That will give Aliyah five months to plan a wedding. Girls like to spend time planning all that stuff. She'll want to finish her year at the Sorrenian, and I'll be working and living here. I can be patient if I know I'm going to be with her in the end."

I'd never been too keen on planning the details of a wedding. The place and decorations didn't matter so much to me. As long as I had the right husband and a priest to marry us, I figured that was enough.

"All right, Henry," King Brian said, his tone weighted. "Bring your mother and Lyle and Aliyah over for tea to formally introduce us. I'm putting my trust in you."

He beamed. "I won't let you down. I promise."

The next morning, hoping to create something nice for the royals, I went to the designated training field to help with the welcome-ball preparations. Queen Averly, Dominic, Falden, a small group of workers, and, of course, my five guards accompanied me. I combined all colors to make a rainbow shield in the shape of a dome, followed by a layer of heat that radiated down to keep the area warm and comfortable. Then I added a floor of the same material. Afterward, I made sparkling stars that hung from the ceiling at various lengths.

"My goodness, Isabelle, this is going to be our greatest celebration yet," Queen Averly said when she surveyed my work.

"I much prefer the fun magic can bring to its destructive properties," I answered.

"Indeed." She waved a hand flippantly. "Carry on."

As I started work on a dais for the royals, Falden and Dominic came and stood on either side of me.

"This is going to be some Lady Champion's ball," Falden said conversationally.

I stilled. "What?"

Surprise flitted across Falden's face. "You haven't heard? That's what they're calling it. Says it right on the invitation."

I felt a flash of irritation. "I was told it was a welcoming ball for the visiting royals."

Dominic spoke. "It is, but they're calling it Lady Champion's ball because they want to acknowledge your deeds on the battlefield. Everyone worth their sundals seeks an invitation. It's going to be a big night."

I frowned. "Great."

When I finished my preparations, we returned to the castle to watch Henry try for a bond with Aliyah.

Henry made introductions to King Brian and Queen Averly. "Lady Aliyah Amdor, daughter of Lord Gregory Amdor of the House of Lords."

Aliyah wore a nervous expression and her hands trembled slightly under King Brian's scrutiny.

King Brian spoke to Aliyah. "You are serious about Henry?"

Despite her grave expression, her voice rang clear. "I am."

Lord Leavesden spoke. "They have been inseparable since the age of twelve. I believe it is a good match."

King Brian nodded. "Proceed."

Malsin went over the basics of the bond and sharing emotions and impressions. Then he reminded them that a mage mate could not be chosen. "It could be anyone, someone in this room or elsewhere. Have you ever felt pulled to anyone?" he asked Aliyah. "Falden or Dominic, perhaps?"

"No, I've only ever wanted Henry," she answered. "Dom and Falden are like brothers."

"I'm not attracted to Aliyah," Dominic said firmly. "She's like a sister to me."

"What he said." Falden gestured to Dominic.

"All right, then. We'll proceed," Malsin said.

The air swirled with anticipation as Malsin took Aliyah's hand. Eyes closed, he and Aliyah glowed bright green while Henry shone a brilliant blue. A silver-and-emerald rope half the size of mine appeared around Aliyah. Abruptly, it shot out and wrapped itself around Henry and connected with an identical-sized silver-and-sapphire rope that came from his heart. They inhaled sharply, then gazed at each other in loving wonder.

Malsin let go. The bond disappeared as they deactivated their magic. Henry stood and pulled Aliyah to him, hugging her fiercely. The room erupted with cheers for the happy couple. Envy snaked around my heart. How simple but fulfilling their bonding had been—not at all like the complicated mess of mine. One girl, one boy, one bond. The simplicity I craved would never be mine. On cue, Andrew and Braidus quietly slipped their hands into mine.

Malsin deemed it wise for Aliyah to stay the night so he could monitor her and Henry and their new bond. "It's a good thing I made a new batch of emotion suppressers this week."

"When do you plan on telling Lord Amdor?" King Brian asked Henry and Aliyah.

"I think sooner is better than later," Aliyah said, glancing at Henry. "The bond cannot be broken, and I'm not sure I can withstand another ball with my father forcing me to do things to get Prince Andrew to notice me." Her eyes darted to Andrew. "No offense, but you've never caught my fancy."

He grinned. "None taken."

"Then I will send a note requesting your family's presence at dinner tonight," King Brian said.

I asked not to join my mage mates and King Brian in the study. After yesterday's experience, I didn't want to spend the whole afternoon watching people cower in my presence. I knew I would be made to get used to it eventually, especially when I decided between Andrew and Braidus and proceeded to marry. But today, I didn't want to deal with it. Since no one objected, I spent the afternoon chatting and playing pilfer with Henry, Aliyah, Dominic, and Falden in Malsin's healing room while Malsin worked in the corner on some experiment. Reminiscent of our days at the Sorrenian, it felt like a celebration.

The boys brought Aliyah up to speed on the inner workings of my life, and time passed relatively fast. I rather enjoyed the newfound sympathy from Henry and Aliyah as they became accustomed to feeling each other.

Rubbing the place over his heart for the umpteenth time, Henry said, "It's so much, and Aliyah's not even upset."

"You're telling me," Aliyah said, dealing out the cards. "Who knew men had a store of emotion locked within them?"

I laughed. "This is great. I'm so happy you two are bonded."

Dinner with Lord and Lady Amdor proved to be interesting. Upon arrival, Lord Amdor's eyes narrowed on Aliyah and Henry sitting together, hands entwined. Lady Amdor smiled politely, but her eyes twinkled. I sensed a kindred spirit underneath the façade.

After a quick greeting, King Brian allowed Aliyah and Henry to break the news to her father. They rose to face Lord and Lady Amdor, and Aliyah spoke. "Henry asked me this morning if I would like to see if we are mage mates. I accepted. We are bonded."

Lady Amdor gasped, bringing a dainty hand to her mouth.

"What?" Shock and anger laced Lord Amdor's features. "You went behind my back." Fury brightened his eyes as he turned his full attention to Henry. "How dare you ask my daughter such a thing without my approval."

"You never would have approved," Henry said calmly.

"Of course not!" Lord Amdor thundered, his blond mustache twitching. "You're not who I intended for my daughter." His eyes briefly flashed to Andrew.

Andrew chose at that moment to wrap his arm around my shoulders. I giggled.

King Brian smoothly interjected himself into the conversation. "Amdor, your aspirations to see your daughter as queen must come down a notch. My son Andrew is in a committed, *bonded*, relationship with our champion, Lady Isabelle. I suggest you take a moment and consider your daughter before your selfish desires."

Lord Amdor glanced at us. "Bonded?"

Aliyah spoke. "Lady Isabelle is in a dual bond with Crown Prince Andrew and Prince Braidus. She is courting them both to decide who she wants to marry."

"Dual bond, you say?" Lord Amdor's bushy eyebrows nearly rose into his hairline.

"That's correct," King Brian confirmed.

Lord Amdor rubbed his chin. "Then there's still a chance Crown Prince Andrew may be available if Lady Isabelle chooses Prince Braidus."

Andrew spoke firmly. "If Isabelle chooses my brother, I will give him the throne. I refuse to be king without her."

Whoa. I touched Andrew's arm. "You would do that?"

"Absolutely," he said, eyes blazing with conviction. "I would rather abdicate than subject myself to a loveless marriage for the needed heir."

His words endeared me further to him. As a prince, he often had to put the needs of his country above all else, and I applauded him for advocating for his happiness. There needed to be a partnership between ruling Aberron and living life. I also appreciated that he'd thought of Braidus over Henry, Braidus's illegitimacy of no consequence to him.

"Humph," Lord Amdor snorted.

Lady Amdor placed a hand on her husband's arm. "Greg, let this go. Henry is second in line to the throne and a nice young man. Aliyah will still become a royal. She will be awarded all the comfort of a queen without the pressure, and she'll be happy. What more could we want for our daughter?"

Lord Amdor pinched the bridge of his nose, closed his eyes, and sighed. Then he nodded. "All right." He opened his eyes and pointed a finger at Henry. "But if you take Aliyah to the high priest without me, I will have your head on a platter."

Henry didn't flinch. "Wouldn't dream of it."

King Brian asked, "Are you in agreement on this match?"

"I am in agreement," Lord Amdor said.

King Brian held out his hand. "Then, welcome to the family."

Lord Amdor smiled and shook the king's hand.

Aliyah rushed forward and hugged him, tears running down her cheeks. "Thank you, Father. You have no idea how much this means to me."

"I think I do," he said, watching Henry gasp for breath as he accepted a pink vial from Malsin that would help suppress the strong emotions.

On the way to our sleeping quarters that night, Aliyah said to me, "I have my father to thank for Henry anyway." She went on to explain how, when Lord Amdor learned Henry would be in her class at the Sorrenian, he ordered her to make friends with him so she might have a better opportunity to get to Andrew. But after developing a deep friendship with Henry, she couldn't see herself wanting any other man. She pretended to honor her father's ambitions, but, in reality, did nothing but cultivate Henry's friendship. My esteem for her continued to rise.

The following morning, the sun shone brightly, with nary a cloud in the sky as I rode with Henry, Aliyah, Dominic, Falden, and my five guards to the Sorrenian. I still wanted to avoid the study.

Henry and Aliyah now wore gold lockets to speak to each other and jewel-encrusted gold rings on their left hands to signify their courtship. When they married, the rings would be switched to their right hands. I wondered why Andrew had never given me a ring during our courtship if that was the norm for Carasmille. He had, however, given me a beautiful bracelet after I nearly died from the poisonous-chains incident. Maybe he wasn't fond of rings. I contemplated asking him about it but then wondered what would be the point since I was now in dual courtship with him and Braidus. A single ring wouldn't make sense.

The ride through the city garnered mixed reactions to my presence. Some called out and waved, earning a return greeting and friendly smile. Others shrank in terror and ran away. Most watched me silently. I noticed a young man's hands slip on a large crate of eggs. With a flick of my hand, I held them up with my magic.

"Thank you, Lady Champion!" he called when he gathered his wits. "You saved me my job."

"My pleasure!" I answered.

In the entry hall of the Sorrenian, I ran into Alzmire, my favorite professor and my first friend when I enrolled there. "Isabelle, what a pleasant surprise!"

"I'll catch up with you guys in a bit," I told my friends. They left while my guards remained with me.

Alzmire and I hugged. "How are you?" he asked.

"Overwhelmed mostly," I told him, "but all right. You?"

"Good, good," he said. "How does it feel to be Lady Champion? You're the talk of Aberron. Tales about you have spread like wildfire. Did you really have a knife and ten arrows stuck in you when you defeated the Dregans?"

"I think ten arrows would've killed me," I quipped. "There might've been a couple, a knife, and some shrapnel, but I'm not entirely sure." I had been too consumed with Stefan's death to notice what had happened to me. My heart seized at the thought of him.

"All the good tales are embellished," Alzmire said sagely. "Still, it's a remarkable feat what you did. Aberron is blessed to have you."

Dominic and Falden sprinted into the entry hall. Behind them, I could hear loud but indistinguishable voices and the pounding of feet.

"Students! A stampede to see Lady Champion!" Falden shouted.

"Time to go." I swiveled on the balls of my feet and raced out the door, my guards and Dominic and Falden chasing after me. "Bye, Alzmire!" I called over my shoulder.

"See you at the ball," he replied, waving.

"Thanks, guys," I said as we reached the stables.

Dominic grinned. "We figured you didn't want to be mauled."

"No, thank you." We moved to reach our horses.

Our plans to hang out with Aliyah and the rest of our Sorrenian friend group had been thwarted. I wasn't that disappointed, though, and hoped the boys weren't too upset either.

"*Back so soon?*" Nisha whickered.

I patted his nose. "Too many people."

Dominic pushed me to the ground and landed on top of me with a muffled cry. What in the Gods? I heard a scuffle. Alarm rang through me. A gravelly-voiced man violently cursed. "Filthy cur!"

Dominic groaned above me, his eyes squeezed tightly shut.

"Dominic?" Panic crept into my voice. I activated my magic.

"Dom's got a knife in his back!" Falden crouched somewhere beside us.

Switching to green magic, I found the injury to be in the back of his left shoulder blade, nicking his heart. I began meshing tissue, muscle, and skin.

"Pull it out," I told Falden.

Dominic groaned and shuddered as I flooded him with green magic until he healed.

"All right. Gently lift him off me, please."

Falden and Zachary lifted Dominic, then leaned him against a stall door. I sat up. My other guards hovered over an unconscious portly man. Micah spoke into his locket.

"What happened?" I asked Falden.

"The man popped out of a stall and threw the knife," Falden said, moving to sit beside me. "Dominic pushed you out of the way and took the hit. Your guards tackled the man and knocked him out."

With a flick of my fingers, I created a rainbow shield that cuffed the man's hands and feet. "In case he wakes up."

"Good thinking, my lady," Weston said.

"Isabelle," I corrected.

"Commander Mirran is on his way with additional support." Micah tucked his locket back into his shirt.

I reached over and grabbed Dominic's hand. His eyes were open but dazed. "Are you all right?"

His gaze darted to mine. "Yes."

"I owe you my life." Gratitude filled my voice as I squeezed his hand.

Nisha snuffled Dominic's head, thanking him for saving me too.

"You repaid it by saving mine," he answered.

I spoke fiercely. "I'd never let you die. Never."

He grinned. "Good." He lifted his shoulder up and down, seeming to test it out. He grimaced. "Gods, that hurts."

Having sustained multiple stab wounds in my lifetime, I nodded. "Yes, it does."

A new sense of understanding lit his eyes. "You are seriously the toughest lady I know."

About twenty minutes later, Joshua arrived with a band of soldiers. Six men went to heave the fat man into a wagon.

"Wait. Let me help." I got up, and, using magic, lifted the criminal into the jailer's wagon, setting him on the floor. The door creaked as a soldier shut and locked it.

"Thank you, my lady," the men chorused.

I fussed over Dominic like a mother hen as he got on his horse. He spoke with amused exasperation. "Relax, Isabelle. You healed me all right."

We took a side route to the castle to avoid people and stopped at the prison in which I had been incarcerated. I put the would-be killer into a cell, then removed the rainbow shield. Joshua told us to return home.

"I'll be questioning him." My brother had a dark glint in his eye as he jabbed his thumb toward the bars.

A guard stopped us at the front entrance and said I was requested in the study.

"I'll stay with Isabelle. You get cleaned up and meet us there," Falden told Dominic.

As I walked into the study, Andrew and Braidus shot out of their seats. I then realized I had some of Dominic's blood on me. "I'm all right. Dominic took the blade for me. He's fine. I healed him. Joshua's interrogating the culprit."

Once Andrew and Braidus were assured of my well-being, I took a seat between them. So much for avoiding the study. I listened to King Brian go over reports with his sons. When Dominic entered, my mage mates expressed their gratitude, and King Brian promised him a raise.

"You're proving to be a worthy companion," King Brian told him.

Dominic smiled, his eyes lighting at the praise.

Joshua returned a couple of hours later with news. "Abominator attack. Kyston, their leader, ordered a few of his loyal followers to kill Isabelle if an opportunity presented itself. Some are willing to die to take out what they perceive as a great threat to mankind."

King Brian grabbed a blank sheet of paper and started writing. "Let's bring Kyston in and charge him. Disband the Abominators. Anyone seen preaching or practicing their ideals will be sentenced. We will install a no-tolerance policy for hate groups against mages. I've let this go on long enough."

"How did you get the killer to talk?" I asked my brother.

He shrugged. "I tied a rope to him and lit the end on fire. As the fire climbed the rope, he started talking."

I grimaced. "That's terrifying."

"Don't worry," Joshua said. "I wasn't actually going to set him on fire."

That relieved me a little. "Good."

Patrol guards found Kyston at a dining establishment early that evening. King Brian wasted no time holding a trial.

"I want this over and done with before the royals arrive tomorrow," he said. "I don't want there to be a single reason for them to refuse trade with us."

We hopped in a carriage and rode to the jail. I shivered as I stepped into the room I'd been sentenced in. Everything looked the same. Ten rows of benches angled to the focal point: a high-backed wooden chair bolted to the ground. Behind the chair stood an ornately carved podium with six plush, dark-blue chairs behind it. Above the stand hung a huge flag bearing the king's crest. A tremor coursed through me as memories of my trial came to life. I fought the urge to bolt.

Andrew took my hand. "You're safe, Isabelle. Don't worry."

King Brian opened a door leading to a room about the size of a broom closet. "Isabelle, hide in here and connect us with your purple magic. I want to read Kyston's mind without him knowing."

I stepped inside.

Falden said, "I better squeeze in there, too, just to make sure someone's got eyes on Isabelle."

Joshua clapped him on the back. "Good thinking."

Despite not liking being constantly watched, I appreciated that Falden took his job seriously.

Several guards brought Kyston, a man in his thirties who oozed with charm, into the room. Once King Brian established Kyston's identity and affiliation with the Abominators, he said, "I'm told you ordered your followers to murder my champion."

Kyston shrugged. "A joke. How could I have known they would take it literally?" His mind said, "*Mages are a plague of the vilest proportions.*"

Ugh. What had some mage done to make him hate us so? Or maybe he was jealous he hadn't been born with a gift?

King Brian brought in my would-be killer. At the sight of a fireball rolling about in Joshua's hand, the man babbled in terror. "I told you everything, I swear."

"Say it again," Joshua growled.

The man pointed at Kyston. "He said, 'Anyone who kills the champion will be rewarded beyond their imagination.' I needed the riches to pay off my gambling debts at the Musing Bard. I owe—" He tried to launch into a further explanation, but King Brian lifted his hand and cut him off.

Kyston's mind said, "*Fool! How dare you betray me!*" Out loud, he drawled, "The man will say anything to spare himself pain."

It didn't take any convincing after that. Thank the Gods I had purple magic, allowing us to see the criminal Kyston was. King Brian sentenced Kyston and the portly man to the Carasmille prison, where they both deserved to be. I prayed this would be the end of it, but I wasn't holding my breath.

# CHAPTER SIX

WOKE WITH A GASP, my heart pounding. I shut my eyes, trying to rid myself of the nightmare and return to sleep. Instead, my body only became more alert, so I slipped out of bed to face a pale morning.

As I made my way to the bathroom, my body became swathed in a golden light and my skin prickled. I cursed. *What in the Gods makes Haldren think I need more magic?* The war with Dregaitia was over. I dropped into my mage core to check my levels. Five full glass spheres greeted me, filled with more gold flecks than before.

Disturbed, I exited my core, hurried into the bathroom, and shut the door. After relieving myself, I stepped up to the mirror to wash my hands. My jaw dropped. "Gods forbid."

My features had been enhanced. My creamy skin now had a healthy glow. I touched it, discovering the softness of a newborn. Vibrant emerald eyes hid behind long, dark lashes. My lips were a rosy pink. My chocolate-brown hair gleamed and fell in soft waves to my shoulders, where it naturally curled into ringlets down to my rear. My hair had grown a finger's length at least.

I shed my clothes to examine the rest of my body and gasped. *I have no moles or scars!* I brought a hand to my mouth as I studied further. My slim figure had expanded. *I have curves.* Everything had grown to healthy proportions. Only my height and birthmark remained the same.

I rummaged through my clothes to find something that would fit, my hands stilling on the dresses I'd shoved in the back of the closet, the ones

Queen Averly had fashioned for me. I recalled her telling the seamstress to make them bigger. "You're much too thin," she'd told me.

I put on a cream dress with green embroidered leaves. The soft material hugged my body. I faced the mirror to see the full picture. My own beauty struck me. Was this me? My breathing accelerated as my anxiety spiked. I'd become an unnatural piece of perfection. I tore my eyes away, sickened. *What will the others think? I can't face them looking like this.*

A soft knock came at the bathroom door. "Isabelle?" Andrew sounded concerned. "Are you all right?"

"I'm not coming out!" I cringed. Even my voice had changed to sound extra warm and feminine, with a soothing lilt.

"Your voice," Andrew said in shock. "Isabelle, I feel your anxiety. Let me in so I can help."

"No." I couldn't let him see me.

Braidus spoke. "Are you dressed?"

"Yes."

When the door handle jiggled, I quickly made myself invisible and hid behind the partition. I felt stupid. Braidus had yellow magic. He'd be able to see me. Still, I couldn't bring myself to move.

I heard the door swing open and my mage mates walk in. They spoke quietly, so I could not make out their words. My heart tugged as they focused on the bond. Suddenly, they appeared in front of me, and Braidus turned on his magic. His mouth fell open, and he grabbed Andrew's arm for support. His attraction to me surged as his eyes roamed over my body. My face grew hot, and I shifted uncomfortably.

Braidus let go of his brother and strode to me, whistling in appreciation. "Gods, Isabelle, you were beautiful before, but this?" He gestured to my body.

"It's awful," I cried.

"There is nothing awful about you," he disagreed. "You're so Gods-forbidden gorgeous I'm struggling to think straight."

Andrew spoke with annoyance. "Isabelle, turn off the magic."

I didn't want to. "*Why, Haldren?*" I complained.

Haldren's voice sounded in my ears. *"You've been doing so well. You deserve a gift for the ball."*

I stilled. *"I appreciate your thoughtfulness, but please take it back."*

*"How very ungrateful,"* he sounded mock affronted. *"No. I like it. Own your beauty. No hiding."*

Haldren shut my magic off, forcing me to materialize. My breath hitched as Andrew's desire hit me full force. He and Braidus were drowning me with their attraction.

I gasped. "Haldren, come on! Be reasonable! I can't live like this!"

*"Accept it, Isabelle,"* Haldren said.

"Meddling God," I grumbled.

His snicker echoed in my ears.

I paced three steps in either direction. "A Gods-forbidden gift. Does he have any idea what this will do to me? Does he care? No, of course not. *'Accept it, Isabelle.'* Well, I won't."

"Isabelle." Andrew choked.

I froze. My mage mates gazed at me with something akin to awe. My eyes widened in panic.

"Why are you so upset?" Braidus asked, gathering his wits. "You're still you."

"An enhanced me. My imperfections made me somewhat normal. Now I'm . . . I'm . . ." I struggled to come up with an accurate description. "Everything is proportionate. I have no scars, no moles, nothing! I checked!" I threw my hands up.

I received dual impressions of my mage mates wanting to see for themselves. Andrew's mouth twitched as he fought a smile. Braidus didn't even try to hide his wolfish grin. I took a step back.

Andrew wrapped me in a hug. "Calm down, love." He inhaled sharply, then groaned. "Gods forbid, you smell so good." In seconds, his lips were on mine, seeking, tasting, devouring. He felt so Gods-forbidden good I kissed him back, completely forgetting why I had been panicking. His hands pressed into my back, passion flooding the bond. "Marry me. Right now," he begged through his kisses.

Braidus yanked him off me. "Control yourself," he snarled. "Don't touch her until you can."

His anger lit a flame in my chest and snapped me out of the moment.

Andrew's blazing-blue eyes slowly cleared of their lustful haze, and remorse flooded the bond. "I'm sorry." He swallowed. "I lost my head."

His emotions had made me lose mine too. It frustrated me that I'd also behaved so recklessly. Thank the Gods Braidus had broken us up. I had no intention of becoming a full-fledged harlot.

I spoke with exasperation as I wondered, "How many men am I going to have to fend off because I look like a Gods-forbidden Goddess?"

My words had the same effect as splashing cold water on their faces.

"We'll just have to stay extra alert." Braidus shrugged. "I doubt there's much else we can do."

Andrew nodded. "Agreed. Let's start by getting the rest of our family and your guards used to you."

At breakfast, I endured the rest of the family's reactions to my enhanced features, except they talked over each other until I couldn't make sense of what anyone said.

Henry shouted over the din. "Her appearance is a little different, but it's still the same Isabelle inside. Let's not lose our heads."

My family quieted after that.

"I love you, Henry," I mouthed.

He beamed. "That's because I'm awesome."

I then went over the same process with my guards as Joshua called them into the study. "The Gods meddled with my sister again," he said, his voice gruff. "Memorize her enhanced appearance and voice."

I shivered as their eyes perused me with appreciation.

Joshua turned to me. "Say something, Isabelle."

"May I please be excused from the ball tonight?" I asked. "I'd much prefer to hide in my room."

"No," my whole family said.

I frowned.

Someone knocked on the door, and King Brian bade them enter.

James appeared. "King Cekaiden and his sons have just pulled up to the castle."

The bond abruptly darkened with Braidus's distaste for King Cekaiden. While I sympathized with Braidus, I hoped he wouldn't choke me with his hatred for the man.

King Brian smiled. "Perfect. I'll be down to greet them." He cast his eyes on me. "Would you please accompany me?"

I wanted nothing more than to run; instead, I squashed the feeling and accepted. "All right." I couldn't forget King Cekaiden's interest in me when we met in Saren, and if I wanted Aberron to succeed in business, I had to do my part even if I didn't like it.

Queen Averly put a hand on King Brian. "Don't keep Isabelle too long. Since her appearance has changed, I need to make sure she'll fit into the dress I got her for the ball tonight."

"I'll just have her say hello, then send her over to you," King Brian said. "She can be excused from greeting the other royals who will be arriving."

"Excellent," Queen Averly said.

King Brian held out his arm to me. I looped mine through his, allowing him to escort me out of the study with the princes, my brother, and the boys trailing us.

"I appreciate you doing this with me," King Brian said.

"Of course," I said good-naturedly. "I want Aberron to succeed."

King Brian smiled at me. "As do I."

We arrived at the entrance hall and waited half a minute before the front doors opened and King Cekaiden, his two sons, and a decent-sized entourage of guards entered.

"Welcome to my home," King Brian said warmly. "We're pleased to have you."

"The pleasure is ours," King Cekaiden said cordially. He gestured to one of his sons. "Allow me to introduce my firstborn, Crown Prince Timtric."

From Braidus's memory, I saw traits of Kiella in him with his onyx hair, purple eyes, and high cheekbones.

King Brian stepped forward and shook hands with Prince Timtric. "Wonderful to meet you."

Prince Timtric murmured something similar.

King Cekaiden's gaze flicked to me, and he smiled. "Lady Isabelle, it is a delight to see you again. You have certainly grown in beauty since the last time we met."

I smiled ruefully. "The Gods have meddled. I woke this morning to see my features enhanced." I switched subjects, not wanting to discuss it. "I trust you had a good journey?"

King Cekaiden nodded. "It was uneventful. I have brought someone of interest to you."

"Oh?" My curiosity rose.

King Cekaiden turned and spoke to his guards in Gaitian while summoning them forward with his hand. The men stepped aside, revealing Danovic, the Dregan soldier I had befriended during our war.

Happiness bubbled inside me. "Danovic!"

The men chuckled, no doubt at my delight.

"Isabelle!" He grinned as he strode quickly to me. Opening his arms, he picked me up, hugged me tightly, then gently set me down. He spoke excitedly in Gaitian while gesturing to King Cekaiden.

Of course, I couldn't understand a word since I didn't speak his language. Laughing, I held up a hand. "Hold on. I need a translator until I can learn Gaitian."

King Cekaiden spoke. "He wishes to tell you of his promotion to my royal guard. In Dregaitia, it is a coveted position and earns him much respect."

I smiled at Danovic. "That's wonderful. Congratulations."

King Cekaiden spoke to Danovic in Gaitian. Danovic took my hand in his, his eyes darting between me and King Cekaiden as he spoke.

King Cekaiden laughed and said to me, "Danovic wishes to know if his new position earns him enough to buy you for his wife."

My eyes grew wide. "Oh." I liked Danovic but as a friend only. I didn't want to marry him. "I'm sorry, I have been claimed already, but I would still very much like to be friends with you."

King Cekaiden spoke to Danovic.

Danovic frowned, then, after a moment, he nodded, his smile in place once more. He spoke quickly. King Cekaiden responded in kind and patted Danovic's shoulder.

"Danovic accepts friendship," the king said.

"Oh, good." I smiled with relief.

King Brian inserted himself. "Allow me to show you to your rooms."

Danovic lightly squeezed my hand, then let go. I waved goodbye as King Brian led the Dregans away.

Braidus came up. "You should know Cekaiden likely only promoted Danovic to such a lofty position to gain your favor. Cekaiden is trying to soften you so you'll acquiesce to his wishes."

"I don't doubt it." To a king, every decision was political. "I'll be on my guard."

"Good." Braidus kissed the top of my head and left to join his father.

The boys walked with me to Queen Averly's sitting room. Once inside, I discovered the queen had her own entourage, including Princess Liliana and a host of workers that included seamstresses and barbers. Elaborate dresses were draped over two of the couches, and on several tables rested containers of jewelry, perfume bottles, and face powders and paints.

Having never seen anything like this, I found myself intrigued and a little terrified. This was a far cry from Adel and me sewing our dresses, doing each other's hair, and applying a few basic face powders and paints. Grief brushed my heart at the thought that I didn't have her with me.

Henry turned to me with a teasing grin. "Gods, I'm glad this is you and not me."

Dominic and Falden nodded vigorously.

I looked up at Henry. "It can't be that bad, can it?"

He laughed. "You don't know my mother."

Queen Averly strode to us with a smile. "Oh, good. You're here. I have everything set up."

The boys started to back out of the room.

"Not so fast, boys," Princess Liliana called before they could fully make their escape. "I won't have any of you coming to the ball looking like you just climbed out of bed. All three of you need a haircut and shave, at the very least." She snapped her fingers, and a barber quickly appeared at her side, scissors in hand.

I grinned at them. "Ha. We're in this together."

The boys groaned.

Princess Liliana made the boys sit in chairs. Meanwhile, Queen Averly grabbed a few dresses for me to try on and directed me to a partition. As I undressed to a breast band and underwear, I felt a little self-conscious over the new changes to my body. This enhanced beauty would only strive to put me more in the center of attention, and I lamented that Haldren wouldn't undo it. Not wanting to look at my body anymore, I hurried to cover it with one of the dresses Queen Averly handed me. Then I stepped out to show her.

She shook her head. "The rose is too pale on you."

After trying on several more in different shades and styles, we settled on a stunning one-shouldered, navy-blue dress with silver embroidery and crystals sewn in. I looked like the night sky. Thankfully, no alterations were needed.

The boys managed to make their escape by the time it came for my hair to be done. I laughed as they practically ran to the door, each carrying a fancy set of clothes Princess Lilliana had procured for them.

Princess Liliana then came over and directed the barber on how to style my hair. Parts of it were braided, then swept to the side, allowing my natural curls to trail over my bare shoulder and down to my waist. Then came the jewelry. Diamond pins were threaded through my hair, and I put on diamond earrings, a sapphire-and-diamond gold necklace, and a matching bracelet. I'd never worn so many precious gems, and it unnerved me.

"You are the guest of honor," Queen Averly said as she caught my expression. "You must look your best." She handed me a matching dark-blue, gauzy shawl, and then, with an exultant smile, deemed me ready.

Once Princess Liliana and Queen Averly were ready, we took a carriage to the field. The sun hung low, minutes from departing for the moon to make its debut.

Along the way, Queen Averly gave me instructions. "The guest of honor is always the last to show, allowing time for everyone else to arrive. Brian will escort me to the dais, then come back for you."

"Don't forget to curtsy," Princess Liliana added.

Queen Averly nodded. "After a welcoming speech, Brian will open the ball with a dance with you." She paused. "Can you dance?"

"I can follow," I said. There wasn't much dancing in Saren, certainly nothing elaborate, but I was quick on my feet. I'd learn.

"That'll do," she said approvingly.

Indiscernible chatter came from outside the carriage as we stopped and a manservant opened the door. Princess Liliana and Queen Averly stepped out first. I didn't move. Anxiety gripped my heart.

Queen Averly poked her head in. "You can do this, Isabelle, you're a strong, capable woman."

*Right.* I forced my feet to move and stepped out. Queen Averly tucked my arm in hers, and together we walked the short distance to the entrance, my guards flanking us. Two soldiers standing attention gawked at me.

A frenzied middle-aged man poked his head out of the rainbow dome's entrance as though he'd been doing this frequently as he awaited our arrival. His relief melted the lines of his face. "We're ready when you are, My Queen." He had the decency not to ogle, but his eyes lingered on me a second longer than necessary.

Queen Averly stepped through the entrance. King Brian turned around, magnificent in his white-and-gold ensemble, a crown perched on his head. His tender expression for his wife melted my heart. He gently took her hand and led them to a dais while the frenzied man announced them.

My guards stood far enough away to make me feel like I stood alone. Andrew's and Braidus's anticipation ate at me, making it hard not to fidget. More impressions flew through the bond. Andrew was annoyed at the hovering crowd of girls. Braidus, standing beside his brother, found his plight amusing.

King Brian returned, a warm smile on his lips. *I can do this.* Andrew and Braidus sent courage and love through our connection. Schooling my features to appear enthused, I walked into the light.

The room hushed. Bright-colored clothing flashed from every direction. Round tables decorated with ice-blue tablecloths and white rose bouquets in silver vases were pushed against the sides of the rainbow dome. A band of musicians stood in a raised corner.

I curtsied.

King Brian extended his hand and pulled me up, grinning proudly. "You are stunning."

"Thank you." I smiled. We turned to face the large crowd.

The frenzied man spoke in a smooth, even voice. "Announcing our guest of honor, Lady Isabelle Elaine Mirran, Champion of Aberron."

With my arm draped over King Brian's, I moved deeper into the room, my eyes sweeping the crowd in search of my mage mates. I found them by the dais, grinning at me like drunken men and surrounded by beautiful young women. They wore nearly identical outfits, white shirts, black pants, and black leather midcalf boots. I noticed Braidus's shirt was embroidered in gold, Andrew's in dark blue. He also wore a thin silver crown, marking him as crown prince. A warmth rose within me. I could hardly take my eyes off them. My lips curved upward. *Gods forbid. They're gorgeous.*

King Brian led me to the dais, where the visiting royalty and my family awaited. Turning on his magic, he spoke to the crowd. "I welcome you to our ball in honor of our visiting guests, our esteemed kings Cekaiden of Dregaitia and Nickoli of Nistier. The magnificent Crown Prince Jakobe of the Jamaylin Islands, Crown Prince Timtric, Prince Kendar of Dregaitia, and Crown Prince Sebastian of Nistier. Also, I bring your attention to our Lady Champion, Lady Isabelle Mirran." He smiled down at me. "We would not be here today without her."

The crowd clapped appreciatively.

Joshua handed King Brian a small black box. King Brian turned to me as he opened the lid to reveal a beautiful, gold, heart-shaped locket nestled on a velvet cushion. Engraved on the top were the king's and Mirran crests, side by side as if united.

"For your services to Aberron, I present to you this locket bearing both the king's and Mirran crests. May you be considered part of the Sorren royal family forevermore."

I gasped.

Braidus's and Andrew's joy hit me hard. Joshua took the box as King Brian removed the locket. I held my hair up, allowing him to fasten it around my neck. I shivered as cold metal touched my skin. King Brian stepped back with a proud fatherly smile.

I curtsied, a soft smile on my lips. "Words cannot express my gratitude. Thank you from the depths of my heart."

The crowd cheered.

King Brian deactivated his magic, making his voice normal. Softly, he said, "You are most welcome, daughter."

I fought tears as warmth filled my heart.

As the clapping died, King Cekaiden spoke. "I also have a gift for Lady Isabelle."

He retrieved a small white box from Prince Kendar. King Brian stepped back, allowing King Cekaiden to face me. He opened the lid to reveal a lovely gold ring with a large red ruby center and some engravings on the side I couldn't decipher. "Saving the life of a king does not go unrewarded. Dregaitia is in your debt. I present to you the ring of my house. May you also be a part of our royal family."

Braidus's suspicion mingled with my own. However, I really didn't see an option to refuse the ring. The last thing I wanted was to offend King Cekaiden and start another war. I allowed him to place the ring on my right pointer finger, slightly surprised it fit so well. I hoped nothing nefarious was attached to his gift.

I curtsied, then flashed King Cekaiden what I hoped was a dazzling smile. "I am honored. Thank you from the depths of my heart."

After another round of clapping, King Nickoli stepped forward. Seemingly around King Brian's age and height with a solid build, he had thick, graying, reddish-brown hair and amber eyes that reminded me of warm honey. His nose was a little crooked, as if it had been broken. The lower half of his face was obscured by a full, gray-streaked beard.

He spoke in a thick Nistieran accent. "We do not know each other yet, but I hope to become well acquainted during our visit. In Nistier, we wear a brooch displaying the family crests of those important to us." He pointed to a large gold pin on his chest that had a row of tiny gold squares engraved upon it. "I give one to you with the crest of my family in hopes of beginning a lasting friendship." He handed me a gold pin with a tiny gold square bearing the royal Nistieran crest.

Joshua stepped forward to help me pin it to my dress. Curtsying, I spoke in fluent Nistieran, excited to put my skills to use. "It would be my pleasure to form a friendship with Nistier. Thank you from the depths of my heart."

A surprised smile graced King Nickoli's lips, and he switched to his native tongue. "You speak Nistieran well. We shall be great friends already."

I laughed lightly. "I shall hope so."

Crown Prince Jakobe approached. His long black hair was braided in thin rows with gold and silver beads threaded through the braids, his beautiful skin the color of milk chocolate. His dark-green eyes scrutinized me from head to toe. "The Jamaylin Islands would also like to form a friendship with you, Lady Isabelle." He had a pleasant, cultured voice. "On our islands, we collect beads as tokens of friendships and family. I wish to give you a bracelet from my house in the hopes that we can become friends." Onto my wrist he slipped a bracelet made of white beads flecked with gold, with a single gold bead in the center that had his family crest on it.

I smiled at him. "I look forward to a new friendship. Thank you from the depths of my heart."

King Brian returned to my side as Prince Jakobe stepped back. "Allow me the pleasure of the first dance?"

I accepted. The crowd melted to the sides as King Brian led me to the middle of the dance floor and the musicians took up their instruments and struck up a soft melody. The king bowed. I curtsied. Then suddenly we were gliding across the rainbow floor in the first dance of the night. The room erupted into soft chatter. I thanked the Gods he led well.

"I know how much you detest attention, but thank you for coming," King Brian said as we danced.

"I'm happy to be here for you." I meant it.

When the last note rang out, Andrew tapped his father's shoulder. "Sorry, Father, but I can't wait any longer."

King Brian laughed. "Take her."

The music started playing a livelier tune.

Andrew picked up where his father left off, twirling me around the ballroom with ease. "Gods forbid, you're gorgeous. Don't be swayed by the other princes' charm. I loved you first." The possessiveness that came through the bond told me he viewed every male besides my family as a threat. He wanted nothing more than to whisk me away and keep me safe from any man who might forget himself and try to win my heart.

I laughed, warmed by his love and desire to protect me. "I love you, Andrew."

Before I knew what was happening, Braidus pulled me from his brother's grasp, spinning me away to dance with him. His impatience surprised me.

"You stole my dance!" Andrew complained.

"I stole nothing. We're sharing," Braidus answered.

Andrew waited about one spin before he stole me back.

"Hey!" I laughed.

Above my head, some silent communication passed between my mage mates. With matching cocky grins and gleeful eyes, Andrew danced me into Braidus. They passed me back and forth, effortlessly twirling and gliding me across the floor and becoming more seductive with each pass. Fingers brushed against skin, slowing my steps, my senses going into overload. I loved every Gods-forbidden second of it.

Midpass, I jumped to the right to slip from their grasp. "Enough," I giggled, holding up my hands.

Andrew and Braidus looked at each other and nodded. They advanced with playful hearts. Andrew had a devious smile, while Braidus made a show of threading his fingers through his hair to push it away from his face. He knew I was a goner for his silky locks. Activating my magic, I sent them flying to the dais. They doubled over with laughter.

As I slowly climbed the steps, I flashed a flirtatious smile at my mage mates. Andrew and Braidus abruptly stopped laughing as their desire for me overtook them. With a flick of my fingers, I bound their wrists with shields they began wrestling with.

A laugh bubbled from my throat. "A lady needs protection from those dangerous hands."

"Our eyes need protection from your exquisiteness," Braidus said.

I made myself invisible, but Braidus summoned his magic to see me.

I sauntered up to him, stopping when my toes nearly touched his boots. "Unfortunately, invisibility doesn't work on you." I stood on my toes and pressed a light kiss to his lips, then retreated five paces to Joshua's side beside King Brian. I revealed myself and removed the shields around my mage mates' wrists.

Joshua leaned down and whispered in my ear, his voice full of amusement. "Your mage mates are hopeless."

I chuckled. "Yes."

The celebration picked up. Others took to the dance floor, the chatter increasing in volume. I caught sight of Henry and Aliyah dancing, silly, in-love grins on their faces. My heart warmed at the happiness radiating from them. Dominic and Falden held court off to the side of the dais with students from the Sorrenian. Like miniature kings, they stood with an air of importance and arrogant smiles. Queen Averly and Princess Liliana entertained a group of spectacularly dressed middle-aged women dripping in jewels.

"Isabelle," King Brian called.

I focused on him. He stood beside Kings Nickoli and Cekaiden and Prince Jakobe.

"Yes?" I asked.

"King Nickoli and Prince Jakobe are interested in a display of your magic," King Brian said. "Will you humor them, please?"

I let Boomer out and activated every color, lighting the dais with my rainbow magic. I shut my eyes. "Let me know when everyone's stopped staring."

"People are going to stare whether you have your magic on or off," Joshua said.

I grimaced and opened my eyes. "You're probably right."

"What is the purpose of the gold and purple magic?" King Nickoli asked.

"The purple gives Isabelle the power of telepathy. The gold extends her magic. She can do more with less." King Brian gestured to the dome and decorations. "As you can see, Isabelle had a bit of fun creating this for us."

The royal guests eyed the room.

King Brian continued. "It is my belief the Gods have blessed Isabelle with additional powers to become an ambassador. She has a sharp mind and a penchant for peace. I believe her talents will be useful for all."

"And yet, as an Aberronian, her ties are to you," King Nickoli said, his gaze severe. "You have great power at your fingertips."

"If you think I control Isabelle, you are mistaken," King Brian said coolly. "Only the Gods have the power to subdue her."

I interrupted before a verbal battle ensued. "If you'll excuse me, I'm not in the mood for politics tonight or to be thought of as a commodity."

Kendar seized the opportunity. "Allow me the pleasure of a dance?"

I smiled. "Of course." I was relieved to be leaving before everyone could rehearse my advantages and disadvantages. I figured I'd hear enough of it with trade talks beginning on the morrow. Why ruin tonight?

I caught approval in King Cekaiden's gaze as Kendar reached for my hand. Together, we walked onto the dance floor. Kendar was so tall I had to settle for putting my hands on his arms, but we somehow made it work and danced comfortably.

Kendar smiled, all charm. "It is good to see you again. You have changed since we last met. Your voice and beauty! My Gods!"

I frowned deeply. "King Brian may think I am meant to be an ambassador, but I firmly believe the Gods use me as a plaything—a live doll, so to speak. The Gods enhanced my appearance as a gift."

"You do not like it," he surmised.

"I do not wish for attention, but they seem intent on giving it to me," I answered. "I am at a loss."

"How grand it would be to be a God, to do whatever you wanted without consequence," Kendar replied dreamily.

"It sure makes it hard for a mere human to fight back, doesn't it?" I answered.

He laughed. "Yes." His expressive coal-black eyes shined with delight as he surveyed me. "You are magnificent."

I smiled, pretending to be flattered. "Thank you."

As the song came to a close, Prince Sebastian of Nistier asked for a dance. I accepted, hoping he wouldn't make me feel as uncomfortable as Kendar had. Prince Sebastian's eyes were bright gold, and I had a hard time not staring at them. We spoke entirely in his native tongue, which seemed to relieve and please him greatly. His voice had a velvet quality to it as we exchanged basic pleasantries.

He then said, "I was told you were a warrior with immeasurable power, but I did not expect you to be so. . ." He paused, seeming to choose his words as his eyes took me in.

"Short?" I suggested.

That brought rich laughter from him as we glided across the floor. "You have wit. A lady of many talents."

Crown Prince Timtric asked for the next dance. He had the seriousness of his father, which I found more enjoyable than Kendar's demeanor.

"You have become famous in our house," Timtric said. "My father and brother raved about you when they arrived home. I must say their words have merit. You do not disappoint."

"Thank you," I said.

"My brother's roguish ways are wasted on you," he said, moving in tandem with the music. "Please do not judge Dregaitia based on his actions."

"And what about your father's?" I asked.

Timtric smiled. "Ah, Braidus has educated you."

"I am aware of Braidus's history and your father's interest in magic for his line," I said.

"Dregaitia has relied on its brute strength for centuries. My father has a vision of embracing magic to improve our standing. I do not see it as wrong," he said. "The Nistieran, Aberronian, and Jamaylin royals have magic. We seek to be on equal ground."

"I don't see your pursuit as foolish," I answered honestly. "Magic used wisely can be a benefit." It amazed me how my attitude about magic had changed.

Timtric gave me what appeared to be a genuine smile. As the song ended, he said, "Thank you for saving my father, my brother, and my first general. It would have been a blow to lose them."

"You're most welcome," I answered.

Prince Jakobe asked for my hand next. I asked him about his home.

"We have white sandy beaches and lush green trees. The weather is usually mild, but when the storms come, they are fierce. We have many watch towers to anticipate storms."

I learned the Jamaylin people revered mages. "We rely heavily on them for storms. To be a mage on our islands makes you instant nobility."

"I see," I answered. "What color are you?"

He smiled, his dark-green eyes lighting up. "Green and yellow."

"A rare combination," I said.

He laughed lightly. "I am the envy of many on my islands."

As our dance concluded, Braidus materialized by my side with a drink. "Had enough yet?"

"Thank the Gods for you." I downed the contents, tasting white grape and peach. I moved with him to the dais. "I've danced with every prince. Can I go now?"

"You've done your political duty. Why not enjoy the rest of the celebration?" he asked.

I gave him a no-nonsense look.

"It wouldn't look good for Father if his guest of honor left early," he explained.

I sighed. "Of course."

"Isabelle, join us!" Henry looped his arm through mine, then pulled me toward his group of mostly Sorrenian students and a few older people. I looked back at Braidus with a pleading expression, but he only chuckled, urging me to have fun. He returned to his father's side.

Aliyah grabbed my hands. "Oh, Isabelle, you are positively radiant." She wore a beautiful peach dress with silver embroidery, her hair curled and laced with silver gems.

"So are you," I complimented. "That dress becomes you."

She beamed.

"Those princes are falling all over themselves for you," Amarilla said with a hint of sourness and jealousy, I suspected. She wore a glittering red dress with a plunging neckline.

"Oh, here! I meant to give you this." Aliyah fished into her reticule and handed Amarilla a perfume bottle. "It's called Catch a Prince. It debuted in Waverly's this morning in honor of all the visiting princes. My aunt picked it up for me before she knew I'd bonded with Henry."

Amarilla sprayed a little on her wrist and sniffed. She shrugged. "A little sweet, but I've smelled worse." She sprayed a little more "Wish me luck. I'm going to catch a prince." With a swish of her hips, she prowled straight to the dais and to the group of princes.

"Amarilla is bold," I said with astonishment as Kendar led her to the floor.

"Trained since birth to up their family's social standing," Aliyah said in all seriousness.

"Hey, Isabelle, will you dance with me?" Dominic asked. "I promised my mother I'd *try* to win you over." He rolled his eyes.

I chuckled. "Of course."

Dominic pointed to his mother while we danced, a hawk-eyed lady dressed in purple who stood beside Queen Averly. She gave Dominic an approving but calculating smile.

He shuddered. "I pray you don't ever meet her."

Out of the corner of my eye, I spied Andrew in the middle of a group of immaculately dressed young maidens. Delving into the bond, I felt his exasperation, but he didn't show it. He spoke to them, words I could not hear. The ladies tittered, their faces aglow with his attention. A giggling blonde in light blue looped her arm through his and put her hand on his chest as if she had claimed him. I read Andrew's surprise at her boldness.

I asked Dominic, "Who is that woman with Andrew?"

He followed my gaze. "Oh, that's Lady Marissa Tenley. She hails from the southwest province."

The name sparked a memory. Could she be the very same Lady Marissa I'd heard Queen Averly had petitioned Andrew to court?

Dominic said, "Her family is just as rich with sundals and titles as mine. My mother considered pairing me with her once but decided she was too haughty, which is saying something for my mother." He leaned forward and said in a secretive tone, "I heard Marissa's father, Lord Marcus Tenley, makes his household staff call him and his daughter King Tenley and Princess Marissa. They're punished if they don't."

I frowned. "That's conceited and wrong."

"Agreed," he said.

My time with Dominic must have signified that I was available to the Aberronians of lesser status. As long as the music played, young men vied for a dance. I said yes because I didn't want them to believe I thought them unworthy. Position meant nothing to me. I tried to be courteous but not encouraging. I wasn't sure it worked because many left looking starry-eyed.

Some of the men asked about my magic. "What does the gold mean?"

"Extends my magic," I'd say.

"And the purple?"

"Telepathy." I had my answers memorized.

Others asked about my feats on the battlefield. "I heard you're just as good with a blade as you are with magic. Is that true?"

"Yes," I answered. "My favorite pastime is fencing."

I noticed Andrew had an equally difficult time getting away from the young women. Lady Marissa had glued herself to his side. I disliked the number of times I saw her putting her hand on him as he chatted with various people. I had the strong urge to march over and tell her to back off. *After this dance,* I thought.

The man I currently danced with—Derrick, I think—seemed particularly interested in my involvement in the battle. "My brother Liam is a lieutenant captain in the First Wave. He works closely with your brother, Commander Mirran. I would have joined, but my father insists only one soldier per household. I aim to take a position in court instead—a magistrate, perhaps."

"I see." *Let's hope you're better than Court Magistrate Philsby—the man who sentenced me to death for robbing the royal treasury without allowing me to plead my case.*

After we briefly discussed the major points of the battle he'd learned from Liam, he said bluntly, "I heard you roasted the Mazika to ash because they killed your first lover—a simple postboy who managed to become an orate judge."

He spoke crudely, as if Stefan had been no better than a homeless beggar. My heart twisted in agony, and tears pricked my eyes. I wrenched free of his grasp.

Derrick's dark-brown eyes widened. "I'm sorry. I didn't believe it to be true."

In seconds, Braidus was at my side, his arms around me. The stress of the constant attention coupled with Derrick's callousness had gotten to me. I lost composure and cried into Braidus's chest. I faintly heard Derrick apologizing again, but Braidus cut him off.

"I'll take over from here," he said as he tucked me into his side. I sniffed, trying to control my emotions to ease the burden on my mage mate. He started to lead me to the dais, but I stopped him when I remembered my plan to rescue Andrew. Reading my intention through the bond, he changed course. We approached Andrew from behind, Braidus releasing me to collect his brother.

Andrew was attempting to disengage from the party. He hadn't seen me yet. ". . . I must see to Lady Isabelle."

Lady Marissa latched on to his arm for what felt like the hundredth time. "But you haven't heard the rest of Mr. Breen's tale."

My patience ran out entirely. I spoke loudly but with feigned civility. "Let go of him, please."

Andrew whipped around, forcing Lady Marissa to drop her hand.

Relief and concern showed on Andrew's face. "Isabelle, my love, I was just coming to find you." He gathered me into his arms.

Lady Marissa looked as if she'd eaten something rancid.

Braidus joined us. "I think Isabelle is done for the night."

"As am I," Andrew answered. Turning back to the small congregation, he said with a smile, "It was a pleasure."

The others murmured something similar, except for Lady Marissa. I could feel her shooting darts at my back as we walked away. *You can't have him,* I thought fiercely.

A laugh escaped Andrew's lips. "Wow, your jealousy is intense."

"Everything about her is," Braidus commented.

"Sorry." I needed to work harder to control myself.

"Don't apologize for who you are," Braidus said.

"You don't need to change," Andrew said in agreement. "You know I'm yours entirely. You've nothing to worry about."

I smiled at him. "I know. I just don't like seeing others trying to claim you."

"Same for you. How many men did you dance with tonight?" Andrew asked.

"Too many," I said with a shake of my head.

As we reached the dais, the three kings and Prince Jakobe turned toward us.

Braidus spoke. "Isabelle has had enough excitement for tonight."

"What happened?" King Brian asked, his eyes darting to me.

Braidus explained, "I believe Isabelle's last dancing partner somehow learned of Stefan and said something uncouth about him." He gestured to his brother with a tilt of his head. "And Andrew cannot go two paces without a particular lady trying to lay claim. Isabelle's claws will come out if she catches the woman near Andrew again."

"Which lady?" King Brian asked.

"Lady Marissa Tenley," Andrew answered. "The women have been more bold than usual in capturing my attention tonight. She clung to me like a leech." His annoyance pulsed strongly through the bond. "Her high-pitched laugh grates on me, as do the glares she fires at other women when she thinks I'm not looking. I don't wish to cause problems between you and Lord Tenley, so I remained courteous, but I do *not* want to be caught by her again."

"Understood," King Brian said. "Feel free to remain here."

The three of us sat at a table with platters of meats, cheeses, pastries, fruits, and vegetables.

Pouring himself a drink, Andrew said with interest, "I've never been able to sit at a ball before. It's nice."

Braidus spoke with disgust. "This ball is no different than any other I attended before my banishment. Illegitimates are always ignored or scorned among high society."

I turned to him, my blood heating. "Who disparaged you?" No one would dare say a bad word once I got ahold of them.

"I will not name anyone," Braidus replied, his tone firm. "I accepted that it will always be this way for me in Aberron when I returned. I suspected it would be worse because no one can forget I tried to murder my father over the illegitimacy laws."

"You did nothing of the sort," I said sternly. "The Fate had control of you."

"No one will believe that. They'll think it's an excuse to get close to my father again for another chance at the throne." His expression darkened, then cleared. "I am not affected by the animosity like I was as a boy. I have grown to value only the opinions of my family."

He didn't want me fighting his battles for him. While I fumed that anyone would dare take a shot at this wonderful, spirited man, I respected his desires. I took his hand in mine and spoke with intensity. "You are no less than anyone else in this room. You are incredibly loved and valued by me and your family."

Andrew raised his glass. "Hear, hear!"

Braidus gave me a rare, genuine smile, the bond surging with his affection. "I know it."

# CHAPTER SEVEN

ATE MORNING THE DAY after the ball, I sat between my mage mates at the table in the study. The three kings and Prince Jakobe sat at the end of the table, easily within hearing distance of each other. The Nistieran and Dregaitian princes and Joshua also joined us.

King Brian gave Henry a stack of paperwork. "I won't be able to review this while entertaining our guests. It's time for you to use your knowledge and common sense to be a leader. Have Dominic and Falden help you. We'll keep an eye on Isabelle in their stead. This will be a good experience for you three."

Henry wore a mixture of happiness for being promoted and distaste for the work of it. I couldn't blame him. I felt proud that King Brian could see Henry's worth, and yet I empathized with the laborious task before him.

Henry handled his promotion gracefully, though. "Thank you for the opportunity to put my skills to use."

Dominic, Henry, and Falden went to meet with some of King Brian's advisors. I wished I was going with them, for my anxiety had steadily risen in anticipation of this meeting. As much as I didn't like it, the kings' and Prince Jakobe's interest in me was strong. I feared I would be the hinge in getting trade reopened for Aberron. That being said, I had no idea what the kings and prince wanted out of me. King Brian hadn't prepared me, and I wondered if it was because he himself didn't know. It wasn't often people encountered someone like me. I prayed no one would ask anything unpleasant of me. I wanted to help Aberron reopen trade, but I still had morals.

King Brian returned to his seat. He thanked everyone for coming, then said, "It is a monumental moment in history for four countries to come together over the prospect of peace and trade. I begin this meeting with a wish for open discussion. Let us forge a bond of friendship and unity that lasts for generations."

"Shall we dispense with formalities, then?" King Nickoli suggested, resting his hands on the table.

"Agreed. I care not for them in this setting," King Cekaiden said. "I suggest we go to the heart of the matter—*her*." He turned his coal-black gaze to me. "Treaty negotiations with Dregaitia reside upon Lady Isabelle."

"As do they with Nistier," King Nickoli said, also turning his attention to me.

"And the Jamaylin Islands," Prince Jakobe said.

I frowned.

"Isabelle?" King Brian invited me to share my thoughts.

I sighed. "All I care about is making sure nobody kills each other." I leaned forward and spoke with intensity. "If you have a question about me, ask *me*. I answer for myself. I will not abide being used as a bargaining chip for anyone."

King Brian spoke, his expression unreadable. "There you have it."

King Nickoli said, "You are Aberronian and bonded to Aberronian princes. Your allegiance must lie with King Brian. Therefore, he has some measure of power over you."

I gestured to King Brian. "If he has any power, it is only because he has earned it through trust and loyalty. I do not blindly follow anyone due to their importance."

"What about the Gods?" Prince Jakobe pointed to my left hand. "You wear their mark. They have claimed you for some purpose."

Andrew and Braidus stiffened. *Haldren's tool*, I thought with disgust.

I lifted my hand. "I was born with this mark. I know not of its reason."

King Cekaiden spoke. "You claim to trust King Brian, and yet he purposely keeps you in the dark. I wonder how a lady of so much skill and intelligence has not figured out the Gods' plan for you."

"Short of reading people's minds, which I consider a breach of privacy, all avenues have been thwarted," I answered. "The Gods have not deemed me ready to learn of my importance."

"What do you know of the Gods?" King Cekaiden asked.

I shrugged. "Nothing of consequence. They appear unannounced, give me trouble, and leave. Frankly, I'd be happy if I never saw them again."

King Cekaiden's eyes glittered like a cat finding a mouse and a bowl of cream. I didn't like it, and neither did my mage mates.

He leaned back. "Dregaitia has been an established country far longer than Aberron. We have extensive records on the Gods. Upon my return after meeting you, I searched through them."

"You're saying you have the answer to this?" I lifted my hand again and dropped it.

King Cekaiden spoke. "I believe I would not be wrong in saying that you are the only person in this room who's unaware of your fate."

The room suddenly felt like ice. Andrew and Braidus seized up.

"The question is, how long do you have, and how can I use that time to my advantage?"

Isaac, the Fate over Fates, whispered in my ear. "*Little Goddess.*"

My head hit the back of the chair as a vision sprang up before me. My mother looked out a window of our home in Korrun, tears streaming down her face as she clutched her noticeably pregnant stomach.

Father came up behind her, placing his hands over hers. "Shh, it'll be all right." He trailed kisses down the side of her cheek and onto her neck.

"No, it won't." Mother wept. "The baby is coming too soon. I thought we had time. We're only at eight months. There are no healers nearby and not enough time to get to Carasmille. Dorothy said she needed to perform another healing for the heart defect. If our daughter survives birth, we'll have an hour at most before her heart gives out." She cried out as a contraction hit.

Father steadied her. "I've spoken to Brian. The healers are on their way as we speak."

"They will not make it in time." Mother panted, squeezing her eyes shut. "The pains are coming closer. Where is Joshua?"

"With Mr. Reden, learning how to hitch a team," Father said.

"I want him here." Sweat dripped down Mother's forehead. "I want him to know his sister."

"Lie down. I'll get him." Father led her to a large bed with a lilac-colored bedcover and then kissed her forehead. "Tilly is coming with hot water and towels." He left to retrieve Joshua.

"Uncle," Mother whispered, staring at the white ceiling. "Uncle, please. I need you."

A bright flash and Haldren appeared. He sat on the edge of the bed and took Mother's hand. Knowledge lit his eyes. His expression was saddened. "She will not survive."

"Please, you can save her," Mother begged, crying out as she gripped her stomach. "I can't lose my child. I've waited so long for her."

"It will come at a price." Haldren straightened, meeting her emerald eyes. "My time is soon at hand. I seek a replacement."

"No!" Mother gasped, horror written on her face. "You will heal her only to take her away. I cannot bear it!"

"You will have many years to raise her," Haldren said gently.

"How many?" Mother groaned, squeezing her eyes shut again.

"Eighteen, until I revert to my human self and another takes my place," he answered.

"Eighteen years to"—her breath caught, "to stop her from becoming—a Goddess."

Haldren smiled, his eyes full of familial affection. "Yes, Anne. Are we in agreement?"

Mother swore loudly, then gritted her teeth as another contraction hit. "Yes! Now heal her!"

Haldren placed his hands on Mother's stomach and closed his eyes in concentration. A bright golden glow bathed them for a few minutes, then faded.

Haldren let go, a wide smile gracing his lips. "It is done. I cannot stop the birth, but your child will be healthy."

"Thank the Gods." Mother sunk into the pillows.

A bright flash and he vanished. Moments later, Father entered with my brother and a matronly woman.

"Mama!" Joshua rushed forward and hugged her with the exuberance of a seven-year-old. "Da says the baby's coming!"

Mother laughed, the sound rich and melodic. "Yes, you'll get to meet your baby sister very soon."

"Joshua, come help me." Tilly waved him over to a nearby table where she set up supplies for the birth. Joshua left his mother's side to assist.

"You're happy *and* sad." Father gazed upon his wife with concern as he rubbed his heart like they shared a bond. "Haldren was here, wasn't he?" He looked about the room as if he could spot him. "What have you done?"

"It's going to be all right." Mother smiled as she took Father's hand. "Uncle healed our little girl. She will live."

"That explains the happy but not the sad. What promise did you give him in return?" Father sat on the edge of the bed.

Mother's eyes widened, and she pulled her hand free. "The baby is coming! Now!"

Tilly pushed Father out of the way. "You need to leave now."

Father grabbed Joshua by the shoulders and steered him to the door. "We'll be right outside. I love you, Anne. You can do this."

Mother gave him a wobbly smile.

The vision then changed. Mother held me against her chest with a blanket over her lap. Tilly stood nearby, wringing out a washcloth. Father opened the door.

"She's here!" Joshua shouted, jumping with excitement.

Father and Joshua climbed onto the bed to see the new tiny baby nestled on Mother's chest. "She's beautiful," Father gushed with pride.

Joshua scrunched his nose. "She's slimy and wrinkly."

Father took the washcloth from Tilly and began cleaning me. "What's this?" He held my freshly wiped left hand out to Mother to show her the fiery-red birthmark resembling a sun.

"The Mark of the Gods," Mother whispered. "Uncle's payment."

Father choked as he dropped my hand. "You—you sold our daughter to Haldren?"

Tears rapidly fell down Mother's cheeks. "There was nothing else I could do. Uncle said she wasn't going to make it. I couldn't let our daughter die."

"How long?" Father asked grievously, pressing a hand to his forehead. "How long before she is taken from us?"

"Eighteen years," Mother said gravely.

"Then she will be our daughter no more." Father fell back against the headboard in dismay.

Joshua touched Father's arm. "What will she be, Da?"

Tears fell down Father's cheeks. "A Goddess for a thousand years."

My eyes snapped open. I lay on the floor in the study. Andrew had my head on his lap, with Braidus and Malsin on either side of me, each touching a shoulder. The kings and princes stood around us, looking on with concern. I scrambled out of their grasp and stood. The room spun, and I threw my hands out to steady myself. My chest rose and fell rapidly, my breathing harsh, as shock pumped through my veins. Andrew, Malsin, and Braidus rose.

Andrew spoke in soothing tones as he reached for me. "Calm down, Isabelle. You're all right, love."

"Don't touch me!" I snarled, jerking away.

Andrew stilled, hurt flashing across his face.

Braidus grabbed Andrew's arm in support. "She knows."

"Knows what?" Malsin asked.

Isaac flashed into existence. He flicked his fingers at me. The ache in my chest eased, suppressing my adrenaline. Another flash and Haldren appeared, scowling. My veins boiled with betrayal, erasing whatever emotion-suppression Isaac had done. Grimacing, Andrew and Braidus massaged their hearts. All the royals and Malsin moved out of the way and watched with a mixture of interest and trepidation. The Gods made them nervous too.

Haldren turned on Isaac. "You should not be meddling in my affairs with Isabelle. She is my charge."

Isaac crossed his arms, undeterred. "It is well past the time she learns the truth. She is halfway transformed already."

"If you felt it was time, you should have spoken to me," Haldren said icily. "It is my duty to reveal her fate, not yours."

"So it should be, but I don't trust you to tell her the truth. You've pulled her along enough as it is." Isaac turned to me, a smirk on his lips. "Want to know another secret, little Goddess?"

I froze, unable to speak.

Isaac took that as a yes because he said, "The real reason your mage mates agreed to share you is because neither will get you in the end. Their talk of marriage is a lie." He casually gestured to the people in the room. "You will lose them, your family, and this life—and soon." He imitated Haldren, by making his voice sound like his. "Both should be given ample opportunity to win your heart and experience love with their soulmate"—he dropped the persona and raised a warning finger—"before you take Haldren's place. Your family's interest in you has only been to protect you until your transformation into a Goddess is complete. Then they'll deliver you to Haldren, and you will cease to exist to them."

A double helping of guilt swept through the bond, confirming Isaac's words. My heart shattered. Braidus and Andrew gasped sharply.

Isaac stepped forward, touched my shoulder, and took my left hand in his. I flinched at the fiery sizzle of his power. His lips curved up. "A parting gift to reinforce the truth."

My birthmark turned molten, like heated metal, then began to bleed, rivulets flowing down my hand and arm. I stiffened at the burning accompanying it. Strangely, no blood dripped onto the floor. He let go.

"What have you done?" Haldren cried to Isaac, his eyes widening in despair.

Isaac shrugged. "She names you the God of trials in her thoughts. I am curious to see how she handles one from me."

"Your trial will end with her death."

Ribbons of gold magic emanated from Haldren's hands, dissipating a hair's breadth before they touched my skin. His ice-blue eyes widened.

He swiveled to face Isaac. "Undo it now!"

"No." A wicked grin slowly spread across his lips. With a bright flash, he vanished.

Scowling, Haldren approached me.

I backed into a bookshelf. "Don't come near me."

He stopped two paces in front of me and schooled his features into something impassive. "Not all is as it seems."

I spoke with venom. "You forced my mother to sell me to you in exchange for my survival. You made the Sorren monarchy accept me as one of their own and maintain a charade that I would be with them forever as a cherished family member." I gestured to my mage mates. "You created a dual bond and advocated that I fall in love with men who knew I could be nothing but a moment's pleasure." I pinned him with a hard stare. "Tell me none of that is true."

Silence permeated the room.

"How cruel you are to subject me to so much deceit," I whispered.

"I take no pleasure in causing you pain, unlike Isaac, who seeks to see you suffer for his enjoyment." Haldren gestured to my crimson hand. The burn traveled upward, nearly reaching my shoulder. "Everything I have done is with a greater purpose in mind—to prepare you for your role as a Goddess over Gods. You will be a better judge of the world if you understand love, pain, joy, and sadness."

Stepping back, Haldren turned his attention to King Brian. "Isaac has put a shield on Isabelle to block the power of the Gods. It is too strong for me to break. It is imperative you keep her alive while the poison runs its course." He paused as if listening to a thought. "Simple magic like the blue you possess will work on her." His last words ended in a growl. "Should

Isabelle die at this juncture, it could very well be the world's undoing." He took his leave.

I read pity in the eyes of the foreign kings, their sons, and Prince Jakobe. I saw remorse in King Brian, Joshua, Andrew, and Braidus. Malsin wore deep concern. I didn't care for any of it. I tore off the two lockets Joshua and King Brian had given me, threw them on the ground, and began walking to the door.

But I stumbled, inhaling sharply as the blood traveled over my shoulder and down my chest, back, and other arm, the pain intense. Andrew reached out as if to steady me.

I ignited my hands in rainbow flames, stopping him short. "Touch me and I'll kill you."

Fear flickered in his liquid-blue eyes. Assured he would leave me alone, I continued to the exit.

Joshua darted in front of me, blocking my escape. "You can't leave. You'll die out there alone."

I saw no problem with that. I didn't want to be a Goddess, and I didn't want to be here either. I'd already had a glimpse of the Realm of Souls. It didn't look bad at all. I'd have Stefan, Nathan, Adel, and my parents with me.

I held my flaming hands out. "Get out of my way before I hurt you."

Joshua crossed his arms, matching my determination. "No."

Malsin ran over and joined him. The blood traveled down my legs, ending at my ankles. Abruptly, the barrier stopping it from making a mess burst, and the pain increased tenfold. I gasped. The flames vanished as I lost my concentration on the magic. My clothes turned crimson, and my legs buckled.

Joshua caught me as I fell, his emerald eyes bright with worry, no doubt concern for the world over any care for me.

"I hate you," I whispered.

He clutched me tighter against him. "I know."

Malsin said, "Let's get her to my room."

I didn't want to go there, but I didn't have the energy to fight him.

Joshua nodded at Malsin, then turned his attention to the others. "Tell everyone to keep their distance as she is still formidable even in her weakened state."

"She harbors much anguish," Braidus said, his voice strained.

Tears stained Andrew's cheeks. I didn't care. He deserved to feel the consequences of his actions. His insides should burn, just as mine.

"She may yet lay this castle and everyone in it to waste for our wrongdoings," Braidus warned.

The concern on the royals' faces deepened into fear. It was warranted, for I had the urge to lash out at those who knew my fate, to be their judge and executioner and let them feel the cruelty they'd bestowed upon me. I was not a malicious person by nature but, today, I imagined changing that.

"I'll try not to let that happen." Joshua opened the door and strode out, clutching me in his arms.

My brother and Malsin walked swiftly through the halls, passing maids, soldiers, and a few nobles. Some shrieked with horror. I suspected word of my state would get around quickly. Halfway to Malsin's rooms, I fell unconscious.

I dreamed of Thimbleton during the Harvest Festival. I watched like a bystander as Andrew gently lifted a sleepy me off Nisha and carried me into Alzmire's house, where he laid me on a bed.

"Sleep," he whispered and kissed the top of my head.

Isaac appeared beside me. "This is what happened while you slept."

We followed Andrew out the door. He looked up and down the hallway for a moment as if deciding where to go. Spotting an alcove not far away, he pulled a white sheet off a chair and sat on it. He reached under his shirt and pulled his locket out, seemingly of a mind to confer with his father. A bright flash and Haldren appeared.

Andrew stiffened, his eyes wary. "Haldren."

"I want you to court Isabelle," he said.

Andrew wore a look of complete disbelief. "You can't be serious."

Pain lashed through my heart at his tone, as if Haldren had just asked Andrew to pay court to a grubby garden worm.

"I sense your attraction to her," Haldren said undeterred.

Andrew shrugged, not denying the claim. "Only a blind man could be impervious to her beauty."

Haldren nodded, the corners of his lips curving into a smile. "So a Goddess should look."

Andrew shook his head. "You have claimed her for your own purposes. It would be folly to court her."

"Regardless, it would be no hardship for you to show her a little romance until my time is at an end," Haldren said. "Keep your heart for a girl of better choosing later."

Andrew eyed him with suspicion. "What for?"

His question struck me as odd.

"She needs the life experience," Haldren replied as if the answer were obvious. "She cannot be a Goddess if she does not understand romantic love."

"If I say no?" Andrew asked, looking disgusted by the prospect.

This couldn't be right. Had he not cared for me at all? Had I not felt his love for me through the bond?

Haldren's godly power flared. "Then my benevolence to Aberron will come to an end."

Andrew's face whitened. "All right, I'll do it," he said hastily.

"Make it believable, or my words stand. I'll be watching." Haldren vanished.

I turned to Isaac. "This can't be true. Andrew cares for me. I've felt it."

A slow smile stretched over his lips. "I wouldn't be so sure if I were you."

I came to with a gasp of pain. I lay on a small bed in Malsin's healing room, Malsin and Joshua hovering over me with pinched faces. I saw blood on their clothes. I glanced down and noticed I now wore a cream shirt with black embroidered flowers and soft black pants. I had stopped bleeding, yet the crimson lines where the blood had run were dried on my skin like a tattoo.

"It won't come off," Malsin said.

The events leading up to this moment came roaring back, betrayal and anger flaring in my chest. I sat up and moved to stand.

Malsin put his hands on my shoulders, stopping me. "What do you think you're doing?"

I gave him my best glare. "Do not touch me," I rasped.

Malsin shook his head. "Oh no, you don't get to use your anger on me. I learned about this Goddess business at the same time you did. I haven't abused you in any way."

I considered that for a moment and decided it didn't matter. He worked for the enemy. I shook him off and stood. Joshua and Malsin moved in to corner me.

"Leave me," I hissed.

"No," both said, voices hard.

Activating my magic, I pushed them out of my way with a gust of air, then headed to the door. They chased after me. Joshua grabbed me around the middle just as I grabbed the handle. I fought his hold, but it was useless.

"Hate me all you want, but I'm not going to let you die," Joshua said.

The crimson lines on my skin flared bright and molten. I gasped in agony, and my vision dimmed.

I dreamed of the night Joshua and Andrew dropped me off at the Sorrenian. Like in my previous dream, I was a bystander. Isaac appeared beside me again. "What you didn't see."

Joshua headed to the door and paused, his hand on the doorknob. "I know you're not eager to stay here, but thanks for putting up with it."

"You're welcome," the past version of me said.

"Good night."

"Night."

Joshua opened the door and strode through, closing it behind him. Isaac and I followed him out. He'd created a red orb to guide him out of the school and back to his horse. We flew through the streets as Joshua hurried home, where he met Andrew on the front steps of the castle.

Joshua grabbed Andrew's arm, his voice a growl. "You know better than to court my sister. She is fated to become a Goddess. We cannot keep her."

"Yes, I know." Andrew's tone matched my brother's. "Haldren appeared to me in Thimbleton and ordered me to court her, claims she needs the life experience romance brings before she can take his place." He spoke slowly so Joshua could not mistake his words. "I am courting Isabelle to protect Aberron against Haldren's wrath, not because I want to."

My stomach dropped at the clarity in his tone. Now knowing my fate, I could accept that perhaps he hadn't wanted to court me in the beginning. But surely he had to feel something for me now, didn't he?

Isaac shrugged, and a large sense of foreboding gripped me.

"Do what you must, then, but keep it quiet." Joshua released Andrew. "Aberron doesn't need to know you're working for Haldren."

"Of course," Andrew agreed good-naturedly. "I pray this doesn't last long. I have only a year and a half to find a wife now that the Walk is over, and I need a lady worth her weight."

The Walk was a rite of passage for the prince. He couldn't ascend the throne without having done this first. The prince started out at the palace in the capital city of Carasmille and walked around the entire kingdom to mingle with the citizens, see the needs of the poor and be humbled.

Andrew continued, "I enjoy your sister's attentions, but I find her lacking in the womanly arts needed to be queen."

Andrew told me I'd make a good queen and that I could take on that role and do it well. Was everything that came out of his mouth a lie?

Joshua laughed. "She speaks her mind, doesn't she?"

Andrew chuckled with him. "She'd never make a biddable wife."

I woke with a cry on my lips, my chest burning something fierce. I lay on the bed again. Malsin touched me, his magic activated. With surprising energy, I pushed his hands away and scrambled off the bed. The room spun for a second as I regained my bearings. My hand went to my heart and came away with blood. Had I dug my nails into my chest as I slept?

Malsin's eyes bore into mine. "Don't run from me, Isabelle. Let me help you weather this storm."

The door opened, and Joshua stepped through, followed by Andrew and Braidus. With the dream still fresh in my mind, my rage stoked the flames within me. Andrew and Braidus gasped sharply, their hands flying to their hearts.

Isaac whispered in my ear. "Want to see more of the truth, little Goddess?"

The crimson lines flared. I cried out in pain, then slid to the ground as unconsciousness took hold once again.

Andrew sat in the study with his parents and Joshua. Reports littered the table.

Clutching a steaming teacup, Queen Averly addressed Andrew. "During one of my garden parties, while you were on your walk, I ran into a Lady Marissa. She appeared gracious and carried herself well among the other ladies of the court. I thought it might be worth mentioning her as a prospective lady to court."

"You know Haldren has me courting Isabelle," Andrew answered, his tone distasteful.

Queen Averly nodded. "I know, but I want you to keep Lady Marissa in mind for when this horrid business is over. She has the potential to be a fine queen. She has a pleasing face, two colors of magic like yourself, and she's on a one-on-one basis with most nobles of the court."

Andrew appeared thoughtful for a second. "If you really think so, I'll make myself acquainted with her when I can."

Oh, Gods, perhaps this was why Lady Marissa clung to him like a leech during the ball. Had Andrew been seeing her behind my back? He hadn't visited me that often while I had been at the Sorrenian. Perhaps he had split his time between us.

A bright flash and Haldren appeared. "Andrew, your courtship with Isabelle is inadequate. She is starting to lose faith due to your lack of communication. She will soon be arriving here with news for Joshua. I suggest you renew your efforts to keep her happy."

Andrew whitened at the malevolent glint in Haldren's eye. "All right. I'll try harder."

"See that you do," Haldren said, then vanished.

One of Joshua's lockets glowed, and a man's voice floated out, announcing my presence. I followed my brother and Andrew as they hurried down to see me. Joshua grabbed Andrew's arm, stopping just before the doors. "Give me a minute with her to get the facts, and then you can romance her."

Andrew nodded, though he didn't look happy about it. Was that dread in his eyes? Was I really that undesirable?

Joshua threw the doors open and rushed down, concern apparent on his features. I watched myself jump off Nisha and run to him.

Joshua clutched my shoulders. "What's the matter, Isabelle? Are you all right?"

"I'm fine. These three escorted me here safely." The past version of me nodded at the guards behind me.

They had discreetly backed away to give us privacy.

"What happened?" Joshua asked.

I handed him the note from the employer. "This was in Nisha's saddlebag."

Joshua brought the note to the light of the torch and read it. His face hardened.

"Joshua, he's still watching me."

Joshua glanced over his shoulder at the doors. I took it as him signaling Andrew because the latter suddenly appeared, flying down the steps.

"Isabelle, my darling." He nearly knocked Joshua aside as he reached for me, crushing me in a hug.

The current me sickened as I saw myself bask in his fake love. It was becoming clear that Andrew was nothing more than a lying cheat.

Isaac appeared beside me. "Braidus is no better. Look."

The scene changed. Braidus sat on a bed in one of the guestrooms in my house in Saren. He started to slip off his boots. A bright flash and Haldren appeared.

Braidus spoke first. "I played the villain for you to absolve my debt, and now you force me into a bond with Isabelle. Why?"

Haldren clasped his hands together. "You are a prince. You know how an heir and a spare works. I won't leave anything to chance when it comes to my successor. Should Andrew die in battle, Isabelle will have you to fall back on until I claim her."

Braidus's displeasure was clear. "What of Stefan? Isabelle cares greatly for him."

"Indeed, but he lacks the connections and experiences a prince of Aberron has," Haldren said, his tone decisive. "I need someone better able to compete with Andrew."

"You know my heart lies with Kiella, though she has passed," Braidus said, his tone serious. "I cannot love Isabelle."

This I easily believed. I had seen and felt Braidus's grief and love for his wife whenever she was mentioned. I had also experienced his utter hatred for King Cekaiden, who had taken Kiella from him.

"I only ask that you commit to her until she takes her place as a Goddess over Gods," Haldren said. "It is not much time in the scope of things."

"And then I'll truly be free of you?" Braidus asked.

"Yes," Haldren answered, a ghost of a smile on his lips. "You'll be able to fully enjoy your life in Aberron without my interference."

Braidus considered this for a moment. "All right. I'll do it."

"Excellent." With a grin, Haldren vanished.

How had Braidus and Andrew fooled me so easily through the bond? I had no doubt of their attraction to me, for I had often heard I had a pretty face. Did their acting skills run deep enough to manipulate their emotions? Had I mistaken their attraction for love? From what Isaac showed me, I must have.

"All royals are taught from birth to be convincing actors," Isaac stated. "It is in their blood, and they quickly rise to be the best in the world. To be a royal means to fake many of one's true feelings for the sake of political gain. It is unbecoming for them to show their true selves in the company of others."

Andrew and Braidus were constantly in the public eye and often had to put on brave faces for the people of Aberron. Hadn't I watched them school their features into pleasant expressions when I knew they were stressed? Hadn't I felt their fear in battle but not seen it on their faces? Their acting skills were unparalleled, I realized, and I had marveled at it before. I just hadn't realized their abilities went as far as being able to control what they projected through the bond. I should have considered that, but I didn't because the appeal of being loved by them was greater.

"Yes." Isaac eyed me with something akin to sympathy as he read my thoughts. "This is why Haldren bonded you to the princes. He knew they could romance you without developing real attachments."

Gods forbid. I had been such a fool.

Isaac waved his hand. We stood in his stone room, empty except for a single torchlight. Isaac faced me, his sea-green eyes calculating. "Now you've seen the cruelty of Haldren for yourself. Your life in Aberron has been nothing but a carefully constructed web of lies. Your family doesn't love you in the way you thought. They care for you because they fear Haldren. Their apprehension is warranted. Haldren can lay Aberron to waste in seconds should he desire, and he is a demon when incensed."

I didn't doubt the power of the Gods.

"Haldren has been pulling the strings on your puppet life since your birth to create the Goddess he wishes to leave as his namesake." Isaac leaned forward and spoke in an unforgiving tone. "The question is, what are you going to do about it?"

I woke to darkness, still on the bed in Malsin's healing rooms. I sucked in a sharp breath as my skin burned with intensity. I brought a hand to my face and watched as the crimson lines faded into nonexistence. Isaac had released his hold on me.

I sat up and swung my legs over the edge of the bed, allowing my bare feet to touch the cool marble floor. Malsin slept in an oversized leather chair nearby. I didn't see anyone else. I waited for the fiery burn to fully vanish before I stood, then quietly walked to the door, careful not to disturb Malsin. Pulling it open, I ran into my five guards, Micah, Weston, Zachary, Oliver, and Eric, who stood attention.

"Lady Isabelle," they chorused.

I frowned as my hopes to depart undetected vanished.

Micah grabbed his locket and spoke into it. "Commander Mirran, your sister is awake."

Malsin woke and dashed over. "Don't you even think about leaving."

I ignited my hands in rainbow flames. "Move out of my way or get blasted. Your choice."

I saw a flicker of uncertainty in my guards' eyes.

Malsin stepped in front of them, not a single shred of fear on his face. "Blast me, then. I don't care."

I hesitated. His bravery surprised me.

"You don't really want to hurt anyone." His voice softened. "There's not a mean bone in your body. There never has been. Put out the flames, Isabelle. Let's work through this."

I didn't want to work through this betrayal. Although, he was right that I didn't wish to hurt him or my guards. They weren't the ones I was mad at. I had hoped my boldness would get them to back down and, instead, Malsin turned it on my head. Sighing, I shut off the flames. I could call them back in an instant if I had to.

My guards stepped out of the way as more family arrived—Joshua, Andrew, Braidus, and King Brian—their presence allowing a simmering rage to take root inside me. I walked backward a few paces, putting some distance between us.

Andrew spoke, his tone soothing. "I know you're angry, love. Gods, you have every right to be. Please, let's work through it together—atone for our mistakes."

I pinned him with a cold stare. "Did Haldren tell you to court me while we were in Thimbleton together a few hours before we went to Silverdens to gather information about the archer?" While the majority of me believed what Isaac had shown me, I knew better than to take his word alone. I wanted confirmation.

Andrew swallowed, indecision written on his features. After a moment, he nodded. "Yes."

I whipped my gaze to Braidus. "And you, while we were in Saren gearing up to battle the Dregans, the night the bond had been discovered? An heir and a spare."

Regret showed in his countenance. "Yes."

My eyes darted between King Brian and Joshua. "You both allowed for these relationships because Haldren ordered them to court me."

Guilt shone in King Brian's and Joshua's eyes. "Yes," they said.

So Isaac *had* shown me the truth. What I saw *was* real. I was never loved by the men in this room. I was tolerated for Haldren's sake. My breath stuttered. My hands went to my stomach as I doubled over, feeling as if I'd been kicked like an unwanted, mangy dog. My knees wobbled as I struggled to remain standing, and tears pricked my eyes.

Braidus and Andrew grabbed each other for support, their breathing unsteady as they felt my turbulent emotions. Malsin stepped in to help me, but I threw up my hands, straightening. He paused.

Joshua stepped forward as if to take me into his arms and offer comfort. "Isabelle."

I wouldn't dare let him get close to me again. We were not family anymore. I scurried backward into a table full of Malsin's healing experiments, inching around it, seeking an escape from this room and everyone in it. My fingers dug into the skin above my heart as pain engulfed it. "Don't, please. I can't take any more of your lies when I've seen the truth."

I sprinted to the windows on the other side of the room. Activating my magic, I blasted the glass, breaking it.

"Isabelle!" The men ran toward me.

Covering my mouth to stifle my sobs, I jumped out the window and into the night, flying as fast as the wind could take me. Through blurry tears, I managed to find Capital Road and kept going south. Hours passed. I charged yellow to keep me in the sky and used red to stay warm. Thimbleton came into view as the sun started to rise. I didn't stop.

Along the journey, I gradually became numb to my emotions. Perhaps it was a subconscious self-preservation thing, but I had somehow imprisoned my rage, pain, betrayal, and whatever feelings my Amora bond gave me. I did, however, feel a resounding thump, like my emotions were pounding at the cell door, begging to get out and go on a rampage. I refused to give in, though. It hurt less to feel nothing.

Clouds rolled in as I flew over the Trivail forest. I created a shield to keep the heavy rain off me and plunged onward. The following evening, I landed on my front porch in Saren. I swiped the key from behind the metal sign reading "Whysten" hanging by the door. Weary, I sat in Nathan's favorite leather chair. I wished he were here to wrap me in his love and support. I refused to believe he'd raised me only for Haldren's sake.

Isaac appeared in a bright flash. "I show you the truth about Haldren and your family, and you run like a cowering dog. You didn't even try to punish them. I'm disappointed."

"There is no point," I answered tiredly. "They acted out of fear for Aberron's welfare. I cannot fault them for wanting to keep our country whole. I might've done the same."

"You reason because you still love them despite everything they've done to you," Isaac murmured, sounding displeased.

I shrugged, not denying his claim. No doubt he could see straight through my heart and read all the little whisperings I'd locked away. I had spent too much time invested in them to not feel anything at all. Despite what they'd done to me, I did admire that they put Aberron first. They were good leaders, and Aberron needed that.

Isaac took my hand. I gasped in pain as the crimson lines reappeared. "You must be broken of that love. A Goddess cannot keep anyone. It is law." He vanished.

I stumbled up the stairs and into my room. Lying on the bed, I closed my eyes, letting unconsciousness claim me.

I dreamed I stood in Isaac's stone room. Joshua stepped into the light. I felt surprised, having expected Isaac. My brother backhanded me, sending me against the wall, and I crumpled to the ground. He then lifted me by the neck, pressing me into the rough stone, his eyes filled with fury. He squeezed until I couldn't breathe.

"You give me nothing but problems. I'm sick of trying to keep you alive. You have no worth."

He disappeared.

Henry then stepped into the light. "You're going to be a Goddess with more power and glory than you could ever imagine at your fingertips. You're small-minded and pathetic to pine after the princes seeking to become Aberron royalty."

Andrew appeared. I cringed at the revulsion on his face. He pressed me against the wall, his arm over my throat. "I hate that Haldren forced me into a bond with you for his purposes."

He whipped out a dagger and ran the flat edge down my cheek. I shivered at the cold metal pressed against my skin.

"Now that the secret's out, I'm taking my bond back." He dug the tip into my chest.

I woke with a cry on my lips, my chest burning again. My crimson-lined hand went to my heart and came away with blood. Andrew's carving. What happened in Isaac's dreamworld became reality.

Activating my magic, I healed the damage, then rose, washed, and dressed. No amount of scrubbing removed the crimson covering my skin. Isaac's idea of breaking me was stupid. Did he think he could make me learn to fear my family by associating them with pain? They'd already done their worst. Any phantoms Isaac created couldn't possibly do as much damage.

I had no plans to return to Carasmille. I'd rather die than step foot inside the castle again. I would not try to keep anyone in my family. Regardless of what Isaac thought he sensed in my heart, I knew when to call it quits. My family and I were finished for good.

I walked down to the cellar in search of food and found it empty. Millie had cleared it out like I had asked. Making myself invisible in case I ran into someone, I went into the tunnels and snuck some provisions out of one of the supply rooms. I didn't care for the residents of Saren to see me this way—broken and under Isaac's curse.

I ate a small breakfast, made myself invisible again, and stepped outside. I slowly ambled over to my maple tree by the creek. Settling my back against the trunk, I spent a quiet day with Nathan, Adel, and Stefan. As night fell, I returned home, the crimson lines flaring to life as I stepped through the back door. I collapsed, falling unconscious on the kitchen floor. Isaac's nightmare played on.

Henry fiddled with a staff similar to the ones used in Professor Lildren's class at the Sorrenian. "I bet Uncle Brian would thank me if I disposed of you and brought our family some peace. Maybe he'd even make me king over Andrew." He stepped forward, a wicked gleam in his eyes. "Shall we try it out?" He raised the staff.

I lost count of how many times Henry whacked me with that stupid staff. Then Falden appeared with a pocket knife and carved pictures into my skin. Patience thin, I threw a fireball at him, but it flew through him as though he were smoke.

He laughed. "You can't hurt me, Isabelle, but I can hurt you." He crouched as his hand shot out and gripped my forearm. Using his knife, he pointed the tip and sliced downward, drawing an arrow.

I woke in the early morning, coughing hard. I groaned, and as I moved to wrap my hands around my aching ribs, I looked down to see Falden's handiwork from my wrist to my elbow, nestled between the crimson lines running up and down my arm. Boomer barked, standing outside his cage. I jumped, caught off guard, then winced in pain. I'd left my magic open. "Heal," I told him. I moaned in relief as the fire abated.

Rising off the kitchen floor, I washed and dressed. I planned to remain hidden here for as long as possible. I loved this house and the memories I had made within it. I had to be careful about it, though. No doubt Joshua had people searching for me.

I resigned myself to a little bit of living as I ate a quick breakfast. Eating had become a chore. I wanted to do as little of it as possible, and hunger pangs had never bothered me. Since the Gods had claim over me and I did not think they truly wanted me to die—otherwise, it would have happened already—I made a little effort to prevent them from forcing food into me.

After breakfast, I made myself invisible and stepped outside to head to the maple tree. I found comfort in being where my loved ones rested. I paused at the sight of a few soldiers approaching my house. I hid behind a tree, just in case one of them had yellow magic and spotted me. I watched as they peered through windows and tried the door, obviously looking for me. I waited until they left before I dashed through the neighboring fields to the maple. I kept watch for soldiers but never saw any. As night fell once more, I made my way back home, careful to keep to the fields and foliage.

On my doorstep, I discovered a letter addressed to me with a wax seal of the king's crest. I suspected the soldiers had placed it there. I chose to ignore it. My family and I were no more. What they had written held no meaning. I would never go back.

Two weeks passed in semi-solitude. I settled into a routine: heal myself from the nightly damage of Isaac's phantoms; eat breakfast; quietly visit with Stefan, Adel, and Nathan at the maple tree; and last, head to bed as night fell. Occasionally, my heart flared with strong emotions—anguish, regret, and anger—from my mage mates. I learned to ignore all feeling.

A regiment of soldiers stayed nearby, checking my house daily, always at random times. I evaded them with magic and never revealed myself to anyone. I made sure the house seemed uninhabited by being meticulously clean and using my powers for everything.

Letters piled up. I didn't dare touch any lest the soldiers take it as a sign that I was around.

Saren had started to return to its former glory as repairs were made. A combined effort to beautify all buildings unified the residents. Harmony like I'd never seen brought peace to the small town.

Winter Jubilee, marking the new year, passed. Saren celebrated in its normal fashion with a huge gathering at Orate Judge Hall with gift exchanges, dancing, music, food, and drink. Invisible, I watched from a corner of the room, failing to gather a shred of feeling.

When I returned home, a new letter had been placed on top of the rest. I was tired of seeing the letters and tired of my family trying to find me when

I didn't want to be found. Frustration and curiosity got the better of me, however. I bent down, snatched the top letter, opened it, and read it.

*Isabelle, if you're there, come home, please.*

*Your loving and concerned brother,*

*Joshua*

*Loving and concerned?* I snorted in disbelief. My brother didn't care for me. He'd only kept me around because Haldren made him. I bet the real reason Joshua never wrote to me growing up was because he was trying to forget me. He probably thought there was no point in trying to get to know me as a sister when I would leave him to be a Goddess.

My veins heated with anger and betrayal. Then my heart suddenly raced as Andrew and Braidus tugged on the bond, seeking my whereabouts. I read their anxiousness and fear, probably over Haldren raining fire and brimstone on them for losing me. It only served to make me angrier. I snatched all the letters and burned them, letting the ashes fall onto the porch. The soldiers would probably report to Joshua when they found the remnants.

I decided to leave in case King Brian sent someone down. The wind whipped through my hair as I jumped into the sky. I worked hard to suppress my emotions lest Andrew and Braidus catch enough impressions to locate me. I flew over the fields and into the trees, seeking a solace I knew I would never find.

A few hours later, the crimson lines brightened to molted steel again, forcing me to land in some random forest. My legs gave out as my feet touched the fern-covered ground, and I fell in a tangled heap. Groaning, I rolled onto my back as darkness claimed me.

Again, I dreamed of Isaac's stone room. Dominic greeted me wearing a maniacal expression. I braced for pain.

I woke spitting blood from a cut and swollen lip. I lay on the damp earth, staring up into a blue sky dotted with clouds. A cold breeze made me shiver. Weary and aching, I passed the day in a paralyzed state. I was tired of running, tired of Isaac and his games to break me of unrequited love, tired of the hurt and betrayal I spent most of my energy suppressing.

Occasionally, my thoughts turned to becoming a Goddess over Gods. The idea of having that much power sickened me, and yet I saw no reason to fight it. Had my family truly loved me, perhaps I would've tried to find a way out—to remain with them. Obviously, that's why Haldren had chosen them to play a part. He trusted they could act well enough to give me the experiences he wanted me to have and yet knew that when the truth came out, I would not fight him to stay in Aberron. I would walk into my fate bringing my heartache and fury with it. *The Gods are mean creatures.* Perhaps to be one, you had to be cruel.

As night fell, Isaac appeared again. Crossing his arms, he stared at me with displeasure. "You are pathetic." He waved his hand, and the crimson lines on my skin disappeared.

Haldren flashed into existence. He raised an eyebrow at Isaac. "Finished playing with her already?"

"She does not perform as she should," Isaac grumbled.

A small smile curved Haldren's lips. "Indeed. Isabelle is unconventional."

Isaac scoffed. "She's boring."

"Does this mean you'll leave her under my charge again?" Haldren asked, his cold eyes intent.

Isaac waved his hand dismissively. "For now." He vanished.

Haldren surveyed me with pursed lips. A flicker of warmth swept through me as I imagined running my sword through him. His frown intensified as he, no doubt, read my thoughts. "It's time you were home and healed." He waved his hand.

Before I could protest, a bright light enveloped me. I shut my eyes, feeling weightless, then stumbled as my feet hit solid ground. My eyes flew open. The forest had vanished, replaced by the entry hall of the castle in Carasmille.

*No!* I swayed unsteadily as I turned for the door. How dare he return me to my betrayers? I refused to stay here.

"Lady Isabelle." My guards moved in to surround me, concern on their faces.

I halted. "Please move."

All five flinched at the soreness they heard in my throat.

"Isabelle!"

I nearly toppled as I swiveled to face the threat. Weston threw his hands out to steady me. Andrew and Braidus raced down the stairs, a mix of relief and panic emanating from them. I backed into Weston, who grabbed my shoulders to hold me in place.

The others moved out of the way to allow my mage mates access to me.

"Isabelle, thank the Gods." Andrew reached out as if to take me into his arms.

"No." I activated my magic and pushed everyone away with a gust of air. He would never touch me again.

I moved to the door, but an invisible shield blocked my exit. I pressed against a solid nothing. Realization set in as a maid walked through it with no problem and eyed me with horror. Haldren had confined me to the castle. In desperation, I created a rainbow fireball and threw it at the door. The shield flashed golden before dissolving it.

Haldren whispered in my ear. "It's over the entire building. No blasting through windows or stone will set you free."

Irritation, then defeat set in. I changed direction and headed for the stairs to go to my room, staggering as I ascended. Andrew and Braidus went to help me, but I pinned them with a death stare.

"Don't you dare touch me." I ignored their hurt. I wasn't going to be fooled by their acting again.

Andrew used his locket to update his father on my arrival. "Isabelle's here. She can't leave the castle. Haldren's locked her in."

As I passed the dining room, my family poured out of it. I spared them one glance as they called my name. Entering my sleeping quarters, I noticed the dust motes in the air and shivered at the overall chill. I created a rainbow shield over the doorway to keep everyone out, then collapsed into a chair and contemplated stuffing my ears to drown out the voices at my door.

Henry sounded aghast. "Did you see the marks on her?"

"Emotional state?" Malsin asked.

"She doesn't want to be here," Braidus said.

"She's holding back her emotions," Andrew said. "She doesn't want us in."

"She's shielded her door," Malsin noted. "I suggest we give her the night and try tomorrow."

"That shield will not come down easily; she harbors much anger for us," Braidus said.

"Nevertheless, we must try," Malsin said. "I'll take my leave."

"We've ruined her. That's . . . that's our fault," Andrew choked, seemingly distraught.

"I know, brother," Braidus said, equally distressed.

"We're monsters. We as good as killed her," Andrew cried.

"We must stick to the plan and prove ourselves," Braidus responded with intensity. "She's here. She can't leave. This is our opportunity."

"She hates us," Andrew said morosely. "She'll never listen."

Braidus spoke with conviction. "There's love underneath it all. I cannot believe otherwise."

My insides twisted. I curled into a ball and covered my ears to block their voices out.

I woke the following morning to Malsin entreating me to drop the shield. "I may not be able to stop the emotional pain, but at least let me fix the physical pain. It's ridiculous to suffer when you don't have to. I honestly can't understand why you do it."

I sunk deeper into the chair and pretended he didn't exist. The morning drifted into the afternoon before the need to relieve myself forced me to drop the shield and open the door. Malsin sat in a chair beside the fireplace, writing in a journal. I breathed a small sigh of relief when I didn't see anyone else.

I ambled to the bathroom, feeling Malsin's eyes on me. When I exited, he stood outside the door, and I had to stop short to avoid running into him. He studied me with a healer's gaze, his lips tugging into a frown.

"Do you mind?" He held out his hands, his green magic activated.

I shrugged. Malsin took my hand in his, then let out a low oath as he ascertained the damage, then healed it. I saw anger in his eyes as he dropped his hands.

When Andrew and Braidus entered the room, I bolted to the sleeping quarters and shielded the doorway. I left the door open so I could see through the shield and returned to my chair. Malsin scowled at me. Andrew and Braidus joined him, supposed concern on their faces.

"How is she?" Andrew asked Malsin.

"She allowed me to heal her physical wounds, so she's stable for the moment," Malsin said, glancing at Andrew and then back at me. "She had three cracked ribs and a host of other injuries indicative of abuse. I'd like to know what sort of trouble she got herself into."

My heart stilled at my mage mates' dismay.

Braidus spoke. "Was she compromised?"

"No, nothing of that nature," Malsin answered, sounding relieved. He then said, "Isaac released his hold on Isabelle right before she left. She had no marks on her when she jumped out of the window."

Andrew stepped forward and touched my shield. His eyes caught mine and held them. A shiver of awareness swept through us, our Amora bond intensifying as we focused on each other. "Then who broke her?"

*You.*

He flinched.

Activating my purple magic, I allowed Andrew into my mind. I took him to Isaac's stone room and let him watch an apparition of himself whisper his truths and pierce my skin with a knife.

Andrew gasped in horror, placing both his hands on the shield to support himself. Satisfied he'd gotten a good enough picture, I deactivated my magic.

Braidus touched his brother's shoulder. "What did she show you?" I felt his annoyance that I had left him out.

"Me, spouting lies and carving her heart with a dagger." Shuddering, Andrew turned to face Malsin and Braidus. "Isaac wasn't done when she left. He created apparitions of us and made us torture her."

"For what purpose?" Braidus asked.

Andrew shook his head. "I don't know. Isabelle is locked up tighter than a clam. I could only see what she wanted me to."

Malsin touched my shield, his expression thoughtful. "So the shield serves not only for her anger but for protection as well?"

"Yes," Andrew agreed. "She is keeping her guard up."

Braidus gazed into my eyes. Our portion of the bond heightened like before with Andrew. I read his desire to come inside and soothe me with his touch. "We must double our efforts to bring it down."

*Never.*

# CHAPTER EIGHT

CURLED UP IN MY chair, forcing myself to be numb so Andrew and Braidus couldn't decipher anything other than what I wanted them to know. They didn't deserve a Gods-forbidden thing from me.

Afternoon faded to night. Joshua, Andrew, and Braidus had taken to standing outside my door, pleading for forgiveness, entreating any softheartedness I might have. I buried my face into the chair and covered my ears. Haldren must have ordered them to keep me happy until I took his place. It wouldn't work.

I mentally called out to Haldren. "*How long am I going to be stuck here?*"

"*Until your eighteenth birthday,*" he answered.

My birthday wasn't till the twenty-first day of the first month of summer. We were currently still in the winter months. That meant several to go.

"*Why can't you just take me now?*" I didn't want to spend another second in this Gods-forbidden castle. I might as well start doing the Goddess job now.

"*No,*" Haldren said, his tone firm. "*I can't take you until you've fully ascended into your new power.*"

"*Then speed it up,*" I said.

"*I can't,*" Haldren said. "*It's out of my hands.*"

I frowned. Some God he was. Weren't they basically equipped with the power to do whatever they wanted? Perhaps I needed to go above Haldren and talk to Isaac, see if he could get me out of here. Then again, Isaac would probably come up with some new way to torture me. I didn't want that. Malsin had food and drink delivered, but I refused to take down my shield lest it lead to them worming their way back into my life. With several months before I became a Goddess, I realized I'd need to find something to occupy my time, but I hadn't settled on anything. Whatever I chose could not involve my family.

Morning came and went, then afternoon. As evening fell, Malsin reached his breaking point. He, Joshua, Andrew, Braidus, and the boys stood near my door, eyeing me with concern.

"She hasn't moved from that blasted chair for well over twenty-four hours. She's not eating, or drinking, or behaving in any sort of normal fashion." He waved his hand wildly. "Somebody needs to come up with a plan to get through to her because nothing I'm doing is working." He pointed at my mage mates and brother. "If she dies, I'm holding you three to blame."

I felt sorry for Malsin fighting to keep me alive while I did everything I could to avoid my family's involvement regardless of the cost to my health. I didn't want them to try and save me when they were the ones who had broken me in the first place. And yet I was reminded that Malsin had learned of my fate the same day I had. Not once had he intentionally tried to hurt me, and here I was, hurting him by letting him see me suffer and not being able to do anything about it. Guilt made me remove the shield.

The men blinked in surprise. Malsin recovered first and strode inside. He crouched beside me, taking my hand in his. The other men quietly filed in behind him.

"Henry," Malsin said. "Could you fetch me a cup of water? She's dehydrated."

Henry rushed out and came back with a cup.

Malsin handed it to me. "Drink slowly or you'll get sick."

I sipped, the water soothing my parched throat. I was tempted to drink more deeply but refrained due to Malsin's advisement. After a few more sips, I raised an eyebrow at Malsin. *Satisfied?*

"No," he said.

I fought back an eye-roll and finished the cup. Malsin wouldn't rest until he saw me taking care of myself. Perhaps if I went through the motions, I'd have a better chance of being left alone. My bones creaked as I rose. I set the empty cup on my desk.

"I suppose a bath and food next?"

"Yes," Malsin agreed.

My eyes swept over the men, seeing a silent plea to end this rift. My anguish flared hot and deep before I quickly reigned it in. Not here. Not now. I walked out of the room, refusing to let them see me crumble.

I took my time in the bath. The methodical motions of washing and drying allowed me to encase my heart in another layer of steel lest my emotions escape again. When I dressed, my clothes hung loose, but I didn't care. Grabbing a brush, I combed through my hair and tried not to stare too closely at the gaunt girl in the mirror. All but Malsin had vacated when I exited.

He eyed me with approval. "That's better."

I followed him to the family dining room for a later-than-normal dinner. Everyone was already seated in their typical spots, leaving me to sit between my mage mates as usual. Except nothing about this was the same. I couldn't forget the truths Isaac had shown me. Digging my nails into my palms, I sat and trained my eyes on the empty white and gold-rimmed plate before me.

Braidus held up a pitcher. "Cider?"

Not trusting myself to speak, I nodded. He poured the amber liquid into my cup.

Andrew selected food from the fare before us and added small portions to my plate. "There's a bit of everything. Choose what you want."

Again, I nodded.

Andrew's cinnamon woods and Braidus's exotic citrus colognes swirled in the air around me, the heady scents infiltrating my senses and sparking memories of breathing them in when they held me. I'd never felt more alive than when I chased a fantasy.

I blinked rapidly as tears pricked my eyes. My nails dug deeper into my skin, drawing blood. The sight of it shifted my attention from the recollections of my mage mates' affection. I let the blood well up, coat the tips of my nails, and run down my palms and onto my tan pants.

Andrew reached over and touched my wrist, his green magic activated. His contact unexpected, I flinched violently and knocked into the table, shaking the dishes. Queen Averly gasped, and Andrew drew back as if he'd been stung.

My heart raced with terror. Isaac's torture room actually held some merit. I had never instinctually feared Andrew physically hurting me.

I read dismay on many faces. Andrew blinked rapidly with unshed tears. Perhaps he was worried about what Haldren would do to him if he couldn't rekindle our relationship. Regardless, his acting skills were phenomenal.

Malsin got up from the other side of the table and came over to me.

"Her hands," Andrew said, his voice thick with emotion.

Malsin activated his magic, healed the damage my nails had done, and wiped the blood with a napkin dipped in water. While he worked, I took slow breaths, forcing myself to calm down.

Malsin smiled gently. "There, good as new." He patted me lightly on the shoulder and returned to his seat. His eyes encouraged me to eat.

Picking up the fork, I speared a piece of roast beef into my mouth and chewed. It went down like sludge, but I did it again and again. I saw appreciation in Malsin.

Talk floated around me, but I couldn't concentrate. If someone spoke to me, I didn't hear them. I ate until I felt sure the next bite would make me throw up. Dabbing my mouth with a napkin, I returned my focus to Malsin, hoping I had done enough to appease him. He frowned, his mossy-green eyes troubled, and yet he nodded. Without a word, I rose and walked out. Returning to my room, I created a shield over the sleeping-quarters door, then kicked off my shoes and lay on the bed. Activating my magic, I put myself to sleep.

I dreamed I stood in a grassy field dotted with wildflowers, a warm breeze tickling my face. The sun, high above my head, felt warm against my skin. I turned and saw Andrew approaching. He grinned, his blazing-blue eyes dancing. My stomach flipped with delight. We ran to each other, arms held out to embrace. He hugged me tight, lifting me off the ground and twirling me around. We laughed together.

Braidus appeared. I held my hand out to him. He took it and pulled me close, stealing me from Andrew's arms, his hazel eyes holding mine with warmhearted affection. He lifted his hand and caressed my cheek. I closed my eyes, basking in his touch.

A cold wind whipped across my skin. Shivering, I opened my eyes and looked up to see dark clouds rolling in. Rain began to pour. Rapidly becoming soaked, I looked around for Andrew and Braidus and found myself alone. Lightning struck a pace away, spraying mud onto me. Scared, I ran, searching for my mage mates, certain I would find protection with them.

Abruptly, the castle appeared in front of me. I sprinted inside. Hearing laughter and music, I followed it to a ballroom where elaborately dressed nobles and rich merchants chatted and danced. I waded through them, ignoring their expressions of disgust. I found Andrew and Braidus standing together, surrounded by gorgeous, elaborately dressed women dripping in jewels. Each had a woman glued to his side.

I pushed my way through the other women to stand before them.

"What are you doing with them?" I asked, gesturing to the ladies. "I thought you loved me."

Andrew laughed as if the thought was preposterous. "You?"

"Look at her. She's wearing nothing but a muddy pile of rags." The blonde eerily resembling Lady Marissa tittered, drawing laughs from everyone. "She's revolting!"

I glanced down to see that my clothes were dripping wet and dirt-coated.

"Don't be ridiculous." Braidus echoed his brother's sentiments. "Why would we share you when we can have all these women to ourselves?"

"You are not queen material," Andrew said, his voice firm. He squeezed the blonde beside him, his expression playful. "But this one might be. She's an excellent kisser." He turned to place a heated kiss on her lips.

The women around me pushed me out of their circle until I once again stood alone.

I woke to darkness, choking, an ache so deep in my chest I couldn't breathe. I sat up, coughing hard and wheezing.

Braidus and Andrew stood outside the room, their hands on my shield. "Take it down!"

I heard the panic in their voices, which only made it worse. Tears came fast and hard. I pulled my knees up and rested my elbows on them. I dug my hands into my hair. My body shook with sobs. I couldn't get a proper breath.

The wall near the door exploded, marble debris flying across the room. I ducked as a piece came at my head. Joshua stepped through a hole made by the explosion. Malsin, Andrew, and Braidus followed. Sprinting to me, Joshua leaped onto the bed and gathered me into his arms, glowing red as he used his magic to heat me. Malsin sat on the edge and took my hand in his, easing the tightness in my chest. I shuddered as my lungs expanded with new breath.

The heart-wrenching ache remained, however, no matter how hard I tried to shove it down. The floodgates opened, and my anguish poured out, again constricting my chest and making it hard to breathe. It killed me that I had fallen in love with a lie.

Malsin kept his hand on me as I labored. Andrew and Braidus wore pained expressions, their breathing unsteady as they felt the onslaught of my emotions. Through it all, I felt a dual desire to soothe me and end this rift between us. Had they become so used to their roles that they'd just as well keep it going until I became a Goddess?

Malsin fished two pink vials from his pocket and handed them to Andrew and Braidus. Undoing the stoppers, they both downed the contents. A few moments later, their expressions cleared.

Joshua smoothed my hair as he held me close. "I've got you, little sister. We'll figure this out together. We'll be all right."

I didn't believe him, though I chose not to voice it. Instead, I soaked up his touch, craving the belief that my brother loved me and that this wasn't just for show. I detested myself for it. Why couldn't I be strong enough to push him away?

Braidus placed a gentle hand on my leg, seeming to want to offer comfort, but I shook him off and curled into a ball, wanting to avoid his touch at all costs. He sighed, a troubled frown on his lips.

Joshua growled, "I told you your relationships would break her."

"It's breaking me too," Andrew replied, his tone just as harsh.

"Gods, you know we're just as much in love with her as she is with us," Braidus said with intensity. "It brings us no pleasure to see her react this way."

"Yes," Andrew agreed.

Their commitment, only in effect until I took Haldren's place, was to save themselves and Aberron from a God's wrath. I would rather they say to my face that they didn't love me instead of maintaining the charade. It would still hurt like nothing else, but maybe I could survive it. Maybe I could learn to cope.

Braidus held out his hands. "Joshua, let me take her, please."

I stiffened, not wanting to leave the safety my brother provided.

Joshua hesitated. For a second, I thought he would say no. He didn't. "Careful," he said as he handed me over.

*Gods, no.* My breathing accelerated. I wasn't ready to listen to Braidus's lies or have him finally spit out what I knew to be true. Malsin started to move around the bed to continue administering to me, but Andrew held up a hand. Activating his magic, he took my hand. I cringed. My mind screamed at me to move, but I couldn't seem to make my limbs work.

Braidus cupped my cheek. His hazel eyes penetrated mine, searing my soul. "The Gods have mixed truths and lies and poisoned you with them." He took a breath, then spoke in a clear, unmistakable voice. "Isabelle, I am wholeheartedly in love with you. I have been since I first laid eyes on you.

Yes, Haldren encouraged me to court you after the bond was discovered, but I already wanted to on my own. I had many thoughts on how I could elevate myself in your eyes to steal you from my brother. I still aim to keep you for myself."

"As do I," Andrew said, taking my attention off Braidus.

*Right.* My heart broke a little more that they preferred the acting.

Braidus and Andrew frowned at each other, no doubt reading the bond.

"My turn." Andrew took me from Braidus and drew me into his lap. He continued to use his green magic to help ease my anxiety. "It's true I didn't want to fall in love with you. When I met you in the forest, I only meant to help you survive and deliver you to Joshua." He gestured to my brother with a nod of his head. "I had to constantly remind myself that you were fated to be a Goddess and that you couldn't keep anyone. I knew it would rip my heart out if I loved you and you left. I was mortified after I nearly kissed you on our way to Thimbleton. I'd never wanted someone or something as bad as I wanted you. But I couldn't. I was supposed to come home from my Walk and court the ladies Mother recommended until I found one I could live with." He spoke with distaste. "I dreaded it."

I remembered him telling me so.

His voice thickened with emotion. "You stole my heart the moment I discovered you. I thought I could ignore it. I tried. It hurt so Gods-forbidden much. Then I started to think that loving you for a little while was better than not loving you at all. If I couldn't make these feelings go away, I should embrace them—enjoy what time I had with you. I worried my actions to pursue you would anger Haldren, but he appeared and gave me his blessing." He smiled. "I was thrilled. Loving you made me the happiest man alive."

He half laughed, half choked as his eyes darted to my brother. "Joshua was furious with me for weeks, months probably. He knew our relationship would break your heart once the truth of your fate was revealed. He demanded I end our courtship to spare you grief, but I had gotten Haldren's blessing, so I refused."

"And spared you nothing," Joshua grumbled at me.

Andrew snorted at my brother. "Spared *us* nothing. My grief over this situation is just as strong."

"As is mine," Braidus said, taking my hand. He rubbed his thumb over my skin in circles.

Malsin said, "I think it's safe to say no one wants Isabelle to leave."

The men all agreed.

Andrew continued. "In light of Joshua's fury, I feared telling my parents and facing their wrath. We couldn't keep you. It would ruin me and potentially Aberron. It didn't fit the plan for becoming king. I started searching for ways to keep you. Joshua helped. We searched every record we had in the castle about the Gods. When that turned up nothing, we went to the temple. The high priest told us what we already knew—that Gods choose a successor and revert to their human state to live out their remaining years, experiencing what they missed. He had no other information. Their records only go back 290 years, when King Aberron first ordered the construction of the temple. None of them said anything about transformations because it hasn't happened since the temple's creation.

"So we sought an audience with the Gods, and Haldren appeared. We asked if he could choose someone else. He told us no, that your fate was sealed." Andrew wore a stricken expression. "My anguish could have rivaled yours."

Braidus placed a comforting hand on Andrew's shoulder.

Andrew cleared his throat. "Then Haldren said, 'Do not forsake her. There may be a chance for her to return.' Hope flared in my heart. He made us promise again not to reveal your true fate but to continue as if you would stay with us forever. So we did."

Passion clouded his voice. His eyes pleaded with mine. "Everything I've said to you throughout our courtship has been the truth. I told you *my truths*—what I desired for both of us. I love you, Isabelle Mirran. I swear it on the Gods a thousand times over. Nothing about us has been fabricated. I love you so Gods-forbidden much it hurts. I need you more than I need air to breathe." His voice dropped to a strangled whisper. "I'll take whatever I can get for as long as I can and hope you'll come back to me."

My heart screamed to take him back. I needed my anchor, my protection. I wanted him to promise that my fears were unfounded. But more than that, I wanted to *believe* in his promise. Except I knew what I'd seen.

"No." I scurried out of Andrew's arms and stood, retreating until my back hit the window. I wrapped my arms around my chest, trying and failing to stave off the ache.

Braidus climbed off the bed and took me into his arms. "We expose our hearts to you, and you still resist us. Why?"

"It's not true," I said.

"What did the Gods tell you?" Braidus demanded. "Show me."

"Show us all, Isabelle," Joshua said. "So we can prove it wrong."

With a sigh, I activated my magic and connected Andrew, Malsin, Joshua, and Braidus. I replayed the visions Isaac had given me, starting with the first one of Andrew and Haldren in Thimbleton while I slept before we went to Silverdens.

I jumped at Andrew's outrage. "That's not what happened!"

"Let her finish, and then you can refute it," Malsin said.

I went to the next scene of following Joshua after he dropped me off at the Sorrenian and the ensuing conversation between him and Andrew about how unsuitable I was. Next was Queen Averly petitioning Andrew to court Lady Marissa and Haldren chastising him for not showing me enough attention. Then the scene of Haldren appearing to Braidus in Saren and expressing his need for an heir and a spare and Braidus telling Haldren he could never love me.

The men's ire increased as the memories spilled forth. I showed them everything. Isaac's reappearance in Saren and the crimson lines returning. Every harshly spoken word, bruise, and mark given to me during the night-mares to break me of my unrequited love. *A Goddess can't keep anyone.* Isaac had made that abundantly clear.

I closed the connection. Andrew's and Braidus's fury swirled around the ache in my chest, making it feel as if on fire. Joshua scowled, his hands flexing as if itching to punch something. Malsin appeared equally disturbed.

Andrew paced in front of me, his rage flaring. "Nothing I said in those visions is true!"

"He took seeds of truth and grew them into lies," Braidus said, holding me securely against him, my back to his front.

Allowing him to touch me like this was bad, but I didn't have the heart to step away, not after showing everyone my memories.

Joshua stood and faced me. He took my hands in his. I looked up into his eyes. "You are not worthless. You have been and always will be a precious sister to me." He squeezed lightly, then let go.

"You never showed it until Haldren sent me fleeing from Saren and put me under your care for his purposes," I couldn't help but say. I had done all my growing up without my brother. I couldn't easily dismiss the idea that he hadn't wanted contact with me because I'd one day leave him to become a Goddess.

Joshua grimaced. I read the pain in his eyes. "A mistake I regret daily."

I regretted it too.

Braidus traced circles on my waist with his thumbs. I followed the feel of his fingers on me, his delight blossoming in my chest. I tensed, knowing I allowed far too much. He reined himself in, careful to keep it simple despite wanting so much more. Andrew's envy brushed my heart. I stepped out of Braidus's grasp. I couldn't let things go back to the way they were before.

Activating my magic, I flicked my fingers and removed the shield over the door. With another sweep of my hand, I collected the marble debris and made a pile beside the hole in the wall. The sun had started to rise, sending its rays through the curtains. The magical orbs the men used for light vanished.

One of Joshua's lockets glowed. He picked it up. "Yes?"

A man's voice floated into the room. "Commander Mirran, there's a large group of merchants assembling in front of the castle, demanding answers concerning trade agreements."

"How many?" Joshua asked.

"A hundred at least, with more arriving by the second," the man said. "There's a volatile feeling in the air. I fear this may turn into a riot."

My brother cursed. "I'll inform King Brian and be down shortly." He tucked his locket back under his shirt.

"May I be of assistance?" I asked. When it came to Aberron, I had no problem putting aside my issues to be a help.

"I could really use you," Joshua answered, sounding relieved.

Malsin spoke. "One second. Just want to make sure you're not hiding any medical concerns."

I appreciated his care and was grateful I could still trust him.

He took my hand in his, his magic activated. After a moment, he let go. "All right, you're good."

I went to the bathroom to quickly wash and dress, then joined my family in the hall.

"Isabelle, walk with me, please." King Brian took the lead.

I quickened my pace to join him.

"Aberron is on the brink of financial ruin. I haven't been able to reestablish a working relationship with Nistier and the Jamaylin Islands or start one with Dregaitia." He cleared his throat. "A good portion of Aberron's income comes from trade, mostly with Nistier and some from the Jamaylin Islands. We barter our natural resources for finished materials, like textiles. Growing conditions in Nistier are poorer than ours, and the Jamaylin Islands need extra help during their storm seasons. Many have turned their efforts into becoming excellent craftsmen. It has been mutually beneficial.

"When Dregaitia started a war with us, Nistier and the Jamaylin Islands stopped all trade. Despite finding peace with Dregaitia, we have not resumed our commerce. Instead, Nistier and the Jamaylin Islands have opened talks with Dregaitia." He scowled. "They seek to work together to exclude Aberron due to our monarchy's magical wealth."

"Can Dregaitia provide the same things as Aberron?" I asked.

"Dregaitia has been self-sufficient for some time," Braidus said, walking just behind me with Andrew. "Cekaiden refuses to rely on anyone but himself regardless of the cost to his people. Whatever resources Nistier and the islands seek, Dregaitia, as large as it is, will be sure to have it somewhere, though I do not think it will be as high quality. Their lands are substandard to Aberron."

"Perishables are going to waste," Andrew said. "The rest is piling up. Businesses are sinking fast. People aren't getting paid. Many have lost their jobs. Families are starting to go hungry."

Hence the angry merchants outside.

When we reached the doors, King Brian paused and looked down at me. "Nickoli, Cekaiden, and Jakobe made a statement to our people before they left, saying peace and trade resided solely on you. Talks would cease until you could be accounted for."

The guilt hit me hard. People were losing their livelihoods because of me. "I will contact them." Activating my purple magic, I pictured King Cekaiden, King Nickoli, and Prince Jakobe. I sent them a mental message. *"Your Majesties, this is Isabelle Mirran. We need to talk. You have one minute before I meld my mind with yours."*

When my minute was up, I connected with the three of them. King Cekaiden appeared to be in a throne room decorated in gold and red. King Nickoli resided in a study similar to King Brian's except with many windows, unlike the cave King Brian preferred. Prince Jakobe stood in a courtyard with his shirt off and a staff in hand. I appeared to have caught him during a training session. I initially felt their amazement, followed quickly by their displeasure at the intimacy. Their Gaitian, Nistieran, and heavily accented Fraison reached me in a garbled mess that quickly quieted as I took control.

*"I apologize for the intrusion, but I don't have much time. As you can see, I have returned to Carasmille—"*

*"Against your will,"* King Cekaiden interrupted.

*"There is still much fury and anguish within,"* King Nickoli said.

He was intrigued that the Sorren family had not been able to regain their standing with me.

*"The fire within you is intense,"* Prince Jakobe said. *"I'm almost sorry for your mage mates."*

I worked harder to clear errant thoughts and feelings, realizing both kings and the prince probed for any information they could glean from me. *"How I got here and what I feel doesn't matter,"* I thought. *"I'm contacting you because I'm willing to open negotiations between us to ensure Aberron's survival."*

They searched for the commitment within me. I stood firm for this cause. Aberron would not fall because of me.

*"You're willing to sacrifice everything, your own life even, for Aberron's future,"* King Nickoli said with surprise.

King Cekaiden added, *"Her life is claimed by the Gods. I doubt they would allow her to sacrifice much."*

Prince Jakobe agreed.

I didn't object. *"So, what will it be? We can continue this mind meld, or you can travel to Aberron."* I could not journey to them since Haldren had confined me to the castle. I'd be lucky if he let me outside to help with the gathering of angry merchants.

*"Travel,"* they said unanimously.

*"Then I shall expect you soon. May the Gods protect your journey."* I closed the connection and met King Brian's eyes. "King Cekaiden, King Nickoli, and Prince Jakobe will be on their way shortly to reopen talks with me."

"Oh, thank the Gods." He breathed with obvious relief. "I didn't know what I was going to tell the people outside."

I managed a weak smile. "Go tell them their fortune has changed." No matter the cost, I would pay it.

"Why don't we do it together?" King Brian extended his hand.

I took it. Two guards opened the doors. I paused briefly at the threshold and held out my hand, searching for Haldren's shield. My hand went through, no problem. He had removed it. Good. King Brian and I stepped outside together. The sun shone brightly, not a cloud in sight. I inhaled the cold air with zeal. *Freedom.* I fought against the strong urge to bolt and never come back.

The ground rumbled lightly underneath my feet, then stopped. My family looked at each other curiously.

"Could have been a small earthquake," King Brian said. "We are close to the mountains and get tremors from time to time but nothing serious."

Hundreds of men and women gathered, with more arriving by the minute. Chatter filled the courtyard, some harsh, some not. Random laughter rang out, but it wasn't particularly cheerful. These people meant business.

"It's Lady Champion!" a man near the front shouted.

"Lady Champion has returned!" another man called.

King Brian let go and raised his hands, his voice magnified by his magic. "Be at peace," he told the large gathering. "Our champion has returned to us."

"Why did she leave?" an older gentlemen with ruddy cheeks asked. The question rippled through the people.

King Brian wore a tight smile. "Unfortunately, during the beginning of our talks with Nistier, Dregaitia, and the Jamaylin Islands, Lady Isabelle received highly distressing news and felt she could not continue negotiations then."

The ground trembled again. Not sensing any concern from my mage mates over it, I tried to ignore it.

"Lover's spat, eh?" the ruddy man said, eyeing me and the princes critically.

Someone else shouted, "Can't choose a prince while we starve?"

My anger spiked. Activating my magic, I magnified my voice and spoke in a hard tone. "Do not think me so frivolous that I would lead Aberron to its ruin over a Gods-forbidden romance." I raised my left hand, indicating my birthmark. "The Gods often interfere with my life, hence my abundance of magic, which has saved Aberron in the past. Sometimes their meddling takes precedence. When I was informed only moments ago of the ramifications of my absence, I immediately contacted King Nickoli of Nistier, King Cekaiden of Dregaitia, and Prince Jakobe of the Jamaylin Islands. They are currently making preparations to resume mediation with me and King Brian. A resolution is close at hand."

"What if the mediations fail again?" a man in vivid green asked. "What of our businesses? My coffers are nearly empty. I will have no choice but to turn away good working men."

The air rumbled with similar stories. I heard the same words repeated. No money, no food, no home.

King Brian spoke. "You all know Aberron has my full interest. As king, I have worked hard to keep our commerce sustainable by being open to new ventures and maintaining good relations with other countries. It has been years since we have faced a business crisis such as this, and I promise we will weather it together." He turned to face me. "Anything you'd like to add?"

"You may not know me personally, but my feats during our battles with Dregaitia speak for themselves. I fight to save lives, not condemn them. I care more for the well-being of Aberron than I do for myself." I spoke with dead finality. "If I must be sacrificed to save Aberron *again,* then so be it." *My life was never mine to begin with*, I finished silently to myself.

King Brian lifted his hands. "Rest assured, trade will be opened as soon as possible. That is all."

I turned on my heel and swiftly walked back inside, not interested in listening to the crowds speculate about me and whether I'd come up to scratch.

"You did great Isabelle," Henry praised, hurrying to follow me, with Dominic and Falden behind him.

"Very convincing," Dominic agreed.

"Let's just hope we can come to an agreement with the other countries," I answered. "I don't care to discover what will happen if we don't."

"Definitely," the boys said.

King Brian, Queen Averly, my mage mates, and my brother stepped back inside.

King Brian reached me. "Thank you, Isabelle. We've managed to quiet the people for now."

I nodded. "I shall retire to my room, then." I couldn't do more until the royals arrived, and I wasn't ready to renew any family relationships. Even if Andrew's and Braidus's soul-bearing was genuine, their deception still hurt.

"As you wish," King Brian said, though he frowned.

"What's it going to take to win her over again?" Joshua asked my mage mates as I turned to leave.

"Our betrayal broke her heart," Braidus said grimly. "I don't think forgiveness is in her nature anymore."

I quickened my pace to my room.

My thoughts remained on the loss of trade. I felt selfish worrying about my problems when people were going hungry and losing their jobs. It would be a few days at least before the royals from Dregaitia, Nistier, and the Jamaylin Islands arrived. I wanted to do something to help the Aberronians in the meantime. I had some sundals in my possession I didn't need, and Haldren had removed his shield around the castle. A walk through Carasmille giving money to those in need felt like a start.

I waited an hour for the crowds to disperse. During that time, I focused on the bond, catching impressions from my mage mates in the study. I hoped to sneak out without them knowing. The last thing I needed was for someone to follow me. Assured the princes were well and truly busy, I hitched my sword to my belt and stuck a dagger in my boot. Then I grabbed a satchel and slung it over my shoulder, stuffing it with all the sundals I had in my possession. I put on a jacket and stepped out.

On my way down, I received a few wide-eyed stares from passing guards, nobles, and workers. I attributed some of it to the fact that I didn't often travel alone. I caught snatches of a conversation between two maids who polished fine silver candlesticks in an alcove.

"I'm telling you, Mia, Lady Isabelle is with child," the blonde said in a knowing tone. "King Brian found out and got angry. Illegitimate child laws and all that. There was probably an argument and she left."

Mia responded. "Who's the father, Lucy? Prince Braidus or Crown Prince Andrew?"

"Could be either. She's cozy with both. But my bet is on Prince Braidus." Lucy sighed dreamily. "The man is walking sin."

"Lucy!" Mia admonished, giggling.

"What?" Lucy didn't sound the least bit ashamed. "I can't think of a single young lady in my acquaintance that wouldn't lunge for his explicit attention—you included."

"Yes, but Crown Prince Andrew is—"

"Hush!" Lucy said, catching sight of me. As I passed them, I heard Mia say, "She doesn't look like she's carrying."

"It's too early," Lucy said, exasperated. "Mark my words, we'll see she's expecting soon enough."

I rolled my eyes. I didn't see a point in correcting them. I figured half or more of Carasmille harbored the same thought. I really wasn't bothered. I had bigger problems to worry about than what people thought of me.

I paused at the front doors, half suspicious that Haldren had locked me in again. I put my hand through, no problem, so I stepped outside, then hurried to the stables in search of Nisha, only to find his stall empty. My stomach dropped. Where could he be?

Haldren whispered in my ear. *"I've taken Nisha home. He missed his herd."*

Oh. Though I felt a pang of sadness, I was relieved to know he was accounted for and safe. Leaving the stables, I set off on a brisk walk, planning to walk straight into the heart of Carasmille.

Out of view of the castle, the tension in my bones eased. I didn't have my mage mates' and brother's melancholy eyes on me. And I wasn't listening to a thousand apologies, as if words could make up for the hurt. Perhaps they knew that, but it didn't stop them from trying.

Two shabbily dressed men with caps low over their heads leaned against a wrought-iron fence in a housing district far nicer than I thought they could afford. Glancing to the mansion on the left, I saw men in similar attire moving furniture in and out. *Not out of the ordinary, then.*

I stopped short as one of the men stepped in front of me.

He leered. "What's a pretty lady like you doing walking all alone?"

His friend nudged him. "Careful, Marty, that's Lady Champion. She could slice you to bits in a second."

Marty puffed out his chest. "I'm not afraid." He flashed me a crooked, scruffy smile. "You lookin' for a little entertainment, Lady Champion?"

I did my best to keep my tone friendly. "Thanks for the offer, but I'm afraid I'm already engaged for the afternoon. Besides, aren't you supposed to be working?" I tilted my head in the direction of the house.

"It's our break time," Marty explained. "We'll be back in the old lady's house in a minute."

"Well then, you certainly don't have time for me," I responded, my tone playful.

Marty smiled. "Aww, everybody's got time for Lady Champion."

Another worker called from the porch. "Hey, break's over!"

I reached into my satchel and grabbed a few sundals, then handed a couple to Marty and his friend. "For entertainment when your work is done."

The men's eyes lit up. "Thank you, Lady Champion," they chorused. Marty stepped back to let me pass.

A little farther down the road, Isaac appeared beside me. "Little Goddess."

My adrenaline kicked up a notch. "Isaac." Was he here to rib me about my fate? Or perhaps put a new nightmare into my head?

He met my stride easily. "Really, little Goddess, I expected a thank-you for having revealed your destiny. Haldren would've stolen you in the middle of the night without warning. I've given you time to prepare yourself for your new role."

*Would Haldren have waited till the last second?*

Isaac's lips slowly morphed into a smile. "Undoubtedly."

I frowned, hating that I didn't know Isaac or Haldren well enough to know the truth. They both wanted to manipulate me. I had no choice but to be amenable to Isaac. After all, he had the power to crush me.

"Thank you."

"You're welcome," he answered, seemingly appeased.

We reached the business district, where people, carts, and carriages flowed up and down the street, like fish in a stream. I found the busyness of it all unnerving. Why so many people enjoyed living in such proximity was beyond me. I breathed in the scent of fish, manure, and a cloying perfume. A lady stood near the open door of a candle and fragrance shop. She sprayed the air with a red bottle. A few paces away, a grizzled man stood near a cart displaying slabs of trout on blocks of ice. I didn't blame her for attempting to remove the fish smell. It wasn't great.

"A rainbow fish for a rainbow lady?" he asked me.

"No, thank you." I smiled while shaking my head.

Isaac and I continued on our way down the street. He spoke conversationally. "You are right to harbor such anger for Haldren and your family. They gave you false hope when there was none to be had. Do you remember the pain you experienced when gold magic first appeared in your core?"

"Yes." Stefan's vase had fallen on me and shattered. In a panic, I'd woken the entire household.

Isaac continued. "Before gold magic takes hold in an individual, it searches the very soul to see if they are worthy enough to possess it. If you were not deemed acceptable, the magic would not have joined with you and Haldren would've found another to take his place."

I had gold magic. "I was found acceptable."

A dark-haired man brushed past me, nearly knocking me into Isaac. He clutched a white cloth bag.

"Yes," Isaac agreed. "The process of becoming a Goddess began when the magic decided to stay. The change is irreversible, much like your bond with the Sorren princes. In the coming months, you will see your mage core slowly fill with gold sand, extending your abilities with the colors you currently possess. When a new ball filled entirely with gold sand appears and joins your other colors, you will ascend into your new role."

"What exactly does a Goddess do?" I asked.

He grinned. "Watch over the world, help or hinder wherever necessary. Like this." He waved his hand and made the dark-haired man who had run past us stop as if frozen.

We stepped aside to allow two patrol guards to race by. Isaac flicked his fingers, and the dark-haired man came to life just as one of the guards tackled him to the ground. "You're under arrest, thief." The guard panted, binding the man's hands.

"As a Goddess over Gods, you will also oversee Amora, Tomas, Nachura, and Zadek in their dealings with the earth," Isaac said.

My shoulders felt heavy at the prospect. I had no interest whatsoever in becoming a leader. I sought a quiet, peaceful existence. *That's not happening,* I thought bitterly.

"You will have your peace after your thousand-year reign," Isaac said, clearly reading my thoughts.

"Everyone I know will be dead," I said, letting my mouth run away from me.

He shrugged. "Such is the way of life. Your loved ones will find someone to replace you, and the world will continue as it did."

My insides turned to sludge.

He stopped and faced me. "Goddesses are meant to watch over the earth. Having attachments can hinder your work. Any time you spend with a loved one can be someone else's last breath, their prayers unheard."

"I understand." I didn't want to, but I did.

"I do not make exceptions to this rule," he said, his tone firm. "If any of my Gods or Goddesses become too attached, I take action."

"Is that what happened to Haldren and my mother?" I asked quietly.

Isaac's lips curled in disdain. "I warned Haldren he spent too much time with Anne, but he could not resist her. I had to eliminate your parents to keep him focused."

He put a hand on my shoulder, and a sizzling jolt of electricity went through me. His power tripled that of any other God I'd met. My stomach lurched in fear.

"Take heed, little Goddess. I will do it to you should you stray like Haldren did." Then, with a bright silver flash, he vanished.

I stood motionless at the edge of the sidewalk, trying to force myself to be calm.

A young boy bumped into me. "Sorry, miss," he said, scurrying to catch up with his mother.

I turned at the sound of arguing. A thirty-something-ish man quarreled with someone at the door of a warehouse. "What do you mean there's no work? I've got seven little ones to feed."

A man seemingly in his fifties with a thick salt-and-pepper mustache said, "I'm sorry, but until trade is reopened with Nistier, I have no work. I'm closing shop."

The younger man raked a hand through his blonde hair. "What am I going to tell my wife? I can't go home empty-handed again."

I stepped forward. "Perhaps I can help." I reached into my satchel and grabbed a large handful of sundals. The younger man's blue eyes widened as I held them out. "Trade will be opened within the next week and a half. Will this be enough to get you by?"

The man accepted the coins. "Yes, thank you. Thank you," he spluttered.

"You're welcome." With a smile, I walked away.

Not much farther down the road, I watched a bony, wizened matron shove a young woman out the door of a brick building. "You're two sundals short on rent." She threw a small carpetbag at the young lady.

"Please, I've nowhere to go!" the young woman cried, tears staining tracks down her cheeks.

"If you can't pay, you can't stay," the old woman said firmly. "I'm not a charity house."

"Allow me." I handed the landlord the necessary money.

The old woman eyed me shrewdly. "Humph. All right, Cora, you can stay." She jerked her head, gesturing for Cora to come inside, and shuffled off. She put a sign in the window stating no rooms available.

Cora grasped my hands. "Oh, thank you. I don't know how I can ever repay you. My job's not paying until trade is reopened."

"No need." I handed her a few extra coins. "To get you by."

She thanked me again and went inside with a bright smile. I stared at the plain redbrick building and contemplated getting a room somewhere in the city for myself. I could still be close enough to the castle to help with reopening trade but separate from my family. I'd have to figure out how to access more of the money Joshua had been keeping to pay for things. Perhaps I could find some information on renting rooms in the ad section of the Carasmille paper. King Brian had one delivered to him in the study daily. Surely he wouldn't mind if I borrowed it.

I continued emptying my satchel and passing out coins to those I saw in need. I gave some to a group of children, a man playing violin on a street corner, a temple priest seeking donations for his charity fund. It wasn't much, but I hoped I had changed a few lives. Once I had emptied my entire satchel, I started the return journey to the castle.

Coming within sight of the gates, I felt the ground shake harder than before. "Whoa." I threw my hands out as I stumbled. It stopped abruptly. I barely regained my balance when the ground rumbled again, more violently.

"Gods forbid!" I fell onto my hands and knees.

My bond heightened with fear as the ground heaved beneath me. Cracking, thumping, breaking glass, and faint screaming reached my ears. I imagined the castle collapsing with my family inside. This terror spurred me into action. Activating my magic, I shot into the sky.

Much to my relief, the castle still stood. I landed on the front steps just as the trembling ceased. I dashed inside. The entry hall was littered with broken pottery and bits of plaster, crystal, and glass. Two older maids hid under a table, quivering but overall unharmed. I flew over the debris in an effort to get to the study more quickly.

The doors hung crooked and slightly ajar. I threw them open with a burst of air, then entered, setting my feet on the ground. Books and papers were scattered about the floor. Chairs had been turned over. A broken inkpot stained the marble floor. The chandelier had fallen onto the table, broken crystal and half-melted candles scattered across its surface.

The royal family crawled out from under the table.

"Are you all right?" I rushed to them, my eyes scanning them for injuries.

"We're fine," Andrew said, lifting his hands to show they were unharmed. "You?"

"Fine. Where are the others?" I asked.

"The boys went to the Sorrenian," Andrew answered. "I think Malsin is—"

"Here. I'm right here." Malsin appeared in the doorway, looking disheveled and shaken but whole.

"And Joshua?" I asked.

"At the forge, I believe," Braidus answered. "I suggest you use telepathy to contact them."

Switching to purple magic, I connected to Henry, Dominic, and Falden. They sat on the floor in the culture room at the Sorrenian beside their friends. A blue shield had been erected over their heads.

*"You guys all right?"*

*"We're good,"* Falden said.

*"Yeah,"* Dominic said, wincing as Amarilla's fingernails dug into his forearm. Through his eyes, I saw she still appeared to be in shock.

*"Gods, that was crazy!"* Henry exclaimed, holding Aliyah tightly against him. His heart still pounded in fear over the thought of something happening to her. *"What about you guys?"*

*"We're all right. Just need to check on Joshua. Be careful out there."* I ended the connection.

"The boys are safe," I said to King Brian. "Checking on Joshua now."

I pictured Joshua's face. Boomer woofed, his tail wagging as he connected with him. *Joshua, are you all right?* I felt his presence, but he didn't respond. Cold fear gripped me. I probed around his brain and sensed he was hurt.

"Something's wrong. I can't hear him. I think he's hurt."

"He might be knocked out," Malsin suggested.

"Which way to the forge?" I asked, having never been there.

Braidus took my hand in his and activated his magic. "We'll fly."

"We'll meet you there," Andrew said.

Rising a space above the floor, we zoomed out of the study, dodging people and overturned furniture. A maid shrieked and ducked as we flew over her head. Exiting the castle, we shot into the sky. *Gods, I can't lose him,*

I thought with a sinking feeling. I remained connected to Joshua despite not hearing anything. I mentally shouted his name over and over, hoping he would come to. Past the stables, a column of black smoke rose into the air.

"Something's on fire," I said to Braidus.

"It's the forge," he said as the burning building came into view.

My heart leaped into my throat. I increased my speed, practically pulling Braidus along with me. I wrapped a rainbow shield around myself as we landed, then sprinted into the building.

"Isabelle, be careful!" Braidus shouted from behind me.

The heat was intense, even through my shield. I could hardly see a thing through the hazy smoke. I coughed at the acridness. Knocked-over basins spilled molten metal. Half-finished weapons and burning timber lay haphazardly on the floor. It was a death trap.

I heard a boy crying and coughing. Hands out in front of me, I followed the sound, stumbling as I bumped into things I couldn't see. The crackling of the flames made it hard to hear the boy. After a few steps, a burning rafter fell right where I meant to step. Splinters flew at me, and I lurched to a stop, instinctively throwing my hands over my head. "Whoa!"

When the pieces settled, I hopped over the beam, calling out, my voice magnified. "I'm trying to find you. Shout as loud as you can."

I heard a wail to my left. I swiveled, following the cries until I found a barely ajar door. I opened it all the way. A boy no older than eleven cowered next to a broom, tears streaming down his face. He coughed violently. I felt a pang of disappointment that my brother wasn't with him.

"You're going to be all right. I've got you."

With a flick of my fingers, I placed a rainbow shield over him, then held out my hand. He took it, squeezing tight. Lifting him, I led him out of the closet.

I stayed close to the wall, searching for a window or door to the outside. I couldn't see a Gods-forbidden thing. Just as I decided I'd be better off blasting our way out, I heard the smashing of broken glass and saw a glint of a sword breaking through a window. Smoke rushed out.

"Almost there." I pulled the boy to the window. Shards of glass protruded from around the frame. "Climb out. The shield will protect you." I helped lift him up and out of the window.

A soldier caught him on the other side. "I've got him."

The boy shouted, his voice hoarse. "Joseph and the commander are still in there!" Two people! Gods forbid, I needed to hurry. I quickly removed the shield from the boy. "I'll find them."

I turned away from the window, intent on rescuing my brother and Joseph. It gave me hope that I hadn't lost my connection to him despite being unable to hear his thoughts.

I waved my hands, trying to use my yellow magic to push the smoke around so I could see better. It didn't work as well as I wished. I cursed the slowness the smoke created. I tried to gather moisture from the air to create water and put out some of the flames, but it didn't work well either. The fire had dried the air.

I kept my eyes close to the ground, figuring I'd find him on the floor somewhere. I prayed he wasn't getting burned alive. *Gods, help me find him.* My coughing increased as I inhaled ash. Another flaming rafter came crashing toward my face. I yelled and jumped out of the way and stepped on a mace handle. The rod rolled under my feet, causing me to lose my balance and fall to the ground. Grief held me in its clutches, and a sob rose in my throat. I hadn't been able to save Nathan, Adel, and Stefan. Would I be too late to save my brother?

Now on my hands and knees, I spotted him. "Joshua!" He lay on his stomach under a large pile of metal of various shapes and sizes. Another man lay on his back nearby, his lower half trapped under a metal shelf. Joseph. Flames came within licking distance of them both.

I scrambled to my feet and dashed over. *Boomer, help me get this off!* Ribbons of Yellow shot from my hands and wrapped themselves around the pieces of metal, lifting them off the ground, then moving them a few paces away. Though free, neither Joshua nor Joseph stirred. My fear increased to a frenzy. I wrapped rainbow shields around them to protect them from the flames. Now to get out. I looked for an exit of some sort but saw nothing. I'd have to break us out. I faced the closest stone wall and raised my hands, forming a large red fireball in them. I threw it at the wall, blasting the rock. Pieces flew in every direction, and a window-sized hole appeared. I threw another fireball, making it big enough to walk through.

Then I turned back to my brother and Joseph and directed Boomer to lift them gently. I guided their limp bodies through the hole, following behind. I coughed violently as I sucked in a lungful of the fresh winter air.

My family waited on the other side, along with a number of soldiers and bystanders. I set Joseph and Joshua on the ground a little ways from the building and removed the shields over them and myself. Oliver and another soldier moved to attend to Joseph while Malsin and I dropped to our knees beside Joshua. As I placed my hands on his chest, my telepathic connection to him had ended.

Malsin whitened, his eyes going wide with despair. I knew that look. I'd seen it enough during the Dregan battles. *No. Gods, no.*

*Boomer!*

He whined, shoving his nose into his paws.

"He's dead."

# CHAPTER NINE

 *o. No, no, no.* I dug my fingers into Joshua's green shirt. I stared at his soot-stained, sleeping face. "No. You don't get to die on me."

Malsin removed his hands, his expression one of regret. Tears formed in his eyes. "I'm so sorry, Isabelle."

Andrew's sorrow hit me hard as he sat down beside me. Queen Averly sobbed as she pulled King Brian onto the ground with her. Tear-stained faces greeted me all around. First Stefan, then Nathan and Adel, and now Joshua. How dare he die on me. I balled my hands into fists as rage consumed me. My mage mates inhaled sharply. I punched my brother in the heart as hard as I possibly could.

Ribbons of gold exploded from me and penetrated Joshua's chest. Boomer danced on his paws and woofed. Joshua's body jumped and twitched as if shocked. From around me came exclamations of surprise. Encouraged by Boomer's reaction, I punched Joshua again, sending more ribbons into his body. His chest expanded. Boomer rolled on the ground, tongue lolling at the power I wielded. I pounded Joshua a third time and swore I heard his chest rattle with breath. I punched him once more, pouring every bit of energy I had into him. A yell escaped my lips as adrenaline and a fiery, prickling pain raced over my glowing golden skin. Gold ribbons of smoke went everywhere, piercing anyone close by. They jumped at the jolt of power.

Joshua's eyes fluttered.

"He's alive!" Malsin cried, rushing to put his hands on Joshua once more.

Queen Averly, Andrew, Malsin, and I joined to heal Joshua. We cleared the smoke from his lungs and healed the damage the metal had done. He coughed harshly, his face tight with pain, as we worked on him.

"Finished." Malsin lifted his hands.

Andrew and I drew back. Queen Averly snatched Joshua by the front of his shirt with surprising strength and pulled him into a sitting position. His emerald eyes went wide as she crushed him against her in a fierce hug, sobbing anew. He lifted his arms and held her tight, a soft smile of affection gracing his lips.

I'd never been more grateful to see my brother whole. He had no business joining the Realm of Souls. Amidst my relief, however, my heartache grew. As King Brian joined the hug, I felt like an outsider watching an unknown family celebrate. I shouldn't be here, selfishly trying to take part in a family that wasn't truly mine.

I scrambled to my feet, unable to stomach another moment. My brother got to keep a family, and I couldn't. It wasn't fair! I swayed, weak and light-headed. My stomach rolled, my chest tightened, my head throbbed, and my desperation to outrun my anguish overruled my sickness. I sprinted away, blinking furiously as the world spun in circles. I ran until my legs failed, then collapsed onto a patch of frost-tipped grass near a wooden fence. I coughed and choked, trying to breathe. My stomach heaved, and I retched, coming up with nothing but spittle. I rested my back against a fence post, brought my knees up, and wrapped my arms around my chest. I willed the tears leaking out of the corners of my eyes to reverse. Crying wouldn't change my fate.

Near the stables with somewhat of a view of the castle, I watched people march up and down the cobblestone pathways with purpose. They carried broken pieces of furniture, pottery, and other debris. Perhaps I should help with the cleanup. Busy work usually helped me become numb. Except I barely had the strength to move. I propped my elbows on my knees and dropped my head into my hands, then shut my eyes as sleep beckoned.

"Isabelle!"

At the sound of Andrew's voice, I lifted my head. He, Braidus, and Malsin approached. King Brian, Queen Averly, and Joshua followed a few paces behind, taking it slow. I averted my gaze, trying to steel myself against their attention. I couldn't keep them.

My eyes caught sight of something flying through the air. Before I knew it, Haldren had appeared in a bright flash and snatched an arrow just before it made contact with my head. Seconds later, Andrew, Braidus, and Malsin arrived.

Haldren turned to my mage mates, his tone full of censure. "You must keep a better watch on my successor."

With a flick of his fingers, he made a young woman appear. She struggled against a gold rope, her eyes angry. A quiver of arrows rested on her back.

"This one hid on the roof of the stables." Haldren waved his hand, and my would-be killer vanished to who knew where.

"Her reason for trying to kill Isabelle?" Braidus asked.

Haldren shrugged as if the reason didn't matter but said anyway, "Orders from her lover—the man you sentenced to the Carasmille prison for leading the Abominators."

"Kyston," Andrew spat. "That man has a reach even from behind bars."

"Perhaps we need to review our prison-visiting policies," Braidus said.

"There will be others who wish to see Isabelle dead," Haldren said, his tone serious. "A woman with her beauty, magic, and princes' affections fosters jealousy. I cannot afford a single misstep in her care."

King Brian, Queen Averly, and Joshua arrived. My brother sat beside me in the grass and tucked me against him. I leaned my head against his chest, hating myself for craving his support.

Braidus angrily spoke to Haldren. "You cannot expect us to keep an eye on her every second of the day and night when she has power afforded to you. She circumvents us at every turn due to your handling of her fate."

"Our connection is broken," Andrew said, his tone troubled. "We are nothing more than jailers to her. She will escape us at every given opportunity."

They weren't wrong. I still wanted to find a new place to stay. Admittedly, my hopes of finding a newspaper with room advertisements were slim considering the earthquake mess, but I could figure something else out.

Haldren turned his attention to me, his gaze as hard as steel. "Give it no more thought, or I will confine you to the castle again."

I eyed him sullenly. Why not continue to torture me with a family I couldn't have? Why not stay with a bunch of betrayers I foolishly craved to be with?

Haldren crouched, meeting me at eye level. "For what it's worth, Isabelle, I have never threatened your princes into a courtship with you with the ruination of Aberron. I only encouraged. Isaac embellished the truth in an effort to stir up animosity between you, your family, and me."

Isaac's warning to eliminate my loved ones still rang clear in my mind. "So I would let everyone go," I surmised.

Haldren half smiled. "Yes, as is the law." He held open his palm, and a black leather journal appeared. He handed it to me. The leather was worn and soft. A gold letter $Z$ had been engraved on the front.

"Isaac might've left you in my care, but he enjoys this rift between you and your family too much. He has been preventing me from explaining the whole truth to correct it." He scowled. "Start with Zadek's journal, and I will try to return to answer any questions you have."

He took a breath. "Now, my other purpose in being here is because, in saving your brother, you managed to access your gold magic and used it like a full-fledged Goddess. You also succeeded in imparting to your family some of your gold power. They now have shields protecting their mage cores."

"Shields?" King Brian's eyebrows rose. "Why?"

"It is possible for mages to tamper with other people's mage cores and cause harm by draining their magic," Haldren explained. "These shields will prevent that." He returned his gaze to me. "No other juvenile God or Goddess has ever done what you just did. We took note of your skill with great interest."

Huh. I'd surprised the Gods. I doubted that happened often—if ever.

Haldren continued, his eyes briefly roaming over my body as if looking inside me. "Your actions caused an imbalance in your mage core. Your next transformation will fix it. Until that occurs—at a time of its choosing—you will suffer the effects of low magic stores. This leaves you vulnerable." He straightened.

I tilted my head up to see him better.

"I'll take my leave." His eyes briefly turned to my family. "Keep my successor safe," he admonished, then vanished in a flash of gold.

Joshua looked at me. "Thank you for bringing me back." He shuddered. "I didn't enjoy the walk down that cold, dark tunnel to the Realm of Souls. I owe you everything."

"Think nothing of it." I smiled, albeit a bit wobbly.

He tightened the arm around me and kissed the top of my head. "I love you, little sister."

I believed him.

King Brian spoke with interest. "My mage core has a coating of gold over the glass." He projected his core to show a ball filled to the brim with blue sand. The glass shimmered with a layer of see-through gold.

"Mine too," Queen Averly said.

My mage mates, brother, and Malsin confirmed theirs had the same change. My heart tugged as my mage mates checked my magic levels. Braidus projected an image of my core and pointed out, "She has very few gold grains." I had less than a tenth of the amount I had before.

King Brian took his wife's hand. "Well, I better go survey the damage to my castle and city." Together they walked toward the castle.

Malsin crouched on the other side of me. "Can you stand?"

I shrugged. Joshua and Malsin helped me into a standing position. I took one step, clutching the journal to my chest, my family rushing to help when my knees buckled.

I held out a hand to stop them as I righted myself. "I can do it."

The men cursed my stubbornness. Stumbling often, I walked at a snail's pace. Through the bond, I felt Braidus's patience wear thin the farther

I walked. My head pounded so fiercely I could hardly see straight, but I prided myself in moving under my own power.

When we reached the front steps of the castle, Braidus snuck up behind me and swept me into his arms. "I cannot stand to watch you manage the stairs."

I didn't fight him.

He carried me to the study. I didn't particularly relish the idea of being there, but Haldren had ordered my family to keep a better eye on me, and they had to run a country in addition. The doors stood wide open with a line of people needing to speak with King Brian, I assumed concerning the damage the earthquake caused. The king took a seat at the head of the table with Queen Averly beside him. On the other side of him, a man took notes, his hand flying across the page as he wrote feverishly.

The man at the front of the line spoke. "We're detecting leaks in the water mains beneath the city. We're dispatching as many people as we can to fix them."

King Brian answered, "We cannot afford a flood on top of everything else. Let's send out some blue mages to shield the broken pipes as a temporary fix until we can handle it."

Braidus deposited me on a soft chaise lounge beside a bookshelf. Malsin took a chair from the table and positioned himself beside me. The others seated themselves at the table to be of help to their father.

I opened the book Haldren had given me to the first page. Black scrawl in an indecipherable language greeted me. I cursed. I couldn't read this.

Malsin looked over my shoulder at the book. "Hmm, that's not a language I know."

Braidus had traveled extensively during his banishment. Through the bond, I projected my wish for him to come to me. I didn't want to interrupt King Brian while he worked on relief efforts.

Braidus caught my wish and walked over. Andrew watched us. His envy that I had requested his brother and not him brushed my heart.

Braidus gave me a teasing grin. "I like feeling wanted by you."

I fought back an eye-roll and held out the book. "What language is this?"

He took it, his eyes scanning the page. "It's Gaitian. I can read it to you."

King Brian called out to us with a strained expression. "I know the book is important, but can it wait until we're not swimming in disaster cleanup?"

I nodded.

"Thank you," he said.

Braidus took the journal as he returned to assisting his father. Everyone kept me under their watchful gaze as they worked. I tried to nap, but the pounding in my head prevented me from getting much rest. My mind traveled to the journal, my annoyance growing as the hours passed with Aberron's business taking precedence.

Henry, Dominic, and Falden arrived around dinnertime, at the close of business.

"The city's a mess out there," Henry said. "No one expected the earthquake to be this bad. Everyone thought we were just having our usual tremors. This one was insane! The Healer's Guild is drowning in patients. Aliyah and her parents have gone over there to help. They're asking for anyone who's a green mage to help."

"What about your mom and Lyle?" King Brian asked.

"Trying to set the Sorrenian back to rights," Henry explained. "They had some issues with damaged pipes, lots of broken windows, and some of the old stone crumbling in the south wing. They've sent all the students home to be with their families."

Falden looked at me with brows drawn. "What's wrong with Isabelle?"

Joshua answered, "She is suffering with low gold-magic stores from bringing me back to life."

"You died?" Dominic exclaimed, eyes wide.

Joshua nodded. "Only for a few minutes."

The boys listened with rapt attention as King Brian told the tale of my brother's survival. At the end, Andrew projected his mage core to show the gold coating his two colors.

Afterward, Henry shook his head. "Gods forbid, she never ceases to amaze me."

A knock came at the door.

Queen Averly rose. "That should be dinner."

She was right. Several maids wheeled in carts of food, drink, and dinnerware. I sighed. Another delay before we could get to the journal. Malsin brought me a simple vegetable soup. I wasn't interested and gave him a look that said as much.

He stared me down, his jaw set in determination.

I knew better than to disobey him when he showed me his stern face. I took the bowl and ate slowly to keep it down. He looked pleased when I finished.

After the meal, we finally turned our attention to Zadek's journal. I hoped beyond hope that it would tell me how to get out of my fate. I also felt much frustration that I had to rely on Braidus to learn the answers. I didn't understand why Haldren seemed intent on pushing me toward my family when I couldn't keep them.

Braidus held the book in front of him. His eyes darted across the first page, then he turned to the next and the next. Ten pages or so into it and he had yet to utter a word.

"Can you even read Gaitian?" Joshua growled, his patience probably as thin as mine.

"Yes." Braidus didn't look up as he turned the page. "Zadek's war tactics against a Kashtine invasion have no bearing on our cause." Another ten pages and Braidus stilled. "There."

"What?" everyone asked.

Braidus read, "Isaac, God of men and war, appeared to me."

"I thought he was a Fate," Andrew said.

"Keep reading," Joshua urged Braidus.

"I have found favor with him. He took my right hand. It burned. A red Mark of the Gods appeared on the back. Isaac said, 'You shall be a God like me.'" Braidus turned the page and continued with what appeared to be a new entry. "I showed the mark to my king. I learned the Gods are not infinite beings as I supposed. A thousand years they reign. I am to be Isaac's successor. My king says it is a great honor. I must prepare for it. I am to tell Yashti, my beloved, to accept Carrick's proposal. We can be no more." Braidus lifted the book, squinting. "The ink is smeared. I can only make out a few words. *Heart. Pain. Honor. Yashti. Sacrifice.*"

"He didn't try to fight it," Andrew said. "He gave up everything."

"It would appear so," Braidus agreed. His finger stopped on a word. "Here. 'I woke bathed in a copper glow. My skin prickled as if tiny fire ants swarmed my body. Isaac appeared. It is the beginning of a power transference into a God. There is copper in my red magic. I can do more with my power. I wish I had it during the Kashtine invasion.'"

"Copper, not gold?" I asked, wanting to be sure I heard right.

"Copper," Braidus repeated, his eyes meeting mine. "Zadek is a lesser God than Haldren. Would it not make sense if their powers are different?"

"Yes, you're probably right," I agreed.

Braidus flipped through the next fifteen or so pages. "Other colors of magic appeared—yellow, green, blue, and purple, all flecked with copper. Zadek took revenge on Kashtine with his extended power." He turned to Joshua. "Zadek is brilliant at war. After we learn what he says about the Gods, it would be wise for you and I to revisit it for the battle strategies."

"I would like that," Joshua said.

Returning to the book, Braidus found another relevant entry. "'The God Haldren came to me. My time as a human is nigh at hand. My mind has been opened in preparation.'"

I tensed.

"'I am to be the God of men and war, joining ranks with Amora, Goddess of women, love, and fertility; Tomas, God of intellect and negotiations; and Nachura, Goddess of nature and animals. Haldren—'" Braidus stopped and cleared his throat.

Andrew poured a cup of water from a decanter and handed it to him.

He drank and then continued. "'Haldren is the God over all living. I believed that to be the end but learned differently.'"

"The Fates," Andrew whispered.

Braidus took another sip of water. "'Above Haldren are four Fates, rulers of the Realm of Souls who watch over the departed. Two men and two women—Cassius, Eli, Ada, Emory. The Fates are infinite—immortal beings made of flesh and blood. They have no time limit like the Gods. They judge souls according to their mortal deeds and place them in one of two levels in the realm—paradise for the good, and a desert wasteland for the evil.'"

"Kind of nice to see that what we know of the Realm of Souls is actually true," Henry said.

"It's a kicker to be good, for sure," Falden said.

Everyone agreed.

Braidus turned the page. "'Above the four Fates is Palina, a Fate over Fates. She rules the living and dead.'"

"How did Isaac get her position?" Andrew asked.

"Keep reading," I told Braidus.

"'Palina answers to the father of our world, a man known as the Creator, who built the earth as we know it. The Gods and Fates follow his structure. The Gods, Fates, and Creator live on a hidden island called Astralind.'" He cursed. "Someone, perhaps Zadek, spilled ink over the next passage. I cannot read it."

Braidus showed it to me. My heart sank.

He read one more line. "'A new ball of copper has appeared in my mage core. I go to the city of the Gods.'" The rest of the journal was blank.

I sighed.

Andrew repeated his question. "If the Fates are immortal and have immeasurable power, how did Isaac take Palina's position?"

"Perhaps the Creator gave it to him," Joshua suggested.

"And did what with Palina?" Andrew asked.

Braidus spoke. "Zadek says the Fates are made of flesh and blood. That means they must eat, sleep, and feel."

King Brian continued. "Immortal but potentially susceptible to bodily harm."

"Murdered," Dominic said.

"Do you think Isaac murdered Palina and somehow stole her power?" Henry asked the group.

"Or the Creator got rid of her and put Isaac in her place," Malsin said. "I don't think the Gods are perfect. Could be she committed a crime and the Creator sentenced her."

"The book isn't going to tell us," I said from the chaise lounge. "I need Haldren."

A bright flash and Haldren was there.

"That was quick," Falden said.

"I convinced Isaac to allow me to explain my plans," Haldren said, "and I've been watching you read the journal."

"You should have just sat with us, then," I said.

Haldren waved his hand, and, suddenly, everyone in the study stood in a wheat field. "Since you are now aware of the hierarchy of the Gods, it is time for you to learn your place in it."

"I'm taking your place," I said.

A slow conspiratorial smile crept over Haldren's lips. "Perhaps."

I stilled. "What?" I saw equal confusion on my family members' faces.

Haldren's cold blue eyes centered on me. "I did more than heal your heart when I chose you in the womb. I gave you blue and green magic in addition to the red and yellow you were already destined to have. I shaped your character, giving you tests and experiences that would make you strong or gentle when the time called for it."

I struggled to get words out. "How I think, what I feel . . . all of that's because you—"

"Not entirely," Haldren disagreed. "Something of your parents shows through in your behavior. Your stubbornness, for example, is a direct trait of your mother, and so is your refusal to eat when you're upset."

"I'm a Gods-forbidden science experiment!" I exclaimed with ire.

Haldren didn't bat an eye. "You are exactly what I need you to be."

He conjured a bead of water, a picture of the Creator frozen inside a glass sphere forming inside it.

"This is the Creator as he is now—immobile, powerless, but alive. He made this sphere to imprison Isaac after he stole Palina's power and then murdered her to become the Fate over Fates."

"The dreams I've had are true," I whispered.

"Yes."

"What dreams?" my family asked.

The scene changed. The Creator and Isaac stood on either side of the large sphere. The ball moved toward Isaac, but he thrust his hands out and propelled it backward, swallowing the Creator. Rays of bright light shot out from the sphere. One struck Isaac. The other beams traveled to find the Gods and two youngish men and two women I supposed to be the Fates.

"The rays of light were the Creator's last wish before his imprisonment," Haldren said. "He left us unable to cause harm to one another. None of the Fates or Gods can kill each other."

A piece fell into place. "I'm not under that rule."

Haldren smiled. "No. Your strikes would ring true."

"He's grooming you to murder Isaac," Braidus said in a low voice.

Haldren's eyes flashed. "Isaac should not be the Fate over Fates. He should have reverted to his human form and let Zadek take his place as set forth by the Creator. At the helm of our world is nothing more than a cold-blooded killer, heady with power. He hurts innocents without reservation—Palina, Anne, Daniel, our Creator."

He flicked his hand and returned to the image of the trapped Creator. "There has been an unbalance in the world since his imprisonment a little over three hundred years ago. It started slow, and we managed to steady the earth during the first few centuries. Over the last century, however, the magnitude of the unbalance has increased. It gave us some struggle, but we still had the ability to manage it. This last fall, it has increased again and put an immense strain on us. The earth is falling apart. Calamities are happening at an unprecedented rate—heavy snow in milder climates, flooding in the deserts." Haldren rubbed his forehead, appearing distressed. "It's rapidly becoming more than we can handle."

King Brian questioned, "The earthquake we had today as well?"

Haldren nodded. Waving his hand, he changed the image inside the bead of water.

I saw the tree with opal bark and a canopy of shimmering leaves in the same colors found in mage cores—red, green, yellow, and blue. I also saw copper, gold, white, and silver. The leaves fell from the branches and turned black, and then black lines climbed up the trunk and along the branches.

"The earth is a living entity. This tree is its heart."

"It's got a problem," Henry pointed out.

"Indeed," Haldren acknowledged. "Like any living thing, it needs nourishment. This tree feeds on magic."

"Like an enchantress plant," Falden said.

"Yes," Haldren answered. "The Creator fed the tree before he was imprisoned. The other Gods and I have tried to nourish it, but it will not accept our magic. I have concluded it is a job meant only for the Creator."

"It's starving," Andrew said.

"What happens if it dies?" Malsin asked.

"The earth crumbles into nothingness," Haldren said bluntly. "And we all cease to be."

"We haven't got much time," Queen Averly said, her eyes on the image. "The disease covers nearly the whole tree."

"Hence our need for the Creator," Haldren said.

I lifted my hands and dropped them. "Surely Isaac realizes he will kill everyone, himself included, should the tree perish. He will have nothing to rule over. Why has he not relented to freeing the Creator in favor of keeping the earth whole and saving countless lives?"

"Isaac still believes he can find a way to feed the tree without using the Creator," Haldren answered. "He seeks to eliminate the Creator in favor of remaining in power. In the past, the Gods and lesser Fates banded together to free the Creator. As you can see, we have been unsuccessful. We have determined it is impossible without the Fate over Fates's help."

As the full picture fell into place, my family looked to me for my thoughts. In truth, I wondered how I remembered to keep breathing.

Haldren placed his hand on my shoulder. "I have spent the last three hundred years searching for a way to free the Creator and save the tree, while Isaac has sought to eliminate him and fuel the tree without him. You are my last effort. If you take Isaac's place and free the Creator, I believe he will give you back your life in Aberron and find another willing to take your place." Stepping back, Haldren gestured to my family. "I have encouraged you and them to build relationships to give you a reason to fight. My hope is that your love for them ensures you'll do anything to keep them."

"How is forcing them to keep the secret of me becoming a Goddess encouraging family relationships?" I asked in frustration, my hand waving wildly. "I cannot look any of them in the eye without questioning if I matter or not. What is truth? What is not?"

A bit of Haldren's godly power flared. "I need you to be resilient enough to handle Isaac at his worst. To get there includes breaking and mending. I take no pleasure in it."

I switched topics. If Haldren was in an answering mood, I'd get every question out. "Why two bonds instead of one?"

"There is no greater love than one forged in a bond. I gave you two because unforeseen accidents, assassinations, sickness, and disease happen. I cannot trust that nothing life-threatening will occur, especially with Isaac at the helm of our world. Thus, should something happen to one, you have another to fall back on."

"An heir and a spare," Braidus reminded. I'd felt his and Andrew's distaste for it.

"I will leave nothing to chance," Haldren said, his tone stern. "Should you liberate the Creator and get your life back, you're free to choose between the princes and live how you want."

Right. Just take on a Fate over Fates with more power than I can fathom. I failed to see how I could beat him to return home. We were all going to die.

I dug my fingers into my hair. "I've no other option to escape this fate . . ."

Haldren spoke slowly. "As it stands, your destiny to be a Goddess and replace me is permanent. There is nothing you or I or even Isaac can do to stop it from occurring on your eighteenth birthday. The only person who has the power to change it is the Creator."

My shoulders drooped. Gods forbid, I didn't want to be a Goddess with the fate of the world in my hands. I would surely mess it up and doom us anew. I sighed, recalling that I was only supposed to live a few hours after birth. My life had been forfeited in the beginning. Did it really matter what happened to me?

Haldren's expression softened. "You matter, Isabelle, and not simply because I need you to remove Isaac and free the Creator. I have kept a close eye on my bloodline over the nearly thousand years I've been a God. I've learned that our family is more resilient than most. Your birth presented an opportunity to shape one of my kin into who I needed, and I took it. But I would have saved you regardless. I never would've said no to Anne." His expression morphed into regret. "I am not proud of tricking your mother into believing that making you a Goddess was the only way you'd get to live. My desperation to free the Creator and save our world guided my actions."

I nodded, close-lipped.

"I've given you much to think about. I will take my leave. Avoid thinking of Isaac or you will call his attention. That would not be wise." Haldren waved his hand.

When the field disappeared, I blinked as my eyes adjusted to the light of the study. I felt the weight of the world on my shoulders as gazes turned to me. I brought my knees up and rested my elbows on them, then rubbed my forehead, feeling overwhelmed by everything. Just the thought of trying to process what I had learned from Haldren was daunting. Where did I begin? Did I want to trust Haldren or not? The words *fate* and *permanent* bounced around my brain, leaving a trail of dread. I shuddered when Malsin placed a comforting hand on my back. I prayed there wouldn't be any more revelations. I doubted I'd survive many more.

# CHAPTER TEN

AFTER HALDREN'S VISIT, MY family agreed to call it a night. I'd petitioned to keep the knowledge of me becoming a Goddess a secret from Aberron. This was my private battle, and I didn't feel like the Aberronians needed to know. Thankfully, everyone agreed.

Before we could sleep, we still had to set our quarters to rights after the earthquake. Letting the others move ahead, I walked with Malsin, my arm tucked under his.

I thought about what Haldren said about encouraging family relationships to make me want to fight for them. His words had dislodged my belief that my family didn't love me. It felt good to know I was legitimately cared for. However, it didn't remove the hurt from their subterfuge concerning my fate to be a Goddess. I still wasn't inclined to renew our family relationships, not after Isaac threatened me with their disposal.

Halfway to my quarters, my stomach violently protested the soup I'd eaten for dinner. Malsin snatched a brass vase from a nearby table, dumped out the silk flowers, and shoved it under my mouth.

He winced as I retched. "I hate that I'm praying for another transformation to fix this." When my stomach quieted, he retrieved a white handkerchief from his pocket and handed it to me.

Young female voices reached my ears as I wiped my mouth. "See? What'd I tell you. The morning sickness has started."

I surreptitiously spied the two maids, Lucy and Mia, if I remembered correctly, peeking out of an alcove, a broom and mop in their hands.

"But it's not morning," Mia pointed out.

"It doesn't have to be morning," Lucy sounded annoyed. "My sister was sick all day and night for three months."

We began walking again, Malsin carrying the vase. "I'll wash it out and return it."

"I should do it," I told him, attempting to reach for it.

He held it away from me. "I'm practically immune to vomit. It's no trouble at all."

"If you insist." I let it go, too tired to put up a fight.

Andrew and Braidus were tidying my sitting room when we arrived. Malsin went into the bathroom to wash out the vase.

Braidus spoke to me. "Your sleeping quarters are put to rights. The swan paintings fell but were mostly undamaged. We hung them back up."

"The bed is made," Andrew added.

I touched my pounding temple, wishing for nothing more than to sleep for eternity. "Thank you."

Malsin exited the bathroom. "I'll watch over Isabelle should you desire." His eyes rested on my mage mates.

Andrew shook his head. "We'll stay and look after her."

"We'll sleep on the couches." Braidus gestured to the furniture.

I was too tired to care who watched over me.

"Alert me if something changes." Malsin left.

I went to the bathroom to wash out my mouth, then walked into my sleeping quarters. Andrew and Braidus followed. The bed had been neatly made, and a fire crackled in a small fireplace. A warm spice permeated the air—a bundle of cinnamon sticks on the mantel.

"It's nice," I said to my mage mates in dismissal. "Thank you."

Andrew's eyes blazed. "I will say it again for however many times I have to. I love you, Isabelle Mirran. I don't want to spend a second holding you at arm's length. I want you for as long as I can have you."

"Same," Braidus agreed.

Tired, I crawled into my bed. Andrew and Braidus sat on the edges on opposite sides.

"I believe you both," I said.

Andrew pled, "Then let us be together now while we still can."

I shook my head. "I will not risk a higher being's wrath."

As much as I wanted to take them back, I feared Isaac would cause them harm. Goddesses couldn't keep anyone.

"What are you talking about?" Andrew asked with concern.

"What have the Gods done now?" Braidus asked angrily.

"Isaac told me he killed my parents because Haldren became too attached," I explained. "He threatened the same to me if I paid too much attention to my loved ones. I'm afraid if I rekindle our relationship, I won't be able to let you go when I'm a Goddess and Isaac will take action. It is better that I end things now to give myself time to adjust to the separation and to keep you safe."

Their vehement rejection swallowed my heart. "No."

I straightened. "I had a taste of the Fate's power. In terms of strength, he is a hurricane, whereas Haldren is a light spring rain. I cannot take him on."

"You are not a full Goddess yet," Braidus replied. "What he says should have no bearing until you are fully ascended."

Andrew nodded. "We can face that battle when the time comes. Please, I don't want to spend my last months with you in arguing and separation."

"Me either," Braidus said. "Most of my life has been nothing but anguish and darkness. You brought light I hadn't experienced in many, many years." His eyes held a burning intensity. "I don't want to lose this light, this joy. Don't return me to the dark by giving up on us."

I tucked a strand of hair behind my ear. Take them back and what? Pretend I had a lifetime with them again? Love them so much it would kill me when I left? *You already do,* a small inner voice whispered. I exhaled slowly, my shoulders drooping. I could feel my mage mates listening closely through the bond.

Looking back at my first encounters with each prince, I could only see Haldren's manipulation behind it all. I doubted it really was chance that Andrew found me in the forest. Haldren had probably led him there unknowingly. Braidus had been forced to play the role of cruel abductor to break and mold me into a stronger person. Haldren had wanted me to believe that Braidus intentionally murdered my parents to see how far I would go. He'd created the dual bond, no doubt initiating the first whisperings of our hearts. Orchestrated relationships—the key to Haldren's success. It left a sour taste.

Andrew took my trembling hand in his. "Arranged or not, it doesn't change that I have these feelings for you. I cannot ignore them."

Braidus took my other hand. "Neither can I. I hold on to the hope that you will come out a Goddess conqueror, as you did with the Dregans, and return to choose me—that we may live out our days with joyful abandon. Should that not occur, at least I'll take comfort in the knowledge that we enjoyed as much time as we could with one another while it was still possible."

"Exactly," Andrew said.

"You said you wouldn't be king without me," I said. "What are you going to do if I can't come back?"

"If you don't return to me before I have to marry, I'll give the throne to Henry," Andrew said with conviction.

"Why not Braidus?" I briefly glanced at him.

"Because I won't marry anyone else either," he said firmly.

"Henry would make a fine king, and he has Aliyah," Andrew said. "It is a good choice."

"Does Henry know this?" I asked.

"No, I'll not worry him yet," Andrew said.

I raised an eyebrow. "If it were me, I'd rather know sooner than later." Being king was a huge responsibility. The more time a person had to prepare, the better.

Andrew conceded. "I'll speak to him when the time is right."

"So, what will it be?" Braidus's eyes beseeched me. "Will you renew the dual courtship?"

Andrew begged. "Take us back, Isabelle, please. Court us, then marry one of us. One of us deserves to have you as a wife before you're ascended."

"Yes," Braidus agreed.

Their earnest pleading tugged at my heart, melting my reservations. "All right."

"Yes!" Andrew shouted, startling me.

Braidus grinned. "Thank you."

Their joy stole my breath away. I prayed I'd be able to let them go when the time came lest I kill them before I could even take on freeing the Creator.

A knock came at the sitting room door.

Braidus went to answer it.

Andrew situated himself so that he leaned against my headboard with me tucked under his arm. My cheek rested on his chest. I listened to his beating heart, feeling his love for me. It felt good to put my trust in him and Braidus again.

Braidus returned a minute later, his eyes on his brother. "It's Father. He's just received word the Kashtine emperor is interested in joining talks with us."

"All right, I'm coming." Andrew helped tuck me into bed and pressed a quick kiss to my lips. "If you need anything, we'll be sleeping in the sitting room when we get back. Try to get some rest."

"Mmm," I mumbled, half asleep already. I didn't hear him shut the door.

I blinked back sleep at the sound of scraping. A cool breeze brushed my skin. *My window is open.* Then I heard the breaking of glass, followed by a hissing sound. Alarmed, I sat up and groaned in pain as I had forgotten about my unbalanced-core sickness. I sensed through the bond that Andrew and Braidus were still with their father.

By the light of my small oil lamp, I could see that my sleeping quarters were filling with green smoke. I choked on the repugnant smell of rotten eggs. A heavy thud and a crunch. Boots. I fought for air. My throat burned, and I struggled to move, as if my body were bathed in thick syrup. A flash of silver caught my eye, and I rolled out of the way. The sound of material ripping hit my ears, and I squinted through the smoke, my eyes burning.

A large, dark form loomed over me—*a man*. My strangled scream came out as a whisper.

His knife came at me again, my body flopping around like a fish as I tried to avoid him. My thoughts turned into sludge, and pain blossomed in my upper left arm. A second blade plunged into my lower right side. My eyes flew open, and I cried out wordlessly.

*Magic.* The word burst through my brain fog, and Boomer lunged from his crate with a growl. The pain intensified to a burning madness. My body pulsed with adrenaline, and I sent a burst of red energy, the room exploding in a brilliant ball of fire. The man flew backward, the flames licking his clothes, the windows behind him shattering on impact. He tumbled out into the night with a scream. The cool wind rushed in, dispelling the smoke.

The door flew open. "Put out the fire!" King Brian ordered.

I sunk onto the bed, exhausted. Dimly, I became aware of the flames retreating and Andrew and Malsin reaching me. I shut my eyes and allowed them to take over. Time moved in a pain-induced haze.

"Isabelle, look at me." Malsin cupped my face with his hand.

I blinked several times.

"Good. You can hear me."

"Mmm." My head felt thick, as if stuck in a fog.

"She's so weak," Andrew said worriedly. "I feel almost nothing in the bond."

"Too much blood lost," Malsin said.

Adrenaline shot through my veins, then quickly dissipated. Andrew cursed. "She isn't taking to the energy I'm giving her."

In a knowing tone, Malsin said, "Her unbalanced core won't allow it."

"But it let us mend muscle and tissue," Andrew countered.

"When a mage core has low stores, it will eat any free energy given in an attempt to restore itself," Malsin explained. "Mending tissue and organs is not plain energy. It's magic with a specific purpose, thus it doesn't alert her core to take it."

"What can we do?" Andrew asked.

Malsin shrugged, his expression regretful. "Watch her closely and hope for the best."

"We should not have left her for as long as we did." Andrew pulled me into his arms and sat with me on the bed. He shifted to cradle me in his lap. I could not understand what I had done to feel so much guilt.

"You may face some wrath from Haldren," Malsin said sagely.

"We deserve any punishment given," Andrew replied.

I turned my head to see the rest of the men in my family surrounding the hole in the wall. Braidus had swept up the glass with his magic.

"There's a dead man down here, Highness," a voice called.

"Any identification?" King Brian asked, his voice too loud.

"No, Sire, his body is charred," the soldier replied.

Braidus jumped off the ledge.

Malsin gave Andrew instructions. "Isabelle will need to rest as much as she can. I don't want to see her moving about unless absolutely necessary." He scratched his chin. "I hate to say it, but now would be a good time for another Goddess power transference."

"Indeed." Andrew kissed my forehead. "You're never leaving my sight again."

Braidus returned.

"What did you find out?" King Brian asked him.

"Trained assassin," he said. "Aberronian, from what I could make out. There's nothing on him."

The men cursed.

Joshua grabbed the rope swinging with the wind by which the intruder had ascended into my room. "What do the men on the wall walk have to say for themselves? Did you question them?"

Braidus nodded. "A weapons cart was expertly placed to conceal the cord wrapped around the marble. Every guard up there swore on the Gods the cart was already in place when they came on watch two hours ago. They insisted the doors were secure and that they didn't see or hear anyone. My theory is someone on the previous shift set it up and the assassin climbed up under the cover of darkness. The man appeared to be built for it."

"Saved them a lot of time dodging the patrols inside the castle, that's for sure," Henry said. "Still, it's a long climb."

"With balconies and ledges to rest on along the way," King Brian said.

I shut my eyes again, unable to focus anymore, the men's voices fading as unconsciousness dragged me under.

I awoke, catching faint traces of Braidus's cologne. I was snuggled against his warm chest. His fingers played with my hair. I tilted my face so I could see him.

He smiled. "You're awake. How are you feeling?"

My body ached like I'd taken a tumble down a rocky ravine, my limbs heavy and weak. Considering the brightness in the sitting room, I suspected I had slept for a while, and yet I was still exhausted and didn't feel quite lucid.

"Perfect." I smiled back.

He laughed softly. "A lie if ever I heard one."

I heard quick footsteps. Andrew leaned over us. "You're awake."

Braidus shifted to help me sit up on the couch, then tucked me under his arm, allowing me to lean against him once more. I was grateful for the support since I felt so weak. I saw I had been changed into a long-sleeved cream shirt with embroidered pink flowers and a pair of soft, tan pants. Probably Malsin.

Andrew sat down on my other side and took my hand in his, his green magic activated. He winced, and a curse fell from his lips. I felt his frustration that he couldn't fix me.

"What news?" Braidus asked.

"Still searching for the maid who secured the rope to the wall walk for the assassin," Andrew replied. "We're told she called herself Dottie to the men up there, but Mother insists there's no one on staff who goes by that name."

Braidus asked, "What about all those workers Father dismissed when they revolted against Isabelle staying here? Could there be a former maid seeking revenge?"

Andrew shook his head. "Mother looked through our staff records. No Dottie working here in our lifetime."

Braidus frowned. "An impersonator, then. Hard to catch."

Joshua stepped into the room, his expression concerned. "There's a growing mob of merchants outside demanding to see Lady Champion. Word that Isabelle was attacked is racing through Carasmille." He scowled. "Someone started a rumor that she died and we're trying to cover it up. They want assurance that she'll still get trade going."

"I'll go." I tried to move, but Braidus stopped me.

"Let's get you bundled up lest you freeze." He helped me to the bathroom to freshen up.

I appreciated his and Andrew's care as they retrieved socks, boots, a warm jacket, gloves, and a hat that covered my ears. Braidus carried me down to the entry hall with Joshua and Andrew flanking us. We met up with the rest of my family, who stood near the front doors.

Malsin took my hand, his green magic activated. He shut his eyes briefly, then frowned as he opened them again. "Not much change." He let go.

"I'll be fine," I told him. I looked to Braidus. "Set me down, please?"

He clutched me tighter. "You haven't the strength."

"I'm not going to assure anyone if I'm not standing under my own power," I told him in a matter-of-fact tone.

I felt his strong reservations as he reluctantly lowered me to my feet. He held my shoulders, keeping me steady, until I nodded at him to let go. My steps slow and shaky, I held my hands out for balance. When Dominic and Falden opened the doors for me, I murmured my thanks. They smiled with empathy in their eyes. The afternoon sun shone through patches of open sky. Hundreds of men and women gathered in the courtyard, chatting amongst themselves.

"It's Lady Champion!" a man shouted.

"She's not dead," was spoken with relief.

I walked across the landing and stopped at the edge of the steps. Shoving my discomfort at the attention down, I activated my magic and amplified my voice. "I apologize for the worry. As you can see, I am not dead. I will be fully ready and able to assist in opening trade when the royals arrive."

King Brian joined me. "We expect them soon."

My strength wavered. I shook with the effort to stay upright. Andrew stepped up behind me and wrapped his arms around my waist. I leaned against him, allowing him to be my strength. He discreetly kissed the top of my head.

"What's to stop someone from getting to her again?" a young man in dark-blue tailored clothes asked.

"Someone wants to see Aberron starve!" another shouted.

"We don't trust your security!"

King Brian answered, "What do you suggest? I leave my champion out here in the cold to be watched by you?"

The chatter increased as merchants conferred. Finding it hard to focus, I didn't try to make sense of any of it.

An older gentleman shouted, "Lady Champion has become Aberron's greatest asset in war *and* business. As such, all of us are forced to put a stake in her welfare if we want our trade to survive. I'd feel better keeping an eye on my investment."

"Yes!" many shouted.

King Brian looked to me.

I shrugged. "If they want me to sit out here so they can guard me, fine. I can't stand much longer anyway." I didn't particularly enjoy the idea, but I wanted to reassure the people I'd help them reclaim their livelihood.

Andrew's concern for me surged through the bond. "I don't think Isabelle should be out in the cold for an entire night or longer. She's barely hanging on as is."

"Perhaps Joshua can join his power with her to create a heat dome for everyone," King Brian suggested. "We need to reestablish good relations with the merchants if we're to make Aberron a success again. You can see as well as I that these people are scared and rapidly losing confidence in us.

Complying with their wishes will go a long way in securing their faith in the monarchy."

Andrew sighed. "Fine, but I'm not taking my hands off Isabelle. I don't believe everyone in this crowd is simply a merchant interested in keeping Isabelle safe for their own profit. That maid impersonator could be here waiting to take another shot at her."

King Brian nodded. "Agreed." He turned back to the crowd and magnified his voice once more. "Lady Champion has agreed to stay on the landing in full view of anyone who wishes to keep an eye on her until the royals arrive." He paused. "Although she may excuse herself from time to time to make use of the facilities."

"Andrew," I warned a half a second before my legs gave out. His grip tightened, catching me as I started to slip out of his arms. He lowered himself to the steps, pulling me onto his lap.

I shut my eyes, fighting to get on top of my aches and exhaustion. I hated feeling weak.

Braidus sat beside us and took my hand in his. Opening my eyes, I smiled at him, grateful for the support he sent through the bond.

Talk amongst the merchants reached a fevered pitch.

"What's wrong with Lady Champion?"

"She's not going to able to open trade if she's unwell. Our businesses are done for."

"It must be serious if green magic hasn't fixed her. We can't afford another setback. We've lost enough as it is."

"She's going to die!"

King Brian raised his hands, his eyes on the people. "Calm yourselves, please. Lady Isabelle is not in danger of death. Her weakened state is temporary." He gestured to Malsin. "We have Aberron's leading healer, Ian Malsin, monitoring her closely."

There were expressions of uncertainty and grumblings among the people. King Brian ignored it and started making preparations with Joshua about heat, extra patrols, and so forth. Joshua relayed the instructions through one of his lockets, then sat on the other side of me and took my hand. I joined my red magic with him, allowing him to direct my power to create a heat dome large enough to cover the courtyard. Queen Averly had workers bring out a long table, dining room chairs, two couches, a chaise lounge, and a few soft chairs and placed them on the landing in front of the doors. Andrew placed me in the middle of a dark-blue couch. He and Braidus took two of the seats. Malsin sat in a chair beside us, keeping watch. King Brian and Henry created a shield in the shape of a box over the entire landing lest someone try to shoot an arrow at us or something else nefarious. They also added a door so we could get inside the castle if needed. I felt like a doll on display in the window of a shop. I didn't like it one bit, but I'd put up with it if it assured people Aberron would once more be successful in business.

Finished with the preparations, King Brian spoke to the people. "Save for excursions to the bathroom, Isabelle will remain within sight until the royals arrive. Should you wish to stay to monitor your investment in her, so be it. However, I ask that you give her space to rest as she is still recovering from last night's assassination attempt."

As afternoon turned into night, the number of people in the courtyard lessened. Some who left returned with chairs and supplies of their own. Twice, Malsin helped me to the bathroom. I hurried, knowing how important it was that I remain in sight. Queen Averly had multiple tables set up with water and platters of bread, cheese, fruits, and vegetables for the merchants. We sat at the long table as a family and had dinner brought to us.

Malsin spoke to me from across the table. "Take it slow and eat something light, like applesauce and chicken soup."

Though I ate as Malsin instructed, my stomach rolled with every bite. Having low magic stores and suffering from an assassination attempt was not something to laugh at. But I didn't regret the low gold storage for a second since I saved Joshua's life. I'd accept staying like this forever if it meant he got to live.

With an unsettled stomach, my thoughts turned to the two maids who believed I was with child. I imagined Malsin would have a remedy for the sickness that came with expecting. While I knew that situation came with its difficulties, I felt like it could be more manageable than becoming a Goddess and losing everything and not being able to do anything about it.

My heart tugged. Braidus turned to me, his expression curious. "You want a child?"

Andrew's gaze whipped to me.

I raised my eyebrows at my mage mates. They were normally on top of the gossip. At least they had been when we were with the First and Second Waves. "Haven't you heard? I'm to have one."

Faster than I could blink, Joshua whipped out a dagger. "Which one gets to die?"

"Not me," Andrew and Braidus both said, eyeing each other with suspicion.

"I haven't detected anything," Malsin said.

I slapped a hand over my mouth, surprised, as a bubbly laugh escaped my lips. I hadn't laughed in ages.

"All right, Isabelle. What's the truth?" King Brian asked, raising an eyebrow.

I lowered my hand. "There are two maids on your staff who believe I am with child with a prince as the father. You supposedly found out at the start of the treaty negotiations and were very angry, prompting me to leave. Their suspicions were confirmed last evening when they saw I couldn't hold down dinner on my way to my quarters."

King Brian's lips twitched in amusement. "Ah."

Joshua sheathed his blade. "Gods, Isabelle, did you have to scare us?"

I shrugged. "Perhaps Braidus shouldn't read the bond so closely."

"I'll keep that in mind," Braidus said, lifting his cup.

"Which prince did they think?" Falden asked.

Henry said to Dominic, "A sundal on Andrew."

"Deal," Dominic said.

"It was a toss-up at first, but the maid settled on Braidus. If I recall, she said she couldn't think of a single young lady in her acquaintance who wouldn't lunge for his explicit attention." I made my tone all breathy, trying to match that of the girl. "The man is walking sin."

Braidus choked on his tea. Andrew cursed. Chuckles filled the landing as Henry grudgingly handed Dominic a sundal.

After dinner, Malsin passed out vials of his stay-awake concoction to everyone but me. "You need the rest. We'll keep watch." I didn't argue.

Returning to the couch, I sat between Andrew and Braidus.

Andrew motioned for Henry to come over. "I wanted to talk to you about something."

"What is it?" Curiosity shone in Henry's gaze.

Andrew kept his voice low so the merchants wouldn't overhear. "It's about being king. If Isabelle does not return to me before I have to marry, I'm giving the throne to you. I would give it to Braidus, but he doesn't want it either if Isabelle doesn't return. We both refuse to marry someone just to produce an heir."

Henry's face transformed into horror. "I don't want to be king!"

"You have Aliyah," Andrew insisted. "Giving Aberron the needed heir will not be an issue for you. Besides, I think you'd make a great king." He grinned. "This past year, you've grown to be smart, courageous, and considerate—all excellent qualities in a king."

A hesitant smile spread over Henry's lips. "You really think so?"

Andrew didn't hesitate. "Absolutely. So, will you do it?"

Henry's shoulders drooped. He scrubbed a hand over his face and sighed. "Yes, I'll be your backup."

"Thank you, Henry." Gratitude colored Andrew's tone.

"You're welcome." Henry's gaze landed on me, his expression transforming into one of desperation. "Isabelle, you have to come back, please. I really don't want to be king."

"I can't make any promises," I told him with regret.

"I know, but try. Please?" he pled.

"I will," I promised. Finding a way out of my fate seemed impossible, but I wanted to be a Goddess less than I wanted to be queen. I didn't want to lose my family forever. Most of my family then partook in a lively game of pilfer. I leaned against Andrew, nibbling on an apple-filled hand pie and offering suggestions about the cards he held. We did not win often but had fun.

King Brian sat at the edge of the landing, speaking through the shield with a line of merchants who were eager to take advantage of his availability. I admired his largeness of heart when it came to the people of Aberron.

My eyes grew heavy quicker than I wanted, and I fell asleep to the warmth of family togetherness and contented laughter.

Much like Haldren often took me to his wheat field, Isaac suddenly pulled me into his stone room. He stood in front of me, glowing a faint silver, eyeing me critically, and giving me the sense he probed my mind for secrets. He waved his hand.

I woke to the glow of torches and the night sky, Andrew and Braidus clutching me possessively. My heart pounded with their anxiety. It didn't take me long to discover why. Isaac stood before us, arms folded. Our eyes met and held.

He spoke to me telepathically. *"So, Haldren has shared his master plan with you."* A corner of his lips curled up. *"How does it feel to know you're being crafted to be my murderer?"*

*"I don't enjoy killing,"* I thought.

*"Nor should you."* He tilted his head slightly, eyes assessing me. *"Although, liking and doing are two separate things. We often do things we don't enjoy. The question is, are you going to try?"*

I couldn't answer that. There was no way I'd win if I got into a fight with him. His intelligence and power easily surpassed mine. It would be folly. However, if I knew with absolute certainty that the tree that fueled the earth would give out before Isaac found a way to save it, I honestly couldn't say I wouldn't try to take him on to give my family at least a chance of survival.

*"Hmm . . . that's not a no."* He waved his hand.

Then the world went suddenly black. I held my breath. My stomach flipped as he transported me to stand closer to him. I stumbled and threw my hands out for balance. The back of my mind registered the sound of gasping, reminding me of the audience of merchants who had chosen to stay outside our shield. I shook with the effort to keep myself upright.

With a flick of Isaac's fingers, a silver rope appeared around my throat. He held the ends. I stiffened, biting my lip as it burned my skin. "*I don't take to threats to my survival. I would kill you and be done with it.*" He pulled, tightening the cord around my neck and restricting my airflow. I imagined my skin sizzling. "*However, Haldren's position is ending, and the gold magic has chosen you to replace him. I cannot change that.*" He scowled, giving me the impression he wished he could do something different. "*The world runs on order, and I adhere to it. To keep everything running smoothly, I have to accept you.*"

His gaze momentarily left mine to stare at my family. My gut clenched, and fear filled the marrow in my bones. He could hurt me as much as he liked as long as he didn't touch them.

"*Your love for your family runs deep. I admit Haldren's molding of you has merit.*" He straightened, his silver magic swirling about him in a show of power.

Black spots swam across my vision. I swayed despite using every ounce of willpower to hold on.

"*Challenge me at any time, for any reason, and I'll deliver your family to the Realm of Souls faster than you can unsheathe your sword.*"

The rope around my neck vanished, and Isaac disappeared in a bright, silvery flash.

I collapsed, my strength spent, my throat burning something fierce. My body convulsed as I coughed and struggled to get air into my shriveled lungs. My ears registered shouting, but I couldn't make sense of it. Multiple hands pressed on me. I choked on the breath someone tried to give me. Several tense minutes passed before I could breathe easier.

Andrew gathered me into his arms, his hand threading through my hair as he pressed me against his chest. "Gods, Isabelle." His heart raced underneath my cheek.

Envy brushed against my heart. I reached out to Braidus and threaded my fingers through his. He eyed me with longing. I read his frustration at having to share me with his brother. I frowned, wishing I had a solution that would make everyone happy.

Malsin moved so King Brian could crouch beside me.

"Are you all right?" King Brian asked.

I nodded.

"You want to tell us what that was about?" he asked.

"No." I cringed. It hurt to talk. "It's nothing." Isaac just wanted to scare me into submission. His intent wasn't to kill me. I didn't want to make a big deal of it.

"Isabelle," my family implored.

"It's nothing," I repeated, my voice raspy but firm. Pulling free from my mage mates, I crawled out of Andrew's lap, then, gritting my teeth, pushed myself to stand.

Hugging myself, I looked at the crowd of merchants and soldiers to see mouths agape, eyes blinking slowly, and a few scowls. I had to say something to reassure them.

Activating my magic, I magnified my voice. "Sorry for the excitement. The Gods meddle with me often, hence the curiosity I've become. This will not affect the trade talks."

Many flinched at the raspiness of my voice.

Turning off my magic, I slowly walked to the couch and sat. Bringing my knees up to my chest, I wrapped my arms around my legs, then shut my eyes, wishing I could make this whole sorry mess disappear.

Joshua sat beside me and tucked me against him in a brotherly hug. I peeked at him from under my lashes.

He spoke quietly. "You're really going to tell us it's nothing when we watched you nearly get strangled to death and couldn't do a Gods-forbidden thing about it?"

"He wasn't going to kill me," I whispered, trying to make light of it. "He just wanted to make it clear not to follow Haldren's wishes to challenge him, that's all."

"Gods forbid, Isabelle, I hate this. I hate seeing you suffer time and time again in the Gods' blasted war." My brother's voice thickened with emotion. "You are so full of goodness. I couldn't ask for a better sister. You don't deserve any of this." He blew out a breath. "What I wouldn't do to see you out of it."

I smiled, also wishing I had a way out, but since I didn't, I'd cherish every second I had left with my family.

# CHAPTER ELEVEN

HE FOLLOWING EVENING, WITH Andrew's support, I stood on the landing outside the front steps of the castle, ready to greet the approaching royals. I didn't need to stay outside any longer and the remnants of our time outside had been removed. King Nickoli advanced first, flanked by his son, Sebastian. Behind them came King Cekaiden and his two sons, Timtric and Kendar, then Crown Prince Jakobe and the guards from all three parties. They curiously eyed the Aberronian merchants and soldiers standing at attention.

As they reached the landing, King Brian welcomed them. "We're delighted to see you return. Thank you for your willingness to give Aberron a second chance."

King Nickoli gestured to the crowd below us. "Why so many people?" The number of merchants had doubled by late afternoon.

"Oh, the merchants wanted to keep an eye on their investment." King Brian waved airily at me.

Prince Jakobe spoke to King Brian, and yet his eyes rested on me, his eyebrows raised. "Your champion appears to be dancing with death."

King Brian frowned. "Yes, we've had a few unfortunate incidents. She's as well as we can make her."

King Cekaiden spoke. "I wish to hear about it."

King Brian led the way to the study. Andrew gathered me into his arms and carried me to a chair at the end of the table, in full view of our guests. He and Braidus took seats on either side of me. Henry, Dominic, Falden, and Malsin sat in chairs against a bookshelf since there wasn't enough space at the table.

King Cekaiden appraised me as if trying to commit my features to memory. I raised an eyebrow, meeting his gaze. A slow smile graced his lips, and I felt like he had the upper hand, though I could not discern from his expression in what way. I found the whole thing unsettling.

King Brian started the meeting by bringing everyone up to speed on the events that led to my illness. He spoke of the earthquake and the fire in the forge, followed by the rescue of Joshua.

"Isabelle brought her brother back to life using her gold magic—a feat, Haldren said, no other fledgling God or Goddess has ever accomplished. She currently suffers from low gold stores and awaits another transformation to be fully healed." He then went on to explain the assassination attempt in my sleeping quarters. "We are still seeking answers on that one." He ended with Isaac's visit, gesturing to the welts on my neck. "I cannot give you any details since they spoke mind to mind. Isabelle refuses to be forthcoming about it."

"You have had your hands full," King Nickoli said, leaning back in his chair.

King Brian chuckled. "Indeed."

"How long must she wait for another transformation?" King Cekaiden asked, his tone unreadable.

King Brain shrugged. "Not sure. We're told it will happen at a time of its own choosing. I hope it's soon because I'm not sure she can withstand another attack."

The visiting royals wore furrowed brows at this. I couldn't fault them. I wasn't exactly in the best shape to make deals with.

"How long before she takes Haldren's place?" King Nickoli asked.

"The twenty-first day of the first month of summer," King Brian said. "Coincidently, Aberron Day—a day to celebrate the birth of our country." He smiled at me.

I nodded. "Growing up, it used to feel like a party just for me."

The visiting royals grimaced at the raspiness in my voice. Malsin had tried to fix it, but whatever Isaac had done was stronger than his green magic.

"That gives us a few months," King Nickoli mused.

I spoke, my tone as firm as I could make it. "Before you all start coming up with plans for me, I want to make it clear. My words and actions are entirely my own. Nothing I say or choose to do should reflect on King Brian and Aberron. You know my fate. We will be separate entities soon enough."

The men nodded, their expressions contemplative.

Prince Jakobe spoke first. "As you know, the Jamaylin Islands rely heavily on mages to keep us safe during our monsoon season. Our storms are fierce and cause significant damage. In return for the services they provide in times of need, we treat them well."

King Brian said, "Many Aberronian mages have traveled to your islands."

"Nistier's as well," King Nickoli said.

Prince Jakobe wore a sly smile. "Indeed, we welcome mages from every country. I would even be so bold to say that we have the best mage university in the world." His expression turned troubled. "When I returned home after our first negotiations with Lady Isabelle failed, I learned that five young and healthy mages had unexpectedly perished in their beds. We could find no explanation for it. Today, that number has risen to ten. I seek help in discovering what or who is killing them."

Huh. I had not expected this kind of request. Although, if mages were randomly, inexplicably dying in Aberron, I'd want answers and to save lives too. Should I be worried for our mages?

King Cekaiden spoke. "You are not alone. I have lost five in a similar fashion in Dregaitia."

"I do not regularly keep track of our mages. Perhaps this is happening in Nistier and I do not know it," King Nickoli said.

King Brian grabbed a pen and wrote on a piece of paper. "I shall make a note to check here as well."

Malsin said, "Might I suggest you start with the Healer's Guild? A report is made and sent to them for every death in Aberron."

"Thank you, Malsin," King Brian said, appreciatively. Focusing on Prince Jakobe, he asked, "What is your interest regarding Isabelle?"

Prince Jakobe's dark-green eyes assessed me. "Simply a pledge that we may call upon you for aid should we need it."

I nodded. "I am always willing to help a friend in need."

Prince Jakobe smiled. "Perfect."

King Brian drafted a decree stating that I would help them should they require it. I signed it, as did Prince Jakobe and King Brian.

Once finished, King Nickoli launched into what he desired. "Come to Nistier. Pledge friendship with me in front of my people. Then help me rid the growing plague in my council."

"I won't kill needlessly," I said.

He shook his head. "No, no killing. I require that the treachery be exposed."

"I do not know you—" I paused as a coughing attack hit me.

Andrew handed me a glass of water, worry in his eyes. I murmured my thanks and sipped the cooling liquid.

I flicked my gaze to King Brian. "Thoughts? You know King Nickoli better than I do."

"He rules with a steady hand. I believe it is a safe bet." He gave me a soft smile of assurance.

I felt no adverse emotions from my mage mates either. Aberron needed trade reestablished.

I said to King Nickoli, "Open trade with Aberron, and we have a deal."

"Where is my insurance that you will come after I open trade?" he asked.

I leaned back and folded my arms. "I'll swear an oath if I have to, but you have my promise."

King Nickoli eyed Braidus and Andrew. "Perhaps I should take your mage mates with me as a token of assurance. It appears you have reconciled."

I shrugged. "Take them."

My family looked at me with surprise.

I gestured to Braidus and Andrew. "I warn you, Haldren uses them as additional eyes on me. It's no secret I have a penchant for trouble, especially when it comes to my mortality. I don't expect you'll get very far before he transports them back to me."

"Hmm . . ." King Nickoli frowned.

I suggested, "Why not consider this a royal visit, reestablishing peace and such." I waved my hand airily. "When Aberron gains, Nistier gains."

King Nickoli leaned back in his chair. "All right. We are in agreement."

"Excellent." A real smile graced my lips. Two down, one to go.

My skin prickled as golden light bathed me. I shut my eyes, waiting out the discomfort of the power transfer. My aches and pains related to the low gold-magic stores vanished. My shoulders dropped in relief.

When it passed, I looked into my mage core to check my levels. Gold sand had started to take over the other five colors. I had reached the halfway point in my transformation into a Goddess.

*No.* I shoved the feeling back. There was no point agonizing over something I couldn't change. Summoning my green magic, I healed myself of Isaac's damage. I now had enough power to do it.

When I opened my eyes, everyone in the room was looking at me. "Sorry for the interruption," I said.

Malsin had moved to stand beside me, no doubt ready to help. "You sound much better," he remarked with a smile.

I smiled back. "No need to worry anymore. I am back to pristine health."

"Let's keep it that way," Henry called from his seat.

My family nodded vigorously. I knew taking care of me exhausted them. It was a full-time job. Not that I meant to be that way. Some things just couldn't be helped.

I turned my attention to King Cekaiden, eager to finish negotiations. "What are your wishes?"

"What are yours?" he asked, his coal-black eyes centered on me.

"Irrelevant," I said with a wave of my hand.

He stared intently. "I disagree."

I had the strong impression he would not be dissuaded. Fine. If he wanted to talk nonsense, who was I to argue? "My desires have not changed since our first encounter. I seek peace and privacy."

"How do you hope to achieve that?" he asked.

"I see no course of action," I said. "My fate has been determined."

King Cekaiden rubbed his bearded chin. "You seek a way out."

My family sat up straighter. I caught glimmers of hope. How dare he taunt my loved ones? My blood ran hot with anger.

"There is no way out. Not even the Fate over Fates can change it."

"Perhaps," King Cekaiden agreed. "I do not claim to possess the knowledge of the Gods. However, I carry something in my possession that may be of great interest to you."

He reached into the satchel at his side and pulled out a small black box. He lifted the lid. Nestled in red velvet was a thick glass ball. He picked it up and held it in his palm. Ribbons of gold smoke swirled inside. A mage core?

King Cekaiden's eyes glittered at my obvious interest. "No mage I've shown it to has been able to tell me its purpose, but they've all agreed it is a powerful relic."

"It carries the magic of the Gods," I said.

King Cekaiden smiled. "So I have deduced. A mage of one or two colors does not have the power to activate this."

"You want me to see what it can do?" I asked.

"I'm interested to see what it can do for *you*," he said. "If you find it valuable to your cause, perhaps we can negotiate an exchange." He held it out to me.

My hands smashed into the table, the weight of the sphere surprising me. King Cekaiden chuckled. I carefully dragged it closer and activated my magic. Boomer barked, seeking direction. *Connect my magic to this. Show me what it can do.*

As tendrils of rainbow magic wrapped themselves around the sphere, the gold inside it gradually grew brighter until it became near blinding. As though I'd accessed my own mage core, I materialized inside the sphere.

Gold magic swirled in smoky ribbons. I reached out and touched one. It seeped into my skin, linking with the gold magic I possessed. I turned around, intent on studying the inside to figure out the sphere's purpose. Then I stopped short and gasped. A man with bright-blue robes, long golden hair and beard, and cerulean eyes rimmed with gold stood before me. *The Creator.* What was his real name? Surely he hadn't been called the Creator his entire existence?

"Haddas," he said, his voice deep, rich, and mellow.

"Isabelle," I said.

"Isabelle," he mused. "Come to take Haldren's place."

Had he gathered the information from my brain, or did he already know?

He smiled. "From inside my prison, my power is limited; however, I am able to take note of the passage of time and the events on my earth."

In the study, King Cekaiden took the ball out of my hands, and Haddas disappeared, bringing me back to reality. I deactivated my magic and rubbed my eyes, trying to adjust to the lower light of the study.

"Well?" King Cekaiden asked.

"What do you want for it?" I asked, trying not to sound too eager.

He didn't hesitate. "The fruit of your womb."

My brother, Henry, and my mage mates jumped to their feet, shouting over each other in a cacophony of outrage. The rest of my family and most of the other royals wore expressions of disgust. Kendar and Timtric remained impassive. King Cekaiden's lips tugged in the barest hint of a frown.

"Guys!" I waved to get their attention.

They paid me no mind.

I stood on my chair and screamed. "Shut it!"

Mouths snapped closed. My brother and mage mates seethed silently, the bond boiling with rage. I rubbed my heart, wishing for a shutoff valve.

"Sit and keep quiet, please. I'll decide after I hear King Cekaiden out."

"You will not," Andrew commanded, blue eyes blazing.

I spoke in low, precise tones. "Don't tell me what to do."

"Andrew, let her be," King Brian ordered. "Listening and agreeing are two different things."

My chest spiked hotter, if that was even possible. Andrew and Braidus fumed at me and King Cekaiden. I didn't want to give away my womb, but I felt like I needed to hear him out.

I settled back into my chair. "Please continue."

King Cekaiden spoke in even tones, stating the facts. "I possess an object of great worth. You have power I want in my royal line. A child born to you would have great magical abilities." He eyed Andrew and Braidus.

They scowled, their hands clenched, their breathing hard.

"Keep your princes. Remain in Aberron. I care not for an outspoken woman in my courts. Allow one of my sons to spend some"—he paused, seeming to search for a delicate way to phrase his request—"quality time with you."

I held up a hand. "One second." I pointed to the door and looked at my mage mates. "Out."

They stared in disbelief.

I grabbed at the tightness in my chest, my breaths coming hard. At times like this, I hated the bond.

"Sons, you're choking Isabelle," King Brian said flatly. "Go with Malsin, get an emotion suppressor, and wait until Isabelle has listened to the proposal. Now."

I'd never seen my mage mates so angry. They shot daggers at me with their eyes as they stormed out of the room with Malsin trailing behind. I huffed. Quiet conversations circulated while I clutched at my chest, struggling to breathe through their fury. I didn't have the mind to pay attention to what anyone said. Minutes later, the intense pressure in my chest eased.

I sucked in a huge lungful of air. "Better. Now, I fail to see how this would work as I only have months before I take Haldren's place." The very idea of doing this sickened me; I didn't think I could ever go through with it. I loved fiercely, and children were especially precious. I'd never be able to give one up. Still, I felt I needed to hear King Cekaiden out.

King Cekaiden spoke. "Goddesses are still made of flesh and blood. The Goddess Amora told me that if you are with child before you fully turn, you can carry to term and then give the babe up to continue your duties. Show proof of conception, and you will be given this orb."

He'd consulted the Gods on this? Gods forbid, he was serious. "What will you do if the child possesses no magical abilities?" I asked.

"Slim chance," he said, clearly not worried.

"Still possible," I stated. "Would you discard the child if not?"

Joshua stood, his revulsion and wrath evident. He moved to the door and paced as if not wanting to hear more but unable to bring himself to leave the room. I wanted to end this conversation just as much as he did, but I couldn't. King Cekaiden possessed an object of great worth, an object I needed. Plus, he deserved the same respect and consideration I had given everyone else.

"No," he answered. "The child would still be of my blood. A place within my halls would be a given."

"A good place or a scrub-the-floors place?" I asked.

King Cekaiden looked affronted. "No blood of mine would be seen in that lowly station."

I smiled. "Had to check."

"You're not seriously considering this, are you?" Henry asked, eyes wide with horror.

"Everything said in this room must be seriously considered," I answered, receiving an ire-filled glare in return.

I leaned back, biting my lip as I contemplated. I'd rather be a Goddess than lose my innocence and become with child in what would only be a business arrangement. How could I acquire the ball without handing myself to Cekaiden?

"Might I suggest a different course of action?" I asked.

"I doubt I will agree to it," King Cekaiden answered, "but as you have taken the time to consider my proposal, I shall do the same."

I smiled, relieved he hadn't shut me down. "Give me a list of those things you seek in women for your sons. Colors of magic, disposition, and so forth. Allow a decree to be sent forth through Aberron and suitable candidates to step forward. Many Aberronian women seek an exalted status and are content to spend their time obsessing over fashion and parties or whatever normal women do."

The men chuckled at my obvious lack of interest.

I continued. "Give your sons an opportunity to find compatible companions. Give the baby a father *and* a mother, as needed. The child will never deal with the pain of being discarded by a mother who suited her needs. You will get a better-tempered one out of the deal."

"Yes," a few people agreed.

I gestured to Timtric and Kendar. "Your sons are exceedingly handsome. It is not hard to gaze into their faces or enjoy their conversation. I do not think you will have any problems finding women to suit your needs."

"You want to play matchmaker," King Cekaiden said thoughtfully.

I spoke with finality. "I am incapable of surrendering a child. Were I to become with child in this business arrangement or even from one of my princes and had to surrender that child to fulfill my fate as a Goddess, the resulting heartbreak and fury would destroy the world."

"Then Nistier strongly opposes this idea of using Lady Isabelle's womb," King Nickoli said.

"As does Aberron," King Brian said.

"And the Jamaylin Islands," Prince Jakobe said.

"Stay in Aberron for a while. Let us find suitable matches," I offered. "To ensure a good fit, I'll even use my purple magic to read minds so you can see what they're really like. Open trade, establish good relations, give a lady ample opportunities to visit home, and I believe you will get everything you want."

Cekaiden conferred with his sons in Gaitian. Both shrugged often and did not appear to be opposed to the idea, but I couldn't be sure. It was clear they had accepted that their father would choose their wives for them.

Finally, King Cekaiden turned to me and said, "All right. Search for suitable matches. If I do not find appropriate matches, you do not get the orb."

"I'll not disappoint you," I vowed.

For the next half hour, I listened to King Cekaiden list what he sought in a woman: seventeen to twenty-one years of age, two colors of magic, social grace, beauty, and an even disposition.

"I care not for blathering women, and I abhor criers over trivial matters." King Cekaiden grimaced.

I smiled. "As do I."

Above all else, King Cekaiden said, "I must be able to stand her presence for longer than five minutes."

I found it disconcerting how Timtric and Kendar remained mute during this time, so I asked what they found attractive in a woman.

"Blue eyes, blonde hair," Kendar supplied. "Those are not often found in Dregaitia."

Timtric agreed with a nod. "And exotic beauty. The lady should stand out in a crowd, like you."

Once I had a good idea of what they sought, King Brian and I drafted a decree. We called all eligible maidens with magic, preferably two colors, to come to the castle to interview to potentially become a royal of Dregaitia. King Brian and King Cekaiden signed it. It was then sent out to be copied and distributed.

Though I was anxious to finish this deal so I could get the ball, I was happy with the progress we had made. I wished two perfect women would materialize out of thin air. Of course, that would never happen.

We determined that I would make a quick trip to Nistier while we waited for the decree to reach all corners of Aberron and for qualified women to come forward. I welcomed the distraction so I wouldn't worry myself silly over fulfilling Cekaiden's request. I prayed the right women would come forth and that none were too afraid of the Dregans to do so. After all, half the people in Carasmille had bought those worthless necklaces to "ward off" the Dregans. Kings Brian and Cekaiden would spend this time hammering out the details of opening trade.

Activating my purple magic, I connected to my mage mates. They sat with Malsin in his healing room. *"Everything is settled."*

"*Are you selling yourself?*" Braidus asked. His and Andrew's ire rattled through my chest.

"*No. I would never offer my virtue, no matter how dire my situation gets.*" I shared with them what had been agreed upon.

"*I would not wish for anyone to live in Dregaitia,*" Braidus said with abhorrence.

"*As long as she is aware, I do not see the harm done,*" Andrew thought.

"*No girl will go under false pretenses or coercion,*" I said with conviction.

"*Then you better make it crystal clear what they're getting into,*" Braidus said.

"*I will,*" I promised.

"*Is the ball worth the price of a woman's womb?*" Andrew asked.

"*You have no idea.*"

# CHAPTER TWELVE

UCH TO MY FAMILY'S annoyance, I refused to tell anyone what I'd seen in the orb. The fewer people who knew, the better. I did my best to shove it out of my mind completely, lest a God or Fate decide to pluck it from my thoughts. I denied any hope in my heart, believing that to be a spark as well. I grew a suspicious nature with every passing minute.

"You're closed up tighter than a clam," Braidus grumbled on our way to the formal dining hall with my family, the visiting royals, and our guards, of course.

I flashed a smile. "Pick a different subject, and I'll give you a pearl."

"All right, when are you going to give up on Andrew and choose me?" He gave me a wolfish smile.

"Give Braidus up, not me," Andrew said.

I laughed. "I've just barely taken you both back. Perhaps I shouldn't give either of you up and hold on to all the love I can until my last day."

"One of us should get to marry you and enjoy life as husband and wife," Braidus insisted. "You should decide before you're ascended."

"I agree," Andrew said. "Think about it."

I could not fault them for their desires, but the idea of hurting one of them by choosing the other was too painful to think about, though I admitted it would be cruel to keep them hanging too much longer. I wanted to experience the joys of marriage, too, though I would have to be careful to not end up in a family way. I couldn't put this off forever when my time was so limited.

"Can we revisit this after I've married off the Dregan princes?" I asked.

"I'll take it." Braidus leaned down and kissed my cheek.

Andrew nodded. "Fine."

During dinner, King Brian received a disturbing report. His eyes widened in despair as he stared at the page handed him. "Aberron has lost twenty mages within the last month."

"That's high," Prince Jakobe said with sympathy in his expression.

"Does it list the reasons for their deaths?" King Cekaiden asked.

King Brian answered, eyes on the page. "Four are related to injuries sustained due to the earthquake. One is old age. Another was a carriage accident. Fourteen mages supposedly died in their sleep."

"This is troubling news," King Nickoli answered, sharing a concerned look with his son.

"Why hasn't a report been made to me from the Healer's Guild concerning the high number of unusual mage deaths?" King Brian asked Malsin.

Malsin answered. "They have been overwhelmed with the number of patients and deaths related to the earthquake. Plus, it's winter, so the amount of illness always rises. I doubt they've had a moment to go through the death records. I will check on it if you would like."

"Please," King Brian said, letting the paper fall to the table.

Worry snaked through my gut. My entire family were mages. What if, like Adel, one of them unexpectedly perished in their sleep? How could I keep my family safe from something I couldn't foresee?

Andrew picked up on my thoughts. "Our family will be fine, Isabelle. I'm sure of it."

Braidus sighed. "Risk comes with everything in life. You just have to trust that everything will be all right and not blame yourself should something unforeseen happen."

Falden spoke. "When I was a boy, my father once gifted me a stunning bloodhound pup—the prize of the litter. Two days later, the pup ran in front of a carriage and was trampled by horses. I was devastated."

"That's terrible," I said sympathetically.

Falden nodded, his expression sad. "Some things are out of our control. We have to live with them."

"Yes." Just like my fate to be a Goddess is out of my hands.

The following morning, I found myself squished between Andrew and Braidus in a carriage with King Nickoli and Sebastian on our way to Nistier. Malsin would have come with us, but King Brian had tasked him to look into the reasons behind the mage deaths.

Malsin's eyes bore into mine. "I won't be there to help you out of a scrape. Please, for my sanity, be on your best behavior. I don't care how powerful you may think you are with your magic, you're not invincible as we've seen time and time again." He pointed a warning finger at me. "Don't do anything reckless."

"I won't, I promise," I answered, trying to inflect as much sincerity as I could into my tone and expression.

He hugged me goodbye. "I'm holding you to it."

Joshua had enlisted my guards, Micah, Eric, Zachary, Oliver, and Weston, to accompany us. They rode with King Nickoli's soldiers behind us. During the five-hour ride to the channel, King Nickoli and Sebastian explained part of their difficulties.

"Ridi is a member of my ruling council, which is comprised of twelve men elected by the people to advocate for their needs," King Nickoli said. "He is a progressive. He campaigns for the lower classes, equal pay for men and women, funding for orphanages, and such. The people love him."

"That sounds nice," I said.

King Nickoli nodded. "His charm made me suspicious. I investigated. We discovered he's routinely siphoning tax money from the charities he campaigns for into his private treasury."

Braidus snorted. "Typical."

I frowned. "That's awful."

"It happens," Andrew said grimly. "Right before my Walk, we caught three lords who'd created a fake shipping tax for the merchants, consequently lining their pockets. Their sentencing was . . . severe." I sensed his unpleasantness over the ordeal. I patted his hand in consolation.

Sebastian crossed his ankles. "Ridi seeks to supplant us with himself. He tries to convince the people to do away with the monarchy in favor of electing a new man over Nistier every ten years."

"Ridi will turn it into his own monarchy," King Nickoli said. "He would not willingly concede a position of that magnitude."

"Why haven't you ousted him?" I asked.

"Ridi is an excellent orator and manipulator," Sebastian said. "He has gained too much support. We would be lynched for removing the people's 'advocate.'"

King Nickoli's gaze centered on me. "We need you to expose his nefarious deeds to the people using your purple magic. If they see he is rotten at heart, I should have no problem sentencing him as he deserves."

"A harsh punishment?" I asked.

Sebastian leaned forward and spoke in a low voice. "Ridi steals from children."

I didn't hesitate. "I'll make sure you get a chance to sentence him."

Traveling across the channel in King Nickoli's magnificent red ship, I used my yellow magic to add extra wind to the sails, increasing our speed and cutting our eight-hour journey to four.

As we docked, Andrew sidled up behind me and slid his hands around my waist. "That poor captain at the bow is begging King Nickoli to keep you."

I leaned my head against his chest, turning my eyes to King Nickoli and the captain, who gestured to the king in a pleading manner. King Nickoli's mouth twitched in amusement.

A carriage and driver waited for us at the dock. Snow covered everything, making it difficult to get a good picture of the land, although I saw many trees and had the impression they had been pummeled by bad weather, just like Aberron had.

It took only an hour and a half to reach King Nickoli's castle in the capital city of Nistella, or King's City.

King Nickoli kept the curtains closed and apologized for not allowing my mage mates and me a look into the city. "When my curtains are open, people know I'm willing to stop with a treat or spare coin for the children. When they're closed, they know I have pressing business." He lifted his hands and dropped them. "I have nothing for the children at the present moment."

"It is sweet to think of the children," I said.

As the sun set, I stepped out to view a stunning five-story castle made of gray stone, with turrets spiraling upward and red flags displaying Nistier's crest. A roaring golden bear stood on two feet with paws out in the middle of a circle of trees and stars. I found the architecture and their crest intriguing.

"The castle is smaller than ours," I murmured.

"They have a separate building for the ruling lords' offices," Andrew said. "This is just a home to them."

I wished Aberron did the same. Having the government in one building did not give the royals much privacy. If I ever managed to return and marry either Andrew or Braidus, I would petition for more privacy.

Stepping inside, we followed King Nickoli to a large dining hall, its décor much the same as Aberron's with gleaming wood furnishings, gilded frames, family portraits, and rich tapestries depicting nature and war scenes.

King Nickoli introduced me to the rest of his family already seated at the table with plates of food in front of them. His wife, Queen Marlee, smiled warmly. She had beautiful, long red hair and large blue eyes that fit her round face nicely.

King Nickoli gestured to his three other children. "These are my triplets, Rylee, Lukas, and Caspiander. They are thirteen and think they know how to run my country better than I do."

Braidus, Andrew, and I chuckled good-naturedly.

"It's a pleasure," I said to the three curious faces.

We commenced eating a variety of fare, from roasted meats to glazed vegetables. All of it tasted just as wonderful as the fare I ate in Aberron.

During our meal, King Nickoli spoke about his plans to expose Ridi. Messengers would be sent out that evening to inform Nistierans to come to a meeting tomorrow. Once there, and with his twelve counselors in attendance, King Nickoli would tell the Nistierans about our new friendship. We would then do a little demonstration with my purple magic, revealing Ridi's nefarious side. It sounded straightforward.

Before they moved into their rooms for the night, Andrew and Braidus made sure I coated the doors and windows of my room with rainbow shields.

Close to noon the following day, we traveled to the court in the heart of Nistella. The chatter was deafening as I got out of the carriage. Hundreds of brightly dressed citizens stood together. We rushed inside, Andrew, Braidus, and my guards blocking most of my view with their height and girth.

I kept my eyes on King Nickoli's back, letting him lead us to a room covered in polished wood with bookshelves lining its walls. A horseshoe-shaped table sat on the far end of the room, around which sat twelve austere men who overlooked a row of empty benches. Behind them, a set of double doors led to a balcony. The men rose and bowed to King Nickoli. Then, straightening, they trained their eyes on me. I worked hard to keep a calm, unassuming expression. I doubted I'd ever get used to the attention.

"Welcome back, My King," a graying man with a warm smile said. "We have company."

King Nickoli spoke formally. "Allow me to introduce Crown Prince Andrew Sorren of Aberron, Prince Braidus Sorren of Aberron, and their Lady Champion, Isabelle Mirran."

The men said their welcomes. We responded in kind.

King Nickoli introduced his council. Most of the names flew over my head except for Ridi—a man appearing to be in his early thirties with a slim build, a mop of golden-brown curls, and laugh lines around his light-green eyes. My eyes locked with his for a second before I pulled my gaze away, not liking the shrewd calculation I saw in the otherwise friendly face.

The head of the council spoke. "Why have you called the people to gather?"

"Per trade agreements, Lady Isabelle has agreed to pledge friendship to me and Nistier," King Nickoli answered. "The people should see the added protection I have provided for them."

"Is her power truly that great?" Ridi asked. "The rumors of her feat against the Dregans—"

"All true," King Nickoli confirmed. "I heard as much from King Cekaiden of Dregaitia and King Brian of Aberron, respectively." He turned to me. "Will you please show them your power?"

With a nod, I activated my magic, letting each color shine. The men gasped at the brightness.

King Nickoli faced the council. "I invite you to stand with me for this momentous occasion."

The men left their seats, I deactivated my magic, and we walked onto the balcony to face thousands of citizens cheering at our arrival. I cringed inwardly at all the attention. Many chanted, "Nickoli! Nickoli!" I clung to my mage mates.

King Nickoli activated his red magic and amplified his voice. "Thank you for your welcome. It is good to be home."

The crowd applauded.

"I went to Aberron to establish better trade agreements and returned victorious." He gestured to my mage mates and me. "I have brought you a gift. I have with me today Aberron's princes, Crown Prince Andrew Sorren, Prince Braidus Sorren, and Lady Champion, Isabelle Mirran." He spoke in a knowing tone. "Her magic alone subdued thousands of Dregan soldiers in battle. Aside from the Gods, she is the most powerful mage I have ever met. I have secured a friendship with her for Nistier's benefit. Today, Lady Isabelle makes a pledge to me with each of you as a witness." Focusing his attention on me, he asked, "Will you show them your power?"

I activated my magic, and the chatter increased tenfold. King Nickoli allowed a moment for it before he lifted his hand and quieted the people.

He spoke to me in an authoritative tone. "Lady Isabelle Mirran, champion of Aberron, will you swear friendship to me and be a protector of Nistier until you take your last breath?"

I amplified my voice. "King Nickoli of Nistier, you have my friendship until my last breath." I curtsied.

King Nickoli took my hand, lifting me up. Facing the people, he said, "To a union of protection and peace!"

Hearty clapping ensued.

He grinned. "Thank you, Isabelle."

I smiled. "My pleasure."

"Ridi, will you please come forward?" King Nickoli motioned for his counselor.

"Ridi!" Many shouted with adoration. Grinning, he waved with effusive charm.

Sebastian caught my eye. I subtly nodded at his "you see what I mean" expression.

"Ridi, will you be our example so Lady Isabelle can demonstrate her purple magic?" King Nickoli asked.

Instant alarm coated Ridi's face.

"I will not hurt you, I promise," I said, trying to sound innocuous.

He nodded his consent. The purple mist that flew out of my hands encircled him. I asked Boomer to project his thoughts loudly to the people.

"*What is this?*" the mist questioned.

Ridi's eyes widened. "*You're reading my mind.*"

The crowd gasped.

King Nickoli gestured to me, exclaiming, "See what power! She has magic afforded to the Gods that will now be shared with us."

Ridi thought, "*Powerful, indeed. Can we stop this demonstration now?*"

"Of course, just one more thing." King Nickoli held up a finger. "Did you or did you not siphon tax money from the Needy Nistieran Charity Fund into your personal accounts?"

"*Not that question!*" Ridi's thoughts cried. It wasn't a denial of the accusation. "*My mind is being read,*" he reminded himself.

"Answer the question, Ridi," King Nickoli commanded.

The color drained from his face. His eyes darted to me, his expression furtive. "*Can she purge answers from my mind with her power?*"

"Ridi," King Nickoli said in warning.

Out loud, Ridi said, "I work tirelessly for Nistier. A few coins will not be missed for my efforts."

Murmurs of shock rippled through the crowd.

King Nickoli pulled a piece of paper from his breast pocket. "I have a report that says you took 40 percent of the taxes from the charity fund last quarter."

"Forty percent!" the crowd cried.

"*Where did you get that? I left no tracks!*" His mind cried.

A lady below yelled, "Ridi said we lacked the funds to improve the orphanages and we needed to pay more taxes!"

"*That was true!*" Ridi protested.

"Because you stole money to pay people to promote you to become prime minister," King Nickoli said, "thus replacing me."

"*Nistier does not need a king!*" Ridi's thoughts bellowed.

The crowd went wild. "Sentence him!" they chanted.

I deactivated the magic.

"Ridi, I hereby strip you of your title and position among my counselors," King Nickoli said. "Your house, lands, and money will be confiscated to repay what you took."

Ridi's jaw dropped in shock.

King Nickoli continued. "I sentence you to a lifetime of working in the mines at Priselouth."

Ridi glanced at the door, but Andrew had created a shield over it, blocking his escape. Ridi backed into the stone railing. He looked over his shoulder at the crowds three stories below us, then at the two guards moving to secure him.

"He's going to jump," I said.

"Let him," King Nickoli said, unperturbed.

The soldiers lunged as Ridi catapulted. I shut my eyes, cringing at the ensuing screams. Braidus pulled me into a hug, and I buried my face into his chest, unpleasant feelings traveling both ways through the bond.

"Evil has been eradicated," Prince Sebastian said darkly.

The Nistierans regarded me with open fear during the three days I remained in Nistella. I sat with King Nickoli and Prince Sebastian in their meetings with their counselors as he reinforced his importance as king. My presence definitely made people more agreeable and subservient to him. He wore a grin practically the whole time. I was happy he was pleased because that meant Aberron wouldn't have any troubles with trade. Candidates for Ridi's position stepped forward. I planned to return in a month to allow the people a glimpse into the mind of the person they chose to ensure a good man was put in place.

As we stood on the dock to return to Carasmille, Prince Sebastian kissed my hand. "You have been a blessing to us. I look forward to your return and pray you'll find a way out of your fate."

I smiled. "Thank you, Sebastian."

My desire to return home great, the ship practically flew across the water.

"You worry too much, Isabelle." Andrew jogged beside me as I hurried up the front steps of the castle upon our return. "I'm sure everything is fine."

"Or Cekaiden has decided we're not barbaric enough and called the whole thing off," Braidus supplied, matching my steps.

"You're not helping, brother," Andrew said.

Entering the dining hall, I breathed a sigh of relief to see Cekaiden, Timtric, and Kendar beside my family, seeming perfectly content.

"See? All is well," Andrew whispered as I slowed my steps.

"Welcome home!" Henry said. "How was Nistier?"

"I'm happy to be home. That's all I'll say," I answered as I took a seat.

"Sons?" King Brian inquired of the princes.

Andrew spoke. "Isabelle struck fear into the hearts of everyone. King Nickoli was absurdly happy with it. Trade should easily move forward now."

"Good." King Brian smiled with approval.

"Any news from Aberron?" Braidus asked his father.

"I've lost an additional three mages." King Brian wore a look of frustration. "The Healer's Guild cannot give me an explanation."

"Nickoli has lost sixteen mages," Andrew said.

King Cekaiden said, "This is a grave problem."

"Indeed," King Brian said, eyebrows furrowed. "In other news, King Cekaiden and I have worked out our agreements. Ladies shall be arriving tomorrow to be interviewed." He smiled in my direction. "It has been quiet without Isabelle."

"Sorry," I mouthed.

The following morning, I sat in the throne room with the boys, Aliyah, Queen Averly, and Princess Liliana as we waited for the ladies interested in becoming a Dregaitian royal. Queen Averly and Princess Lilliana had enthusiastically agreed to help me with the interviews. I appreciated their help more than words could say, considering their expertise as royals.

My feelings toward being queen were rapidly changing now that I knew the role would never be mine. I had spent much time adamantly despising the job and public spotlight, but now, with my fate to be a Goddess, being queen didn't seem so bad. It would mean I had a family I got to keep. My thoughts briefly touched on King Cekaiden's orb, and desperation clawed at me. I needed that link to the Creator to free myself. My determination to help Cekaiden find a suitable match for his sons overshadowed anything else. There was no room for failure.

By Queen Averly's side sat a huge basket filled to the brim with letters. We chatted leisurely as she sorted through it. A slew of messages had flooded the castle, demanding to know whether Andrew had found his bride. Queen Averly showed me the notice King Brian had sent out, stating, "My son, Crown Prince Andrew Brian Jason Sorren of Aberron, is in a happy, committed courtship with Champion Lady Isabelle Mirran. He desires her hand in marriage. Henceforth, consider my son firmly unavailable."

This put the people in a funny predicament of wanting to state their objections but not wanting to receive my wrath. "The complaint mail we're receiving is unusually polite." The queen held up a letter. "'We respectfully ask that Crown Prince Andrew end his courtship with Lady Isabelle as she has been seen encouraging the attention of other men, particularly

Prince Braidus. In exchange, we offer our dearest wishes for a happy union between Crown Prince Andrew and our daughter Olivia."

"Olivia Portersmith?" Princess Liliana asked.

Queen Averly nodded.

"She doesn't like Andrew. Rumor is she's been trying to elope with wealthy merchant John Vinzlen."

"It's the Portersmiths' feud with the Mindle family that prompted the letter," Dominic said.

"It's been, what, twenty years at least since that started?" Princess Liliana asked.

"Yes," Queen Averly said.

Dominic explained, "The Mindles said they'd make their daughter—remember Iris from the Sorrenian?"

"Prince stealer," I mocked. She'd tried to throw paint on me at the Sorrenian and caught Henry instead.

My fellow students half chuckled and half grimaced.

Dominic said, "The Mindles swore they'd see Iris made a princess to show they were better than the Portersmiths once and for all. Of course, the Portersmiths claimed their daughter Olivia would be chosen over Iris. Olivia has never been of the same mind as her parents, unlike Iris, who truly believes she is queenly material."

Queen Averly shuddered. "I have never believed Iris Mindle to be a good fit for Andrew. The Dregans, on the other hand, might enjoy her."

"Does she have magic?" I asked.

"Yes, one color," Henry said.

"She's still sixteen, though, isn't she?" I frowned. "Her age doesn't meet the requirements."

"A pity," everyone echoed.

"Have there been any ladies in the court you liked for Andrew?" I asked Queen Averly.

"There have been a few I've considered," she said. "Every summer, I host a party for the younger ladies of the court to try to get to know them and get a good idea of where our future is headed with the younger generation.

There were a couple who stood out to me at this year's party, namely Ladies Dorothea and Marissa." She waved her hand as if it were of no consequence. "Of course, there's not a lady in our court who can compare to you. Had I seen you at one of my parties, you would have stood out to me. You bring out the best in Andrew and are by far the finest choice."

I smiled, warmed by her words. "Thank you."

Queen Averly was exceptionally sweet, and I would love to have her as my mother-in-law.

A soldier entered and bowed. "The ladies are starting to arrive."

Queen Averly smiled. "Send them in."

Twenty young women dressed in their finest walked down the blue carpet to form a horizontal line before us. I spotted Lady Marissa among the women and smiled inwardly. Perfect. She's given up on Andrew to be queen elsewhere. I hoped the Dregans found favor in her. I never wanted to see her hands on Andrew again.

My family remained seated while I stood at the edge of the dais. A few, particularly Lady Marissa, openly glared at me. Others held interest or were indifferent.

"Thank you for coming," I said. "King Cekaiden of Dregaitia has appointed me to oversee this venture."

The door opened, and a young woman in a pale-pink dress hurried down the carpet. "Sorry I'm late. Carriage wheel broke," she said. "I'm Calliope."

I smiled at her. "Welcome." I clasped my hands together. "I will be explicit on what King Cekaiden desires. I ask that you be clear as well, as your interests are important to the Dregans. Do not hesitate to tell me if you disagree with anything discussed. Do not feel pressured. This is entirely your choice. If you feel any sort of coercion, please do not participate. Any questions?"

Lady Marissa spoke up, her expression suspicious. "Is Crown Prince Andrew really unavailable?"

The other girls murmured their interest in the question and eyed me expectantly.

I bit back a sigh. Gods forbid, would these women never give up? "Yes."

Undeterred, Lady Marissa asked, "Have you lost interest in Prince Braidus, then?"

"Is it not common knowledge that I share an Amora bond with both princes?" I asked, lifting my hands and dropping them. "I am currently courting both princes to decide which one to marry. Until I choose, consider Andrew out of the question."

Lady Marissa didn't relent. "Prince Andrew has a time limit now that his Walk is completed. How long are you going to wait to make a decision?"

"Yes." The other girls echoed Marissa's eagerness for an answer.

I held up a finger. "One moment please." Activating my magic, I connected to Andrew. "*These women are not ready to give up on you. Will you please come in here and tell them your beliefs around matrimony? I cannot proceed unless they believe there is no hope for them.*"

"*Certainly,*" Andrew said.

"*Thank you.*" I deactivated my magic. A minute later, the side door opened, and Andrew stepped out with Braidus, their appearance causing more than one inquiring glance and blush. And here I'd hoped they'd given up.

Andrew turned on his princely charm. "Good morning, ladies."

Faces lit up at his attention. I found it painfully obvious that Andrew would be their first choice if given.

"My brother and I want to wish you well in this endeavor with the Dregan royals. I pray you'll find love and happiness like I have with my darling Isabelle."

Lady Marissa spoke to Andrew. "I have heard Lady Isabelle does not wish to be queen of Aberron, nor does she care about class. Therefore, Prince Braidus's chances of being chosen may be higher than yours."

I stiffened at the subtle jab at Braidus's illegitimacy. I had a strong urge to put Lady Marissa in her place. Braidus wrapped his arms around me, my back to his chest. He'd silently stopped me from laying her flat.

Andrew answered her. "It is true I face stiff competition against my brother." He looked over his shoulder at Braidus, giving him a playful smile. "He has many loveable qualities that would make any woman proud to have him at her side. Indeed, I could not be more lucky to have him as my brother."

I appreciated Andrew's defense.

Lady Marissa wore a hint of a triumph. "So you admit your chances of being chosen are slim."

Andrew shook his head, still as charming as ever. "Oh, I didn't say that. My bond with Isabelle is without words. My hopes are high."

"But if you're not chosen, what then?" Lady Marissa asked, her tone insistent. "You are to be king. You must marry to continue the royal line."

The other girls nodded.

Andrew's tone turned unyielding. "If Isabelle does not choose me, I will abdicate the throne to my brother. I will not be king without Isabelle. I'm sorry ladies. Your best chance at becoming queen is with the Dregans."

I read the disappointment on the girls' faces. Lady Marissa's eyes glittered with what I suspected was suppressed anger.

Andrew walked over and stole me from Braidus. His lips tangled with mine in fiery passion. Pulling back, he asked softly, "How was that?"

Gods forbid. I clutched him tightly to keep from falling over. "Good, thank you." While I wasn't overly fond of having an audience, in this case, I felt it was warranted. The ladies needed to know Andrew was off-limits.

"You're welcome." Andrew pressed a light kiss to my forehead, then released me.

Braidus kissed me quickly and followed his brother to the study.

Catching my breath, I focused on the women once more. "Now that you've heard Andrew's sentiments, if any of you have come here in hopes of gaining his attention, you may leave."

Not a single lady moved.

"All right, then, let's proceed. In this first round, I ask that you reveal your mage core to prove your magical status, along with answering a series of questions to show your suitability magic-wise." I waited a beat, then said, "I warn you, now, I will be using my purple magic during the interview process."

"That means Isabelle will have direct access to your thoughts," Henry said.

"That should be private!" a brunette exclaimed. Ripples of agreement went down the line. Many ladies scowled at me.

"It's simply to ensure you're genuine," I said evenly. "Dregaitia's army is greater than Aberron's. I will not give them a lady with ill intent, lest Dregaitia retaliate. I had a hard enough time saving Aberron. I do not wish to battle again." I gestured to the door. "If you do not desire to continue, the exit is on the left."

Again, no one moved.

I walked down the three steps and stopped at the head of the line. Lady Marissa. "Please show me your mage core."

I stepped to the side to allow a sphere to form in front of her. She displayed two colors, blue and red. No wonder Queen Averly had found her suitable. She had physical and magical wealth.

I forced a smile. "Thank you."

She quit projecting.

I asked about her heritage. "How far can you trace your magic?"

"Generations," she said. "The line has not been broken for the last five on either side."

*Perfect.* I wanted her out of Aberron.

Three people later, I discovered another with two colors, yellow and red.

"A yellow-and-red combination is the rarest of all," she said proudly.

"Indeed," I agreed.

One had a surprising history with her green magic. "My parents and grandparents don't have the gift, but my third great-uncle on my father's side was a great healer. It was a surprise when it showed up in me."

"I was surprised to discover magic within myself as well," I said.

Five of the twenty-one women had two colors. I considered them top contenders. Magic that skipped generations I put at the bottom of the list. I needed strong lines, a near guarantee that any child they bore would have the gift.

I returned to the dais to confer with Queen Averly. "I think I should turn away the women with weaker lines of magic."

"I agree," she said. "How many will that eliminate?"

"Seven," I answered. "It leaves us with fourteen."

"We'll further narrow it when we test them," Queen Averly said.

I called forth the ladies who didn't quite make the cut. "Unfortunately, I do not think you match King Cekaiden's requirements. Do not despair. You are all queens in your own right."

Several hung their heads in disappointment. One muttered, "At least I don't have to get my mind read." Dominic and Falden showed them out.

I focused on the remaining women. "We will now go over leadership qualities with Queen Averly and Princess Liliana, followed by a physical health assessment with Malsin, my healer. If you pass both, you will be invited to meet with the Dregan royals."

"Ladies, if you'll follow me?" Queen Averly gestured to a side door.

We moved into a large sitting room that had cream-colored furniture with gold accents. Choosing a soft chair by the fire, I watched Queen Averly and Princess Liliana speak to the ladies.

Queen Averly said, "Being queen is not tea parties and fashion. There are grueling decisions to make and duties to perform that revolve around your supreme role over your household."

"It is the woman's job to keep everything running smoothly," Princess Liliana said. "As queen or even princess, you will be expected to keep your house immaculate and on schedule for your husband. Some of that entails surveying all the work done by the staff, hiring and letting go, and being responsible should something go wrong."

"You must have a ready opinion on everything," Queen Averly stressed. "It is not up to the staff to decide whether the draperies should be gold or white. It is their job to carry out *your orders*."

Some of the women seemed particularly excited by the prospect of ruling a household. Lording over people didn't sound fun to me. To test the ladies, a line of servants arrived and presented a real problem to be solved.

"There is a discrepancy on the second floor," one middle-aged lady said. "Lord Javen is refusing to let the maids into his office, and it is starting to smell. He claims the maids shuffle things around and it takes him hours to put everything back in order."

"Perhaps he should supervise the maids in the room," the lady named Mila answered.

"He refuses," the servant answered.

"Then have a servant of higher standing watch the maids to ensure nothing is moved out of place," Mila said firmly.

During these proceedings, I activated my purple magic, allowing the girls to see my glow. It noticeably put them on edge, but I didn't give Boomer a command. I simply wanted the ladies to think I read their minds. I would use it later when the girls met with the Dregan royals.

By lunchtime, Queen Averly and Princess Liliana had excused four women who did not seem proficient at making abrupt decisions. That left ten women to see King Cekaiden.

"Now that we have proved you are equipped on the working side, we must go over the most important job a queen will ever have." Queen Averly clasped her hands as she faced the ladies. "Producing an heir."

I sent a mental message to Malsin, telling him it was time to ensure they were capable of producing a child.

"*On my way,*" he said.

Disconnecting from Malsin, I spoke to the women. "King Cekaiden seeks magic for his royal line. Dregan mages are scarce. Therefore, he comes to us to make this possible. If you agree to marry Crown Prince Timtric or Prince Kendar, you must be willing to immediately become with child."

"Would there be no time to get to know the princes beforehand?" Suzanna asked, unease written on her features.

"You will have time during your confinement and many years after that," Princess Liliana said.

"Aberron law requires the queen to be with child within the first year of marriage to ensure an heir," Queen Averly said. "I was expecting Andrew within two months of my marriage to King Brian."

Suzanna rose. "I'm sorry. I do not believe this is right for me. I will take my leave."

"Me too." Beatrice rose to follow Suzanna. "Good luck, ladies."

My heart sank. Suzanna and Beatrice had two colors. Eight remained, only three of whom had two colors of magic—Marissa, Mila, and Calliope. Hopefully, the Dregans found favor with them. I needed to talk to the Creator again.

Malsin arrived. Each contender sat with him behind a partition at the far end of the room and went over her health. We excused another lady when Malsin believed she would have difficulty producing a child. An unexpected blow to the girl, she left in tears.

"Regular visits with a healer are important," Malsin said to me.

"Indeed," I agreed. "Malsin, I don't remember you ever checking me to see if I'd have problems having children despite my being engaged to Andrew at one point."

He smiled. "Oh, you're perfect in that regard. I always ensure there's nothing strange going on in your womb when I assess you. It's a routine procedure all healers do when they examine a lady to ensure she's in good health." His smile turned sheepish. "When I don't detect anything wrong, it's easy for me to forget to tell the person where all I've checked, especially if I'm doing a full-body assessment."

"Oh." This knowledge was bittersweet. I had always wanted children, but given my fate, that would likely never happen—unless I found a way out of it. I had to have that ball at all costs.

I then brought Braidus in to explain some of Dregaitia's history and customs. Tucking me close against him on a couch, he spoke first about the terrain. "Dregaitia's lands are larger than Aberron's. It is a rugged terrain with many rocky mountains, deep lakes in the north, and a desert in the southern province. It is not as lush as Aberron, but there is beauty to be found."

He then spoke of their temperament. "Dregans are naturally coarse and do not often convey emotion. Do not expect them to use words to profess their love. If they are pleased with you, they will show it in the form of gifts. From royals, it will most likely be jewelry."

Ruth giggled. "What lady doesn't love a pretty bauble?"

The other girls agreed.

"Most women are subservient," Braidus said. "You must be willing to defer to your husband as the head of your family—especially to King Cekaiden." His gaze and tone turned severe. "It would be unwise to cross him."

I read some uncertainty in their countenances. I could not fault Braidus for saying this, however. The ladies deserved to know. My anxiety ratcheted at the thought that his statements might cost us a good candidate.

Queen Averly must have also noticed the discomfort because she said, "As it is in Aberron. I do not openly challenge my husband." She leaned forward and spoke in a conspiratorial tone, as if sharing a secret. "I *have* found that my feminine wiles go a long way in securing what I want." She winked.

The ladies tittered, and the tension vanished. *Thank the Gods for Queen Averly,* I thought with relief.

Braidus gave them a bit of information on the armies and fighting skills. "Every firstborn son, outside of the courts, is delivered to King Cekaiden at the age of five to become a soldier in his army. They can take on a wife at the age of thirty and leave the king's service at forty, having spent their lives learning how to be effective killers. It is encouraged they then produce an heir to give to the king. Dregans take pride in their combat. Tournaments are considered a favorite pastime for many. Be prepared to see men fight to the death."

Many women grimaced. I noted Lady Marissa seemed unaffected.

Braidus finished his lecture with an unexpected smile. "If you play your cards right, you will live like a Goddess."

The girls smiled broadly.

The one named Lorraine spoke up. "Excuse me, Prince Braidus, I was wondering how you know so much about the Dregans? I'm told they haven't opened their borders to outsiders in years." The other girls murmured their interest.

"For a time, I was married to Cekaiden's eldest daughter, Kiella," he answered.

"What happened to her?" Mila asked softly.

"She was executed for rebellion," he answered bluntly. "I do not suggest it."

Eyes widened in horror.

I spoke. "I believe that is the last test I have. My job is done. I will now inform King Cekaiden of my findings. You shall meet with him and his sons shortly."

Braidus and I exited the sitting room together. "Thank you, Braidus."

"My pleasure." He drew me in for a heated kiss, sending my senses haywire.

I gave him a questioning glance as we caught our breath.

"Andrew kissed you senseless earlier. It's my turn."

I laughed softly. "Of course." The princes didn't actually take turns, but I could understand Braidus's need to kiss me when he felt how much Andrew had affected me earlier.

The conversation in the study halted as we entered. Clearing my throat, I spoke. "I've come to report my results concerning the candidates for Dregaitia."

"What have you found?" King Cekaiden asked.

"I have narrowed it down to seven," I explained. "All have strong lines of magic. Three have two colors. All are adept at handling the household duties of a queen with grace and leadership. They are also fully capable of producing a child." I flashed a smile. "Now, it's up to you to decide if you like their personalities."

"Bring them in," King Cekaiden said with a wave.

"Certainly." I sent a thought to Queen Averly, relaying the order. I then turned my attention back to King Cekaiden and his sons. "At this stage, I believe it would be prudent to connect minds, allowing you to read their thoughts in case ill intent lurks."

"I do not like you in my head, but for this one instance, I believe it might be useful," King Cekaiden reluctantly agreed.

"You have nothing to worry about if you keep your thoughts in Gaitian," I answered. "The same for your sons, as I believe they should be a part of this."

"Yes," he said.

"I will need to leave so the ladies aren't aware I'm using my magic on them." I turned to King Brian. "When the ladies walk in, will you come up with an excuse for me to leave? I don't want my absence to be suspicious."

"Of course," he said.

Moments later, Queen Averly entered with the seven ladies in tow. I inclined my head to King Cekaiden. "As requested."

King Cekaiden offered his thanks.

King Brian addressed me. "Isabelle, I'm due for my monthly meeting with my hot-springs delegate. He should be arriving any minute now. Since you've finished your business with King Cekaiden, would you be so kind as to meet him in my stead? Take your friends with you." He gestured to Henry, Dominic, Aliyah, and Falden.

"Of course," I said.

The second I left the room, I connected King Cekaiden, Timtric, and Kendar. Their instant displeasure at the intimacy struck me hard enough that I lost my breath. I gently brought to their remembrance the help this would give them, and they settled some.

*"Show me what you know,"* King Cekaiden said.

I brought the candidate to mind and rattled off information, giving them a clear picture of each lady and her abilities so they had a good idea of who was who. *"What did I tell you? Valuable,"* I thought with pride.

They grudgingly consented.

We moved to an office a few doors down. Sitting at a round table, Henry, Dominic, Falden, and Aliyah launched into a game of pilfer.

Timtric pointed out, *"You wish us to take an interest in this Lady Marissa."*

Kendar's lips curved into a smile, his amusement evident. *"Could it be the famed Lady Isabelle considers her a threat?"*

I huffed, causing the boys and Aliyah to stare at me. The Dregans had taken special notice of my dislike for Lady Marissa.

*"Jealous, indeed,"* Kendar said with satisfaction.

The idea that I could be resentful of another woman with all the power and beauty I possessed piqued their interest. They requested her mind be listened to first.

"Lady Marissa, I am told," King Cekaiden said.

She executed a perfect curtsy. "Yes, Your Majesty." She repeated a mantra in her head. *"Calm, cool, collect, Queen."*

"You have two colors, blue and red," King Cekaiden stated. "Will you demonstrate your power for me?"

She conjured a fireball in her left hand and an ice ball in her right.

Kendar and Timtric turned their thoughts to their native tongue, but I sensed they found her tall willowy frame, fair complexion, and blonde hair appealing.

"Why have you come?" King Cekaiden asked, focusing on the woman before him.

Lady Marissa's ambitions were ruthless. *"Prince Andrew needs to see he's making the biggest mistake of his life in choosing a harlot over me. I won't waste my hard-earned efforts to be anything short of queen somewhere."* Out loud, she said, "I believe we can benefit each other. I seek the title of queen, and you have need of the magic I possess."

*A wolf underneath layers of silk.* Ugh, I wanted her gone. Anywhere. Kendar mentally chuckled at my animosity.

"If you marry one of my sons, where would your loyalty lie should Aberron and Dregaitia fall into war?" King Cekaiden asked.

*"Whoever treats me better,"* Marissa thought. Out loud, she spoke sweetly. "With my husband, of course."

Her telling thoughts garnered an instant rejection from the Dregan royalty. I couldn't blame them in the slightest. I quit listening to her as

King Cekaiden thanked her and called forth another. *A pity,* I sighed. I'd have to find another way to send her packing.

"Why do you want to be Dregaitian royalty?" King Cekaiden asked Ruth.

"*Money, luxury, thousands under my supreme control,*" Ruth thought with an unsettling vindictiveness.

Violet's salacious thoughts made me flush as she imagined disrobing Kendar. "*I'll put those muscles to good use.*" Kendar found this entertaining until she started thinking of Timtric in the same manner. "*Mmm . . . maybe I could get a two-for-one deal, like Lady Isabelle. Two princes worshipping me . . .*"

We all opposed her wandering eye.

Jacquelyn's entire inner monologue resided around Andrew crushing her dreams. I saw through the Dregans' minds that her eyes glistened with angry tears as she repeatedly glanced at Andrew. "*How dare he give his attention to a Gretlin. I'll make the Dregans see I'm worthy material, and then I'll show Andrew what he missed out on. He'll be sorry.*" She entertained the idea of him begging for forgiveness.

I found it distressing that Ruth, Violet, and Jacquelyn had mindsets similar to Marissa's. I found their thoughts to be frivolous and rude. *Beautiful outsides, rotten cores.* I shuddered to think of any of them in elevated positions. Surely Aberron had better stock than this. The Dregans began to wonder the same thing.

Calliope stepped forward, flipping her blonde hair over her shoulder. Her soft blue eyes, the smattering of freckles across her pale skin, and curvaceous pale-pink dress warmed Timtric. He took extra time studying her.

King Cekaiden started in his round of questioning. "Please demonstrate your two colors of magic."

She held a fireball in one hand and a green, smoky ribbon in her other. "I have the power to destroy and heal. I enjoy the adventure both bring." She smiled and thought, "*A means of defense and a means to be helpful.*"

"Why do you seek to be queen?" King Cekaiden asked.

"*No point in hiding the truth*," she thought grimly. "To get out of Aberron. It's either this or be forced into an engagement with a man twice my age to save my family from financial ruin. Frankly, I find this option more appealing."

"Who?" King Brian asked.

Calliope made a face. "Lord Astor—nice gentleman but physically unappealing and rather dull in conversation."

The expression on King Brian's face made me think he agreed.

Calliope placed her hands on her collarbone. "I have too much vigor to be matched with an old man who simply wants a caretaker with bed-warming benefits. I need a little excitement and purpose. I'm not finding it here."

"In Dregaitia, a man's word is law. Are you willing to submit to that?" King Cekaiden asked.

Her thoughts said, "*Why else would I be forced into a marriage with Lord Astor? Gods, don't let me be stuck with him. I'll die out of sheer boredom and misery within a week.*" Out loud, she said, "Father's word is law too. I have not known differently."

I sensed no ill will, just desperation and a need to put her stamp on life. I liked her.

Lorraine, a tall redhead with startling green eyes also turned out to be nice and in a bit of a desperate spot. "I contemplated seeking employment with my blue magic, but as a lady of noble standing, I'm told it would shame my family. My parents, my mother specifically, refuse to acknowledge the trade loss we've suffered. I decided to take matters into my own hands and make my own path. One less mouth to feed, per se."

Mila, a tanned, dazzling brunette in a shapely red dress, was blunt but in a good way. When King Cekaiden asked why she had come, her thoughts questioned, "*Am I being silly for basing this whole thing on one amazing dance?*" Out loud, she explained, "At Lady Champion's ball, I danced with Prince Kendar. He made me laugh in a way no one else has. I liked him very much."

"You wore red then too," Kendar replied, placing her in his memory.

Her thoughts danced. *Hallelujah, he remembers me*! To him, she said, "I thought it would help you remember me."

"Indeed," he agreed with a charming smile.

Despite their rapid thoughts in Gaitian, judging by the two ladies they kept their eyes on, I found their choices to be clear. Timtric liked Calliope, and Kendar liked Mila. King Cekaiden approved as both possessed seemingly sound minds and two colors.

Finished with the interviews, I closed the connection. "Back to the study," I told the boys and Aliyah.

King Brian smiled at our return. "What have you to report from our delegate?"

I mentally cursed as I scrambled to come up with an answer. "All operations concerning our hot springs are in good working order," I lied in my best convincing tone. "Nothing new has been discovered, but they're hopeful the recent earthquake might've unearthed something new. They're sending more people to scour the land."

Henry added, "The guy cowered in Isabelle's presence. He spewed information like a bubbling spring. It was pathetic, really."

Dominic, Aliyah, and Falden nodded vigorously.

"Excellent." King Brian grinned. "Thank you, Isabelle."

"My pleasure," I said while finding my seat between my mage mates. "Did I miss the choosing?"

King Brian shook his head. "No, we were just about to hear a judgment."

King Cekaiden spoke to me with praise. "You have done well. The ladies are of exceptional stock."

The women flushed and smiled under his approval.

His gaze swept across the room. "I thank all who helped in this endeavor." He turned to his sons and spoke in Gaitian. After a response, all three rose. King Cekaiden then said, "I will leave it to my sons to choose."

The room held its breath as Timtric moved forward. He took his time, eyes lingering on each candidate until he faced Calliope. "I would be honored to know you better."

Complete disbelief crossed her features. "Me?"

He nodded.

She leaned forward. "Really?"

Timtric entertained a smile. "Yes."

"Oh, thank the Gods," Calliope said as she placed her hand over her chest. "No Lord Astor." She blushed and stammered. "I mean to say, that is . . . yes, I'd be honored to know you as well." She executed a quick curtsy. "Thank you."

Soft chuckles went around the room. Timtric took her by the hand and led her to a seat beside him.

Kendar wasted no time moving to Mila. "Will you accept me as a permanent dancing partner?"

Mila beamed. "I would love to."

Kendar took her by the hand and sat beside her.

King Cekaiden addressed Lorraine. "I would like to offer you a place within my halls," he said. "Come to Dregaitia, and you will have my entire court to choose a husband from."

She didn't hesitate. "I accept." She curtsied. "Thank you, Highness."

King Cekaiden bade her to sit beside him and addressed Marissa, Ruth, Violet, and Jacquelyn, still standing with sour expressions. "Thank you for your willingness to be a part of my family. I wish you a prosperous life in Aberron." To King Brian, he said, "I believe that concludes Dregaitia's business with Aberron for today."

"Quite," King Brian agreed. He addressed the boys. "Would you three please show these ladies out?"

Dominic and Falden led the girls out. Henry took up the rear, right behind Lady Marissa. She halted at the door, Henry rocking on his heels as he lurched to a stop.

Lady Marissa swiveled around, her eyes landing on Andrew. "I think you're making a mistake in choosing Lady Isabelle. You love a high-class harlot who will break you. As crown prince, you should put your country first and choose someone who's passionate about Aberron and being queen over getting your baser needs met."

"That's it." I shot to my feet, smoky tendrils of power swirling around me. "Leave before I throw you out."

"You are the wrong choice," she snarled, not moving a step.

I spoke harshly as I closed the distance between us. "I may not want to be queen, but my loyalty to Aberron and my bond is unparalleled. You claim you have passion for Aberron, but that's a lie. You wouldn't think twice about throwing Aberron under the blade if it meant you would be treated better. You disgust me with your disloyalty. Aberron would not benefit from a selfish and narrow-minded woman like yourself.

She gasped. "You read my mind during the interview!"

"Yes." I didn't bother to hide it since the decisions had been made. "I know what evil lurks behind your pretty façade." I lowered my voice to not be overheard. "You are not capable of loving my sweet Andrew the way he deserves. You will never be *his* queen."

Lady Marissa's eyes bulged with rage. "Gretlin!"

"I've got this." Henry handcuffed her with a shield and shoved her out of the study, her screams echoing all the way down the hall.

My fingers slowly unclenched as Lady Marissa left my sight, though Boomer jumped to the forefront of my mind, seeking direction. *Not now,* I told him. I put him back in his cage and then returned to my seat.

Queen Averly frowned. "A shame she turned out to be so awful. I really liked her at my garden party."

"Her sweetness was only motivated by her selfish desires to be worshipped," I said.

Mila spoke, her lips tugging downward. "You read all of our thoughts during our interviews. You had your magic on during our tests. I thought you were reading us then."

I shrugged. "A ruse."

My eyes darted between Calliope, Lorraine, and Mila. They all wore furrowed brows and frowns of discontent.

"King Cekaiden, his sons, and I felt you three passed with high marks. Your insides are as beautiful as your outsides."

Their faces transformed into complacent smiles.

I turned to King Cekaiden. "Please let me know when I've finished holding up my side of the bargain."

The girls eyed me curiously.

"When Timtric and Kendar are married, you may have the ball," he said.

"How long does it take to marry someone?" I asked no one in particular.

King Brian smiled. "Patience, Isabelle."

The weddings were planned for the following Gods Day—giving time for members of the Dregaitian court to arrive and witness the union. I lamented having to wait a week.

The parents of Calliope, Mila, and Lorraine were invited to dinner with the royals, allowing their daughters to share the news. It came to light that Lorraine had neglected to tell her parents what she'd been up to, having pretended to visit a friend.

The poor mother burst into tears when she learned of her daughter's doings. "You're—you're leaving me!"

"It's for the best," Lorraine soothed, patting her mother's back. "You can't pretend any longer. The trade losses we suffered broke us. I have no dowry, nothing to offer a man here. I'll have better opportunities in Dregaitia. I'll be living in comfort. I won't be the only Aberronian girl there either. I'll have Calliope and Mila."

Calliope's parents clutched each other in shock as they learned the news. "Queen," they half whispered. Much to everyone's relief, however, they seemed to have no qualms about it.

Suddenly, Calliope's father's expression turned to one of dread. "What will I tell Lord Astor? The advance he gave me . . . I have no way to pay him back."

"Dregaitia will cover your expenses," King Cekaiden said breezily. "You shall not want."

The man spluttered. "Thank you, Highness."

"You are certain you want this?" Mila's mother studied her daughter carefully.

"Yes," Mila said firmly. "I like Prince Kendar. I haven't been able to stop thinking about him since the ball."

Kendar wore an exultant smile.

"What if it's just infatuation?" Mila's father asked, eyeing Kendar with suspicion.

Mila shrugged. "Then I've cast my lot. I'm not turning back."

Retiring to my quarters for the night, Andrew inquired after my "spat," as he called it, with Lady Marissa. "What did you say to make her crazy with rage?"

In the sitting room, I ran my fingers through my hair, undoing my braid. "I said she wasn't capable of loving you the way you deserve and that she would never be *your* queen."

"Ouch." Andrew pretended to be wounded for Marissa's sake, while Braidus chuckled.

I cupped Andrew's cheeks, locking my gaze on him. "Promise me you won't consider her if I'm unable to come back. Her thoughts were really rotten."

"Henry will get the throne if you can't come back, remember?"

"Yes, but if something happens to him, it will fall back on you."

Andrew cursed. "You're right. I promise, Isabelle. I won't consider her."

# CHAPTER THIRTEEN

T HE FOLLOWING MORNING, JOSHUA walked into breakfast with information on the maid who had helped the assassin. "It's the Gods-forbidden Abominators again." He scowled. "Kyston has a sister who's taken the lead of their now 'underground' operation. She's sneakier than a rat. I have patrols combing Carasmille for her."

"Those mage discriminators don't know when to give up, do they?" Henry said.

"No, dispatching my sister would be a great accomplishment for them," Turning to me, Joshua said, "Until I find Kyston's sister, I'm assigning your guards back to you."

I didn't object. "Fine."

Micah, Zachary, Weston, Oliver, and Eric now watched me inside and outside the castle.

To ensure they were prepared for anything, Joshua let them know of my fate to be a Goddess and to expect meddling from the Gods. "Not all attacks my sister faces are schemed by ordinary people." Growling, he then said, "I'll have your heads on plates and served for dinner if you let word of my sister's fate out to anyone. Understood?"

"Yes, Commander," they chorused.

I didn't enjoy the additional eyes on me, but I also didn't relish the prospect of another assassination attempt. I'd suffered enough of them to last me a lifetime.

I immersed myself in planning over the week leading up to Timtric's and Kendar's weddings. I was prepared to give Calliope and Mila anything they wanted to ensure they followed through. Sunflowers and dahlias in the middle of winter? Done. Sparkling red hearts floating over our heads? Done. Their weddings would be the talk of the year.

Through playful banter, Andrew and Braidus hinted at me making a choice between them. Their desire to have me as a wife before I ascended only increased as time passed.

"How about yellow roses at our wedding?" Andrew asked, his mouth twitching in a smile.

"I suggest tulips colored like a sunrise at my wedding with Isabelle," Braidus said in response.

"We could have it under the stars," Andrew suggested. "It would be romantic."

"Nothing is romantic about freezing to death," Braidus said. "How about we forgo the court's attendance and have it in one of our sitting rooms with just our family? No unnecessary attention."

I chuckled softly. "Both ideas are lovely."

A private wedding would always appeal to me, but a ceremony with the whole court in attendance would let all the ladies know that the prince I'd chosen was officially off-limits. I found that to be more important, especially if I chose Andrew. Too many women tried to stake their claim on him.

The day before the Dregan weddings, Mila, Lorraine, and Calliope cornered me.

"Why are you so eager to see us married?" Calliope asked. "What's so important about that—?"

"Ball," Lorraine supplied.

"Ball," Calliope corrected.

"Are you keeping something about the Dregans from us?" Lorraine asked.

Gods forbid. "There is nothing wrong with the Dregans, I swear. They are exactly as they appear to be."

"There is more going on here than meets the eye," Mila said, hands on hips.

"You're right, but it affects only me, not the Dregans," I answered. "They will treat you well as long as you are willing to have a child."

"Then this ball they have . . ." Calliope's light-blue eyes probed mine.

"May very well ensure my survival," I answered.

"Are you dying?" Lorraine asked softly, compassion in her expression. "I've noticed the way your family looks at you. It's as if they're trying to commit you to memory."

"She has so much power. Surely that isn't the case," Mila said with an eye-roll at Lorraine.

I lifted my left hand, showing my birthmark. "I am a slave to the Gods. I seek a way to break their hold. What King Cekaiden carries in his possession may help me secure my freedom."

I read sympathy on their faces. Suddenly emotional, I managed a weak smile. Everything rode on these marriages.

Calliope took my hand and squeezed it. "I'll help you, Isabelle. I'm not backing out of a marriage to Timtric. He's sweet to me."

"Kendar is too," Mila answered. "I want him as my husband."

"My trunk is already packed for Dregaitia," Lorraine said. "I've said my goodbyes."

I sniffed, blinking back tears. "Thank you."

The weddings took place in a private ceremony at ten in the morning with close friends and family in the throne room. A Dregan high priest named Rask, and Aberron's high priest, Jorrun, presided. I practically held my breath during the recitation of the wedding prayers, then nearly cried out of sheer relief when everything went smoothly.

Jorrun spoke, with Rask repeating his words in Gaitian. "I present to you Crown Prince Timtric Kai Zayne and Crown Princess Calliope Luanne Zayne, husband and wife. I also present Prince Kendar Numore Zayne and Princess Mila Marie Zayne, husband and wife."

The room erupted in cheers as Timtric and Kendar kissed their wives.

A wedding celebration for the Dregan and Aberron courts was planned for late afternoon, giving family and friends time to meet and greet beforehand. People lined up to congratulate the newlyweds.

King Cekaiden handed me a familiar box. "As promised."

I reverently clutched it to my chest. "Thank you."

King Cekaiden returned to his sons. I ran through the side door into the study, with Braidus, Joshua, Andrew, and my guards scrambling after me.

"Are you going to tell us what that is now?" Joshua asked as we settled into our respective chairs.

"My possible salvation." I lifted the lid, my hope flaring.

I held the ball, cool to the touch, and activated my magic. I materialized inside the sphere, facing Haddas. "Hello."

He smiled. "Welcome, Isabelle. I commend you for your efforts in retrieving my ball from the Dregans. Your determination is admirable."

More like desperation, but I'd take it. "Thank you."

He strolled around the sphere, hands behind his back. "You have come with questions. Ask."

"Do you have the power to change my fate—if you are freed?" I blurted.

He nodded. "Freed, yes. But you must go through Isaac to do so."

"How was Isaac able to trap you?" *How could a being of immeasurable power not anticipate . . . ?*

Haddas spoke. "I see infinite possibilities based on choices. When Isaac murdered Palina for her position, I crafted a ball to imprison him lest he use his new powers to wreak havoc on my earth. I knew my creation could be turned against me when I made it, but I considered it a small chance and took the risk." He frowned. "Isaac was quicker than I thought."

"What about the tree Haldren mentioned?" I asked. "Is the earth really so connected to it that we could be destroyed should the tree perish?"

Haddas nodded. "Yes. Haldren has not lied about the severity of the death of my tree and earth. We are well on a path to death with Isaac at the helm. I estimate the tree will die by the end of this summer."

Dismay hit me. I didn't think Haldren had been dishonest, but it was good to get an estimate from the Creator himself. My eighteenth birthday fell on the twenty-first of the first month of summer. That meant when I ascended to be a Goddess, I would have a little less than two and a half months to fight Isaac, free the Creator, and save the tree, or we would all die. Then I'd never be able to reunite with my family in Aberron. I wanted that more than anything.

"What must I do to free you?"

Haddas stopped to meet my eyes. "You must—"

In the study, a cold hand violently snatched the glass ball from my hands. I flew out of my chair and hit a shelf with a sickening crunch, pain erupting in my back. Heavy books tumbled off the shelves and onto my head. I blinked through tears to find Isaac hovering over me, his expression murderous. I stilled in absolute terror.

"You are not to speak to the Creator," he snarled. In a fit of rage, he threw the ball onto the marble floor, smashing it into a million pieces.

*No!*

Isaac cinched his hand around my neck. He pulled me out of the pile of books and held me away from him like a wiggling worm. I choked. He turned me so I could see my guards, Joshua, Braidus, and Andrew seated at the table and motionless with fear, knives hovering at their throats. *Oh, Gods.*

"Must I give you a visual reminder to not defy me?" Isaac said.

Isaac branded an image of a dagger on the men's throats in the same fashion as a cattleman would brand his livestock. The men gasped in pain.

I tried to speak, but Isaac crushed my vocal cords. "*Please!*" I mentally cried out. "*I wasn't trying to fight you. I was only trying to find a way out of my fate and let the world run as it has been with you at the helm. I know better than to fight you. Please.*"

Isaac considered me, his head cocked slightly to the side. "Did you think the Creator would tell you differently than Haldren or I?"

"*I hoped he knew of a different way.*"

His hold loosened just enough to let me breathe a little easier. "Did he?"

"*No.*" Despair swallowed me whole. "*It's over. I'm giving up. I'll never be able to fight you and win. You're too powerful. Haldren was wrong to think he could mold me into the Goddess who would ensure your ruin.*"

Isaac had hundreds of years of experience over me. He had outsmarted the Creator—the literal maker of our world. My abilities were paltry compared to Isaac's, and any further moves on my part would surely get my family killed. There was nothing I could do but accept his superiority and take Haldren's place as a Goddess over Gods.

Isaac smiled triumphantly. "Claiming defeat already. Interesting."

I didn't like seeing Isaac victorious, but I knew when to quit. It killed me to lose everything, but he had me in submission. I went limp, and tears leaked from the corners of my eyes.

"I'll grant you some leniency for your allegiance." The knives vanished, along with the brands on their throats, as Isaac released me. My left arm snapped as it broke my fall onto the pile of glass. His lips curled in amusement. "I'll see you soon, *little Goddess.*" Then he disappeared with a bright flash.

Gasping for breath, I sobbed uncontrollably.

"Someone get Malsin!" Andrew shouted.

Eric sprinted out the door and into the throne room. Micah and Braidus swept up most of the glass, allowing Andrew and Oliver to kneel beside me. They placed their hands on me.

"Fractured spine, broken arm . . ." Andrew's voice faded into the background amid my cries.

My heart tugged as Andrew pulled magic from my stores. Malsin dropped to his knees and put his hands on me. They worked fast, healing the damage Isaac had inflicted.

"I need tweezers to pull out the pieces of glass," Malsin said.

Joshua rose. "I've got it."

Malsin carefully plucked each shard out of my skin and then repaired the injuries. My guards, the rest of my family, the boys, and Aliyah had also arrived. They watched with worried expressions.

"Finished." Malsin lifted his hands.

Tears rolled down my cheeks despite Malsin having eradicated the physical pain.

Andrew gathered me into his arms and pressed kisses to my forehead. "It's all right, Isabelle. It'll be fine."

"No, it won't," I disagreed. "Isaac destroyed the ball. I've lost my link to Haddas."

"Haddas?" Henry asked.

"The Creator," I cried. "He was about to tell me how to free him when Isaac appeared."

I could see the realization go down their throats like a muddy slime and settle sickly in their stomachs. Braidus took me from Andrew and pulled me against him.

"Did you learn anything?" Joshua asked.

I sniffed. "Haldren was right about the tree and my fate to be a Goddess. Haddas said he expects the tree to die by the end of this summer. When it does, the earth and everyone in it will be destroyed. He also said he could change my fate if he was freed. He said I must go through Isaac to do so." A fresh wave of tears spilled down my face. "But I told Isaac I was giving up and offered him my allegiance to keep you all alive. I will never be able to fight him and win. It's over."

"Don't say that," Braidus said, smoothing my hair.

I wouldn't take my words back. Hopelessness ate at me. Haddas hadn't mentioned another way for me to get out of my fate, and Isaac had too much strength for me to go against him. We had lost before we even began.

Braidus rested his forehead against mine. "I'll carry hope for the both of us. Rely on me."

"And me," Andrew said with conviction. He leaned in and kissed my cheek while threading his fingers through mine.

"Me too," Joshua and Malsin said together, each placing a hand on one of my legs.

"Count me in," Henry said.

"Us too," Dominic, Falden, and Aliyah said.

"And your guards," Micah said, speaking for my five protectors.

"Yes," Weston, Eric, Zachary, and Oliver chorused.

Emotion clouded my voice. "I love you all."

My mage mates and I returned to our separate quarters to wash and change into something suitable for the wedding celebration. Through the bond, they gave me their unyielding support. I knew without doubt that they believed in me and that I would come out victorious. I wished I had the same faith in myself. I feared Isaac more than any living creature.

Andrew, Braidus, and I met with King Brian, Queen Averly, and the Dregan royals outside of the ballroom. Inside, guests assembled for the wedding couples' debut.

"Everything all right?" King Brian asked us. "Henry said the Fate over Fates appeared and caused a commotion in my study."

Andrew scowled. "Isabelle found a way to talk to the Creator using the ball. He confirmed what Haldren said about her fate. Isaac destroyed the ball, severely injured Isabelle, and nearly murdered us in retaliation. To save our lives, she swore her allegiance to him."

"What?" Queen Averly said, gripping her husband's arm.

"You will need to send some maids to put it back to rights," Braidus added.

King Cekaiden spoke to me. "I take it my gift did not help your quest."

"It did help, just not as much as it could have," I said, inflecting as much gratitude as I could into my voice. "Thank you all the same."

A man stepped out and bowed to the royalty. "Highnesses, we're ready for you."

Stepping into the ballroom, I paused to take it in. Windows—more than I could count—lined one side of the enormous rectangular room, the orange glow from the setting sun filtering through them. Two doors led to a terrace. Chairs and round tables decorated with white tablecloths and red rose bouquets in gold vases were pushed against the sides of the room. Several long tables pressed together at the end of the room sagged with food and drink. A string quartet stood off to the side. I found the whole thing incredibly opulent, but I doubted a royal wedding demanded anything less.

Three hundred or so people, some coming into adulthood and others quite elderly, all lavishly dressed members of the Dregan and Aberronian courts, milled about the dance floor. Interspersed, staff held trays of food and drink. I wanted to blink against the brightly colored clothing assaulting my eyes but resisted.

Kings Brian and Cekaiden spoke about how Timtric's and Kendar's marriages to Calliope and Mila united Dregaitia and Aberron under a new reign of peace. After their speech, the new couples stepped out. We clapped heartily as they walked off the dais for their first dance. I was pleased to see genuine smiles on all four faces.

I leaned against Andrew and sighed. I wished my life was as simple. I wanted an eternity with my family.

As the song ended and a new one began, Andrew tugged on my hand. "Dance with me."

I allowed him to lead me to the floor, where he pulled me flush against him, dancing far too close for polite society, but neither of us cared.

He leaned close and whispered, "Gods, I wish this was our wedding. I want you all to myself."

Since I had no hope of escaping my fate, I wanted to embrace every moment I had before I ascended. I wanted to be married, even if it was only for a few months. "I want to marry too. I think it's time I make a decision."

Andrew's surprise and excitement rippled through the bond. "Truly?"

I laughed. "Truly. I want to experience marriage before I ascend."

"What can I do to help you decide?" Andrew waggled his eyebrows. "Perhaps a few more of these." He cupped my cheeks and pressed his lips to mine, kissing me with sweet, gentle passion.

I felt a tap on my shoulder and pulled free to see Henry. "Braidus sent me to tell you the song ended a while ago, yet you still seem to be kissing his brother."

I looked to Braidus, who stood on the dais beside his father. He eyed me with desire. It sent tingles up my spine and butterflies fluttering in my stomach. Choosing between them was going to be the most difficult decision I ever made, but I was ready.

Andrew cursed under his breath. "Just when I was getting somewhere, Braidus steals the show." He took my hand and began to lead me to his brother. "You'll tell him you're going to decide?"

I nodded. "Yes, I'll have a decision by tomorrow night." I didn't want to give myself too much time; otherwise, I would fret myself silly.

Andrew smiled at me, his expression radiating gratitude. I could tell he was ready to end the dual courtship too.

"Prince Andrew, might I have a word?" An unfamiliar older gentleman called out to him as we passed. We paused.

"Go," I told Andrew. "I'll be with Braidus."

"All right." He moved to speak with the man.

Four steps into my approach to the dais, Lady Marissa fell in step with me. She wore a soft smile and an intense stare. I frowned. Who'd invited her? I didn't bother to play nice. "What do you want?"

"I want to concede to the better warrior for winning Prince Andrew's heart," she said evenly. "I'll never be of interest to him with you in his life."

Was this some sort of an apology? As I turned to study her, cold steel plunged into my chest.

"You have to go."

My heart ceased to beat.

# CHAPTER FOURTEEN

I STOOD ON A COBBLESTONE path at the entrance of a tunnel barred with opal. I touched the bars, cold to the feel, and shivered. Not sure what to do, I turned around and saw the ballroom as if I hovered over it. I watched my body fall to the ground, blood pooling beneath it. *Dead.* Lady Marissa rapidly retreated, quickly stashing the knife in the folds of her dress.

"Isabelle!" Braidus's and Andrew's agonized yells shook the room. I shuddered at their gut-wrenching horror. I could still feel them. Even in death, my soul was bound to theirs. It surprised me. Perhaps we still would have been bonded had I become a Goddess.

The music stopped, and people craned their necks to discover the commotion. A lady in vibrant plum screamed as she backed away from my body, prompting nearby women to join her. My family and guards hurried in from all directions.

A young, curly-haired man glowing green with magic touched my hand, then abruptly pulled back. "She's dead!"

The news rippled through the crowd. "Lady Champion dead?" many whispered to each other in shock.

Braidus activated his magic. With a blast of wind, he pushed people aside, giving everyone a clear view of Lady Marissa attempting to exit. With a pulling motion, he used a blast of air to drag her to the center of the ballroom. She screeched, arms flailing, eyes wide. Braidus pinned her upright with his magic, then reached into the folds of her dress to retrieve the bloodied knife.

Fireballs exploded from Joshua's, Dominic's, and Falden's hands. Andrew, Henry, and King Brian launched ice spears, Queen Averly and Malsin ribbons of green smoke. A pile of ash marked Lady Marissa's spot.

My guards, now hovering around my body, moved out of the way to allow my family to drop down beside me. Magic activated, Andrew and Malsin touched me, no doubt searching for life.

"Nothing," Malsin said, his voice choked.

"No." Andrew snatched my body off the floor and clutched me to him. "You're not dead. Gods, you can't be." He rocked my still form back and forth. "Wake up, love," he begged through tears.

Braidus took me from Andrew and buried his face in my hair. "Don't do this to me, Isabelle. I cannot live through this again." Grief poured through my soul.

"Can you feel her at all through the bond?" Joshua asked.

"No," my mage mates said.

Not a dry eye could be seen among my family and guards.

Haldren and Isaac flashed into existence. Haldren looked distraught as he crouched down and touched my body, a curse escaping his lips. His eyes flicked to Isaac in some silent communication.

Isaac shrugged, his sea-green eyes alight with interest. "She's not in the Realm of Souls." His lips curved into a sly smile. "It would appear you need to find a new Goddess to take your place."

Haldren's expression hardened as he straightened to his full height. "Her soul must be found for that to happen. At the moment, not even you know where she is."

Isaac gestured to my body. "She's deader than a pile of bones. Your plans for her to challenge me have all come to naught."

A fresh wave of grief hit me as Braidus and Andrew listened to Haldren and Isaac. I moved to them, needing to do something. I couldn't let them suffer.

A dark-skinned man with a head of long, thick, black braids interspersed with jewels appeared beside me. "Eli, a Fate over the Realm of Souls." He dipped his head in greeting, sending one of his braids over his face. He pushed it out of the way with his hand. "You cannot enter the Realm of Souls because you have been chosen to take Haldren's place as Goddess over Gods. This is something the Creator put in place for ascending Gods and Goddesses. With growing power comes much fear from the weak." He grinned, showing a full set of pearly whites. "Haldren and Isaac were not informed of this protection. Isaac searches fruitlessly for you in the Realm of Souls." I had the sense he enjoyed a laugh at Isaac's expense. Eli's expression sobered. "Touch your body, and your soul will return."

*Better than wandering around like this.*

Eli further explained, "When you come back to life, you will be awarded all the power of a Goddess over Gods. Your time in Aberron will then be finished. You must immediately step into your role as set forth by the Creator. Should you die again, that will be your true end in the mortal realm."

"Good to know," I said with gratitude. "Thank you."

"I'll see you soon." Eli smiled toothily, then vanished.

A Goddess already. I wouldn't get to choose between Andrew and Braidus or experience marriage after all. Regret pulsed through me, followed by anger that Lady Marissa had taken that from me. At least as a Goddess, I could keep busy. It would help me lock all my sad and angry feelings in a little box. I worried Isaac would punish me if I dwelt on my misfortune too long.

I touched my lifeless arm, and the world went black, then spluttered to life in a golden glow. Tissue knit together, healing the hole in my heart. Fresh blood pumped through my veins. My left hand burned as my birthmark dissolved. I coughed as my lungs expanded with air. In a blur of motion, Andrew seized me from Braidus.

"I'm not a doll!" I cried.

A fresh round of tears and happy shouts circulated the room.

"She's alive!" the crowd spouted with wonder.

Haldren crouched down again and took my hand. "She has the full power of a Goddess over Gods."

"Your magic?" Isaac asked Haldren.

A slow, exultant smile spread across Haldren's lips as he let go of my hand and stood. "My powers are still fully intact despite Isabelle's elevation. I suspect I will retain them until my thousand years are truly up."

"Humph." Isaac scowled. "A few months means little in the scope of eternity."

"Indeed," Haldren said, his voice cold. "Since I am still here, it should fall upon me to train her until my time has ended."

Isaac grudgingly agreed. "Fine." His eyes swept the ballroom. "Do not tarry." Then he vanished.

Haldren looked down at me. "It is time, Isabelle."

Andrew clutched me tighter. "I'm not ready."

I cupped his cheek. "You were never going to be ready, love." I got to my feet and faced Haldren. I pleaded, "*Let me say goodbye, and I'll come willingly.*"

He nodded.

I held my hands out to my family. "Give me hugs because it might be a little bit before I see you again."

Sniffling, Joshua squeezed me tightly. "Come back soon, little sister. I love you."

"Don't get killed again," Malsin said as he enfolded me in a bear hug.

"I'll do my best," I answered.

Next came King Brian and Queen Averly. "You'll always be a daughter we happily gained," Queen Averly said with King Brian murmuring his agreement.

"Show those Gods what you're made of, then come back," Dominic said as he released me.

"There's only so much normal I can take," Falden said. "Don't be gone long enough for life to get boring."

I chuckled. "We'll see."

"We're really going to miss you," Aliyah said.

"This better not be the last hug I give you." Henry lifted me off the ground and squeezed me tightly. "We'll be cheering for you down here."

I didn't become truly emotional until I stood in front of my mage mates. Then the tears cascaded. Andrew reached into his pocket and pulled out a small white box. "We meant to give this to you tonight." He handed it to me.

I lifted the lid and gasped. Three silver rings entwined with ruby, sapphire, and gold were nestled in silk. "Our bond. It's beautiful." The different threads split apart, allowing me to separate the two bonds into individual rings.

Andrew picked up the smallest ring. Taking my left hand, he slid it onto my third finger. "Courting couples wear identical rings on their left hands and move them to the right when they marry. I had planned on making rings ages ago, but time slipped away," he explained with a rueful smile. "Now we have this bond. Braidus and I thought this would be more appropriate."

"I love it," I gushed. Quickly, I grabbed the other two rings and put them on my mage mates.

Andrew picked me up and hugged me close, pressing a soft kiss to my lips. My heart cried out as he gently released me. I wanted more time with him. Appearing too choked up to speak, he handed me to Braidus.

Braidus's hazel eyes glistened. "This isn't goodbye."

"Quick vacation," I agreed.

Braidus crushed me against him, cocooning me in his love. I soaked up his encouragement to return as he pulled back and pressed a light kiss to my forehead.

Turning to the Dregan royals standing on the dais, I apologized. "I'm so incredibly sorry for causing a scene at your wedding celebration. I didn't mean to be murdered by Lady Marissa. I give you my warmest blessings for happy unions."

Mila and Calliope looked rightfully shocked. King Cekaiden, Timtric, and Kendar inclined their heads in acknowledgment.

I retreated to Haldren, not sure my heart could take much more of this too-short goodbye. He took my hand, and with a bright flash, I stepped into my fate.

We arrived in a white stone courtyard surrounded by flowering pink trees lit by the moonlight. I stood on the Mark of the Gods inlaid with gold. It was pretty, but it wasn't home, and I fought against the urge to run. I didn't care how inviting the place looked. There wasn't a single part of me that wanted to be here.

Haldren let go of me. "Welcome to Astralind, home of the Gods, Fates, and our Creator."

He took my hand again. I blinked and found myself in a sitting room decorated with accents of gleaming wood and forest paintings, like a posh cabin for the rich. Nachura, Tomas, Amora, and Zadek sat in chairs around a roaring fire. They smiled in welcome. Haldren bade me to sit in a luxurious white chair. With a flick of his fingers, I suddenly held a steaming mug of hot chocolate. My tears had dried, leaving cold resignation in their place.

Haldren spoke to me. "Before his imprisonment, the Creator took all recruits under his care and instructed them. As you know, Isaac has granted me permission to be your instructor until my time is up."

"Bit of a sad welcome without Haddas, isn't it?" Nachura said, aimlessly turning her cup into a flowerpot with pink roses and vines.

Others murmured their agreement. Doom and gloom had descended with the mention of the Creator. *Lovely.* My fate now resided with a bunch of depressed Gods and Goddesses.

I set my untouched mug of chocolate on a side table. "When do we start training?" I needed to get my mind off my bleak fate and working was the only way I knew how to shut off my feelings.

"You've created a tenacious one," Zadek said to Haldren, the corners of his lips curving up.

He chuckled. "That is all her."

This had nothing to do with eagerness to start the job. The sooner I learned everything, the sooner I could make better choices in keeping my family safe. I felt wildly uncomfortable with a bunch of strangers whose motives I could only guess at. Haldren had been pretty clear on what he wanted out of me, but what about the others? Did they support him or Isaac? Out of terror of what Isaac would do to my family, he had my allegiance. However, I also had the Creator's timeline for the tree to think of. If Isaac couldn't figure out how to save the tree by the end of summer, the earth and everyone in it would be destroyed. Somehow, I would form an allegiance with Isaac and figure out how to save the tree by whatever means to ensure my family's survival. To start, I had to study with all that I had on how to be an excellent Goddess. It would put me on a better footing with the other Gods and Fates and help me navigate the best steps to take for my family's sake.

The way the Gods studied me, I had the distinct impression they read my thoughts.

"Tomorrow," Haldren finally said.

"Then, if I'm not needed, I'd like some space." I rose.

"First door on your right down the hall. You may stay there," Haldren volunteered.

"Thank you," I murmured.

The wood theme seemed to carry throughout the house. I located the room Haldren had indicated, discovering sleeping quarters decorated in forest green, a bathroom, and a large closet. My clothes from home had been transported, along with my sword. I suspected Haldren had done it. I appreciated that he'd thought of my sword. It was my favorite possession aside from the new bond ring Andrew and Braidus had given me. I grabbed a nightgown, then slipped into a bath to wash off the dried blood.

I stared at the clear patch of skin on my left hand. Seventeen years of seeing the Mark of the Gods and now nothing. I half wanted it back, if only for a bit of normalcy, something to ground myself. I washed, dressed, braided my hair, then lay down in bed.

I let my thoughts drift to the bond. Officially a Goddess and leagues away, I still felt Andrew's and Braidus's hearts beat in tandem with mine.

And they could probably feel me once more. I was surprised and grateful that the bond was unbroken. It made me wish all the more that I was home.

I pictured Andrew's blazing-blue eyes and full lips curved into a smile. I imagined the smell of his woodsy cologne and the feel of his arms wrapped snugly around me, exuding safety. My anchor against the wind.

I thought of Braidus's long, wavy, blond-streaked hair, the intensity that never ceased to make me lose my breath, the feel of his beard against my cheek, and his signature smirk. My pillar of strength and resilience.

I closed my eyes and basked in the love that came through the bond.

The following morning, I sat in the comfy white chair in the sitting room, holding a new cup of hot chocolate from Haldren. This time I drank it. Having not seen anyone as I moved from the bedroom to the sitting room, I wondered how the Gods sustained themselves. Did they do all their own cooking and cleaning?

Haldren chuckled, obviously reading my thoughts. "We have servants—cooks, maids, groundskeepers, hostlers, and the like—people who have suffered in their earth lives and found favor with us."

"No conjuring food out of nothing, then?" I asked.

"No." He flicked his fingers, and an apple pastry appeared on the table beside him. "I transported this from the kitchens, made by Edgar. Our powers allow us to see things happening far away from us."

"The cook doesn't get mad when his food randomly disappears?" I asked.

He shrugged. "It is expected." He made an additional pastry appear in front of me.

The other four Gods arrived as we finished breakfast. I sensed anticipation in the air. After a quick greeting, Haldren began my instruction. "Look into your mage core. Tell me what you see."

I dropped into my mage core. Six glass balls—red, blue, yellow, green, purple, and gold—greeted me. "Six balls."

Tomas projected his core. I saw six glass balls there also—red, blue, yellow, green, purple, and copper this time. "Our God powers are sourced from copper instead of gold since we have less power."

Haldren spoke. "The power of the Gods goes as follows." He gestured to Zadek, Amora, Nachura, and Tomas. "Copper for these four." He pointed to me and him. "Gold for you and me. White for the four Fates over the Realm of Souls, and silver for Isaac as Fate over Fates."

"And the Creator?" I asked.

"Opal," everyone answered.

Haldren continued. "The magic afforded us must be charged by touching the same element as the color. For you and me, it is gold." He gestured to the other four Gods. "For them, it is copper."

"What about the Fates?" I asked, curious.

"Eli, Emory, Cassius, and Ada take their power from gemstones—rubies, emeralds, and amethysts." Haldren waved his hand airily. "Essentially, any natural crystal will work. Isaac takes his power from silver."

"And the Creator?" I asked.

"The Creator gets his power directly from the sun." Haldren's tone turned awed. "He is the only man in existence able to harness the sun fire."

"Impressive," I said, imagining it would be hotter than the brightest flame.

"Our gold magic feeds into our other mage balls, allowing us to do more with the other colors. It also enhances the abilities of the color we're currently using. For example, blue magic is known for the power of creation. You have used it in the past to construct figurines and bridges. Previously, anything you created would look like—as you put it, a blue syrupy substance." A smile came to his lips. "Now that you have come into your full power, the blue magic will convert itself into the exact object you are trying to make, like this." With a flick of his fingers, a dagger appeared in his hand.

I raised my eyebrows. "A big difference."

The others chuckled. Haldren made the knife disappear.

"The sand in your gold ball will lessen as it continually transfers its grains into your other colors, allowing you to do more. You must keep a close eye on your levels to ensure you don't become sick." Haldren held up a finger.

"It does not matter how many colors of magic you possess. If you empty just *one* of your balls, you die."

"I'll keep that in mind," I said, duly noting the seriousness. "What would happen to the gold magic if I died? Would it transfer to a new person?"

Haldren shook his head. "No, not unless you were nearing your thousand years, like me, and had already selected a successor who had been approved to take on the power. If you were to die right now, your gold magic would disintegrate, and then, when I reverted to a human in a few months, it would be lost to us entirely. It would add an immense amount of chaos to our already tumultuous world. As it is, each of us Gods is pressed to mitigate the damage our dying tree causes the earth. To lose the gold magic would be devastating and send many people to their deaths."

"Is that why Isaac hasn't been so quick to kill me?" I asked.

Haldren nodded. "Isaac needs you if he wants to keep the earth running as it has been, which he does."

"Why couldn't you choose another successor?" I asked.

"Because I don't have that ability anymore," Haldren explained. "When you became a full-fledged Goddess, that power transferred to you, and when you reach the last twenty years of your time as a Goddess, you'll be able to use it."

I sighed. I wanted to use it now and find someone to take my place so I could return to my family. I hated being here.

"It will take time and practice to work with your amplified colors, but I believe we can mold you into an excellent Goddess." Haldren smiled.

My mind caught on the word *mold*. I scowled, reminded that I was Haldren's science experiment. Now that I had the same level of power, I wondered if it might do him and me a bit of good to kick him where it hurt.

Tomas burst into sudden laughter. Zadek, Amora, and Nachura snickered quietly. Haldren frowned very much like a disapproving uncle. My mouth twitched as I fought back a smile of my own.

Haldren continued with the lesson. "A king looks after the needs of one country, one people. Nachura, Tomas, Amora, and Zadek look after *the specific* needs of *all* people. Amora focuses on women, Zadek on men. Tomas on business arrangements and the working world, and Nachura on land and weather management, farming, animals, and the like." He gestured to me and him. "You and I care for *all* requirements of the living. We are not limited to one cause."

"You're saying we can do all their jobs," I said waving my hand at Tomas, Nachura, Zadek, and Amora.

Haldren smiled. "Yes. We have more freedom to pick and choose who we want to help or destroy." He leaned back in his chair and clasped his hands together. "As a Goddess over Gods, you will oversee the judgments made by the others"—he pointed to the two Gods and two Goddesses—"and weigh in when they are unsure about a course of action. When they are not in need of anything, you can listen to prayers and choose who you want to assist, lessening the burden for the others." He rubbed his chin. "It is a full-time job."

"What if you are not sure what to do?" I asked.

"The God or Goddess over Gods is supposed to directly answer to the Fate over Fates as ruler over the living and dead." Haldren's expression darkened. "That makes Isaac our superior. The Fate over Fates is *supposed* to answer to the Creator, Haddas."

*Who is currently locked up, not feeding the tree, and allowing Isaac to run rampant.* "You don't really work with the other four Fates, do you?" I entertained seeing my loved ones in the Realm of Souls again.

"No, not really," Haldren answered. "They focus solely on the Realm of Souls and have done so since the beginning of our world."

For the rest of the day, the five Gods taught me how to work with my extensive power. I learned how to conceal the glow of my magic and planned to keep it hidden forevermore, as they did, albeit for different reasons. The others didn't seem to mind being the center of attention, while I reveled in the idea of being able to hide.

Amora said, "I enjoy an air of mystery."

I learned how to see the world with my mind using purple magic. I didn't have to move from my comfy chair to observe Chef Edgar mopping the kitchen or patrons drinking in Silverdens. I could count all the gold in King Brian's treasury and take a bag without being physically present. My magic could go anywhere it wanted, and no one would see it but me, the other Gods, the Fates, and the Creator.

"How am I supposed to see something I can't already picture?" I asked Haldren. There was much of the world I had yet to discover.

"You listen to the prayers, pick one, and follow it. You see in your mind's eye the situation, look at the cause and effect, then send a bit of magic their way to help or hinder depending on what they deserve," he said, perched on the edge of his seat.

"Follow the prayers. Got it," I said. "What is considered a prayer?"

"Anytime the word *God*, or *Goddess*, or even our true names are uttered in thought or spoken aloud, we hear it," he said.

"Even in casual conversation like, 'Gods forbid, I hope he's not late'?" I asked.

Haldren nodded. "Let's try one." He took my hand.

He directed my magic to listen to prayers. Thousands of voices filled my mind. I cringed. Haldren removed them until we could focus on just one.

A young girl's voice pled, *"Gods above, please help me find my bunny."*

Haldren instructed Boomer to show us the situation, and a scene formed in our mind's eye. A little redheaded girl no older than ten searched under a table in a living room. Haldren took an image of the rabbit from the girl's mind and then told Boomer to find him. A black-and-white, floppy-eared rabbit appeared under the couch, pressed against a wall and chewing on an old celery stick. Haldren lured the rabbit out with fresh leafy greens transported from our kitchen.

"Rex!" the girl cried in sheer relief when she saw him. She scooped the rabbit into her arms.

Haldren removed his hand from mine, the view dissolving. "There you have it."

"And we do this all day, one prayer after the next," I stated.

"Nights as well," he said. "We take shifts."

"Great." No break.

# CHAPTER FIFTEEN

**A**FTER LUNCH, HALDREN TOOK me on a tour of his rustic cabin. It was built on one level and had five bedrooms, three bathrooms, a kitchen, dining room, living room, and library. I hadn't envisioned a God's house to be this small, but I liked it. His themes of forest and wood also appealed to me. It felt a bit strange to see a commonality between Haldren and me in our love of simplicity. Perhaps we were related after all.

With Haldren's time nearing its end, he gave me the freedom to make some creative changes to his house. "You're more than welcome to it. This will be your house soon." He teased, "You can add twenty rooms if you want."

I laughed. "No, thanks. I like it just the way it is." I didn't need much, and I enjoyed the warm coziness he had created.

"Good." Haldren seemed pleased.

"What are you going to do?" I asked. "Where are you going to go?"

"I have a nice cabin in the mountains above Carasmille, which I'm rather fond of," he said. "I'll be reduced to green and blue magic again. Perhaps I'll return to my old profession, a healer."

With a thousand years of knowledge. "Would you stay if you could?" I asked.

"Without hesitation." Haldren's blue eyes settled on me. "Isaac and I are much the same. We go about it differently, but in our hearts, we revel in power. It would be a lie to say I look forward to leaving this to you."

"Well, I'm not excited about it either," I grumbled.

Haldren chuckled. "Such is our lot."

Somehow, I needed to change that. Haldren was better suited to be a God over Gods than I was. If the Creator was ever freed—and I wouldn't say that I would be the one to do it—maybe I could convince him to keep Haldren and let me return to my family. He certainly had invested himself in freeing the Creator. Surely that had to count for something.

Haldren smiled. "Come, I have more to teach you."

We returned to the living room.

Once settled, he covered transportation. "Previously, you flew with the wind to get to places faster. Now you can use yellow magic to transport yourself, persons, and objects anywhere in the world. Picture the place in your mind's eye, then express a desire to be there."

I imagined the white courtyard and Mark of the Gods, gold against white. *Take me there,* I told Boomer with intent. I shut my eyes against my own bright flash. I stumbled as I landed outside. Momentary excitement raced through me. *It worked*!

I fought against a sudden urge to return to Aberron. I had the power, but so did Isaac.

I sighed with resignation. *Back to my chair.* I materialized, standing on the white cushion. I threw my hands out for balance. *Oops.* I hopped down.

Haldren laughed. "It's best if you picture an open space in the room instead of a specific piece of furniture."

I flushed. "Right."

"Using the same principle, take a book from my shelf." He gestured leisurely to the wall behind him.

I picked out a red spine with gold lettering and expressed a desire to Boomer to have it. I held my palm out as it appeared in my hand. I gripped it tightly to stop it from slipping.

"Good," he said. "Now, let's expand that. Take a rose from Nachura's garden and deliver it somewhere in the world."

A week passed as Haldren and occasionally the other Gods trained me. Despite my wish not to be a Goddess, I enjoyed the lessons. It felt good to exercise my mind and new abilities. The more I learned, the more independent I could be. I thrived on self-reliance, and my goal to study hard so I could be on the same footing as the other Gods increased with everything taught. I hoped to be a force for good, especially when it came to keeping my family alive.

The Creator's timeline that the tree would die by the end of summer never strayed far from my mind. As it stood, we had practically reached the end of winter. Spring was on the horizon and, with it, I neared Haldren's reversion to a human and the tree's death—two things I desperately didn't want to happen.

I found it interesting how often the Gods transported around the island. I wondered how they stayed in shape since they seemed to do more transporting than walking. They never knocked at the front door and often randomly appeared in the kitchen, dining room, or living room with something to say or accomplish. The bedrooms and bathrooms seemed to be the only places they didn't show up, thank the Gods. The lack of privacy unnerved me, but I seemed to be the only one bothered. The sudden flashes of light accompanied by their appearance put me on edge, and I had to work hard to get used to it.

I sat at the dining room table, nibbling on a piece of apple bread when Haldren took his leave to help Nachura with a spring storm and Tomas appeared in his place to continue the lesson on prayer.

"Ooh, I love Edgar's apple bread." With a flick of his fingers, he transported a piece to his hand and took a large bite.

"It's very good," I agreed. Wanting to get to know Tomas a little better, I asked, "How long have you been a God?"

"Six hundred and fifty-two years," he answered between mouthfuls. "The Creator himself chose me after my predecessor, Jacqueline, fell in love with a man from Kashtine and asked to step down to spend a lifetime with him." His chest puffed up with pride, seemingly at the honor.

This surprised me. "The Creator didn't punish your predecessor for falling in love while on the job?"

He shook his head. "The Creator is not callous. He is known to make exceptions if the cause is warranted. Of course, the terms are laid out that we're not to get involved with humans, and we do our best to adhere to them. However, life doesn't always go the way we plan it. Jacqueline wasn't looking for love when she found it. The Creator saw that those two were a good fit and let her go. She went on to have ten children and an extremely happy life."

This gave me hope that maybe one day I could return to my loved ones. "Do you miss the Creator?"

Tomas's expression saddened. "Most of the Gods and Fates do." He cleared his throat. "Now, on to the lesson. Your purple magic will allow you to hear the prayers of those in need. It will also translate all languages into your native Fraison tongue so you may hear the pleas of all nations." He grinned. "No more melancholy about not being able to understand Gaitian."

"What about reading?" I asked, thinking of Zadek's journal.

"The words will rearrange themselves into Fraison," Tomas said. "Over time, you will learn the languages without needing purple magic."

A book appeared in his hand. He held it out, showing me that it had been written entirely in Gaitian. I watched, mesmerized, as the letters transformed to Fraison with a simple command to Boomer using purple magic. "Great, isn't it?" He grinned.

"Definitely," I agreed.

"Oh, I've taken the liberty to help the Nistierans find a new worthy council member." He smiled at me. "I know you had planned to assist them before you were murdered, but now that you're a Goddess, it is better for you to focus on your training."

"Right," I agreed. "Thank you for covering for me." It was thoughtful of him to step in to ensure the Nistierans had a good man in place.

He smiled. "You're welcome."

Later, I learned how to morph magic into matter with Amora.

"This is where creativity shines." Amora smiled. "Design the product in your mind, then relay the order to your blue magic."

I created a white silk dress with crystals sewn into the bodice. Amora then transported it to a lady whose wedding gown had just been ruined by a jealous former lover of the husband-to-be a few minutes before the union. We laughed as we watched the antagonizing lady's jaw drop as the bride glided down the aisle in the new dress, grinning from ear to ear. The outfit she originally had was nice, but I felt mine made her extra spectacular.

"I just love weddings," Amora said dreamily.

"They're sweet, aren't they?" I said wistfully, wishing I could have experienced a wedding myself. I ached to be home with my family in Aberron and to have a husband and the promise of children, like the bride I could see in my mind's eye. The bond heightened as Andrew and Braidus read my feelings. I fought back tears as I felt their love and mutual desire for the life I wanted.

Amora put a comforting hand on my shoulder. No doubt she also read the struggle within me. "No one should be forced into a role they don't want. I have hope for you to return to Aberron, choose between your bonded, and marry."

I smiled, appreciating her support. "Thank you."

The following day started with a lesson from Zadek. We stood in the courtyard, each clutching a steaming mug of apple tea, his mouth curved in a half smile as he surveyed me. "I wish to tell you how much I enjoyed watching you fight my people during the war. Your ferocity impressed me. You'd do well as a Dregan."

I blinked, caught off guard by his comment. The God of war was impressed with me? Somehow that didn't seem real. "Thank you . . ." I didn't quite know what to say.

He laughed.

"Can I ask a personal question?" I ventured. "Why did you give up your life in Dregaitia and accept the position of a God? I got the impression from your journal that you weren't dissatisfied with your life."

"No, initially I was not," Zadek said, his expression reflective. "I was highly favored among my people and by my king. I had a woman I cared for. But I was restless. Nothing I did fulfilled me. Isaac saw that I had the aptitude for more, and he was right. I would've made Yashti unhappy within a year or two of our marriage. Becoming the God of men and war has been a blessing to me. It's given me the purpose I lacked in mortality. I am grateful Isaac chose me."

I smiled. "It's good to do something you love."

We moved on to the lesson, first focusing on red magic.

"Red is still mostly destructive," Zadek said. "However, we can create fire-forged materials I would wager are stronger than whatever blue creates." Blue flames emerged from his hand, then suddenly diminished. He clutched a black shirt with a gold Mark of the Gods stitched on the front. He handed it to me with a wry grin. "Impervious to flame and other forms of destruction."

I smiled, abashed. Because of my penchant for bodily harm, I had destroyed many articles of clothing. Playing around with the fire forging, I made myself several new outfits that were resistant to destruction and then transported them to my room.

Zadek then spoke of his duties as God of war. "As Gods, we do our best to remain neutral during times of war and let the kings of each country work out their problems on their own. Oftentimes, we choose an individual, like a struggling soldier, to help during battle. I helped many Dregans stay warm as they fought the Aberronians."

I shuddered as I recalled our harsh winter. "The snow was awful."

Zadek nodded. "Nachura was beside herself."

"How hard is it for you to remain neutral in war?" I asked. "You are originally from Dregaitia. Do you favor them?" I wondered how evenhanded I would be when it came to Aberron.

"I favor justice and equality," Zadek said decisively. "It doesn't matter who it is—Nistierans, Jamaylin Islanders, or Dregans." He waved his hand airily. "What matters is their cause. Whose is more worthy? Are they fighting for a better life for themselves? To retain their freedom? Or is it merely out of prejudice and greed? Those who fight for survival over gluttony get more help from me."

I was of the same mind. "As it should be."

We moved on to listening to and answering prayers. Zadek had me give a boost of energy to a scrap of a boy fighting against three bullies, allowing him to escape.

"They'll be back, but our boy will be stronger." He directed the child to find a few silver coins peeking out of the dirt. Picking them up, the boy promptly ran to the nearby bakery for food.

I doubted half the people we helped ever noticed the hand of higher beings in their lives.

Haldren gave me a short break by taking me to see Nisha. He transported us to an expansive grassy field that sloped upward onto a hill with an apple orchard. At least fifty horses grazed at the far end of the field, their coats a myriad of colors—white, cream, gray, brown, and black. On their foreheads, the horses had swirls like the inner part of the Mark of the Gods.

Haldren left to inspect his orchard while I visited with Nisha and met his friends. The sweet scent of apples drifted on the air, reminding me of Saren at the end of summer. I loved harvest time. My thoughts lingered on Saren as I transported back to Haldren's house for more training.

I landed on a dining room table laden with food, facing Mava and Carl. Mava screamed and started to fall out of her chair, but I saved her with my magic. Carl threw a bowl of hot gravy at me. Drenched in burning brown liquid, I let loose a stream of curses. In my mind's eye, I watched and heard the Gods laughing from Haldren's sitting room.

"Good reflexes, Carl." I jumped off the table and waved the mess away.

"Isabelle!" they cried, eyes wide.

"Turns out my birthmark meant something, after all," I explained. "I have been elevated to a Goddess in training, hence the unexpected visit on both our parts."

An awkward silence descended.

I shifted on the balls of my feet. "Well," I cleared my throat. "Sorry to interrupt your meal. I guess you can pray to me if you need aid. Goodbye."

Haldren surprised me with full-belly laughs when I returned to Astralind, cheeks flushed with embarrassment.

After dinner, Haldren sent me to work with Nachura.

"There's a harsh wind threatening a village in the plains of Kashtine," she said. "Search for it with your mind."

I did as instructed and discovered the howling storm. Trees whipped back and forth, and branches cracked as the wind ripped them off. Rain pelted the ground in large, heavy droplets. Lightning struck a large oak, slicing it in half and sending a good portion of it toppling onto a field of peas.

"Gods forbid." I cringed at the devastation.

"The wind shouldn't be this strong for this area," Nachura said, her tone frustrated. "Their fledgling crops will be ruined, and they will starve to death if we don't help."

In my mind's eye, I saw families huddled together in their little houses. Children cried into their parents' chests, fear evident on their faces. Anxiousness and desperation permeated the air. Their whole world was shattering right before their eyes.

Nachura and I sent our magic out, managing to lessen the storm and save their crops.

When we finished, I asked, "Does this chaos come because of the tree?"

"Yes." She growled. "I could kill Isaac if the Creator hadn't taken that ability away from me. Just look at all the destruction!"

Taking my hand, she showed me image after image of natural disasters. A volcano eruption in Hestas. Flash flooding in Sondrei. Avalanches in Nistier. Death followed in the wake of each event. I watched people—sometimes whole families—get swept up in water, fiery ash, and ice, their screams echoing in my ears.

My stomach twisted sickeningly. "The world is literally falling apart."

"It is." Anxiety showed strongly on Nachura's face as she let go. "With the tree as starved as it is, I have been working twice as hard as the others to keep the earth from falling to pieces. I swear every minor storm now becomes a hurricane. I've needed Haldren's help almost constantly, and it's only going to get worse as we near the tree's death." Her lips quirked in a humorless smile. "It's nice to have a third set of hands. Perhaps one of us will finally get a breather."

After training with Nachura, I went to Haldren and asked to see the tree in person. "I'm aware I probably can't do anything about it with the Creator locked up, but I'd like to at least see the damage and keep abreast of it."

Haldren's ice-blue eyes brightened, but his face remained serious. "All right, we'll go, but you must be careful. Isaac guards the tree. He keeps an eye on it no matter where he is in the world. No doubt he will appear when we do. It would be best not to anger him at this time."

"All I'm asking for is a look. Nothing else." I pressed my lips together in a grim line, gearing up to be on my best behavior.

"Then let's go." Haldren took my hand.

We transported to another courtyard made of stone, except this one was triple the size of Haldren's. Two things caught my eye—the tree and the Creator. They resided next to each other.

Isaac arrived in a bright flash, his gaze severe. "What are you two doing here?"

I lifted my hands, trying not to appear threatening. "I just wanted to see. Nothing more."

Isaac's head tilted slightly, and an uneasy feeling washed over me. I had the distinct impression he searched my mind for an ulterior motive. After a moment, he straightened. "Fine, but don't go near the Creator."

"May I touch the tree?" I asked.

Isaac nodded.

I took a few steps forward, my head craned upward as I stared at the multicolored canopy. A blue leaf, eerily the same shade as found in a mage core, fell from the top and turned black as it touched the ground. I frowned, saddened to see the destruction of something so beautiful. Lines of black, syrupy sludge, stretched up the tree. I spied the Mark of the Gods underneath the lines, near eye level. It appeared to have grown naturally on the trunk. Like a beating heart, it pulsed and dimmed with white light.

I reached out and touched it. The soul-wrenching anguish that hit me was so forceful I gasped, caught off guard by the depth of feeling the tree possessed. Unexpected tears formed in my eyes and spilled down my cheeks. Haddas flashed to the forefront of my mind as the tree cried out to me for its caretaker and friend. I recognized a kindred spirit as I too had been denied my loved ones. I desired to be reunited with my family just as much as this tree craved to be with the Creator. We both suffered a cruel fate. I pressed my forehead against the trunk. *I'm so sorry,* I whispered. A bleak existence loomed before us both. I wondered if I would end up like the tree, slowly dying, starving for the touch of those I cared for.

The tree shuddered underneath my touch. I lifted my head but kept my hand on it. The Mark of the Gods suddenly flared white, and an opal ribbon of smoke rose from the mark, then swirled around me before penetrating my heart. My breath caught, and my eyes flew open at the sizzling, raw energy I felt.

Isaac grabbed my shoulders and yanked me away. Haldren hurried over. My heart pounded loudly against my rib cage as it adjusted to the magic the tree had given me. Thump. Thump. Thump. My bond went wild with fear. Whatever had just happened, Andrew and Braidus felt it too.

Still holding my shoulders, Isaac assessed me, eyes intense. Haldren wore a look of astonishment. I squinted against many bright flashes as the Fates and Gods arrived, every eye zeroing in on me.

"What did I do wrong?" I asked in a shaky voice. Sudden terror gripped me. Had I angered Isaac enough to make him retaliate against my family? I hadn't meant for whatever happened to happen. *Oh, please don't be upset with me,* I thought frantically.

Isaac's lips curled in amusement, no doubt at my fear of him. He had me right where he wanted me, and he knew it. "You made a connection with the tree. It gave you a gift. Look into your mage core."

I shut my eyes, and six balls materialized, each protected by a shimmering opal shield. *Huh.* The tree had put a protective layer over my mage core similar to what I had done for my family when I saved Joshua's life. Haldren had told me shields over mage cores would protect them from being tampered with. However, I wondered if this protection from the tree meant something different than what I had done for my family. Did this affect Isaac in any way that would make him want to strike back at me? I was afraid to ask. I opened my eyes hesitantly, still unsure whether Isaac was angry or not.

Isaac dropped his touch, took a step back, then stared at the tree and back at me with interest. "The tree has never linked with anyone but the Creator."

Oh. "It's never given anything to any of you?"

"No," everyone said, eyeing me with wonder and fascination.

"I didn't ask for it," I said quickly.

Isaac turned to Haldren. "Continue training the little Goddess. I may have use of her later."

Haldren inclined his head. "As you wish." He held a hand out to me. "Come, Isabelle."

I took his hand, grateful Isaac didn't rain fire on me. We returned to Haldren's sitting room.

Haldren seemed unnaturally pleased. "You never cease to surprise me. Your mage core now carries the protection of the Creator. No God or Fate will be able to meddle with it or cause you harm. You've just become harder to kill."

# CHAPTER SIXTEEN

D AYS MORPHED INTO WEEKS as I trained under Haldren and occasionally the other Gods. I often found myself struggling with cause and effect. I once led a quail to a starving man who then jumped and shouted praises to the Gods. Shortly thereafter, I heard him crying for the Gods to give him food again. I learned that my act of kindness had given him a sense of entitlement. If he prayed hard enough, the Gods would provide and he didn't need to leave his hut.

"They're called wailers," Tomas said with an eye-roll. "People who cry to the Gods for every little thing."

"A little help or hindrance here and there is good." Haldren raised a finger, stressing his next point. "But we must not allow people to take advantage of our power, or be too much of an influence that we alter the natural course of things."

"This is ridiculously complicated," I complained. "How am I going to know what the natural course of life should be? The gift of prophecy was not handed to me by the Creator."

"But you can guess a future based on the past and present," Haldren countered. He created an orb and showed me a plump, rosy-cheeked grandmother putting bread in a large oven. "What can you tell me about her?"

I noted her silver hair, bright-blue eyes, and rough hands. With yellow magic, Boomer sent me information through a series of quick images, like sketches of moments in her life that explained her up to this point. I rattled off a bit of the information. "Lola. A widow of fifteen years. Runs late-husband's bakery. Has three grown children. Rises at three-thirty every morning."

Haldren smiled in approval. "And has done so for the past forty years except on her birthday or when she's sick. Based on this, what can you expect for tomorrow?"

"Same routine," I answered with confidence. "She's in good health, and her birthday isn't for another three months."

"Yes," Haldren agreed.

That was how I became acquainted with guessing the future of strangers. Haldren assured me that time and experience would make my predictions as close to accurate as a Goddess could get *without* possessing the gift of foresight.

Weeks turned into a month. I felt I had a fairly good idea of where the Gods' loyalties lay. Zadek favored Isaac, while the others favored the Creator. It made sense considering Isaac had chosen Zadek to become a God and aided in his training. Like me, Zadek wasn't given the opportunity to train under the Creator. Therefore, how could he be loyal to a man he hardly knew?

My family had taken to praying to me, usually a word or two, to remind me that I was not forgotten.

"*Thinking about you, little sister,*" Joshua said. "*I miss you.*"

Henry cried, "*Andrew's telling everyone he's giving the kingdom to me. I don't want it! Come back soon so I don't have to be king.*"

"*Gods, I miss you,*" Andrew said with longing. "*Your laughter, your kisses, your tenacity. Your absence is felt everywhere. Father's getting frustrated because I'm struggling to focus in the study. You're in my thoughts constantly. I thought Braidus was doing better than I was, but I learned differently when he flat-out said to Father, 'What's the point in all these reports when the world will be destroyed when summer ends?' Tensions are high without you.*"

"*Wish you were here to liven things up,*" Falden said. "*Everyone's walking around like a lost puppy. It's not pleasant.*"

*"I crave your presence,"* Braidus said. *"Tell me that you're training hard and doing everything you can to return. You're in my heart and on my mind always."*

At the risk of Isaac finding out, I took a chance and sent a group message back. As long as I didn't talk to them often, I figured I could get away with a few words here or there, especially if my family spoke to me in a prayer fashion. *"I hear you. Don't stop talking to me even if I can't respond. I'm training hard. I'm not giving up. I love and miss you all so much."*

Terrified of Isaac, I never set foot in the castle or purposely sought them out. However, my Amora bond could not be easily disregarded. I rebelled in the smallest ways possible, allowing my heart to fill with warmth for Andrew and Braidus before I closed my eyes each night, allowing them to see that I had not lost sight of my goal to return. I dared not do more, however, lest Isaac think I pined too much for what I had lost. *I will return,* I vowed to myself. I prayed it wouldn't take me before summer's end to do it.

Two months in Astralind passed swiftly. Every day, I grew in experience and knowledge. I could now compartmentalize my mind to see multiple things at once: a flood in the Jamaylin Islands, a market riot in Reechi, and a woman going into labor on the side of the road in Dregaitia. So many people praying. So many issues. It filled my days and nights until Haldren began reminding me to eat.

"Your mother never ate when she worked or was upset either." Haldren handed me a bowl of potato soup. "Daniel often hand-fed her."

"They were a good match," I said, picking up the spoon.

Haldren smiled, his eyes misty. "Indeed, although Anne didn't think so in the beginning. I remember on more than one occasion Anne coming to me to complain about Daniel's antics. 'He's always laughing,' she would lament. 'He never takes anything seriously.' Of course, she couldn't see what I saw—that Daniel was madly in love with her and it was his nerves that made him appear as though he constantly jested. When I encouraged her to give him a chance, she did so, though reluctantly. It wasn't until they bonded that she realized that there was more to Daniel than mischievous-ness. I never heard a single complaint after that."

I smiled, loving to hear stories of my parents. "Tell me more."

Haldren obliged, and I spent an enjoyable evening learning about my parents, starting with how my father's parents had been lost at sea and Daniel had been taken in by King Jason and raised as a brother to King Brian, much like Joshua had been taken in by King Brian after my parents' deaths. I learned how my grandparents on my mother's side were nearly fifty years old when they were finally blessed to have my mother. Haldren had been concerned that his generational line would end with them. They passed away shortly after I was born due to age-related issues. Haldren then spoke of how my mother and Princess Liliana had been inseparable, thus putting my parents together often and sparking their journey to love. I enjoyed every second of learning about their heritage and history.

As my knowledge of the duties of a Goddess expanded, Zadek, Nachura, Amora, and Tomas began consulting me. Haldren's living room became our designated meeting place. We removed some of his furniture, allowing everyone to create a chair to their liking. Not a single chair matched, but no one minded. Comfort mattered more when we worked as hard as we did.

"I need an extra set of hands on the flood cleanup in Jamaylin," Nachura said as she sat down.

"This treaty is unfair." Tomas raked a hand through his hair as he stared at a magical copy of the document. "The girl deserves way more livestock for her dowry. Her father needs to see he's making a bad deal."

"I've cut out the tongues of three men who swore wrongly on me," Zadek said, crossing one leg over the other. "I'm debating on making the fourth blind. Which do you think is worse?"

That one made me pause. "Seriously?"

Zadek replied, "There is no greater oath than swearing on the Gods. When people do so, they must be punished lest people lose faith in the pledge."

"Granted," I said, albeit with a frown. "I think I'd take blindness over losing my tongue."

Zadek grinned. "Agreed."

Amora appeared in a bright flash and sang, "I have happy news to share." She skipped to her chair and sat down. "Crown Princess Calliope of Dregaitia is expecting a child with Crown Prince Timtric. I thought you'd want to do the honors of keeping her pregnancy healthy."

"When do we find out if the child has magic?" I asked.

"As soon as the heart is fully formed," Amora said. "We have two weeks."

Despite using an exorbitant amount of power daily, I'd only had to recharge once so far. I marveled at the amount of power I held, and yet it still wasn't enough to get me back home.

Mava and Carl spread the word of my transformation into a Goddess through Saren, Aberron Cliffs, and Prastis. People from that province, some I didn't even know, specifically prayed to me with praises like omnipotent and supreme attached.

Many of their pleas were based on their fears for their crops and livestock. The weather was still colder than it should be, making their crops struggle. Much of Aberron's food came from that province. I helped as much as I could.

Initially, their prayers made me wildly uncomfortable. I didn't see myself as an almighty Goddess, and the thought of people worshiping me sickened me. Noticing my distress, Haldren tried to comfort me, but his words fell flat. I hated being a Goddess something fierce and lamented my ability to change it.

On a sunny spring afternoon, I walked around Haldren's courtyard, soaking up the good weather and answering one prayer after another. I listened to a particularly heartfelt plea from Malsin. *"We're still losing mages at an extraordinary rate. I'm at my wit's end trying to find an answer for King Brian. Any help you could give would be greatly appreciated."*

My worry over my family increased. They were all mages. *"I'll look into it,"* I told him.

Rather than doing a ton of investigating on my own, I went straight to Haldren for answers. No doubt he would have an explanation concerning the mage deaths. He sat at a table in the kitchen, inspecting an array of apples.

"Why are so many mages dying in their sleep without good reason? We're up to a hundred mages."

"I know," Haldren answered. "I have been keeping track."

"Well?" I asked, my eyebrows raised.

Haldren scowled. "Isaac is delivering them straight to the Realm of Souls."

A touch of anger hit me. "What for?"

"To help with the taxation on the tree," Haldren explained. "All magic given to mages, including the Gods and Fates, comes from the tree. The Creator is the only person in existence who does not take from it. When a mage charges their magic by touching the element they are associated with—fire, water, copper, etc.—they're actually gathering power sent from the tree. Isaac hopes that by eliminating some mages, there will be fewer people needing magic from the tree, thus slowing the starvation."

"He's trying to buy himself some time to find a solution to feed the tree without needing the Creator," I said.

"Yes," he agreed, his eyes severe. "The others and I have voiced our objections, but, unfortunately, it hasn't done us any good. Isaac threatens more devastation to the world if we try to stop him."

"Mages are heavily relied on in many parts of the world," I pressed. "This cannot continue."

Haldren laughed without humor. "Don't I know it. Tell me, what do you think is worse—a few mages lost or entire villages set on fire? Isaac's threats have weight to them. We have to consider the cause and effect when going against him."

I threw my hands up in exasperation. "The Gods cannot keep watch over everyone every second of the day. People's problems fall through the cracks at a constant rate. One mage at the right place at the right time can be the difference between saving an entire village or letting them fall to ruin should some catastrophic thing happen and catch us unawares."

"Indeed." He rubbed his goatee. "What do you propose?"

I put my hand on my chest. "I made a connection with the tree, didn't I? Perhaps I can help it and get Isaac to stop killing mages."

"I doubt it," Haldren said immediately.

"It's worth a try," I insisted.

"All right, but expect disappointment." He rose and took my hand.

We transported to the tree. My eyes flicked to the Creator with a pang in my heart, but I resisted the urge to go over to him.

A bright flash and Isaac appeared. He crossed his arms over his chest. "What do you want?"

I swallowed back my initial fear. Something had to be done. "I wanted to see if I could convince you to stop killing mages."

"Is that so?" Isaac's eyes flashed, reminding me to tread carefully.

I took a breath, trying to maintain my courage. "I thought I would see if I could help the tree since I connected with it."

Haldren spoke. "You have nothing to lose by letting Isabelle try. The disease continues to grow despite your attempts to stop it."

"All right." Isaac gestured to the tree. "You may go to it."

"Thank you." I walked over to it. Inhaling and exhaling slowly, I placed my hand on the bark over the Mark of the Gods.

The soul-crushing anguish once again held me in its grip as the tree cried out for the Creator. Tears came to my eyes. "*I know. I want my family back too. Gods, I need them to survive just as much as you need the Creator to live.*" I felt like I was nothing without my loved ones. They gave me the strength to push through and do the impossible.

I thought of the struggle Malsin faced trying to find answers for King Brian concerning the dying mages. My anger sparked at Isaac for creating this mess—for trapping the Creator and now killing mages who didn't deserve to die—all so he could stay in power. I told the tree, "*You shouldn't be starving due to someone else's greed.*" I wanted to help in any way I could.

*"You gave me a gift. I wish to return the favor. I offer what magic I have if you wish to take it back."*

The anguish I felt from the tree lessened a smidge, giving me the impression that it contemplated my offer. I didn't have the means to free the Creator at this time, but I couldn't stand back and do nothing. I wished to see the tree thrive, thus saving my family from annihilation—especially with Isaac killing mages.

The tree shuddered, the Mark of the Gods flared white, and an opal ribbon of smoke shot out and penetrated my chest. I gasped at its fiery power, and my body trembled with a surge of adrenaline. I put both hands on the tree to steady myself. The ribbon connecting us deepened with a mesh of my six colors as the tree pulled strength from my core.

My strength diminished rapidly. Aches and pains emerged as my levels plunged. I fell to my knees, hands sliding down the tree, as it took everything I had to offer. My chest burned something fierce. Black spots swam in front of my eyes. My head pounded like a beating drum. I found it hard to catch my breath. I could feel the tree's hunger gnawing through my insides as it soaked up my magic. It would take every grain of sand I possessed, and I would never come close to satisfying it. A sense of my mortality hit me as I realized I'd just offered myself as a sacrifice. Not yet ready to die, I cursed my foolishness.

"The tree will kill her!" Haldren wrenched me away.

The connection between me and the tree ended, and Haldren gathered me into his arms and stood, concern on his features. My eyes fluttered open and closed as I fought to stay lucid. I felt much fear in my bond with Andrew and Braidus.

Haldren spoke to Isaac. "The tree needs more than Isabelle can give."

"Indeed, but she brings progress," Isaac answered with interest. He gestured to the canopy. "Only a few leaves now fall. We should try this again."

"No." Haldren's vehement rejection came swiftly. "Using Isabelle is not a solution. She will feed the tree till her last grain of sand only to take from it again to recharge. The only person who can truly fix the tree is the Creator, who does not take from it. Relinquish your desire for power and free him before you send us all to our deaths."

"Never," Isaac said, his voice firm. "I will find another way."

Haldren transported us to his house, where he set me on a couch and conjured several bowls containing natural elements. "Charge, Isabelle."

I stuck one hand in dirt and the other in water, charging two colors simultaneously. Next, I charged purple and gold by holding a lump of gold and sticking my other hand in a bowl of flames. Haldren then helped me outside to catch the wind. When finished, we returned to his sitting room.

Haldren turned his powerful gaze on me as we sat. "Well, you've managed to excite Isaac and nearly get yourself killed. What have you to say for yourself?"

I swallowed, cowed by his censure. "Thank you for pulling me away."

"Humph," he grumbled, seeming only a little mollified.

"I don't suppose Isaac will stop with the mages?" I asked.

"No," he said.

I sighed. "I guess I'll tell Malsin, then."

"Be careful lest Isaac think you pine too much over your loved ones," Haldren warned.

I nodded, then searched for Malsin with my mind's eye. I found him in the study, conversing with King Brian, Andrew, and Braidus. Using purple magic, I connected to his mind. "*I have an answer for the mage deaths.*"

"*Isabelle!*" Malsin cried with surprise and relief. "*Are you all right? Andrew and Braidus have been beside themselves over you. They're insisting you were playing with death again.*"

"Malsin," King Brian said.

Malsin held up a finger. "One moment. I'm talking to Isabelle."

"How is she?" Andrew clutched Malsin's arm.

"*I'm all right. Tell them not to worry.*" I relayed the reason for the mage deaths and my attempt to help by feeding the tree. "*I'm sorry I wasn't able to do much good.*"

"*My goodness,*" Malsin said in dismay. "*Thank you for trying all the same. I appreciate your help in this matter.*"

*"You're welcome. Tell everyone I send my love."* I ended the connection.

Haldren and I resumed training, except this time, things took a different twist.

"You have the basics of being a Goddess down," Haldren said. "Listen to prayers, help or hinder depending on the need to keep the world running smoothly—"

"And work so hard I can't have any personal time unless it's to eat, wash, or sleep," I added dryly.

My sentiment, of course, launched Haldren into an age-old lecture. "We have a duty to the world. Anytime we spend on ourselves could be life-or-death for someone else—"

I interrupted again, using a particularly bored voice. "Which is why Gods and Goddesses are not allowed families. The world could go to waste while we focused on them."

Haldren nodded seriously. "Not to mention you will outlive a husband."

"Unless I somehow figure out how to share my powers," I suggested with a sly smile.

"Don't even think it," Haldren countered.

The fact that I was not under the same protection as the other Gods and Fates, meaning I could cause injury or be harmed, had Haldren teaching me defensive magic. It wasn't fireballs or ice spears anymore. A simple relay to Boomer and I threw a volley of knives into Haldren's gold shield. He sent arrows raining down on mine. I encased Haldren in a steel box. He blasted it to smithereens and put me inside a bubble of water. I burst through, spluttering like a drowned rat. A fight like this could go on for days.

Our training sessions became a great source of entertainment for the Gods and Fates. Often, one or two or sometimes all came to observe. I didn't mind them coming as I had begun to be more comfortable around them and count them as friends. It was easy to endear myself to people who selflessly worked to help others and better the world.

Haldren claimed he wanted me to be the best Goddess I could be before he stepped down. "The Creator can't give you the protection he gave us, so you have to watch out for yourself."

Haldren's near thousand years of life had definitely made him creative. I lost count of how many times he knocked me down with something unique.

"Think past swords and knives. There are a million ways to kill someone." To prove his point, he whacked my face with a massive book.

Dizzy, I shook my throbbing head to clear it. He sprayed To Catch a Prince perfume in my face. As I choked on the fumes, he wrapped a pearl necklace around my neck and pulled it tight.

"All things found in a lady's room."

*Amarilla's, maybe.* Tired of getting beaten, I switched tactics. I worked on a shield that sunk into my skin and gave it a healthy glow while strengthening it to a hide that resisted a blade.

"Well done, Isabelle!" Haldren heartily approved when a spear tip with the power of the Gods bounced off it.

I grinned. For once, I had done something right in these sessions. As a Goddess, it was imperative to keep my magic open at all times. *Always be on the ready.* I kept the shield as I prepared to move on to a new task.

Haldren cocked his head as if listening to a thought. "Edgar says dinner is ready."

We transported to the dining room and sat at the table. Edgar brought over plates of food. We thanked him before digging in.

"There is something else I want to teach you," Haldren said, stabbing his fork into the roast beef. "Shielding our thoughts."

My fork hovered halfway to my mouth, my interest piqued.

"As you may have noticed," he said, "the Gods are always listening in."

"Like some collective hive." One section or another of their brains always seemed to be listening to the others' thoughts. My complaints about it had fallen on deaf ears.

"Telepathy is faster," Nachura had said. "Some things can't wait."

"I need to know what the others are doing so I don't intervene with someone else's work," Zadek said.

"Really, we wouldn't be Gods if we didn't listen in and conspire against each other," Tomas said. "I'm currently ahead in a bet with Amora because of it."

"Ah. Not anymore." Amora grinned wickedly, making Tomas curse.

Haldren put a hand on my shoulder, bringing me back to the present. "Not everything we do deserves to be known by all. We do enjoy our privacy from time to time."

Yes! Finally something really useful. "Teach me."

Haldren grinned. "There are two parts to this. The first is sending shielded thoughts to another person. For that, all you have to do is tell your purple magic to conceal what you're going to say, much like you would shield yourself before battle. When someone sends a shielded thought to you, it enters your mind with a zing attached to it, thus alerting you that this is private. I'll show you first by sending you a regular thought, then a shielded one."

"All right." I straightened my spine, eager to learn.

"*The roasted potatoes are particularly excellent this evening.*" Haldren speared a cubed potato and held it up for emphasis.

I smiled. "Edgar is a great cook."

I stiffened as I felt a zap of energy, followed by Haldren's words.

"*Isaac is watching us in his mind's eye this very moment,*" Haldren said. "*He doesn't like that I'm giving you this lesson.*"

"I see the difference." It would take a minute to get used to.

"Try it out," Haldren encouraged.

First, I focused on Boomer and relayed the command to conceal my thoughts to Haldren. He wagged his tail and barked. I was startled when

I felt the zap of energy course through my mind. It felt like a current of energy.

I spoke to Haldren telepathically. *"How often does Isaac watch our lessons?"*

He smiled. "You've got it." He sent me a shielded thought. *"Often. He looks for signs that I'm teaching you how to kill him."*

*"Are you?"*

He didn't bat an eye. *"Yes. Every day that you grow stronger in your knowledge of Goddess work makes you a bigger threat to him."*

I frowned, not liking the idea of being groomed to be a killer, but the world was at stake with the dying tree, and we had a limited amount of time to save it. Something had to be done. Would I be the one to do it? Despite growing in knowledge and power, I didn't know if I would ever have that type of strength, but I wanted to try.

I deactivated the purple magic and sighed in relief as the zapping energy vanished. "So what's the second part of shielding thoughts?"

"Building a safe haven in your mind." Haldren picked up his cup. "It's a place you can go to relax and ponder without worrying about others barging in."

"A free-thinking place," I said, already loving the idea. I craved privacy like no one else among the Gods.

"Yes, exactly," Haldren said. "I often go to my safe haven when I want a break from my life as a God."

"What does yours look like?" I asked as I took a bite of meat.

"A wheat field," he answered. "You've been to it many times."

Indeed. I pictured the field of grain and bright-blue sky. "Why wheat?"

Haldren shrugged. "I grew up on a wheat farm. It symbolizes hard work, growth, and nourishment. I have always been very fond of it. The other Gods have places of their own they go to. Amora's is a beach, Zadek's the woods. Nachura has a garden and Tomas a cave of jewels."

That one made me pause. "Jewels?"

Haldren nodded. "He's fond of the way the light reflects off them."

"How do I make one?"

"Build an empty room within your mind and tell your magic to protect it with its strongest shield," he instructed. "Then envision what you want the room to look like, a library or orchard, a place you feel most comfortable in. Once you have that image firm in your mind, transfer it to the room, and there you have it: a safe haven. To access it, simply tell your magic you want to go there, just like you would ask your magic to take you to your mage core to study your levels of magic."

I understood. "I'll have to think on it a bit to see what I want to build as my safe haven." I contemplated the castle in Carasmille, but then I worried it would make me homesick.

"Of course," he readily agreed. "It took Amora months to decide on a beach."

The end of spring fast approached as I walked alongside Nisha one early night. I had been a Goddess for nearly three months now. Every day closer to summer filled me with dread as I thought of Haldren leaving and me remaining in his stead. I relied on his guidance more than I cared to admit. How was I going to be a Goddess without him? How was I going to ensure the tree's survival before the end of summer?

Isaac sent me a mental message. *"Come to the tree alone."*

Great. "Isaac calls for me," I told Nisha with a frown. "I'll see you later." I gave him a quick kiss on his nose and patted his neck, then transported to the tree.

I expected to find Isaac but found myself alone. Seizing the moment, I walked over to the Creator. I gazed upon the man frozen in a glass sphere. Long blond hair cascaded around Haddas's shoulders, which were garbed in a bright-blue robe. His eyes were closed, his lips curved into a soft smile, his chest softly rising and falling. Sleep.

I reached out and touched the glass. A jolt of energy shot through my veins. Words burned into my mind. *"Hello again, Isabelle."*

I gasped.

A bright flash and Isaac appeared, forcefully pushing me away. I nearly fell before I righted myself with a bit of magic.

"Don't touch!" he snarled.

"This isn't right," I cried. "You need to free him."

He spoke pointedly. "And lose my position? I think not."

I let my mouth run away from me. "Why are you so cruel? What has Haddas done to make you hate him so?"

Isaac appraised me. "You are a Goddess now. You have the world at your fingertips." He conjured an orb and showed me two lustful men advancing on a crippled young woman in a darkened alley in Nistella. "Will you do something?"

I found the situation in my mind. I went to transport the woman to a safer place, but Isaac blocked my magic with a silver shield. My frustration surged, causing alarm from Andrew and Braidus.

"Why aren't you letting me help?"

Isaac's wicked smile sent shivers down my spine. "The exact question I asked our Creator when my time neared its end. Why should he and the Fates be granted eternal life and power and not I? Had I not proven myself every day—for a thousand years, even!—helping those in need?"

I bit my lip, considering. "Maybe he saw something he didn't like." I stiffened, worried I'd been too bold.

Isaac focused on the Creator. "Or maybe he is the cruel one, making us slaves to his will, giving us a slice of his power, then taking it away when we have done nothing to deserve it." He leveled his eyes at me. "Forcing us to be weak again when we don't have to be."

I opened my mouth and then closed it. How could I argue with that?

Isaac crossed his arms, smug. "I want to try an experiment with you." He conjured a glass ball filled to the brim with blue sand. A mage core. "Take this and give it to the tree."

An ominous feeling pooled in my gut as I took the ball. "Where did you get this?"

He shrugged. "I took it from a mage."

*Gods forbid.* This ball had been inside a person Isaac murdered. I held a piece of death. My stomach rolled with nausea. My grip loosened, the ball starting to slip out of my fingers. I fumbled with it before clutching it tighter.

Isaac scowled.

I turned and walked toward the tree, my heart racing as Andrew and Braidus noted my abhorrence. I didn't question Isaac lest he turn on me and hurt my family. Taking a shuddering breath, I held the mage core against my chest with one hand and placed the other on the tree over the Mark of the Gods.

I fought to keep a clear head. It sickened me to no end to be forced to join Isaac in his wrongdoings. The Creator needed to be freed. Turning my full attention to the tree, I thought, *"I have this blue magic to offer to you. Will you take it?"* A part of me wished it wouldn't out of principle, but a stronger part wanted to keep Isaac happy for the sake of my family.

The tree trembled as it sent out an opal tendril and penetrated the mage core, the smoky ribbon darkening with blue as it soaked up the magic. As the last grain of sand disappeared, the glass ball disintegrated in my hands.

I stepped away from the tree and turned to face Isaac. A smile played on his lips. I doubted I'd ever been more disgusted in my life.

"You may go." He waved me away.

I transported to Haldren's courtyard. Walking into the house, I searched in my mind's eye for the lady Isaac had shown me. I found her in the midst of the assault, her eyes wide with pain and terror, a knife pressed against her throat so she wouldn't scream. Seeing only darkness in the two men's hearts, I ripped their souls out of their bodies and delivered them to the Realm of Souls without a shred of remorse.

Isaac spoke approvingly in my ear. *"You're getting better, little Goddess."*

I scoffed, finding little pleasure in his approval. My heart thudded with Andrew's and Braidus's concern. They sat at the dinner table with the rest of my family. I ached to be there. Feeling rebellious, I broke the rules and sent them a mental message. *"I'm all right, my loves. I swear it on myself."* I chuckled humorlessly. *"I just had to do something unpleasant is all."*

My mage mates calmed at the sound of my voice, and my heart filled with their love for me, bringing tears to my eyes as I sent my love back.

Haldren appeared. "You shouldn't be talking to them."

"When are you going to deem me ready enough to get out of my head?" I countered. "I don't go looking into yours."

"I have a limited amount of time before you succeed me," he said. "Every second I have counts."

"*Yes, use me to free the Creator.*" I directed a shielded thought to him.

"*You've seen the Creator,*" he said, his words also shielded. "*Death would be a better alternative than his state.*"

I met his cold blue eyes. "*Isaac blocked my magic with ease. I cannot fight him and win. This whole thing is fruitless.*" And now I had become complicit in offering mage cores to the tree.

He spoke with intensity. "*No. If Isaac, a lesser God than me, managed to steal Palina's power, then so can you.*"

"*How did he do it?*" I asked.

Haldren took our minds to his wheat field.

"I believe a visual will make it clear." He conjured a glass orb and put regular white beach sand in it, creating a representation of a mage core. With startling force, he threw the ball to the ground, shattering it into a million pieces. He then crouched and touched the spilled sand with a finger, much like someone would when recharging. The sand vanished. The glass disintegrated. Palina died because her mage core had been emptied.

Haldren straightened. "Unexpected simplicity. Isaac used his charm and managed to convince Palina to let him into her core. While inside, he smashed her silver ball and stole her magic." The corners of his lips curved up. "You are fortunate the tree gifted your colors with opal shields that have the power of the Creator. Your core is nigh unbreakable."

"Yes," I agreed as I fully realized the tree's gift.

However, as I thought of Haldren's wish for me to take Isaac on, my frustration grew.

"Isaac certainly isn't going to sit still, let me sneak into his core, and take his magic." I didn't have a clue how to fight him.

I hadn't seen my family in nearly three months, and I felt their absence acutely. I worried I'd never get them back because all of this was too Gods-forbidden hard.

Haldren sighed. "I pray we don't regret this." He pulled my family's consciousnesses into the wheat field, all nine of them materializing in front of us. "Five minutes."

"Yes! Group hug!" Arms outstretched, I barreled into my family.

"Isabelle!" they cried with joy.

I hugged them all. "I miss you all so much."

"Tell us what's going on that's so horrible," Andrew said.

"Isaac is collecting the cores from the mages he's killing and has made me feed one to the tree since I connected with it," I said with all due seriousness. "Please watch yourselves."

"We lost Ethan from the Sorrenian yesterday," Henry said grimly. "You need to stop Isaac before all mages are sacrificed."

Joshua scowled. "The Abominators are rising in triumph over the amount of mage deaths. They whisper fear into many hearts, causing an abundance of mage-discrimination complaints for my patrol guards to handle. We're hard-pressed to squash them."

*Not good.* Mustering false cheer, I said brightly, "Well, don't give up on me yet. I'm training hard, I swear."

Braidus chuckled. "Yes, on yourself." This normally would have earned him a cheeky response but, instead, I gave him a quick peck on the lips.

"Time, Isabelle," Haldren said when I pulled back.

"One second." I pulled Andrew to me and lightly brushed my lips against his.

"Fight for us, love," Andrew whispered against my lips.

"I will. I promise." I stepped back, wiping unexpected moisture from my eyes.

Haldren waved his hand, and they vanished. "Better?"

I curled my fingers as fire raced through my veins. I was more determined than ever to take back my life. "Better."

Haldren grinned. "Good."

# CHAPTER SEVENTEEN

HE FIRST DAY OF summer arrived. In twenty-one days, I would be eighteen and Haldren would lose his Godly power, thus ending my training. I wished he would remain and I go home to Aberron. I sighed. If only it worked that way. Perhaps if I somehow managed to free the Creator.

Per Isaac's demands, fifty-two mage cores had now been fed to the tree. The black ooze growing on the uppermost branches had slowed. Every couple of days, he brought me to the tree to offer it magic. I made no effort to hide my revulsion, but I doubted he cared. Until a better option became available, I would do as told.

Haldren agreed with my logic. In a shielded thought, he said, "*Making Isaac comfortable in his authority over you will help our cause. He won't feel the need to layer himself in shields. His arrogance will be his undoing.*"

I strolled in Nachura's rose garden, listening to prayers, when Tomas appeared. "Isabelle, have you taken a look at what is happening in the Aberron courts?"

"No," I answered. "I've been warned against paying too much attention to my family."

"Sage advice," Tomas agreed. "But I think this warrants consideration."

I let my mind travel to King Brian's study. Stacks of papers covered half the large table. King Brian, Braidus, Andrew, Henry, Dominic, and Falden sat there in deep conversation.

Braidus stood and rested his hands on the table. He leaned forward. "Grandfather wrote the laws out of spite." He spoke to his father with intensity. "He has been dead for almost fifteen years, and you've done nothing to change it. Lustful indiscretions have not decreased. It was ridiculous of Grandfather to think he could control the heady desires of the Aberronians. Innocent children are being discarded because their parents cannot give them everything they deserve. The number of children in our orphanages has exploded. Our charitable fund cannot cover the needs like it used to. I've searched the record books, so I know."

The illegitimate-child laws—one of Braidus's most passionate causes.

"Many also gained from those laws," King Brian replied calmly. "They will be loath to relinquish ownership. The resulting riots would turn the streets into rivers of blood."

"Did they not fight when the laws first came out? Did Grandfather not send the First and Second Waves to enforce it?" Braidus struggled to keep his tone even. His passion for this cause burned through our bond. "Greed ran rampant. People were thrown out of their homes and left to starve on the streets while legitimate family members took possession. Hundreds went to the Carasmille prison for disputing. He turned perfectly good citizens into criminals for something they had no control over." He took a breath and spoke calmly. "Children should not be blamed for the misconduct of their parents."

King Brian grimaced, the pain in his eyes obvious. This had to be a particularly sore subject with him. Braidus's expression softened, and I could tell he didn't enjoy hurting his father.

Andrew spoke up. "I agree with Braidus. I think we should reverse the laws."

King Brian's gaze flicked to Andrew. "That would make Braidus king."

Henry spoke before Andrew could respond. "The court has no love for Braidus. The illegitimate-child laws Grandfather put in place made Braidus an enemy in their eyes. Not to mention people still remember that he was banished for a while for treason. If you were to reverse the laws and make Braidus Crown Prince, the court would rise against it." To Braidus, he said, "I am in no way trying to shoot you down. You've proven to be a good man. I'm merely stating the facts."

"I know," Braidus said, expression grim.

"Isabelle is the deciding factor on Braidus or I becoming king," Andrew said, voice eerily calm and resolute. "If she cannot return and choose between us, the throne falls upon Henry. The laws could be reversed, and it would not matter for us."

"Yes," Braidus agreed, flipping his long hair back.

"No!" Henry held up his hands. "I am not going to be king."

"You have Aliyah. You don't get a choice," Andrew said sternly. Ignoring Henry's glare, Andrew tapped his chin thoughtfully. "What if we reversed the laws from this point forward? Help the future generations?"

"And do nothing for the ones who've already suffered?" Braidus asked. "These laws are a wrong on our part. It must be fully rectified. All those people tossed aside need to know they are worth something. We must recognize them, not just future generations, as full citizens of Aberron entitled to all inheritances and legacies."

Dominic spoke. "My father has a large investment in old Mr. Trevledger's mining operation. Harry, Trevledger's illegitimate firstborn, works harder than anyone else at the business. His mind sucks in information like a tornado and spits it out with perfect clarity. He's made his father and mine very wealthy. However, when Mr. Trevledger dies—which my father expects to happen within a year—his business will be given to his second-born and legally legitimate daughter, Meredith, and her husband, Corvis." His tone lowered as if he shared a great secret. "Word has it, neither has a lick of sense about business and Corvis squanders their money in pilfer and drink. Their company will end up in shambles within months, if not weeks. Father's been quietly preparing to pull out of the venture to avoid Meredith and Corvis and save our sundals."

"My older brother, Rhys, is good friends with Harry," Falden said. "I heard Meredith has offered for Harry to buy the business from her but at twice the inheritance value to repay their creditors and secure their future. Harry can't afford it."

"I've heard many similar stories," Braidus said, his expression frank. "Retracting the laws from this point forward would do nothing for people like Harry."

King Brian rubbed his chin. "What are people like Harry's sister, Meredith, going to do when they have been relying on that inheritance to secure themselves? It is not their fault to be on the receiving end either."

"I'd better see if they need any help," I said to Tomas.

"Wait." Tomas put his hand on my arm to stop me. "There's something you should know."

I stilled. "What?"

"King Jason was incensed when he found out his son had defied him by secretly bonding with Hannah and getting her with child," Tomas explained. "Jason wanted to punish Brian enough that he would not defy him again, so he created the illegitimate-child laws. Brian said it didn't matter. He would reverse them when he became king, thus making Braidus his heir. Their feud caught the attention of Isaac."

An ominous feeling pooled in my gut. "Uh-oh."

"Isaac sided with Jason and offered to ensure he got his way," Tomas said, his expression grave. "Jason agreed, and Isaac tied Braidus's life to the illegitimate-child laws."

My brow furrowed. "Wait, you're telling me that if King Brian reversed the laws, Braidus would die?"

"Yes," Tomas said.

"Oh, Gods," I whispered. No wonder King Brian has been so insistent on Andrew becoming king.

"It gets worse." Tomas grimaced. "Isaac put a silencing spell on Brian. He is physically unable to tell anyone why he won't reverse the laws. His body locks up every time."

I thought of how I'd circumvented Braidus when he held me captive by writing in the snow. "He can't write it or anything?"

"No." Tomas shook his head. "Isaac has given Brian the opportunity to break the curse. He created a room in their library only King Brian can enter every six months."

The king's personal library and record room. I recalled the time Henry took me to the library to help me get information about the Gods. He had shown me the door and warned me not to go near it. He had severely burned his hand when he touched it. "I know of it."

"Every six months since Braidus's birth, Brian has entered that room to try to break the curse," Tomas said. "He fails every time because Isaac enjoys Brian's persistence and watching him lose."

Why wasn't I surprised? "What must he do to break it?" I asked.

"It's really rather simple," Tomas said. "All Brian has to do is retrieve a crown meant for Braidus. However, Isaac puts painful and life-threatening obstacles in his way, and they are never the same. Every time Brian goes into the room, he has no idea what to expect. Here, I'll show you." Tomas took my hand in his.

A vision of the past appeared. King Brian stood beside the gate to the door with the king's crest on it. His lips were set in a thin line, his brows furrowed. His eyes were glazed, and his body quaked as if a gentle wind would push him over. He took a fortifying breath, his shoulders rising and dropping as he exhaled. His hand shook hard as he walked through the gate and reached for the door handle. The king's crest flared brightly as the door opened. He stepped inside a pitch-black room. A glowing orb appeared at the end of the small room, shining down on a black marble pedestal. A blue velvet pillow rested upon it, a thin silver crown on it.

King Brian stared at the crown with an expression of longing. It appeared only a few paces away, well within his grasp, but he made no move to retrieve it. He flexed his hands, his chest rising and falling rapidly. Then, as if not giving himself another second to deliberate, he strode forward.

Abruptly, the room grew to the size of a dining hall. The crown resided at the end, twinkling under the light of the orb as though taunting him. King Brian glared and continued to march toward it. Thick manacles attached to chains and two fiery balls appeared out of nowhere and latched on to his wrists. He stumbled as the weight pulled him down. Gritting his teeth, he trudged forward, leaving a trail of fire as he dragged the two balls behind him. He made it a few paces when an additional set of fire-ball manacles fastened themselves to his ankles. His veins popped as he strained to pull the load, a guttural yell escaping his lips. He made it another few paces, eyes never leaving the crown.

Five silver arrows whistled through the wind as they zoomed toward the king. He ducked, allowing one to fly over his head. Two struck the fiery balls attached to his wrists, and the balls exploded like black-powder bombs, the shrapnel embedding in his skin. Flames licked at his clothes. He cried out and dropped to the ground, rolling to put the fire out. Blood blossomed from all the little cuts he'd received.

Tomas took the vision away. "I think you've seen enough to understand."

I shuddered, disgust, anger, and horror filling my veins. How dare Isaac make King Brian suffer so? My hands curled into fists. I wanted to punch him with the power of a Goddess over Gods. "Why hadn't King Brian shielded himself with his blue magic?"

"His magic doesn't work in there." Tomas scowled. "Another one of Isaac's ploys. The room spits him out once he's passed out, hovering between life and death, and tally marks are burned into his chest for each failed attempt. It was wise of him to marry a green mage."

"This has to stop," I said, a hard edge to my tone.

Tomas nodded. "Haldren and I have tried, but Isaac refuses. I thought perhaps you might convince him."

I put a hand on my chest. "Me? What makes you think I can do it?" Already, I had to tread carefully around Isaac to keep my family safe. Challenging him over this might send him over the edge.

Tomas spoke animatedly. "You might not think it, but you have leverage. You're the only one among us who can feed the tree with the mage cores he's collected. He needs you if he wants to stay in power. Refuse to feed the tree unless he breaks the curse and sets Brian and Braidus free from the illegitimate-child laws."

"That is a big undertaking." I put a hand to my forehead, my body jittery with nerves.

Tomas put his hand on my shoulder and smiled encouragingly. "You can do it. I have faith in you."

I took a shaky breath and exhaled. "All right, I'll try."

I searched in my mind's eye for Isaac. Naturally, he stood by the tree, guarding it. I transported there.

He crossed his arms as he eyed me. "What do you want?"

I refused to let my fear show on my face. "I want to talk to you about the curse you've put on King Brian and Braidus over the illegitimate-child laws."

I stiffened as I felt his magic probing me. "Ah, you've been speaking with Tomas."

I straightened to my full height. "I think King Brian and Braidus have suffered enough. Remove your magic and let them reverse the laws, please."

His gaze narrowed, no doubt at my boldness. "If I say no?"

I matched his stance, allowing my anger at the injustice to overpower my trepidation. "There shouldn't be two classes of citizens within Aberron. You're making people suffer needlessly and for what? Some sick, twisted enjoyment? Remove your Gods-forbidden curse or you can forget about me feeding the tree."

Isaac's eyes flashed dangerously. "I don't give in to ultimatums."

I shook my head. "It's not an ultimatum; it's a compromise. You do something for me; I do something for you."

I didn't dare push my luck any further. Isaac still had me firmly in his grasp. I made sure he knew I looked at the broader spectrum with a focus on *all* the Aberronians these laws affected. My love for my family was not my main priority.

"All right, I'll agree to this, but don't expect me to be so lenient again." His eyes took on a faraway look. He waved his hand, then made a pulling motion. "I've eliminated the curse. Take King Brian to the room, and he will be able to retrieve the crown to place on Braidus."

"Have you also given King Brian the ability to speak about his experiences?" I asked, wanting to be sure he had truly undone his meddling.

"Yes, now go." He shooed me away.

I fought hard to hold back a smile as I transported to King Brian's study, my insides dancing. It was a miracle! I'd never been so proud of myself, although, it didn't embolden me enough to think I could take Isaac on to free the Creator and save the tree.

The second I landed, Braidus and Andrew shot out of their chairs and crushed me in a group hug. They showered my face with kisses. Their soft lips tickled, and I squirmed, laughing. Our hearts raced with excitement.

"I'm going to get in trouble!" I cried. "This is official Goddess duty."

Andrew and Braidus reluctantly pulled back. I snatched their hands, unwilling to let them go completely. Gods, I missed them.

King Brian gave me a genuine smile. "Welcome, Isabelle. We're delighted to see you."

"Hear, hear!" the boys chanted, their hands raised in a cheer.

"It's a pleasure for me as well." I couldn't keep the grin off my face as I viewed my family members. We were missing Joshua, Malsin, and Queen Averly. "Before I state my purpose, the whole family needs to be here." I pulled my hands free of Braidus's and Andrew's and searched my mind's eye for Joshua, Malsin, and Queen Averly. With a wave of my hand, I transported Joshua from the forge, Malsin from his healing rooms, and Queen Averly from the kitchens.

"What in the Gods?" Queen Averly cried as she appeared in the study.

My brother and Malsin blinked with confusion until their eyes landed on me. "Isabelle!" all three exclaimed.

I bit back a laugh. "Sorry to catch you off guard, but you need to be part of this. We're taking a trip to the library." I waved my hand and transported us all to the gate leading to the library door with the king's crest.

King Brian looked at me with uncertainty. "Isabelle . . ."

"Do not worry." I smiled at him, hoping I conveyed assurance. "It is my great pleasure to inform you that I have successfully convinced Isaac to allow you to reverse the illegitimate-child laws." With a flick of my fingers, I opened the door, revealing the darkened room. "The crown is yours. Go in and retrieve it."

King Brian's eyes nearly popped out of his head. His mouth opened and closed as if he didn't know what to say. Hesitantly, he took a step forward, his body trembling.

I put my hand on his arm. "It's all right. Nothing will hurt you. I promise."

I watched his expression change from one of fear to one of trust. Straightening his shoulders, he walked through the gate and into the pitch-black room with the confidence of a king. When the darkness swallowed him, I watched his journey in my mind's eye, the orb of light appearing and shining down on the pedestal holding the crown. King Brian quickly strode the few paces to it and reached out his hand, his fingers closing over the crown. A gasp of disbelief escaped his lips as he picked it up. He turned and walked out of the room at a fast pace.

Once he went past the gate, the silvery sparkle of Isaac's magic appeared and absolved the room, leaving nothing but a blank wall in its place. Clutching the crown to his chest, King Brian dropped to his knees and burst into sobs. Queen Averly swooped down to hold him against her, tears flooding her face. King Brian might not have been able to tell her what the room was about, but I had no doubt she had a good idea.

I hastily wiped my eyes as their emotional state started to undo me. Goddesses were meant to be stoic.

Malsin whispered to me. "Is there something I should be doing for them?" He gestured to the king and queen.

It was then I noticed the rest of my family looking between me and them in confusion and helplessness.

"No," I said quietly. "They need this. When the shock has worn off in a few days, set up some healing sessions so King Brian can talk to you about his experiences. He has been unable to tell a soul what happened to him in that room."

"What happened?" everyone asked.

"I should leave it to King Brian to answer," I said, nodding at him.

He looked up at me, his expression earnest. I read his thoughts. *"Ease their confusion. I don't have it within me to speak just yet."*

"As you wish." I turned to the rest of my family. "The reason King Brian hasn't reversed the illegitimate-child laws is because Isaac and King Jason put a curse on them." My gaze flicked to Braidus, then back to the group. "Isaac tied Braidus's life to the illegitimate-child laws. If King Brian reversed them and made Braidus heir, Braidus would die."

Braidus's face paled. My heart seized with his shock.

I gestured to the wall where the door had been. "A room was also created for King Brian to break the curse."

With a flick of my fingers, I allowed them to see images of his efforts to retrieve Braidus's crown, like climbing a tower of sand only to fall back down again and getting swallowed up. Showing his wrists bound by chains as he tried to outmaneuver a bull made of flames. Horror and anguish flooded the bond as Andrew and Braidus watched their father repeatedly get tortured near to death until the room released him and seared a new tally mark on his chest.

"Unfortunately," I said with regret, "Isaac put a silencing spell on King Brian, preventing him from being able to tell anyone. Every six months since Braidus's birth, King Brian has entered that room to try to break the curse and reverse the illegitimate-child laws. Isaac enjoyed watching him struggle and therefore never allowed him to win—until today."

Braidus sat down, his face ashen. Tears sprang to his eyes as he gazed at his father, who clutched the crown with a viselike grip. Braidus's heartache for all the times he'd argued over the laws and every ill thought he'd had about his father growing up poured through the bond. It was an incredible amount of regret to process. I trembled from the weight of his emotions and resisted the urge to enfold him in a hug.

"Please tell me this is the last of the Gods' meddling in our lives," Andrew said to me, his gaze pleading. "We can't take any more of it."

I flinched. I was a Goddess now. How cruel had I been, making them hope for my return when I honestly questioned if I'd ever be able to do so? Hadn't they suffered enough? Perhaps it was best that I cut ties and let them focus on what they had and could achieve in Aberron. It would certainly be more realistic to hope on what you could see—and to find love with someone who wasn't already promised to another cause.

My heart tugged as Andrew read the bond, catching impressions. His eyes widened as he caught how I'd interpreted his words. "Isabelle, I didn't mean—"

I held up a hand. "No, you're right. Our family has certainly had enough trials to last several lifetimes, and I am sorry to be involved in your reasons for it." I asked Boomer to check for any magical enchantments on them. He pointed out two things—the bond Haldren had made and the shields I had created over their mage cores when I brought Joshua back to life. "The only meddling left is the bond and the shields on some of your mage cores." A hole opened in my chest as I forced my next words out. "If you'd like, I can remove the shields and see what can be done with the bond." It killed me to offer this, but they deserved better. I was not a guarantee to happiness. "Then you'll all be truly free of us Gods."

"No!" An immediate refusal came from everyone.

Joshua put his hand on my shoulder. "You're not a problem, little sister. Since coming into our lives, all you've tried to do is good. We don't want to erase you."

"Yes," the other family members echoed.

"All right." I gave them a soft smile, appreciative of their support. Amidst that, I worried I was spending too much time with them and Isaac would get mad. "I must go. I'll come back and check in on you concerning the reversal of the laws when you're ready."

"Thank you, Isabelle," King Brian said.

I smiled. "My pleasure."

When I transported back to Haldren's living room, Tomas and Haldren rose from their seats and clapped.

"Well done, Isabelle!" Tomas exclaimed heartily.

"Excellent job," Haldren said.

I flushed at their praise. "Thank you."

Andrew's and Braidus's emotions coursed strongly through me the rest of the day, making it hard for me to focus as I returned to answering prayers. The royal family had chosen to take the rest of the day off and potentially the next day to come to terms with the torture King Brian had endured to reverse the laws. Our fury and anguish flared hot. I rubbed my chest, trying to ease the ache so often that I felt sure I bruised myself. I knew I could easily quiet the emotions from the bond with a flick of my fingers, but I didn't because I craved their closeness. Whatever they went through, I wanted to understand and be there for them.

It took two days for King Brian to return to the study to discuss the reversal of the illegitimate-child laws with the family. From Haldren's living room, I watched them through my mind's eye.

King Brian rested his forearms on the table and clasped his hands together. "I have a solution in mind."

Braidus smiled. "We're listening."

"Let's reverse the laws and give both parties that were wronged a dual partnership," King Brian said. "For example, the mining operation Mr. Trevledger runs—when he dies, make his legitimate daughter, Meredith, give the illegitimate son, Harry, dual partnership." He took a shaky breath and then exhaled. "They should be equal since both were wronged by the actions of their parents."

Yes! Turns out I didn't need to help after all. King Brian knew exactly what to do. "What about being king?" Andrew asked.

"You and your brother should both act as king," King Brian replied. "It would show that we're not leaving anybody out, including the monarchy. Also, it would give you two the freedom to have a life outside of this study. Overall stress levels would decrease and productivity increase as long as both of you do your part."

Henry grinned. "Yes! I don't have to be king."

"Who gets to be king after them?" Joshua asked. "Would both have to marry?"

"I think as long as one of them marries and produces an heir, we should be fine," King Brian said. "If both marry, then the first to have a child should be heir. The line will continue much the same after that. This dual kingship should only last for this generation."

"Not a bad thought," Braidus mused.

It's perfect.

Andrew looked at his cousin and then back at his father. "Henry is still on the docket to become king if Isabelle can't return and choose between Braidus and me. I refuse to be king without her."

Braidus's expression turned serious. "Same goes for me."

Henry groaned. I listened to his mental plea. *"Isabelle, get me out of this madness!"*

I sent a shielded thought to him. *"Believe me, I want to."*

Everyone gave Henry a strange look as he felt the zing and jumped. "Isabelle," he said simply.

King Brian leaned back. "If we push for the dual kingship, and Andrew and Braidus go on a new Walk around Aberron together, promoting the reversal of laws and each other, I could push back the time limits on marriage, giving you an additional year and a half."

The princes' eyes lit up.

Braidus pushed his hair away from his face. "Then, if Isabelle is still not able to come back within that time frame and Henry becomes king, will that affect the reversal of these laws?"

King Brian rubbed his chin. "We might get some backlash for promoting something that didn't end up happening; however, it should not directly affect the new laws. Those in this generation who have suffered will still have dual ownership of all the rights and heritages afforded them."

Andrew and Braidus looked at each other. I didn't feel any ill-will through the bond as they considered.

Braidus spoke first. "I am in agreement."

"I too," Andrew agreed.

I transported to the study, following through with my promise to check in with them. My gaze landed on King Brian. "I heartily approve of your plan." Pride seeped into my voice. "Andrew and Braidus are amazing as a team!"

Everyone chuckled. My heart grew warm as my mage mates' affection for me surged through the bond.

"I would be happy to offer my backing as a Goddess over Gods." I smiled brightly. "You could even call it the will of the Gods as it really is the best solution to avoid civil unrest."

King Brian grinned. "Excellent. May I call upon you to voice your support if I organize a meeting with the Aberronian people?" King Brian asked.

I smiled. "Absolutely. Work out the details, and I will return to ensure all goes smoothly," I said.

The prayers of a family in Aberron Cliffs screamed through my head. "*Gods, help us! Fire!*" I pressed my hands to my forehead. A father tossed buckets of water on a barn engulfed in flames. My heart went out to the desperation and exhaustion I could see on his face. I contained the fire with a bit of blue magic. Most of the animals had gotten out except for a batch of orange kittens no one knew existed. I found the mama cat crushed under a burning log. Gone, poor thing. Luckily, the kittens were old enough to survive without their mother's milk. I debated on leaving them since it was clear the family had too much on their hands to care for them. My family, on the other hand, might be able to help. I created a large wicker basket and set it on a clear spot on the table, then transported the four singed, mewling kittens to the basket. With a flick of my fingers, I healed the damage the smoke and fire had caused.

"Aww, they're so cute." Falden picked one up and snuggled it against his chest.

"Keep one if you want," I said. "Their mother just died in a barn fire in Aberron Cliffs."

Falden looked to King Brian for permission. Dominic and Henry now each held one. They smiled softly. The last orange tabby, no doubt the boldest of the bunch, jumped out of the basket and straight into King Brian's lap.

"Nachura will find homes for them if you don't want them," I said.

King Brian didn't look particularly happy to have a kitten foisted on him, but he said, "We'll keep them, Isabelle."

I smiled. "Perfect. They'll cover the seriously-lacking feisty department for me."

My family chuckled.

"I better go." I had finished what I needed to do, and any moment I tarried would be a provocation for Isaac.

"Wait." Braidus rose and took my hand in his. "I wish to thank you for the support you lent me through the bond over these last few days. You carried me through a difficult time, and I am extremely grateful for it." He squeezed lightly before letting go.

Andrew joined us. "I also would not be this strong without you. Thank you, love." He pressed a light kiss to my forehead.

My cheeks grew hot as I soaked in their gratitude. "You're welcome."

A bright flash and Isaac appeared. "Goddesses don't have time for casual conversation. You do what you came here to do and leave—unless you want my warnings to come true."

I blanched. "All right, I'm going." With my eyes, I offered an apology to my mage mates and returned to Haldren's courtyard.

Isaac again flashed into existence in front of me. "You have fifteen days before I'm considering your training over. Then I won't be so lenient. Visit your family in anything other than strict Goddess capacity and I will send them all to the Realm of Souls."

Fear and anger coursed through my veins. "I wasn't doing anything wrong! I helped with the illegitimate laws and found those poor kittens a home!"

"You gave in to your mage mates' affection," he countered. "A Goddess doesn't allow inferiors to touch her. From here on out, you are dead to them." The ring on my finger signifying my bond vanished. Isaac held it in his hand and turned it to glittering dust.

I inhaled sharply, forcing myself to not react. My family mattered more to me than anything else in the world. I didn't want to jeopardize them by doing something stupid.

Isaac's eyes danced with a twisted mirth. His lips curved in the barest hint of a smile at my submission. "You are under my rule, Goddess. Know your place." He vanished.

I balled my hands into fists, furious—yet defeated. I transported to the tallest peak in the Fraison Mountains. Snow swirled around me, and the wind threatened to knock me down. I pounded my fist into the ice and screamed.

My heart thumped hard against my chest. I caught impressions of Andrew and Braidus on the floor as they caught the brunt of my fury. I stilled, willing myself to calm down for their sake. A fleeting, traitorous thought raced through my mind. I let it go as quickly as it had come, knowing someone could be listening.

I closed my eyes and began building a safe place where I could release my traitorous thoughts. I pictured a flat, white surface. A floor. I added walls and a ceiling, then reinforced the structure to make it impenetrable. *Cast your weapons against it, and it will remain standing.* I pictured my favorite place in the whole world—the maple by the creek in Saren. I remembered the softness of the grass underneath my feet, the thick trunk of the tree, its roots digging into the earth. I could hear the creek's steady rush. The sky burst with oranges, pinks, yellows, and purples as the sun dipped below the horizon. The image firmly in my mind, I transferred it to the white room, my haven—a place I could think without being spied upon. The only thing missing was Stefan. My heart clenched. His death would always weigh heavily on me.

Once my haven was made, I turned my attention back to the real world. I remade my bond ring by searching with my mind's eye for silver, ruby, gold, and sapphire and transporting them to my hand. I molded the raw materials into an entwining circle, then slipped the new ring onto my finger. Then I returned to Astralind to resume my Goddess duties. Any thoughts I wanted to have in my haven would have to wait until I didn't have the Gods' eyes on me.

As I burst into the kitchens, I caught Haldren sampling an onion soup simmering on the stove. Edgar nodded at me as he pounded a ball of dough.

"You made Isaac mad." Haldren set the spoon on a sideboard, the air around him thrumming with excitement. It repulsed me. Anytime Isaac antagonized me, it was fuel for his fire.

"He made me madder." I snatched a clean spoon and sampled the soup too. "Needs a pinch of salt, I think."

"Agreed." Haldren reached for the salt. He sent me a shielded thought that radiated with pleasure. "*What are you going to do about it?*"

"*I'm going to throw you into Isaac's den while I make my escape,*" I thought back.

He turned to appraise me with cold blue eyes. I put on my most serious expression as I ladled the soup into two bowls. Something must have flickered in my head because his lips quirked. He said nothing, though, choosing instead to grab a plate of roast beef and two slices of buttered bread.

We kept to relative silence during dinner. I couldn't get rid of the feeling that Isaac watched us, probably expecting me to do something exceptionally rash in light of the anger I felt earlier. Maybe Haldren felt it too.

The other Gods popped in for dessert—a lemon tart with fresh berries.

Tomas grinned at me. "Mountaintop screaming looked refreshing. I might have to try it."

"Don't," Nachura said to Tomas, then spoke to me. "You nearly caused an avalanche."

"Your poor mage mates," Amora said as she licked the last bit of cream from her spoon. "I felt sorry for them."

I defended myself. "I had to do something to get my frustration out. Isaac would crush me to powder if I acted out on him." I'd barely gotten away with my little stunt to get the illegitimate-child laws reversed. Surely, I'd never be able to do something like that again.

"Yes," everyone but Haldren agreed.

"It is hard to follow orders when you're a natural rule-breaker," Zadek said sympathetically. "There have been times Isaac censured me over decisions I've made that caused me to want to strike out at him."

"Yes," everyone said. I smiled without humor. At least I wasn't alone.

# CHAPTER EIGHTEEN

HE FOLLOWING WEEK, I visited every temple around the world as Haldren introduced me as his successor to the priests and priestesses.

Jorrun, Aberron's high priest, said, "Word has quite gotten around already."

"Unfortunately, my transformation wasn't a quiet affair," I responded.

Jorrun chuckled. "Indeed not."

During my visits, I learned more about the temples and their purpose in serving the Gods.

Reginald, high priest of the Jamaylin Islands, explained, "Primarily, we are a gateway for the people to get direct help from the Gods, but we also have charging stations available at all hours of the day." He pointed to a bright flame in a bowl. "These flames are never allowed to go out."

Haldren said, "Each temple is equipped with every element needed for a God or Fate to refuel their magic."

"Thoughtful," I said.

Throughout these interviews, I remained subdued, waiting for the uneasy feeling that Isaac was watching to vanish. When it did after what felt like an eternity, I took Haldren to my haven.

Haldren surveyed my space with appreciation. He complimented me on the vividness before saying, "So you're finally ready to tell me what you've been stewing over in the recesses of your mind."

I rolled my eyes. "You know as well as I do that we have been watched."

"Yes," he agreed, a soft smile curving his lips.

"I need you to distract Isaac so I can speak to the Creator," I said.

"For how long?" Haldren asked.

"Five minutes at most," I said. "I'll be quick."

"Five minutes is a long time to distract Isaac." He rubbed his chin, considering.

"Time is running out," I urged. If I could free the Creator before my eighteenth birthday when Haldren had to leave, maybe I could convince the Creator to keep Haldren while I went home to Aberron. "You don't want to revert to your human self, do you?"

He wore disgust at the prospect. "No. I'd prefer to keep my position."

"Then you'll do it?" I asked.

He dropped his hand. "I'll do it."

"Dare I ask how?" I asked, suddenly apprehensive.

His eyes narrowed with fire and determination. "No, there's no reason to concern yourself. Do what you need to, and leave it to me."

"All right, just don't burn up the world or something while you're at it," I said.

We returned to Astralind. Haldren nodded at me, then vanished. The minute I waited seemed like an eternity.

Haldren sent me a shielded thought. *"It's safe. Go now."*

I set my sights on the Creator and transported, beads of sweat dotting my brow. I hoped no one would suddenly show up and stop me. I put my hand on the glass sphere and sent shielded thoughts to the Creator. *"Hello, Haddas."*

His deep voice penetrated my mind, and a familiar jolt struck my veins. *"Isabelle, risk taker."* I sensed this intrigued him.

*"Tell me how to free you."*

*"Gladly."*

His thoughts consumed me. I pressed both hands against the sphere for support, blind to the outside world. He spoke about so many things I struggled to keep track. His plan seemed just as insurmountable as Haldren's desire for me to fight. I prayed I could pull it off.

Haldren's voice broke through. *"You're out of time."*

Haddas released me. "*You have what you need.*"

I pushed away from the ball and transported to Haldren's sitting room. Taking a seat in a comfy white chair, I locked my knowledge of Haddas's plan into my haven. I itched to implement the first step, but I had to wait until three in the morning, when, as Haddas had said, Isaac would be sleeping and it was safe.

Haldren appeared beside me. "*The world does not burn, though we came awfully close to destroying it.*"

I leveled my eyes at him. "*It may still burn yet.*"

Around two in the morning, when I knew my family was asleep, I pulled them into my haven—much like Haldren had done to me with his wheat field. "I'm going to be doing some magic on you to keep you safe. It is imperative you stay calm no matter what you see happening to your bodies. Don't draw the attention of the other Gods. They can't know I'm doing this."

"You're scared," Andrew said. "Why are you so scared?"

I met his eyes. "I'm preparing to take my life back. It's time. I love you all." I waved them away.

I recharged my magic, then stepped inside and went to the kitchen, where I made a cup of hot apple cider and sat down at the table. Time appeared to move at a snail's pace as I waited for the clock to strike three. I listened to and answered a few prayers. Nachura was on duty tonight and was entirely focused on trying to fix a drought in Dregaitia, courtesy of the tree. Out of all the Gods, she was the least nosy, so I didn't think I had to worry about her peeking in on me. When the clock finally struck the appointed hour, I breathed a sigh of relief. Now, I had exactly two hours to place protective layers on my family before Isaac awakened. I felt jittery. Hopefully, nothing disturbed his sleep.

I looked upon my family in my mind's eye, most in their beds, except for Andrew and Braidus, who sat together by the fire in Braidus's rooms, conversing quietly. I searched for the bright glow of a soul deep in the recesses of their hearts. When I found it, tendrils of my gold magic wrapped around it. I envisioned the gold twine as a thread with the strength of the most powerful shield I could muster, then sewed their souls into their bodies. Should Isaac try to rip them out to send them to the Realm of Souls, it would weaken his magic to the point that I could kill him. I doubted Isaac would dare leave himself in such a vulnerable state.

I leaned forward and rested my head on the table, dangerously close to passing out. I reached into my pocket and felt the piece of recharging gold. Energy shot through me, awakening my senses. I sewed my soul into my body the same as I had for my family. Afterward, I placed golden shields over Henry's, Dominic's, and Falden's mage cores. I wouldn't make it easy for Isaac to take them. Last, I knitted golden shields into my family's skin, like the one I constantly wore, and then recharged my gold magic a third time. Pleased, I crawled into bed as the clock struck five. My two-hour window was up. Isaac would be awake now.

At breakfast, Haldren eyed me much like Malsin did when he turned into healer mode. I supposed he suspected something had happened during the night, but I wasn't sure he knew what.

Isaac sent me a mental message. *"Come to the tree, now."*

"Isaac calls," I said to Haldren, then shoveled a forkful of eggs into my mouth and transported over.

Isaac stared at the tree, his arms crossed over his chest, a frown on his lips. Twice as many leaves fell as before. I moved to stand beside him.

He conjured a yellow mage ball. "Feed the tree. It's been awhile."

"You're going to run out of mages," I muttered as I took the ball.

Isaac had me give thirty mage cores to the tree one after another, bringing the total to eighty-two now sacrificed. Every ball that disintegrated in my hands felt like a slash to my heart. I doubted I'd ever forgive myself for assisting Isaac in this.

Another week passed in subdued monotony. I kept an occasional eye on King Brian, waiting for him to finalize the details for the reversal of the illegitimate-child laws. I wanted to see that finished before I challenged Isaac. I felt a constant thrum of anxiousness from Andrew and Braidus as they waited for an update concerning my wish to free the Creator. I wished

I could ease their worry, but I couldn't bring attention to them yet. *Soon,* I said to myself.

I also had to keep a low profile because Isaac had become concerned that we Gods were using too much magic and thus overtaxing the tree. He lit into all of us, including the Fates, one day in Haldren's living room.

"I'm ordering you all to ration your magic." Isaac eyed us all severely. "No more frivolous uses—like transporting your meals from the kitchens. Use your two legs and walk to get them. It will be better for the tree if we can reduce the number of times you have to recharge."

Haldren had been so bold as to ask, "Will you be rationing your magic as well?"

"I might," Isaac said, but his tone and posture implied otherwise.

I fought back an eye-roll. Far be it for him to suffer. The other Gods and Fates seemed to be of the same mind, for I saw frowns everywhere.

"No more taking on big projects by yourselves either." Isaac paced as he spoke. "Connect your magic with others to lessen the amount of power you use." He stopped and pointed a finger at Nachura. "Especially you. Controlling the weather takes more grains of sand than answering prayers."

Nachura didn't argue, but I could see the fire in her eyes. She had closed her mind to listeners, but I had little doubt she felt none of this would be a problem if the Creator were freed.

Cassius folded one leg over the other and stared at Isaac pointedly. "We already have our feet in our graves. Making Isabelle feed mage cores to the tree is a pittance of what it needs and will only stretch the tree's lifespan so far. Are you going to wait until the dirt covers our heads before finally agreeing to free the Creator?"

"Yes," everyone including myself echoed.

Isaac snarled. "Do not question me."

He flared bright with power, and I stiffened, hating it when he got angry. The other Gods could stomach it better. The Creator had given them protection I didn't have.

It was silent for a moment before Isaac said, "I'll be checking in to ensure you're rationing." With a bright flash, he vanished.

There was much grumbling after.

"I guess I'll be walking to my house from here," Amora said sarcastically.

Astralind wasn't big enough to be called a country, but the island wasn't tiny, either, and all of us Gods and Fates were fairly spread out from each other. It would take hours before Amora reached her house on the other side of the island.

"You're welcome to take one of my horses," Haldren teased.

Amora laughed. "You know I detest riding."

"I haven't employed a cook in three centuries," Eli said. "Ada's cooks have been making an extra plate for me, and I've simply transported it over." His braids swung around his face as he grinned at Ada. "Guess I'm going to have to move in with you so I can 'walk' to the kitchens."

Ada tapped her chin thoughtfully, but her eyes sparkled with humor. "I might have a closet you can stay in."

Eli mock gasped. "A closet!"

We all chuckled.

It was stressful to be more mindful of my magic, especially after spending the last several months being trained to let it do practically everything for me. Although, I believed the other Gods had it worse than I did. They had been using their magic in excess for hundreds of years. Isaac often appeared unannounced to snap at them for not rationing enough. Some choice words were said when he wasn't around.

My tension ratcheted when the day finally arrived for King Brian to unveil the new law. After it was revealed and everything was settled with the people, I planned to make my move to free the Creator.

"I promised King Brian my support," I told Haldren. "I want to be by his side and instill a feeling of peace and goodwill in everyone so they'll accept it."

"I think it would be wise if the other Gods and I accompanied you," he said.

My lips curved into a half smile. "You think I'm going to destroy a monarchy by showing too much affection?"

He chuckled. "Something like that, yes."

I watched in my mind's eye as thousands gathered in front of the castle for the unveiling. The official notice had simply called people to congregate for important news. King Brian had refused to give details to anyone. No one knew what to think. The whole city of Carasmille had shut down for this.

Prayers came in. *"Gods, don't let this be bad."*

Dressed in their finest, my family stepped out onto the landing in front of the castle doors. The boys, Malsin, and Joshua gathered off to the side. King Brian, Queen Averly, Andrew, and Braidus moved closer to the edge to be seen. King Brian took one more step, putting himself in front of the others.

I signaled the other Gods with a thought. *"I think it's time."*

Wide-eyed spectators greeted us as we transported to the landing.

"Welcome." King Brian smiled, though I sensed his uneasiness—a perfectly normal reaction to having all six Gods and Goddesses appear out of nowhere when he only expected me.

I joined King Brian and spoke loud enough for Andrew and Braidus to hear. "The others are here to make sure I don't show affection lest Isaac take action."

"Oh." King Brian cleared his throat. "Shall we get started, then?"

I smiled. "Yes."

King Brian faced the crowd and magnified his voice. "Welcome, my beloved Aberronians. I acknowledge with me Haldren, God over Gods; Tomas, God of intellect and negotiations; Amora, Goddess of women; Nachura, Goddess of nature; and Zadek, God of men. Beside me you may recognize Lady Isabelle, Aberron's champion, now exalted to a Goddess over Gods."

Murmurs of fear ran rampant through the crowd. "All the Gods here?"

King Brian waited for things to die down before continuing. "I have gathered you here to discuss laws that have affected Aberronians—including myself—for twenty-seven years. The illegitimate child laws."

Two different sets of prayers flowed through my mind. *"Please, Gods, remove these cursed laws."*

*"Gods, please! I can't give up my inheritance. I have nothing to fall back on. I'll be ruined!"*

King Brian spoke in a firm tone. "Henceforth, the illegitimate child laws will be reversed. All those considered illegitimate will be fully recognized and entitled a share in the inheritances and legacies of their parents and family."

Exclamations of surprise rippled through the crowd. People shushed each other so they could continue to listen.

"In its place, we are implementing a new law called United Families. Those who gained from the illegitimate child laws must now have dual ownership with those who lost. Full details of the United Families Law will be posted in every city in Aberron."

"Share?" The congregation looked to their left and right for confirmation that they'd heard right.

King Brian angled himself toward his sons, who stood to his left. They took a step forward to be seen better.

"The United Families Law will also affect the monarchy," King Brian said. "Even a king must abide by the regulations placed on our people. As such, my cherished firstborn son, Prince Braidus, previously known to the law as my illegitimate child, will now be recognized as Crown Prince Braidus Alexander Sorren. He is to join his brother, Crown Prince Andrew Brian Jason Sorren, as a dual ruler of Aberron. Together, they will share in the duties of king, bringing forth a union of peace and equality for all."

Shock crashed over the people like a tidal wave. "Two kings?"

Prayers of a different nature rose up. *"Please, Gods, save us! Our king is insane!"*

King Brian deactivated his magic and said to me, "I think it's your turn."

I raised my hands, calling for silence. "It is the will of the Gods that the United Families Law roll forth. We have seen an imbalance in Aberron since the illegitimate child laws came into effect during the reign of King Jason. Thus, we hope to see the United Families Law ease the inequality. We bless the Sorren Monarchy in this new venture of fairness and peace."

I raised both hands and created a wall of green-and-gold mist infused with feelings of goodwill and rightness. I pushed it forward, and it moved through everything—buildings, trees, people. The Gods mentally chuckled at the trick to make the people believe we'd blessed the whole of Aberron with something powerful.

King Brian signaled Henry, who stepped forward bearing the thin silver crown King Brian had spent twenty-seven years trying to retrieve to reverse the laws.

King Brian took the crown and turned to Braidus. "I give you this crown, with our people and the Gods as witnesses." Grinning with pride, he placed the crown on Braidus's head. "You shall now be known as Crown Prince Braidus Alexander Sorren, dual heir to the throne of Aberron."

"Thank you," Braidus said in shock. It was a giant leap to go from banished, illegitimate prince to crown prince and future king.

My heart soared.

Andrew raised his hand. "To Braidus!"

"To Braidus!" My family saluted.

I resisted the urge to join them.

Slowly but surely, the Aberronians started clapping. The ones I suspected were previously considered illegitimate whooped and hollered. With the largest grin I'd ever seen, Braidus bowed regally to the crowd—all those years of believing he was no better than a speck of dirt lifted off his shoulders. With his hair blowing in the wind, he stood taller, prouder, a glorious sight to behold.

A joyful laugh escaped my lips, and Braidus's gaze snapped to mine.

Haldren appeared at my side. "Isabelle . . ." He gently grabbed my elbow and started pulling me away.

But I stumbled backward, aching to run in the opposite direction. Braidus stepped forward, reading my wishes. Out of the corner of my eye, I caught Joshua holding Andrew back as well.

King Brian threw his hand out to stop Braidus. "No, you cannot touch her. Let her go, son."

I read the apology in Braidus's face as he stilled. King Brian patted his back in consolation. Braidus shoved his hands in his pockets, his regret racing through the bond as he turned his back to me.

My tentative allegiance to the Gods shattered. I couldn't stand another minute away from my family. I didn't care that it was a little earlier than I planned and that Aberronians were still congregated. *The fight starts now.*

Haldren stiffened, his cold blue eyes appraising me. He sent me a shielded thought. "*You realize what this means.*"

"*I do,*" I responded. "*Stop anyone who gets in my way.*"

"*You have my support for as long as you need it.*" Haldren released me.

I strode to Braidus. Grabbing his arm, I pulled him around to face me.

"Isabelle," he gently objected. "You shouldn't."

I cupped his face in my hands, feeling his soft beard against my fingers. "Trust me."

I pressed my lips against his, kissing him with all the pent-up fervor stored within me. Braidus pulled me flush against him, his surprise giving way to passion. Gods, I could get lost in his kiss.

I pulled back as Isaac appeared in a bright flash. *Right on time.*

Braidus's eyes widened. "You used me."

I pleaded forgiveness with my eyes. "A good memory to keep my demons at bay."

"I warned you, little Goddess," Isaac growled. "Now suffer the consequences."

Isaac waved his hand, transporting Braidus and me to the white stone courtyard with the tree and the Creator. I allowed myself a moment of panic despite knowing I needed to be near the tree for the next part of my fight. I didn't want Isaac to believe I was pleased to be here lest he get suspicious.

Haldren and the other four Gods also flashed into existence.

"You disobeyed me, and now you must watch your prince die," Isaac said. "His two colors will help the tree."

Braidus's eyes went wide.

I stepped in front of him protectively. "I won't let you lay a hand on him."

Haldren waved his fingers, and my sword appeared in my hand. I sent him a mental thank-you.

Isaac laughed, eyebrows raised. "You wish to fight me? Have you lost your mind?"

"Perhaps," I acknowledged. "But it's my life to give up."

"No, not your life. Your family's."

He snapped his fingers, and the rest of my family appeared beside me, alarmed. King Brian clutched Queen Averly to him.

"Say goodbye." Isaac made a pulling motion with his hand, and family members jerked, some crying out in surprise. His eyes nearly popped out of his head. "What have you done?"

"Protected them from you," I said.

With a blink of his eye, Isaac conjured a volley of daggers and hurled them at my family. Instinct told me to deflect them; strategy told me to wait and save my magic. Queen Averly screamed, but the blades bounced harmlessly off them. My knitted shields had done their job. *Thank Haddas.*

"Leave them alone," I demanded, jaw set. "This is my fight."

Isaac's expression hardened. "So be it."

Nachura darted over to my family. "I'll protect them! You take care of Isaac." She ushered them over to stand by the Creator, out of harm's way.

"I love you guys!" I shouted to my family as I angled myself to face Isaac, sword at the ready.

In my mind, I heard Haldren shout to Amora, Tomas, and Zadek, *"Either you help Isabelle against Isaac to free the Creator or you do nothing. That's an order."*

*"I choose nothing,"* Zadek said.

I didn't suspect otherwise, not after Isaac had granted him the life of a God.

"*Jerk*!" Amora said. "*I'm helping*!"

"*Long live the Creator*!" Tomas said.

I sent shielded thoughts to Amora, Tomas, and Haldren. "*Help me deflect*!" I twisted out of the way of a large mace hurtling toward me and set my sights on the tree. It was crucial I get to it for the next stage.

Masses of sharp objects—knives, swords, arrows, spears, anything with impaling capabilities—zoomed in my direction. Haldren, Tomas, and Amora blasted the weapons as they neared me. I dodged the few they missed as best I could while inching toward the tree. Suddenly, a series of explosions shook the courtyard. Would I be crippled before I made my destination? I needed to save my magic as much as I could, but I also had to fight back. With a flick of my hand, I turned and sent several weapons flying back at Isaac. They vanished as they reached him.

I saw an opening and sprinted toward the tree, banking on the hope that Isaac wouldn't try something drastic and inadvertently damage it. Sweat dotted my brow. Adrenaline raced through my pounding heart. Blood rushed through my ears. *This is it.* I coated my sword in blue flames.

Isaac advanced, his expression hard.

My heart seized when I realized that my family watched, helpless and terrified, from near the Creator, but I knew they were safe under Nachura's watchful eye. "I'm done following you." I plunged my fiery sword into the trunk, straight through the Mark of the Gods.

A series of gasps reverberated through the courtyard. Time slowed as the Gods and my family stared in horror. The four Fates arrived, eyes wide, mouths agape.

Blue fire danced from branch to branch as it went up in flames. Opal ribbons shot from the uppermost limbs and swirled in the air. In seconds, it crumbled, coating me in ash and smoke. My sword clattered to the ground, the blue flames extinguished.

"You've killed our world!" Isaac thundered.

Isaac's anger was fully directed at me, where I hoped it would remain, off my family. With the tree gone, he had no reason to protect me so I could feed it mage cores. I suspected he would put more effort into taking me out, but I planned to do the same to him. Our fight was about to get substantially cutthroat.

He created a tiger of smoke and shadow with red, burning stripes and eyes. The tiger grew until it was the size of a house. It then opened its mouth and roared, flames shooting forward.

*Gods forbid.*

Haldren shouted to the other Gods and Fates, "If we're all going to die, let's make sure it isn't with Isaac ruling!"

Dark clouds rolled in and covered the sun, plunging the scene in near darkness. Lightning curled around Isaac's hands, forming whips. He struck the beast and sent it charging, jaw open to reveal the inferno inside.

I dodged it by jumping into the air and then searched for a way to get close to Isaac without losing my life in the process. I had to be near him to finish him.

"Down, kitty!" Tomas threw a mammoth water bead at it, but the liquid evaporated on contact. The tiger hissed, then turned around and began the chase, passing right through Tomas as though he were a soul. *Haddas's last wish.* Protection for the Gods.

Isaac joined me in the sky. A lightning whip hit my shield, jarring my senses. I cried out as I was catapulted through the air and bright flashes of color darted past me. My family had joined in the fight. I smiled at their courage.

I flinched as a streak of light cut through my shield and nicked the flesh underneath, singing my cheek.

Emory and Cassius created holes through the dark clouds, allowing streaks of light to shine through so I could better see Isaac. Four additional tigers prowled the sky, keeping Haldren, Amora, and Tomas busy. Ada and Eli joined Nachura as she protected my family in the fight. Zadek hovered under a ray of sun, arms folded, eyes watching with interest. *Jerk.*

I ducked as another lightning whip grazed my skin. A tiger roared above me, spewing molten fire over my head. I transported across the sky. I had to do something about those cats or I'd never get close to Isaac. I held my hands out. Out of smoke and shadow, I created a house-sized version of Boomer. Ice blew out of his mouth. "Be a good boy and chase the kitties!" I told him.

Boomer barked, then bounded off, shooting frosty breaths at the cats to extinguish their flames.

"Very clever," Isaac whispered in my ear.

I whipped around. He'd managed to sneak up on me. I cried out as his lightning whips snaked around my wrists. He pulled them tight, threatening to pull my limbs from their sockets. Then he leveled a good kick to my gut, and I doubled over as my shield disintegrated. Lightning surged through me, sizzling my insides. High-pitched screams tore from my throat.

Haldren appeared. "No!" He tried to grab the whips but his hands passed through them. Magic flared from his fingers but did nothing. "Stop, Isaac!"

"She's killed us all!" he yelled. "She deserves to be demolished!" He yanked on the ropes, sending additional jolts into my body.

I screamed until my voice gave out. Abruptly, the pain lessened, and I choked, trying to get air into my lungs.

Isaac transported all of my family members to surround me. They gazed upon me in dismay, their cheeks stained with tears. None of us could speak. The rest of the Gods and Fates gathered as well.

"You knew you couldn't fight me and win." Isaac snarled. He gestured to my family with the tilt of his head. "You knew the only way you could be with your family was if you joined them in death."

*Yes.* I thought of my loved ones already in the Realm of Souls. Patterned after our current world, the place appeared comforting and peaceful. I remembered the happiness on Stefan's and Nathan's faces as they fenced. Their souls were safe. Nothing could hurt them there. My eyes flicked to my loved ones, hoping they saw the apology in them.

Haldren exhaled loudly, no doubt having read my thoughts.

"Your soul will never see them in the afterlife." Isaac snapped his wrists.

The lightning cords cinched tighter, digging into my soul. My head fell back as I howled in pain. Regret surged through my heart. I wished it wasn't ending this way. A fleeting childhood memory floated through my mind. I felt a sudden urge to protect it, though I could not think of why.

Joshua and I stopped in front of the redwood tree Da had been making into a playhouse. It looked like a plain tree on the outside, matching all the others. The magical illusion hid the door and window.

I touched the bark. "Is this the right one?"

"Say the password and find out." Joshua shrugged.

I giggled. "Bubbles."

Above my head, a circular window appeared, and in front of me, a small red door. I grinned and bounced on my feet. "It worked!"

Joshua turned the handle. "Go inside. I have a present for you."

I looked up at my brother. "You only give me presents when you don't want Mama to know you snuck off."

"Come on, Isabelle. I've been chasing you around the forest for an hour," Joshua begged, hands out in front of him. "I won't be long. Promise."

I frowned. "Mama says I'm not old enough to be on my own."

"Mama said that when you were four. You've been five for a week." Joshua leaned against the doorway. "Just stay there till I come back. You promise?"

"All right." I hoped Mama wouldn't get mad if she caught me. I'd tell on Joshua if she did.

Joshua smiled wide. "You're the best little sister."

I stepped inside. As the door shut, I heard him say, "Pop." I knew that meant the magical illusion was back in place. I hurried up the stairs. On the floor of the empty room, I found a soft pink bear with a white bow.

I ached for my childhood and to be five again with laughter, pink bears, and bubbles. Boomer flashed in front of my mind, whining. *Bubbles,* I told him. *Make me happy one last time.*

Isaac's harsh laughter cut through the air. My head fell forward, not of my own will. Isaac gripped the lightning with one hand. With the other, he reached out to touch the hundreds of golden glowing bubbles coming from my fingers. They floated and popped as they collided with a family member or God.

Isaac roared with laughter. "So much power and this is all you come up with?"

Haldren gripped his forehead, ashamed. Conquered. The other Gods and Fates looked upon me with pity. Out of the corner of my eye, I saw Boomer's and Isaac's tigers join in a quest to chase the spiraling bubbles. I read disappointment, sympathy, and love on my family's faces. No judgment for my last moments.

Isaac's amusement overrode his concentration on the lightning he was using to kill me. He held his hand out, popping the bubbles that floated his way. The small part of my brain I'd spent my energy protecting suddenly came to life. I thought of Haddas trapped inside that sphere, deceiving those who gazed upon him into believing he slept. *No more.*

A bubble formed in my palm, fueled by all but one grain of gold sand. My hand twitched, releasing it to land upon Isaac's outstretched finger. My heart stopped as I watched the perfectly formed ball begin to spin. An eternity seemed to pass before it collided with Isaac.

*Pop!*

The bubble sucked him inside and grew to fit his stature. Simultaneously, the outside hardened. *Immobilized.* Shock twisted Isaac's features. I had led him straight into my trap, just like he had the Creator.

The dark clouds dispersed. The tigers departed. The lightning holding me upright vanished.

I fell.

# CHAPTER NINETEEN

FELT STRONG ARMS AROUND my middle and briefly looked into the gaze of my rescuer before my eyes dimmed.

"Isabelle!" Braidus screamed.

My eyes fluttered open. My head lay on Andrew's lap, with Haldren and Braidus hovering over me. Boomer lay on his stomach in his cage, head down, eyes closed, unmoving. I started to slip into the comforting darkness. *Rest.*

Andrew shook me awake. "Don't you dare!"

Haldren took my hand in his and closed his eyes in concentration, his body brightening with a golden glow. My veins tickled. The feeling intensified, morphing into the familiar buzz of adrenaline. Boomer opened his eyes and lifted his head, showing signs of life. Haldren let go.

I attempted to sit up, Haldren, Andrew, and Braidus helping me to do so. I cried out at the intense pain radiating from head to toe. I took several slow, even breaths as tears leaked onto my cheeks. *Gods, this hurts.* I searched for the source of pain, but I appeared to be whole.

Haldren grimaced. "Your soul is torn beyond our repair. I fear you may be in agony for eternity."

Wide-eyed, I sought Andrew and Braidus. "Is this affecting you?"

"The bond is not broken," Braidus said, placing his hand on mine. "We feel your pain but not to your extent."

"It's more like the ghost of it," Andrew explained. "Like using green magic to heal someone. We can handle it."

"I'm sorry," I whispered.

"Don't be, love." Andrew kissed my forehead. "You're alive. That's all that matters."

I moved to stand, and the pain intensified threefold. I bit my lip, drawing blood. Haldren stepped back, and with my mage mates supporting me, I shakily stood on my two feet. I had to get to Isaac and take his power so I could free the Creator and save our world from annihilation. Gritting my teeth, I took a tentative step forward, but my legs buckled, and my breath hitched. Andrew caught me. I trembled in his arms.

He gently cradled me against his chest. "Let me be your legs."

I blinked back more tears. Andrew turned so I could see the courtyard. My family huddled near the Creator. The Gods and Fates stood in the ashes of the tree, their faces anxious. Isaac, now trapped in the sphere, had been placed beside the Creator.

The ground rumbled with the beginnings of the world's destruction. I didn't have much time.

"Take me to Isaac."

Andrew brought me to the bubble with Isaac in it. My family and the Gods and Fates gathered behind us. I wondered how Isaac felt, falling for the same ruse he had used on the Creator. I pressed my hand against the glass. I flinched at the sudden loudness in my head. *"I underestimated you. Release me and I'll help you free the Creator."*

*"No,"* I said firmly. *"Your reign is over."*

*"Gretlin!"*

I inhaled and exhaled slowly, trying to focus through the pain. I opened a section of the glass to reveal the tip of Isaac's finger.

*"No!"* he cried.

I pressed my finger to his, then shut my eyes and delved into his core. Haddas had warned me that Isaac could still do damage if he could materialize beside me, but I had followed his instructions, making sure Isaac couldn't touch me when I created his prison.

Smoky silver ribbons streaked about. For a moment I just stood there, entranced by their brilliance. Shaking it off, I brought forth Isaac's six cores. He had a fourth or less of every color. I grabbed the silver ball. Gold tendrils wrapped around it. I envisioned the glass as malleable, much like the bubbles I had created, and there was a burst of light and then a ribbon of gold that penetrated the glass to touch the grains of sand.

I bit back a cry at the intense heat that filled my body as Isaac's power transferred to me through the ribbon of gold. As I took his magic, he reverted to a simple mage with one ball of red sand.

I drew back, exhausted, and fell into Andrew's arms, my fight with Isaac having taken its toll.

Haldren placed his hand on the sphere, and his eyes widened. "Isaac's not dead. You made him human."

The other Gods and Fates touched the sphere to confirm Haldren's words, exclamations of surprise rippling through them.

The ground trembled again, this time harder. We had to free Haddas before all the magic left by the tree was gone. Isaac hadn't left me with enough power to do it on my own. Without the tree, I couldn't recharge.

"I need every mage in the world here immediately," I ordered the Gods and Fates. "Transport them now. We have to free the Creator immediately."

Zadek spoke, his tone objective. "The tree is gone. What can Haddas do but stand with us as we die?"

I leveled a steely glare at Zadek. "Just do it."

The Gods and Fates spaced themselves a few paces apart in a line in front of the Creator and Isaac and got to work. Bright flashes dotted the courtyard as mages appeared one after another. They looked around in fear and confusion. Some flinched against the brightness of additional mages arriving. I saw mages from Nistier in the north, Sondrei in the south, Kashtine in the east, and Aberron in the west. Young and old, rich and poor. A cacophony of languages filled the courtyard as people questioned being there.

Activating my yellow magic, I stepped out of Andrew's grasp and rose above everyone's heads so they could see me. The wind pushing against me helped calm my trembling. I spent a good portion of my energy pushing the pain back to focus. Using purple magic, I made sure all tongues would understand my words.

I magnified my voice. "Do not fear. No harm is intended."

The Gods and Fates continued bringing people as I spoke. I guessed there to be a thousand congregated, with more arriving every second.

"I will explain when everyone has arrived. Until then, please remain calm."

Another few thousand arrived, some I recognized, like King Nickoli and Amarilla. The ground now rumbled steadily, bringing with it fresh rounds of fear and apprehension. In my mind's eye, I could see storms brewing over the oceans, the waves forming whitecaps. Multiple avalanches occurred on mountaintops. A humungous tornado formed near the Sea Traveler's channel between Aberron and Dregaitia.

Squabbles broke out amongst a few mages from countries that considered each other enemies.

I repeated my plea for all to remain calm. "This is not the time to fight."

Haldren called to me. "Everyone of an age to help is here."

Amora leaned against Tomas. "My arms are tired."

Tomas chuckled. "Mine too."

"Thank you," I said to the Gods and Fates. I turned my full attention to the masses and raised my hands for silence. "I have assembled you all because we need every mage's help to save our world. The magic holding our earth together is running out. We face annihilation at this very moment." I gestured to Haddas. "An evil Fate trapped the Creator of our world in this ball. I ask your help to free him and save us all from death."

The air rippled with unease.

"Will you all join hands so that we may connect our magic?" I asked. "It will take every one of you to make this happen. Not a single mage can be left out."

The ground shook more violently. People screamed as they tried to steady themselves.

"Please, we don't have much time."

The courtyard glowed with magic as one by one, the mages grasped each other's hands. My family, the Gods, and Fates joined the ranks. I lowered myself to the ground, putting myself at the head of the line in front of Haldren, my body trembling with the effort to remain upright. I breathed slowly, in and out, to combat the excruciating pain, praying for the strength to complete the task at hand.

I took Haldren's hand. "Are we ready?"

"We're ready," Haldren said, his expression determined.

A fiery buzz of adrenaline raced through my veins as I joined my magic with that of the others, then put my hand on the sphere. Boomer barked, seeking direction. *Break the glass.* Multicolored light flared from my hand and hit the sphere, the glass splintering and cracking.

"It's working!" Nachura shouted.

A cry escaped my lips as I poured more power into it, giving it everything I had. The ball shattered, showering me with fragments of glass. Haddas stumbled forward, throwing his hands out for balance as he opened his eyes.

"Yes!" Cheers rent the air.

I sat clumsily in the pile of glass, my energy spent. Andrew and Braidus rushed over and sat beside me, allowing me to rest on them. They grimaced at my shuddering breaths. Emory and Ada clung to each other, weeping with joy. Tomas swept Amora into a hug and kissed her cheek.

Haldren approached Haddas.

Haddas spoke. "Allow me a moment to recharge."

He lifted his hands. Opal light flared about him as he harnessed the power of the sun. The rest of the Gods and Fates gathered around him.

When the opal glow diminished, he said, "Now, I must see to the tree."

"But the tree has been destroyed," Haldren said, gesturing to the ashes.

"Indeed." Haddas stepped into the masses.

Andrew scooped me into his arms and followed behind the other Gods and Fates trailing the Creator. The multitude of mages quickly moved out of the Creator's way. He stopped on the other side of the courtyard in front of a Mark of the Gods inlaid in the cobblestone. We formed a circle around him.

Haddas waved his hand, and the stone beneath his feet crumbled. Everyone took a healthy step back to avoid falling into the rapidly growing black hole. A wide set of stairs appeared. Haddas descended, and we followed, flaming torches lighting our way into an expansive cavern. Millions of crystals in a multitude of colors hung suspended from the ceiling. Haddas raised his hand, and suddenly, all of them glowed with light, brightening the room.

"Whoa," Andrew said.

"Gods, this is crazy," Henry said from somewhere behind us.

Haddas strode across the smooth cavern floor at a fast pace. At the end of the room, a sheet of water fell from the ceiling into a pool. We stopped before it. Haddas flicked his fingers, and the waterfall disappeared to a chorus of gasps. We gazed upon a humongous glass ball inside of which stood a full-grown tree with opal bark and multicolored leaves.

The second tree.

Haldren turned toward Andrew and me, then met my gaze, his expression accusatory. "You knew."

A soft smile graced my lips. "I did."

Haldren shook his head while muttering, "You never cease to amaze."

Haddas touched the glass, opal light flared from his hands, and the ball disintegrated. He strode into the water and onto the small island upon which the tree resided, then put his hand on the darkened Mark of the Gods on the trunk. Opal light blazed around his form. The Mark of the Gods flickered, then brightened to a brilliant white. The tree shuddered, its branches and leaves dancing as it came to life. Opal ribbons of smoke burst from the tree and swirled around the cavern in a spectacular show.

Abruptly, the cavern ceiling fell away as though there had never been a roof of crystals in the first place. The sun shone through, and the water Haddas had walked through to get to the tree vanished. The ground rumbled more violently, and Andrew gripped me tightly. Exclamations of surprise went all around as the cavern floor lifted us all to the surface. *Whoa.*

Haddas grinned as he patted the tree in a friendly manner, giving me the sense that fond words passed between them. With his smile still in place, he turned to face the multitude. "The earth is saved."

Exclamations of joy echoed through the hosts of participating mages. I spied Nachura hugging Haldren, tears in both their eyes. Braidus clapped his brother on the shoulder and took my hand in his, squeezing softly.

*It is done.*

Haddas raised his hands, quieting the people. "I wish to offer my heartfelt thanks to everyone who helped free me." He gestured to the tree behind him. "And for making this possible. The earth surely would have been destroyed without your help. Consider yourselves heroes. I will now return you safely to your homes with my blessing that you may lead peaceful, enriching lives."

With a wave of his hands, the congregation of mages vanished. Only my family, the Fates, and the Gods remained.

Haddas walked over to our group, where Ada embraced him.

He laughed softly as he hugged her back. "I've missed you, my dear friend."

My family and I watched with soft smiles as the Gods and Fates each hugged him.

After a few minutes of warm reunions, Haddas said, "I would like to see to Isaac."

Braidus took me from Andrew as we followed the Creator. My family sat on white benches close to Isaac's prison. The Gods and Fates grouped behind Haddas. He lifted his hands, and the sphere holding Isaac melted away, with Isaac stumbling as he regained his footing, fear evident in his features.

Haddas assessed him much like a disappointed parent. "Isaac, son of Nistier. What have you to say for yourself?"

"You know my mind," Isaac said, hands clenched.

"Yes," Haddas readily agreed.

"Kill me and be done with it, then," Isaac said, jaw set.

"No, I think not. Death would be a reprieve." Haddas shut his eyes and stilled.

Isaac glowed red with the activation of his magic. Alarm filled his face as he examined himself. The light vanished.

Haddas opened his eyes. "I have confiscated your magic. You will be sent back to Nistier to live out your life as a commoner. You will die at an old age as nature intends and then be sent to the Realm of Souls to be judged there. No one will recognize you for your power again."

Haddas waved his hand, and Isaac vanished. I searched Nistier and found him cursing in the midst of a flock of sheep on a country mountainside. Haldren shook with silent laughter.

"What's so funny?" I asked him.

"Haddas sent Isaac back to his humble beginnings. *Hate* is not a strong enough word to describe how Isaac feels about sheep." Haldren grinned.

I did not know Isaac well enough to judge his sentence, but I figured Haddas did. Despite all the wrongs he had committed against me and my family, none of us had been trapped in a ball for some three hundred years.

My thoughts turned to my shredded soul. How could I fix it? Was it something that couldn't be fixed? Would I be stuck in eternal pain? I decided it would be all right. What mattered most was that I had saved my family and the world by freeing Haddas. Besides, I'd always been good at handling pain. I could learn to stomach this too. I would not let it define me.

Shifting my focus to what was next, it struck me that, despite of what I'd done, I didn't get to decide my fate. Haddas said he had the power to change it, but he'd never said he would. Sudden fear stole my breath. My mage mates stiffened.

Andrew kissed my forehead. "It'll be all right, Isabelle."

"You worry too much," Braidus said. "I'm sure you will be rewarded for your efforts."

Despite their assurances, I couldn't dislodge the terror. By the time Haddas approached us, silent tears poured down my cheeks.

"Please, don't take me away from my family."

Haddas surveyed us. Andrew and Braidus clutched me protectively. The rest of my family closed in around us. I knew it down to my fractured soul—I needed them just as much as I needed air. I would not survive without them.

Haddas spoke to Haldren with a hint of surprise. "You made a family strong enough to defeat my magic and free me."

Haldren smiled. "The best way I knew how to ensure your freedom."

Haddas clapped Haldren's shoulder. "Love is a powerful tool. It allows us to do impossible things."

"Indeed," Haldren agreed.

Haddas faced me. I shrunk into my mage mates, shuddering through the pain that gripped me. He smiled with gentleness in his expression. "Do not be afraid, Isabelle. I will not take you from your family."

I dared not hope. "Truly?"

Haddas laughed, his voice rich and melodic. "Truly." He gestured to my loved ones. "Your love for each other is so deeply ingrained in your souls it would be a travesty to separate you."

I covered my mouth with my hand and burst into sobs. Delighted shouts fell over my ears. I was pulled from two different directions as Andrew and Braidus pressed kisses to my face. Joshua and Henry each clapped a hand on my shoulders.

Joshua voiced a question. "What about Isabelle now being a Fate over Fates?"

"Yes," Haddas answered. "I would like to discuss this."

Tomas spoke. "The Aberronians are panicking without their king."

King Brian nodded. "Better send us back, then."

"Braidus and I will stay with Isabelle," Andrew told his father.

"Apprise me when you're home," King Brian said.

I waved goodbye, hoping it wouldn't be too long before we were reunited.

Tomas sent everyone but my mage mates back to the castle.

Haddas took my hand in his, and a jolt of electricity traveled up my arm. "Allow me to fix your soul and regenerate your magic." He shut his eyes.

My body flamed with energy. The pain and trembling melted away, clearing my mind and restoring my body. I'd never again take it for granted.

"You are whole once more." He dropped my hand.

I exhaled in relief. "Thank you."

"You're most welcome."

Haddas then transported all of us to an ornate dining room about the size of the family room King Brian usually used. Gold and cerulean blue dominated much of the décor. With a flick of his fingers, the table filled with food. I saw cookware from all the Gods' and Fates' kitchens.

"You'll forgive me for discussing business over a meal, but it has been some time since I've eaten." He sat at the head of the table.

The rest of us took our seats.

Haddas studied the fare before him and transported portions of what he wanted onto his plate. Once he began eating, the others dug in. Haldren wiggled his fingers and filled my dish with food. This did not escape my princes' notice.

"Yes, Haldren has had to feed me too," I admitted ruefully. "He's been as diligent as you two in ensuring my health."

Andrew's and Braidus's approval of Haldren rose. Perhaps they recognized that he might actually care for me as more than just a tool for his quest.

Haddas cut into his roast chicken. "You have a gift for bringing people together. Men with no blood connection have become true brothers. The loyalty you have garnered is astonishing."

"Everyone deserves a good support system," I said. "It doesn't matter whether they are connected through blood."

Haddas smiled. "A fighter for the right cause. I have waited some time for someone like you."

Alarm bells rang. I spoke vehemently. "You're not taking me away from my family."

"I wouldn't dream of it," he said evenly.

"Then what are you suggesting?" I asked. "If you want the Fate magic, take it. Bestow it on someone who can accept your rules of all work, eternal solitude, and celibacy."

Haddas laughed. To Haldren, he said, "By the earth! She is perfect."

Haldren's lips curved in a conspiratorial smile. "I knew she would be."

"This may earn you another thousand years," Haddas said, picking up a spoon to dip into a chocolate pudding.

Haldren's expression brightened considerably. "That would be most welcome."

"If she agrees, consider it done," Haddas said.

I wasn't entirely sure what was going on, but I had a strong urge to clock Haldren over the head with my sword—as soon as I found it among the ashes of the tree and transported it into my hands. My mage mates had similar feelings.

Haddas turned his gaze to me. "We work well together, don't you think? You came up with an excellent plan to free me, and I am grateful for your fortitude in accomplishing it. Not many could have withstood the opposition that came with it. I want you to remain as Fate over Fates—with your bonded by your side."

I gestured to Andrew and Braidus. "You would make them immortal?"

"Yes, I would give them the power of the Fates," he agreed.

I eyed him with suspicion. "Why?"

"You said it best." He turned my words on me. "Everyone deserves a good support system. Love is not lost on me. One day I, too, will have need of a wife."

My eyebrows rose in surprise.

He took a breath. "I have been searching for a person of your caliber with a strong bond for millennia."

I decided to be forthright. "I can't be a Fate and have my life in Aberron. The two roles do not mix."

Haddas sipped from a mug. "Do not underestimate my power. I built this world." He paused as if listening to a thought. "Indeed, my interaction with Isaac did not serve me well, but perhaps I was better for it since it brought me you."

I shivered, not liking the possessiveness I saw in his eyes. Had Haldren forced me to defeat Isaac only to offer me up to a more formidable beast? The last thing I wanted was to be owned. Under the table, I gripped Andrew's hand. I just wanted to go home. Was it too much to ask?

Haddas spoke, his eyes assessing again. "I will give you till your seventy-fifth birthday. In the scheme of eternity, it is not so long. You may have your life in Aberron, marry, have children, the whole dream. You'll even experience growing old. On the day of your seventy-fifth year, I claim you and your bonded to be Fate over Fates for me. I will give you a grand estate, regenerate your cells, and make you young again. You will be able to walk through the world of your progeny and ancestors at your leisure."

I looked to my mage mates. Both wore furrowed brows.

"Seventy-five years to be bound for eternity," I whispered.

"You would not have to be celibate with whomever you marry," Haddas said.

"What about the person I don't choose?" I asked him. "Say I marry Braidus. How can I expect Andrew to be by my side as a friend for eternity? Or vice versa."

"You face that problem now," he answered pointedly.

"Yes, but a lifetime compared to an eternity is different," I replied.

"I could break the bond with whomever you don't marry," Haddas said. "Then you won't have to worry about your happiness affecting them on an emotional level."

"That's certainly something to think about," Braidus said, sounding intrigued.

"I'm not sure I'd want to break the bond if Isabelle didn't choose me," Andrew said. "I've gotten so used to her presence, I think it would hurt too much."

"Hmm," Braidus sounded like he might agree. "Perhaps we should re-visit that idea after Isabelle has chosen."

"Agreed," Andrew said.

"Haldren manipulated two bonds for you out of caution." Haddas sipped from his mug again. "However, bonds are meant to be between one man and one woman to continue a line of magic through procreation. All mages, young and old, share a bond with someone. One of your princes has another companion. If you do not choose him, he will join with his other intended—giving me four Fates instead of three."

I leaned forward. "Who?"

Haddas's eyes twinkled. "I will not influence your choice of a partner." He touched my hand, my veins momentarily buzzing with the activation of my magic. "I have taken your ability to search for bonds."

"Who will act as Fate over Fates while I am human?" I asked.

"I will take over that role," Haddas said. "Haldren can remain as a God over Gods, and life will continue as it has."

I bit my lip, contemplating. I turned to Andrew and Braidus. "This affects you just as much as me. What do you think?"

"I want more time to think about it," Braidus said.

"What if we agree and we're stuck in an eternal nightmare?" Andrew asked. "What if being a Fate is awful? How are we to know?"

"The work of the Gods is strenuous," I told them. "I answered prayers even while I bathed. But it can be rewarding. We'd have the power to visit our loved ones in the Realm of Souls and we'd still be active participants in the world. If one of our progeny goes insane, we can knock some sense into them."

Braidus's eyes lit with the appeal, but he said, "It is a lot of power and responsibility."

"Yes," Andrew agreed, rubbing his clean-shaven chin.

"As kings of Aberron, you'll have decades to get used to responsibility," I said. "You've been trained since birth to handle big decisions."

"It sounds as if you've made up your mind," Andrew said.

I took a breath. "I trust myself. I trust you two. We've gone through so much together. Our bond is the strongest thing out there. I felt you even as a soul. Would you rather leave the world in someone else's hands, someone you didn't know, couldn't trust—or in ours?"

"We do not know the Creator," Braidus said, gesturing to Haddas with a tilt of his head. "What if this benevolence is an act and you reach seventy-five years for eternal miserable servitude? How much of our lives will he control?"

I pursed my lips. Braidus had an excellent point. I suddenly found myself no closer to an answer.

Haddas spoke. "The terms laid out for the Fates are similar in nature to those for the Gods. The main difference is the ability to care for the Realm of Souls."

"I generally like to keep busy, but I don't envy the prospect of working *all* the time," I said.

"That will change. I will seek additional bonded pairs like yourselves to fulfill similar roles, allowing you more time for leisure," Haddas said. "You will be the first and therefore highest-ranking Fate, other than myself."

"Why didn't you start out this way?" I asked.

"My earth is young, barely two thousand years old," he answered. "Populations have increased. I have a greater need of Gods who can keep my world running smoothly than I did before."

"What happens if the population outweighs our resources?" Andrew asked.

"A new Creator is then born. After extensive training with the current one, he or she will make a world with a new tree and take a portion of the people to it to begin anew," Haddas explained.

"Hence your need of a wife," Braidus supplied.

"Yes," Haddas said simply.

Andrew raked a hand through his hair. "You would swear an oath that we get to experience a full life in Aberron first?"

Haddas nodded. "I will reduce Isabelle's powers, lessening her responsibility to the world. When your time is finished, I will elevate the three—perhaps four—of you to Fates over Fates."

I waited for a bad feeling, some sense of dread that I'd be making the worst decision in the history of decisions. I felt Braidus and Andrew doing the same. We looked at each other, reading the bond and each other's facial expressions. Braidus shrugged. Andrew cocked his head. When nothing ominous surfaced, a mutual decision was made.

I turned my gaze to Haddas. "We accept."

"Excellent." Haddas stood. He waved his hand over the table, making the dishes disappear.

The other Gods and Fates, save for Haldren, resumed their duties. I found it a little disconcerting that after the day we had had, it was back to work as usual. Then again, the world couldn't stop just because we had an eventful day.

Haddas transported us to a sitting room also decorated in blue and gold.

"Now I will lessen your power." He took my hand in his and activated my magic. My skin began to glow with each of my six colors. He let go. I dropped into my mage core to check. Five glass balls materialized—yellow, red, blue, green, and purple—with a healthy amount of silver grains interspersed.

"The silver magic will automatically transfer as you use your colors. The others you will need to recharge," Haddas said. "I want to ensure you have enough should you mistakenly empty your core doing something you previously could."

"Good thinking," I said.

He smiled. "Now, to ensure you won't end up in the Realm of Souls." A cool opal mist descended upon the three of us. I felt no different afterward. "As a reminder."

My left hand burned. I looked down to see the Mark of the Gods had reappeared. *Well, that was short-lived*, I thought. Braidus and Andrew now wore marks as well.

"It is complete. Enjoy your lives in Aberron."

# CHAPTER TWENTY

BEFORE WE KNEW IT, we stood outside the castle under the light of the moon.

We looked at each other, eyes wide, mouths agape, none of us entirely sure if this was real. Then Andrew grinned, Braidus smirked, and I laughed. We raced up the stairs. Down the hall of the royal living quarters, I pounded on doors. Then I stood in the middle of the hall and waited. One by one, our family members stepped out, some rubbing sleep from their eyes.

I held my hands out, grinning recklessly. "I'm home!"

"For good?" Joshua asked.

"For good," I confirmed.

My brother crushed me to him. "Thank the Gods!" Shocked, I didn't protest the inability to breathe. Hot tears wet the top of my head as Joshua spoke through thick emotion. "I'm so happy. I love you, sister."

My heart warmed. "I love you too."

Henry stole me from Joshua and pulled me into a hug. "I'm so excited you get to be here for my wedding! Aliyah will be thrilled."

"I wouldn't dream of missing it." Sheepishly, I asked, "When is it?"

He laughed. "It's in two days, on Aberron's Independence Day. I'm pretty sure I told you in my prayers."

Independence Day, coincidentally my birthday.

"Sorry, I wasn't allowed much time to think about family," I responded.

"I want explanations," King Brian said.

He ushered us into the sitting room. Joshua, Dominic, and Falden lit lamps as well as the fireplace. The air thrummed with excitement as we settled in, taking up couches and chairs. I glanced at my mage mates. *Where to begin?*

Queen Averly spoke, her tone concerned. "Sons, why is the Mark of the Gods on your hands?"

"We've made a deal with the Creator," Braidus said.

"You what?" the family exclaimed.

Andrew raised his hands. "Calm down. It's not that bad of a deal."

We spent the better part of the night discussing the agreement over cookies and hot drinks. The others digested it with amazement and suspicion.

"You're sure Haddas won't go back on his word?" Joshua asked.

"We're not entirely sure, but we feel like he's being truthful," I said.

Henry spoke enthusiastically. "Seriously, you'll never taste death again. How awesome would it be to grow old, then get to be young again and be given power for eternity?"

"I guess you won't need me around, then, will you?" Malsin asked, hands resting on his knees.

"Of course I will!" I cried. "Haddas never said anything about putting a protection over my life. I can still get hurt—or worse."

Malsin chuckled. "Just checking."

I stood. Emotion clouded my voice as I looked at everyone. "We are a family. I trained hard as a Goddess. I fought Isaac and freed the Creator. My soul was literally torn to keep us together. If you're going to leave me, you better have a Gods-forbidden good reason."

"There's the Isabelle we know and love." King Brian's blue eyes shone with pride and affection.

Joshua's brow furrowed. "I've been going over the fight you had with Isaac in my mind, and there's something I wanted to ask you." At my nod, he said, "Isaac said you killed the tree because you knew you couldn't defeat him and wanted to join your family in death, but that wasn't the real reason, was it?"

I shook my head. "No, I had to kill the tree because I was the only higher being, other than Haddas, with a connection to the tree and the ability to feed it." I shuddered at how many mage cores I'd sacrificed to it. "I had become Isaac's lifeline to success. He never would have actively fought me but instead put all his power into killing you guys as a punishment for my actions. I gave you every ounce of protection I could, but Isaac's power could've broken through had he really tried. I couldn't allow that to happen."

Some time passed with everyone lost in their thoughts. As the clock struck five, everyone but I, Andrew, and Braidus vacated the room for a much-needed nap. On the couch, I pulled my mage mates close and fell asleep. When I woke up, I refused to open my eyes. It had been a long time since I felt this comfortable, and I didn't want to lose it. My head lay in Andrew's lap; my legs rested on Braidus. Both were sitting up and talking quietly. I feigned sleep.

"I never actually believed this moment would come," Andrew whispered. "Since I first set my eyes on her, I've lived with this gut-wrenching fear that I would lose her. I nearly did several times. Now she's here and safe. I don't know what to do."

"I know what you mean, brother," Braidus said. "When Isaac had her in his clutches with the lightning whips. Her screams—Gods, it haunts me."

"Mmm, I can still hear it ringing in my ears," Andrew said.

Regret laced Braidus's tone. "I am ashamed to say I lost faith in Isabelle when she made the bubbles. I truly believed Isaac had broken her. At that crucial moment, all I could think of was how grateful I was that she tried. If I could go back, I'd give her the encouragement she needed." He sighed. "She told me to trust her, and when she needed me most, I didn't."

"We were all fools," Andrew said, sounding disgusted. "I don't think anybody gave her the support she needed, myself included." He choked on emotion. "We should have been cheering for her till her last breath. We let her down."

"She should be disappointed in us, but I haven't detected it. Not even a breath of it," Braidus said in wonder.

Andrew gently brushed a strand of hair from my face, his love for me burning through my heart. "That's Isabelle for you. She loves us when we haven't earned it—selflessness at its finest."

"Yes," Braidus agreed.

A beat of silence passed. I almost decided to wake up.

Then Braidus asked, "Who do you think has the second bond?"

"No clue." Andrew gently rubbed my cheek with his thumb. "I'd be lying if I said I didn't wish it was you. I want Isabelle for myself."

"Same, brother," Braidus said with grim conviction.

"She could end up choosing whichever of us has the second bond, leaving the other with nothing," Andrew said.

"Perhaps that would be best," Braidus replied. "I do not care to think of another woman after enjoying Isabelle's attentions."

Andrew chuckled softly. "She feels intensely. Can you imagine experiencing another woman's emotions on top of hers?"

Braidus shuddered. "Say no more. I think I would break my bond with Isabelle just to avoid that."

"Isabelle is unique," Andrew mused. "It's possible other women don't feel as intensely as she does."

"True," Braidus agreed.

"I can't imagine ever wanting to break my bond with her," Andrew said.

Braidus sympathized. "I understand that." He lightened his tone. "You know she'll probably turn matchmaker for who she doesn't choose, like she did with the Dregans."

Andrew mused. "No doubt the second she makes her choice, she'll be seeing who has the second bond. She'll not want to see either of us without a partner. Father was bonded to your mother but found love again with mine."

"How much can your heart take before you call it quits, though?" Braidus asked. "I loved Kiella, now Isabelle. Opening my heart a third time might be too much."

"Isabelle has loved three men. Stefan, me, and you," Andrew said. "You know that if Stefan were still alive, she would be happy with any of us. At least only one of us has to marry. I don't envy the prospect of being forced into a marriage just to stay king."

Braidus snorted. "All of Aberron knows we are bonded to Isabelle. Only the wealth and fame hunters will not mind that our affections lie with another woman. I do not care to align myself with that filth."

"Neither do I," Andrew said.

I opened my eyes, deciding I'd heard enough. Not quite ready to leave the comfort of my mage mates, I slowly stretched. I knew it was time to make a choice. I wanted to marry and have children and be blissfully surrounded by love, but I was scared of the pain I would feel in letting go of a piece of my heart and hurting whoever I didn't choose. It frustrated me. Why did love have to be so complicated?

"Isabelle," Andrew spoke. I knew he and Braidus had been reading the bond, catching impressions of my thoughts. "This has to end soon. You can't lead us along forever."

I stood. "I'm not planning to. I know it's time to end the dual courtship. I want to choose between you and get married. I just . . . I just don't want it to be today, all right?" I folded my arms, more emotional than I wanted to be.

I read the sympathy in their expressions.

Braidus stood and enfolded me in his arms. "Promise me you won't keep putting this off."

I pressed myself into him, inhaling his cologne. "I won't, I promise, but what you're asking is harder than facing Isaac," I mumbled into his shirt. "It will hurt."

"We'll always share a bond, Isabelle. We'll still be in your heart." Braidus kissed the top of my head.

Full-blown anxiety coursed through my veins now. "This is going to kill us."

Andrew spoke, eyes blazing. "Regardless, it has to be done."

"Soon," I agreed.

Henry popped his head in. "There you are. Uncle Brian is looking for you three—something about a treaty with the Dregans, Nistierans, and

Jamaylin Islands now that Isabelle is back. We're having lunch in the study. Meet us there."

I walked hand in hand with my mage mates, a rush of excitement enveloping me. I had until my seventy-fifth year to walk these halls. Fifty-seven years of freedom with a family I loved more than anything. Nothing could be better.

King Brian greeted us with a smile as we entered. "Have a seat, eat something, and then we'll talk."

The rest of the family already sat with plates in front of them.

Over our meal, King Brian spoke. "The other royals put a clause in our treaties that in the event you did manage to escape your fate, we would renegotiate. You may not have the full power of a Goddess anymore, but you're still formidable."

"And not as governed by the Gods," Joshua added.

"We must contact them immediately to alert them of your new status lest all our hard work go to waste," King Brian said.

"Allow me." I activated my magic and sent a mental message to King Cekaiden, King Nickoli, and Prince Jakobe. "*This is Isabelle. In exchange for freeing the Creator, I have been granted life in Aberron. I'm told we need to renegotiate our treaties. In a couple of minutes, I'll meld our minds so we can discuss how you want to proceed with the treaties.*"

I watched the clock for the two minutes, then connected with them. King Nickoli sat at a dining room table with a report in his hand. King Cekaiden strolled in a rose garden. Prince Jakobe waded in a pool with a waterfall.

All three wanted to know the details of my return to Aberron.

I briefly recounted my fight with Isaac, freeing the Creator—which King Nickoli and Prince Jakobe took part in as mages—and the agreement with Haddas. The royals watched my memories with rapt interest. "*I have close to the same amount of magic as before I ascended. To ensure trade and peace with Aberron, I am willing to share.*"

"*Nistier will come to talk,*" King Nickoli said.

"*As will Dregaitia,*" King Cekaiden added.

"*And the Jamaylin Islands,*" Prince Jakobe said.

"*Excellent. I shall await your arrival.*" I closed the connection and turned to King Brian. "They will be on their way."

"Good. Now, I need to make a statement to our people. The Aberronians should be apprised of your return." King Brian pushed his plate away to make space to compose the statement.

Andrew announced, "I think we should plan a wedding for Isabelle."

I sucked in a sharp breath. *What in the Gods is he thinking?*

"Has she chosen?" Joshua asked, eyes darting to my mage mates and me.

"No," Andrew said, seeming entirely unconcerned. "But we've already agreed it's time to end the dual courtship."

"Yes," Braidus said. "Our feelings have been made clear. It is time for a decision."

Annoyance flashed through me. While I agreed with the princes, I'd just barely returned from being a Goddess. Couldn't they see I needed a few days to adjust? "How am I supposed to plan a wedding without a groom?"

Braidus shrugged. "Perhaps the choice will become clear as you plan it."

I could see minds considering. "What about Henry and Aliyah's wedding? We should be focusing on their blessed event." I didn't want to steal any of the attention they deserved.

"Or we could make it a double wedding like the Dregans," Henry suggested. "The whole court will already be here. It'll save a lot of time and expense. We could do a sunrise-sunset wedding or one after the other."

"Seriously?" His offer stunned me. There weren't many people willing to share their wedding day with someone else.

"Yes!" Henry laughed. "This will make it a whole lot easier. You'll fret yourself silly trying to organize a wedding and figure out who to marry. With my plan, all you need to do is walk down the carpet in the throne room in a pretty dress and pick a prince. Quick and easy."

"How gracious of you to offer, Henry." King Brian smiled at his nephew.

"Are you sure Aliyah won't mind?" Queen Averly asked.

"I'm sure I could talk her into it," Henry said confidently. "She should be here with her parents within the hour."

I got out of my seat and paced. My emotions were a jumbled mess of eagerness to marry, fear of the pain that would come when I chose, and uncertainty about taking some of the focus off Henry and Aliyah by marrying on the same day. "I'm not so sure about this."

"No one is going to force you into anything." Braidus moved to get out of his seat. "If you really think we should wait, we will, but I know Andrew and I are ready, and I think underneath your worries, you are too." He took my hands in his. "We're wearing thin waiting for your answer."

I bit my lip, weighed down by Braidus's words. My eyes found Andrew. I read confirmation in his expression.

"Our dynamic will change, but you're not going to lose anyone," Andrew said. "We'll be here as a family, always."

I sighed. "All right. I'll give you my decision on the morrow."

"Then you'll proceed to marry that person so you don't start second-guessing," Henry said in a tone that brooked no argument.

I detested bittersweet moments, but it made sense. "Yes, Henry."

Braidus pressed a light kiss to my cheek. "It'll turn out all right, I'm sure of it."

I wished I had his confidence.

Henry scrambled out of his seat. "Aliyah is here." He ran out the door.

She must have used the bond to get his attention. I had done that a time or two.

"Now, on to my statement." King Brian held a pen over a blank sheet of paper.

Queen Averly said, "We should make it simple. Isabelle abdicated the role of a Goddess in favor of following her heart. Her magic has been reduced. She is Lady Isabelle, Aberron's champion, once more."

"Sounds good to me," I said.

King Brian wrote quickly, then handed me the pen. "Please sign next to mine."

I signed my name and gave it back. Using a locket, King Brian summoned someone to make copies and distribute them.

Henry entered the study, leading Aliyah. Both wore grins. Aliyah's parents trailed behind them with pinched faces. I had the stark impression they did not like whatever had been decided.

"Aliyah agreed," Henry said excitedly. "We can proceed with the two weddings tomorrow."

"I'm so happy you've returned, Isabelle," Aliyah said warmly. "You've made so many sacrifices. I think you deserve some happiness. Henry and I are delighted to help."

I felt bad. "I really don't want to take the attention away from your big day."

Aliyah's parents nodded subtly behind her, just as I figured.

"Certainly, I can—"

"Nonsense." Aliyah shook her head as if she wouldn't hear any more of it.

Henry's blue eyes blazed. "You already said yes. You can't take it back."

Right. "If you insist."

"We do," they said together.

"Then I give you my heartfelt thanks." I smiled, feeling blessed to have such good friends.

*Gods help me, I'm getting married tomorrow.* Happiness and anxiety wrapped themselves around me. I was ridiculously excited to see my dreams of having a husband and eventually children fulfilled—especially after believing it would never happen. Simultaneously, I was concerned about choosing between the princes. I loved them both deeply, but which would make me happiest? What if I ended up making the wrong choice?

Along with Aliyah, Queen Averly, Princess Liliana, and Lady Amdor, I attempted to help plan the last-minute details for tomorrow's festivities. Most of what they said went unheard. I only hoped I nodded in the right places. The men deemed wedding details women's territory and remained in the study.

Queen Averly put her hand on my arm.

I blinked. "I'm sorry, what was that?"

"Dresses," Queen Averly said.

"What about a dress?" I asked, clueless and way out of my depth. The last thing I remembered was flowers, or was it dessert? *Gods, I'm doomed!*

A bright flash and a gorgeous white silk dress with diamonds sewn into the bodice appeared in my hands. A note fluttered and landed on top. *Deep breaths, Isabelle—Amora.*

Queen Averly seemed the only one not surprised. She smiled. "Excellent. That's taken care of. Now, I was thinking about a seating arrangement that would . . ."

I clutched the dress, lost to the world again.

Sometime later, Queen Averly led me to the dining room for dinner.

As I approached the table, I heard Andrew ask Braidus, "Do you think we pushed her too soon?" I heard the worry in his tone and felt it in the bond.

"Time will not make a difference," Braidus said. "This is a difficult decision. Her reaction to it won't change even if she has a hundred years to decide. It is best we do this now."

"Maybe this dual courtship was a bad idea to begin with," Andrew said, feeding off my emotions. "Neither of us thought we'd actually be able to marry her. Now we've made this harder on ourselves."

"True," Braidus agreed. "But doesn't it also feel good to know that Isabelle has conquered her fate? That we've reached the point of marriage?"

Andrew nodded vigorously, his expression brightening. "Indeed. The impossible has happened. We should celebrate it."

As I sat between my mage mates, both reached out and took one of my hands in theirs. Their compassion brought tears to my eyes. I loved them more than life. How could I choose between these incredibly good men?

# CHAPTER TWENTY-ONE

O N THE DAY OF celebrations—Aberron's Independence Day, my birthday, and now the wedding—I woke to find my sword lying by my side. It had a pretty pink bow tied around the hilt and a note that read, "Happy returns—Haldren." I hugged my blade to my chest.

I slipped out of bed and stretched. *Eighteen.* In the span of eternity, it seemed short, yet I doubted I would ever forget it considering what was planned. I didn't suppose I would lament a single birthday since I would revert to a youthful state at the end of a long life in Aberron.

I grabbed my robe from the back of a chair and slipped it on. Opening my door, I stopped short. "*What in the Gods?*"

Stacks of brightly wrapped presents filled the room, rising above my head. I couldn't see a path to the bathroom or the door leading to the hall. A note fluttered in front of me. I snatched it. "Happy birthday from Haddas, Eli, Ada, Cassius, Emory, Haldren, Nachura, Tomas, Amora, and Zadek."

Knowing they would hear me, I said, "Dear Gods in Astralind, thank you for the gifts. You're all very thoughtful." *Now, how am I going to get to the bathroom?* I swear I heard chuckling.

I started taking packages to my sleeping quarters to get enough space to fly above the rest when someone knocked on my door. "The entrance might be blocked!" I shouted.

I heard some pushing and what sounded like boxes scraping across the floor. Joshua cursed. "What in the Gods, Isabelle?"

"Help a sister!" I cried. "I can't get to anything." I managed to clear enough space to fly. Thank goodness for the tall ceilings. "The Gods apparently go to the extreme for birthdays."

"Figures," he said. "I'll get the boys to help. Happy birthday, by the way. I wanted to be the first to tell you. My present will probably get lost in all this." His gaze swept the room.

I grinned. "Thanks, Joshua. That means so much to me."

I flew to the bathroom to wash up. Afterward, I dressed in soft black pants and a cream-colored shirt, then flew out of my room to find Queen Averly. She held my wedding dress for me. I sucked in a deep breath and exhaled as I landed in the hallway, enjoying the open space.

I stepped into the family room, where Princess Liliana and Lady Amdor hovered over Aliyah with hair brushes.

Queen Averly clutched her heart in relief. "Oh, Isabelle, you're here. I was beginning to worry you'd run away."

"I'm sorry," I apologized. "The Gods filled my room with birthday presents, and I couldn't get out. I had to fly to reach the door."

Queen Averly shook her head. "There's always something with you." She put her hands on my shoulders and gently steered me to a seat beside Aliyah. "Happy birthday, by the way."

I smiled. "Thank you."

Aliyah reached over and squeezed my hand. "Happy birthday and wedding day."

I returned the gesture. "Thank you. Happy wedding day to you too."

"Have you chosen?" she asked.

Everyone stilled to listen.

"No." A bundle of nerves and despair hit me.

"I'm sure you'll make the right choice when the time comes," Aliyah said, trying to be encouraging. She rose to put on her dress, a stunning off-the-shoulder cream creation.

Queen Averly styled my hair with diamond pins. I slipped into the floor-length silk dress Amora provided and did the buttons running up the side. It hugged my curves.

"These showed up this morning." Queen Averly handed me a pair of silver slippers. She then put a diamond necklace around my neck. Glittering earrings graced my ears, and sparkling bracelets encircled my wrists.

Queen Averly's eyes glistened. "I've always wanted to dress a daughter for her wedding. You are gorgeous."

Princess Liliana bumped shoulders with Queen Averly. "One of your sons is going to be very lucky, just like my Henry."

They chuckled softly. Aliyah blushed as Lady Amdor beamed at her daughter.

Despite earnestly wanting to get married, I trembled head to toe at the thought of having to decide between my mage mates. I'd never been more indecisive in my life, and that in itself scared me. Maybe I wasn't cut out for this, after all. "On second thought, I think running might be prudent." I went to make a mad dash for the door.

"Isabelle!" the ladies cried.

A bright flash and Amora appeared. A flick of her hands and I was frozen. "You're not escaping this one, my dear."

"I can't do this!" I exclaimed, wishing I had the use of my limbs. "I don't know who to choose!"

I'd spent all night trying to tell myself it would be all right and Haddas had given us the option to break the bond with whoever I didn't marry, thus making it easier. But nothing I said to myself stopped the panic seizing my heart. It was like a faucet had been turned on and the knob had broken, preventing me from shutting it off.

"You will when it's your time to walk down the aisle," Amora said, undeterred. She briefly turned her attention to Aliyah. "Don't be nervous, Aliyah. You and Henry are perfect for each other. Your love is powerful and will see you through many happy years."

A maid stepped in and bobbed her head. "Majesties, we are ready."

"Excellent," Queen Averly said. Her eyes darted to me with a question.

"I will keep her with me until her time," Amora said to Queen Averly.

Aliyah, Princess Liliana, Lady Amdor, and Queen Averly exited.

Amora took hold of my arm. "Let's find a nice spot to watch a lovely couple get married, shall we?" A bright flash and we stood on the dais in the throne room. "We're invisible. If your mage mates see you now, they'll be distracted from Henry and Aliyah's nuptials."

*Good thinking.*

I inhaled a heady aroma. Flowers of every kind imaginable, from roses, delphiniums, and lilies to dahlias, sunflowers, and so much more floated above our heads in an explosion of color. I sensed Nachura's hand. The blue carpet had been switched to white. White-and-gold banners hung between the pillars. Rays of morning sun shone through the windows. Hundreds of ornately dressed men and women sat in white chairs lined up along the sides of the carpet. The entire court, no doubt. They chattered softly. A few women fanned themselves.

A man in the back sneezed loudly and repeatedly. "It's these Gods-forbidden flowers!"

Amora snapped her fingers, and the man quit. A quartet of violinists played soft melodies in a corner near the front. The men in my family plus Lord Leavesden, Lord Amdor, and High Priest Jorrun stood at the foot of the dais, all dressed immaculately. The sight took my breath away.

Henry shifted nervously. He adjusted the sleeves of his white shirt. Lord Leavesden put a gentle hand on his son's shoulder and whispered what seemed to be encouraging words because Henry's stance relaxed.

I focused on my mage mates, sensing a bit of apprehension but mostly resignation. I had the stark impression both were convinced they were not going to be chosen.

Queen Averly, Princess Liliana, and Lady Amdor strolled down the carpet and reached their husbands. Jorrun, Henry, and Lord Amdor remained standing while everyone else found seats nearby. Then we turned our attention to Aliyah standing alone at the back of the room.

I smiled. I'd always loved weddings and was thrilled that Henry and Aliyah had found happiness. For a moment, my anxiety lessened as I hoped I would be equally content when it was my turn.

High Priest Jorrun motioned to Aliyah, who glided forward. Flower petals descended from the ceiling, landing on top of people's heads and dusting the floor. She and Henry broke into delighted grins, eyes riveted on each other. Happiness radiated from them, filling the room with warmth.

Lord Amdor took his daughter's hand and placed it in Henry's. "I trust you'll take good care of her."

Henry nodded solemnly. "I will."

Lord Amdor kissed Aliyah's cheek, emotion in his expression, then sat beside his wife.

Jorrun recited the wedding prayer, and Henry and Aliyah repeated it. Tears sprang into my eyes at the all-encompassing love I saw. Since the moment I met them, it was easy to see how dedicated they were to each other. I admired their faith in each other. When they slid rings onto each other's fingers, a red ribbon of smoke wrapped itself around their hands and seeped into their skin, signifying their tie to each other. Nonmages used real ribbon.

"Now, seal it with a kiss," the high priest said.

Henry gathered Aliyah into his arms, his lips touching hers in a passionate kiss. When they pulled back, their cheeks were flushed.

With a wide smile, Jorrun said, "I present to you Lord Henry James Sorren and Lady Aliyah Madeline Sorren, husband and wife."

The crowd stood and cheered.

After it went on for a few minutes, Jorrun raised his hand for silence. "Please be seated."

Everyone sat, confusion evident on their faces.

He turned to King Brian. "I believe I have another wedding to perform."

"Indeed," King Brian confirmed. "Lady Isabelle, now returned, must choose between my sons."

I read the surprise on many faces. The chatter increased, but I did my best to ignore it. Andrew and Braidus walked to stand beside Jorrun, their faces a picture of grim acceptance. I shielded my eyes as Haddas, the four Fates, and the four other Gods materialized.

The crowd gasped. "The Gods are here!"

Haddas spoke to King Brian and Jorrun. "We support our own. We have come to witness Isabelle's choice and the ensuing union."

King Brian smiled and held his arms out. "Welcome."

Amora flashed me a delighted grin. "It is time, Isabelle."

"What? No." I held my hands up, terrified.

She flicked her fingers, and I found myself standing at the beginning of the white carpet. People turned in their seats to ogle me, and full-blown panic set in. I wasn't ready. I stepped backward, ready to run, but a nudge at the small of my back propelled me forward. I dug my heels into the carpet. Another prod sent me stumbling forward. The blood drained from my face, and the room swayed.

*"Focus on your bonded, and your answer will be clear,"* Amora whispered in my ear.

My heart beat out of my chest. I trembled all over. I halted and shut my eyes. *How can they do this to me?* I jolted at a touch on my arm.

Joshua's emerald green eyes probed mine. "You've fought so hard for this moment. Don't let fear stop you now. If you're stressed about choosing, you can't go wrong. Both love you more than life itself and will do their utmost to make you happy." He looped his arm through mine to lead me down the aisle. "I suggest you take a hard look at your heart as we walk, see which prince speaks to you more, and choose that one."

I took a breath and exhaled. Joshua was right. "All right."

Joshua's encouragement encircled my heart. My mage mates' resignation turned to a sweet sense of calm. I turned my gaze on them. Braidus wore his signature smirk. Andrew flat-out grinned. I took a step forward and halted, eyes darting between them. I flushed at their desire. I took another step, then stopped. I raised an eyebrow at them, questioning if they really wanted this. They nodded. My heart flooded with their feelings on the matter. I caught impressions of an earlier conversation between them. *Won't do it. Hurts worse the longer she holds on. Help her choose.* They needed this.

I sucked in a breath and exhaled slowly, then opened my heart, inhaling sharply as emotion enveloped me. I let my mind drift back to the conversations and experiences I'd shared with each of them. I remembered my first encounter with Andrew in the woods as he pulled the arrows out of my body. I had fixated on his chiseled face, noticing how focused he appeared, his full lips in a tight line, his bloodied brow furrowed and damp with sweat, his stunning blue eyes darting back and forth in concern.

I had bit my lip. *Gods forbid, he's gorgeous.*

I then thought about the moment I laid eyes on Braidus. His wavy hair—medium-brown streaked with blond—fell a little past his shoulders. His sun-kissed beard was short but well-groomed against his chiseled face. I thought about his straight nose and full lips and the scar above his right eye. He'd worn sturdy clothing that day—a dark-blue, long-sleeve shirt, black pants, and boots that rose to his knees. His hazel eyes had caught mine and penetrated deep into my soul.

Even kidnapped, he had affected me more than I'd cared to admit.

Memories washed over me. My first kiss with Andrew in Silverdens. The way my heart overflowed with love when he proposed to me before the Dregan battle. Discovering the bond and believing it to be a tragedy.

"I don't want it," I had shrieked. "Get it off." I had pulled on the rope, digging my nails into the fibers as if I pierced my heart. I had slid my knife under the couch as Andrew struggled to pry my hand off. Braidus joined the fray. Together, they had restrained me.

"It's unbreakable, Isabelle," Braidus had reminded me. "You're only causing us pain."

"No, I'm not going to be tied to two men. It needs to go. Now."

I didn't know then that the bond would be the best thing that ever happened to me. It made me stronger, braver. I owed my life to it—to Braidus and Andrew.

I thought back to the first moment I knew I loved Braidus.

I had scrambled for a plan as I'd walked toward him. Nothing immediate had come to mind. No words or . . . "Gods forgive me." Not thinking twice, I had cupped his face, pulled him toward me, and kissed him. Surprise had consumed me, then Braidus's soft lips had moved with mine in perfect symphony, a collaboration of two souls playing the same melody.

I remembered when Andrew begged me to take him back after I'd learned of my fate to be a Goddess.

"You stole my heart the moment I discovered you. I thought I could ignore it. I tried. It hurt so Gods-forbidden much. Then I decided that to love you for a little while was better than not loving you at all. If I couldn't make these feelings go away, I should embrace them—enjoy what time I had with you. I've never regretted that decision," Andrew had said. "Loving you made me the happiest man alive."

How Andrew had clung to me as I ascended to be a Goddess.

"I'm not ready."

"You were never going to be ready, love."

I'd put him through agony with near-death experiences, caring for Stefan, loving Braidus, leaving to be a Goddess, and fighting to return to this moment.

"I love you, Isabelle Mirran. I swear it on the Gods a thousand times over. Nothing about us has been fabricated. I love you so Gods-forbidden much it hurts. I need you, Isabelle, more than I need air. I'll take whatever I can get for as long as I can and hope you'll come back to me."

My heart burned. His love was faithful and true. He pushed me to be the best version of myself.

In seconds, his lips had been on mine, seeking, tasting, devouring. His hands had pressed into my back, passion flooding the bond. "Marry me. Right now."

I looked up and discovered I'd stopped in front of Andrew, my feet having moved of their own accord. Joshua released me, and Andrew held out his palm. A silver ring braided with ruby and sapphire vines flashed into existence, our part of the bond.

My heart seized, as Braidus struggled to accept my decision.

Braidus kissed my cheek. "I'm happy for you."

My lower lip trembled as I met his glistening hazel eyes. Tears filled mine and spilled over, my throat tightening. He took my hand and placed it in Andrew's. "It's all right, Isabelle. Marry Andrew and be joyful." He stepped back, allowing Andrew and I to be the center of attention.

I turned with Andrew to face the high priest, my heart breaking into a thousand pieces. I wouldn't take back my choice, however. I wanted Andrew more than I wanted life. But it didn't make giving Braidus up any easier. He carried a large part of my heart and soul. I loved him irrevocably.

Jorrun assessed me through intelligent blue eyes. "You are certain?"

I opened my mouth, but my throat thickened with so much emotion that nothing came out. I tried again and barely managed a whisper. "Yes."

Andrew's eyes searched mine, ready to give me to Braidus if I didn't mean it. "You promise?"

I was addicted to the way he made my heart flame and never wanted to give up the passion between us, not now or in a millennia. I gave him a wobbly smile. "I promise."

Jorrun smiled. "Then let us begin."

I turned to face Andrew, tilting my head back to meet his gaze, his undiluted joy consuming me.

The high priest began the wedding prayer. "Two bodies, two hearts, two souls come together to join as one . . ." The words grew faint as Andrew caressed me with his eyes. His delight at being my chosen brought a grin from me.

I was brought back into focus as Andrew repeated his part. "I, Crown Prince Andrew Brian Jason Sorren, give my body, my heart, and my soul to you, Lady Isabelle Elaine Mirran, to love, treasure, and respect in the eyes of the Gods, our king, our family, friends, and ourselves, from this day forward and into the Realm of Souls." He slid the ring onto my finger.

An identical ring, slightly larger, materialized in my palm. I surprised myself with an even voice as I said my part. "I, Isabelle Elaine Mirran, give my body, my heart, and my soul to you, Crown Prince Andrew Brian Jason Sorren, to love, treasure, and respect in the eyes of the Gods, our king, our family, friends, and ourselves, from this day forward and into the Realm of Souls." I slid the ring onto his finger.

We joined hands. A red ribbon of smoke wrapped itself around our wrists and seeped into our skin, signifying our tie to each other.

Jorrun grinned. "Now, seal it with a kiss."

Andrew swooped me into his arms and crushed my lips with his, setting my heart ablaze. I faintly heard cheers and crying in the background.

Andrew then rested his forehead against mine, breathing heavily. He closed his eyes. "I can't believe it," he whispered.

"Believe it," I whispered.

Jorrun spoke in bright tones. "May I present to you Crown Prince Andrew Brian Jason Sorren and Crown Princess Isabelle Elaine Sorren of Aberron, husband and wife."

*Married at last.*

The Gods took their leave, and the crowds dispersed. The court would return for the Independence Day ball tonight. I caught sight of a few ladies falling into the arms of family and friends, sobbing that Prince Andrew was officially taken.

Now that I'd aligned myself with Andrew, I pulled free. "I need a minute, please."

Andrew, still in complete bliss that I'd chosen him, frowned. "Are you regretting this?"

I locked eyes with him. "No, but I just gave up a huge part of my heart, so I need a minute."

His expression softened, and he nodded. I moved past him and sat on the top step of the dais near the windows, resting my elbows on my knees, my head in my hands. The world around me faded, and I shuddered as I fought to control my emotions and adjust.

Joshua sat beside me. "I thought brides were supposed to be happy."

"I am," I said.

"No, you're not," he said bluntly.

I dropped my hands and straightened up. "I'm secure in my choice."

"But you suffer the sharp sting of losing Braidus." My brother wrapped an arm around my shoulder and pulled me close. "With two bonds, I suppose Andrew could not hope to have a cheerful bride." He kissed my forehead. "Time will ease the wound, little sister."

"I know," I agreed. "I just wish it didn't hurt so much. This should be a day of celebration, and I don't feel like it at all."

Dominic and Falden approached, and Joshua took his leave.

"I heard your room got swamped with presents." Falden grinned at my nod. "Need some help unwrapping?"

I waved my hand flippantly. "Have at it. I'd like my room back in order."

Dominic chuckled. "You're a married woman now. You think Andrew's going to let you return to your room out of his sight and bed?"

I flushed at the implication. "Forgive me for being a bit slow. I've been too preoccupied with choosing and didn't think about it."

Their expressions sobered some. Dominic said, "I do think they pushed this marriage on you a bit too fast, but they did try to make this as quick and painless as possible."

I sighed. "I know."

Falden nudged Dominic. "Come on, let's go open Isabelle's presents."

I rose, knowing I'd spent enough time wallowing. I cast my eyes upward, again enjoying the abundance of flowers.

A warm hand brushed against my shoulder, drawing my hair back. I smelled the woodsy cologne. I shivered involuntarily as Andrew pressed his lips against my neck, his breath hot on my skin. "How long will you stay upset?"

"Indefinitely," I murmured even as I tilted my head to give him better access.

He pulled me back against his chest. He wrapped his arms around my waist, then rested his chin on my shoulder. "Would an apology help?"

"You're not sorry," I said, reading the bond. Andrew was positively euphoric. I'd chosen him, taken his last name as my own. I was his for eternity.

"I could try to be, for you." A desperation to win me over threaded through his bliss. I knew he'd do anything for me—except take back pushing me toward this marriage choice.

"Can I have a moment with Braidus?" I asked.

"All right." He reluctantly let go.

Braidus stood on the dais with his father and Jorrun. Noticing my approach, he stepped down to meet me.

I threw myself at him, engulfing him in the biggest hug I could muster. "I'm sorry." Tears threatened. I wanted him to know I still cared for him, that it hadn't been an easy choice. He mattered to me. He always would.

As Braidus held me tight, I could feel his acceptance. I wondered how he could be so strong when I was not. "It's all right, Isabelle. Andrew would sacrifice his life for you. He is a good choice. I'm grateful you gave me a chance."

When Braidus and I stepped back from each other, Haddas appeared in a bright flash. Seeing what was going on, Andrew hurried to my side and tucked me against him.

Haddas spoke. "Braidus, it's time you found your happiness so you can be a Fate alongside Isabelle and Andrew. You have the second bond." He waved his hand, and an opal mist floated through Braidus. "Your lady will be at the celebration tonight. Amora has been to see her. She is aware she will meet her bonded at the ball."

"Who is she?" Braidus asked.

Haddas smiled conspiratorially. "We enjoy keeping your identities a secret. When you see each other, you'll know."

"Is she good enough for Braidus?" I asked. There was no way I would let him find himself entangled with an unworthy woman.

"Her heart is true," Haddas said. "She will be a good addition." His gaze swept the three of us and then centered on Braidus. "Because you have the option to bond again, I wish to give you the choice to break yours with Isabelle."

Braidus nodded slowly, his expression grim. "I think that would be best since Isabelle has made her choice."

Even though I understood, I stared at Braidus in dismay.

Andrew's gratitude for Braidus raced across my heart. "I am indebted to you," he said to his brother.

Braidus inclined his head in acknowledgment, a soft smile on his lips. His expression softened as he stared at me, both of us fighting through an onslaught of emotions. "We'll still have each other as friends."

"Best friends?" I questioned.

"Best friends," Braidus agreed. Stepping back, he looked at Haddas. "Break the bond."

"As you wish." Haddas flicked his fingers, and our bond, a silver nautical rope entwined with silver, ruby, sapphire, and gold appeared. Haddas made a series of twisting motions with his hand, and the threads of silver and gold unraveled, separating Braidus from me, our portion of the bond disappearing and leaving a single tie between me and Andrew. A sense of emptiness engulfed me. I gripped my chest as my heart adjusted. A sigh of relief escaped Braidus's lips.

"It's done," Haddas said. "I will take my leave." He vanished with a bright flash.

I allowed peace to chase away the remnants of my sadness. Braidus had given me a gift. I could now focus on Andrew without worrying about how my actions affected Braidus. Joy danced across my heart as I envisioned a lifetime of love with my new husband.

# CHAPTER TWENTY-TWO

ALSIN APPROACHED. "IF YOU wouldn't mind coming with me, I have something for you in my room."

Andrew and I followed him out of the throne room. Malsin's healing room had taken on a new level of experimentation, every table covered with papers, bottles, and healing supplies. A pot of yellow liquid bubbled under a small flame, giving off a strong lemon scent.

"You've been busy," I said, taking it all in.

Malsin smiled. "Indeed. I've made several breakthroughs on a cough syrup. I plan to introduce my findings to the Healer's Guild soon." He went to the window and retrieved an orange calendula plant. Affection shone in his eyes. "Happy birthday and warmest congratulations for finding your heart."

I smiled. "Thank you."

Andrew and I stopped by my room to check on Dominic and Falden. They sat amongst a mountain of wrapping paper. Beside them sat empty boxes and a pile of books, clothes, weapons, colored flasks, and more. The sheer monstrosity of it overwhelmed me.

Dominic pointed to a stack near the far wall in white wrapping. "Wedding presents. Those arrived a few minutes after we did."

"We're not touching those," Falden said.

"Take whatever is of interest to you," I told them both.

"We've got to sign some papers for our wedding." Andrew kissed me lightly.

"Send someone by with food," Dominic said. "And some helpers to clear away the boxes and wrapping."

King Brian had the needed document in a folder on the table in the study. Upon entering, we found Henry and Aliyah signing their papers with their parents, King Brian, Queen Averly, and High Priest Jorrun witnessing.

Henry handed the paper to King Brian. "Finished." With a grin, he turned to Aliyah. "You're mine."

She blushed. "Always."

"I was just about to send someone to find you," King Brian said, turning his attention to me and Andrew.

"No need." Andrew reached for the paper signifying our marriage agreement. He quickly signed his name and then handed it to me. "This will be the last time you write Mirran." His smile sent butterflies through my stomach as I wrote my name. "You are now Isabelle Sorren forever, my beautiful, feisty wife."

I flashed him a delighted smile. "I'll take it, dear husband."

Andrew dropped the papers and crushed me to him, his lips firmly on mine. "Say it again," he whispered in between kisses.

"I love you, husband," I whispered.

Andrew groaned, his desire turning the room to a haze.

Henry cleared his throat. "Guys, I'm just as anxious to kiss my wife with abandon, but at least I have the decency to wait till after the ball."

"Preferably without an audience," Aliyah said.

Andrew released me but grabbed my hand. "Let's forgo the ball."

"No," King Brian said. "It won't look favorably on the monarchy if you two aren't there."

"Then we absolutely need to be there," I said.

Andrew cursed. He wanted to hide us away from the world and delve into untold passion, but he relented at my determination. "All right."

Henry laughed at Andrew. "Isabelle is so in charge of your marriage."

Andrew arched a brow. "And Aliyah's not of yours?"

"Conceded," Henry acknowledged.

Before the ball, we enjoyed a private feast with my family. Andrew spent the entire time hand-feeding me to be sure I ate. Three two-tiered cakes completed the meal. A lemon for my birthday, a vanilla with a spiced peach filling for my wedding, and a strawberry cream for Henry and Aliyah.

The sun had nearly descended when we stepped out for the Independence Day ball. With the gardens swarming with nobles in bright attire, I wished I hadn't eaten so much. My stomach rolled as we stood on a raised pavilion.

King Brian magnified his voice and addressed the crowd. "Welcome, all, to our Independence Day celebration ball. I hope you'll enjoy the magnificent gardens, food, music, and dancing. May we take this time to remember my forefather, King Aberron—the man who boldly shaped a disarrayed Fraison into the Aberron we know and love." He raised a glass. "To Aberron Sorren and our independence!"

The crowd cheered and raised their glasses in salute. As the din quieted, King Brian said, "As this is also the day my son and my nephew married their respective brides, I wanted to start this ball a little differently. It has been some time since we had a bonding party."

The court tittered.

"What is a bonding party?" I asked Andrew.

"Mages line up and see if they can discover their Amora bonds," he explained. "It is something kings do when their sons or daughters have found and married their mage mates."

At King Brian's insistence, a small group of young men and women came forward—less than thirty people out of the hundreds of court members in attendance.

King Brian turned to the unmarried men in our family. "Will any of you try?"

Falden shrugged. "Why not?" He joined the men.

Dominic shook his head. "No, thank you."

"Not on my life," Joshua growled.

I sidled up to my brother. "Joshua, you need a good woman." I pushed him down the steps, ignoring his protests. "You have no excuse. Andrew is taken, and Braidus will be soon. You're next."

He eyed me spitefully. "You'll pay for this."

I met his glare. "Shall we set up a time in the training room?"

"Definitely," he agreed, flexing his hands.

I bit back a grin as I retreated. Joshua folded his arms, wearing an intimidating scowl. That didn't stop the ladies on the opposite side from admiring his muscular manliness.

"Are we ready? Excellent." King Brian then proceeded to direct the mages to search for their bonded. Silvery ropes shot out and connected, and six people found their matches.

"Oh!" I gasped in surprise as Joshua bonded with—Amarilla? Sapphire entwined with ruby against a silver setting, connecting their hearts. *Gods forbid.* Amarilla had a love of the finer things in life. Joshua was a hardened commander. How in the Gods were they matches? Wide-eyed, I caught Henry's glance. He shook his head, apparently equally surprised.

Joshua's gaze locked on Amarilla.

She bounced with excitement. "Yes! I got the commander! Those muscles are mine!"

"Oh, Gods."

Just as I was about to apologize for insisting my brother participate, he cracked a smile. I halted.

He approached Amarilla. "Your name?"

She executed a perfect curtsey. "Lady Amarilla Decoyden."

Joshua took her hand in his. "A pleasure."

Amarilla's cheeks flushed bright red, and Joshua smiled.

I backtracked. "That certainly went differently than I imagined."

"Tell me about it," Henry said with a laugh.

Falden jogged back up the steps empty-handed. "My lady isn't here."

"Better luck next time," Dominic said, clapping him on the back.

King Brian motioned for the music to start, and people began moving about. I pulled Andrew with me over to Braidus.

"Have you seen her yet?" I asked.

"No." With a barely concealed frown, he eyed a group of girls sidling their way over.

"Let's look together," I said.

We descended into the gardens, where roses of various shades scented the air. I looped my arms through Braidus's and Andrew's, unwilling to let Braidus be a victim of scheming women. A few people congratulated Andrew and me as we passed. My intent on helping Braidus, Andrew answered for us.

"Perhaps she decided not to come," Braidus said as we made a full turn.

"Amora is pushy," I said. "She will not let the girl run."

As we turned around, Braidus stopped. I followed his gaze. A woman approached, eyes scanning as if searching for someone. She hadn't spotted us yet. She was close to my height and had auburn curls, creamy skin with a smattering of freckles, a pert mouth, a straight but small nose, high cheekbones, and a softly pointed chin. A gorgeous teal dress hugged her willowy figure.

Her eyes caught Braidus's, and she halted, awareness flooding through her as it clearly had Braidus a moment ago. Her small hand went to her mouth, and her eyes widened as if she couldn't fathom this turn of events. I could see now that she had two different eye colors—a vibrant blue on her left and a deep green on her right.

I pulled my arm free from Braidus's and nudged him forward, getting the impression that he knew her from ages ago. I was right when he spoke her name.

"Brielle."

She dropped her hand, recovering enough to extend a curtsy. "My prince." Her voice was soft and sweet.

"Braidus," he corrected her. "It has been some time."

"Thirteen years since we last met," she said evenly.

"Why haven't I seen you?" he asked. Genuine concern laced his words, and I could see he had once cared much for the girl. "Your father?"

"A few years after you were banished, my father died of unexpected heart failure," she explained, nervously gripping her dress. "His wife cast me out. I managed to secure a position in the Healer's Guild to avoid the streets. I've been there ever since, working with the less fortunate. It's been my calling."

"A healer?" Braidus studied her.

She smiled with care. "Yes. My green magic has been my lifeline."

"And now you're here," Braidus whispered.

"You reversed the illegitimate-child laws." Admiration shone in her gaze. "I could not be denied entrance."

I stepped forward and gently laid an arm on Braidus. "Should I leave you here?"

"Forgive me," Braidus spoke quickly. "Isabelle, this is Lady Brielle Courell. We were close friends before my banishment. Her father often brought her along to play in the nursery with me as a child."

"We illegitimates must stick together." Brielle winked at him.

The corners of Braidus's lips curved up. "Quite. Brielle, allow me to introduce my sister-in-law, Crown Princess Isabelle Sorren."

"Your mage mate as well, or are the rumors false?" She focused on me with a healer's gaze. I found I preferred that scrutiny to the jealousy I usually received.

Braidus answered, "She was, but the Creator broke our bond as Isabelle has married Andrew."

"Oh." Her eyes brightened with interest, and then she turned her attention to my husband with a smirk. "Little Prince Andrew all grown up and looking well."

Andrew laughed. "Indeed."

"I find it hard to believe you and I are mage mates," Brielle said to Braidus. She cast her eyes downward, again fidgeting with her dress. "I had always hoped . . . but then you were banished, and I was cast out . . . and I decided it was the imaginings of a foolish girl's heart."

"Would you like to take a walk with me?" Braidus asked suddenly.

Brielle smiled. "I would like that."

Braidus extended his arm, and she looped hers through it. Braidus said over his shoulder at Andrew and me, "Good night. *Pleasant* dreams." He wore his signature smirk as they strolled off into the night.

Andrew grinned at me. "I think Braidus is in good hands."

"You think so?" I asked, trying not to worry.

"As a child, the illegitimate-child laws closed Braidus to himself and others. Facing the same lot, Brielle was a rare exception of true friendship. She and Braidus used to chase me around the nursery. They had much affection for one another." His tone brightened as he led me down the path toward the crowd. "I want to dance with my wife."

In the middle of the dance floor, Andrew held me against him. I rested my head on his chest as we swayed to the soft melody. I couldn't keep from smiling. Though unable to see Andrew's face, I could feel him grinning like a drunken man. The world faded until it was just the two of us under a canopy of stars. I couldn't think of a better place to be.

As the song ended, he swept me into his arms. I threw my head back, laughing. "Hey!"

His eyes blazed with delight and passion, stealing my breath. "You're claimed, *wife*." He clutched me to him with an iron grip. I closed my eyes and snuggled in as he moved through the gardens to the castle doors.

Andrew didn't release me until we'd stepped over the threshold of his room. While he lit a fire, I took in the deep-green and mahogany décor. Like me, Andrew kept his things in order down to the way his pencils lined up, short to tall, on his desk. I suspected organization had been ingrained in him from a very young age.

As I took my slippers off and placed them by the door, Andrew snuck behind me and wrapped his arms around me. "You're tense."

He then lifted me and carried me to his bathroom, where steam rose from the tap as he started a bath. He helped me remove the jewelry from around my neck and wrists and then the pins in my hair. I pulled the earrings free. He set everything on a clean marble countertop.

"Relax. I'll collect you in a little bit." He kissed me lightly, then left the room.

I stared after him, loving his gentleness and need to see me well. I fumbled with the buttons on my dress, grateful Amora had the insight to run them down the side for easy access. The hot water loosened my tense muscles.

As comfortable as I could be, I stepped out of the bath and slid into one of Andrew's green robes. It drowned me, but I found it soothing, perhaps because it smelled like him—cinnamon and woodsy. I started to turn the door handle when it opened and Andrew stood there, his eyes taking me in. He laughed softly. "We'll have to move your things over."

I lifted my arms, my fingertips the only thing visible from beneath the sleeves. "I like it."

He reached for my hand. "Then wear it all you want."

I allowed him to lead me to his sleeping quarters, where he stopped at the door and gathered me into his arms. I tilted my head back to meet his tender gaze. One hand pressed against my back, the other cupped my cheek, and his fingers threaded through my hair. "My soul, my heart, my body are yours."

My heart swelled. So choked with emotion was I that I couldn't speak, but Andrew understood the unspoken words. He pushed the door open, and I followed willingly, losing myself in his liquid-blue eyes.

# CHAPTER TWENTY-THREE

ARM BREATH TICKLED MY neck as I woke to the late-morning sun. Andrew held me to him. I flushed as memories of our night together flashed through my mind. I didn't think there were strong enough words in Fraison to describe how incredible our time had been. Andrew's chest rumbled with soft chuckles as he caught impressions through the bond. I turned around to face him, watching love fill his eyes.

We didn't need to leave Andrew's rooms that day, but I contemplated a future routine. Sword fighting with Joshua in the morning, then sitting with Andrew and Braidus in the study, helping them and King Brian with ruling Aberron. I had a lot of Goddess knowledge they might find useful. Or I could always take an active part in Queen Averly's duties as I, and potentially Brielle, if Braidus ended up with her, would take them over one day.

When I voiced my thoughts to Andrew, he protested. "The prince gets a week—all that ensure- an-heir-protocol stuff."

I laughed at the suggestive hint in his gaze. "We don't have a week. I've got to negotiate with Nistier, Dregaitia, and the Jamaylin Islands. They should be here soon."

Andrew cursed. "I forgot about that."

"Of course you did," I said.

He snuggled close. "Fine, a bit of negotiating, and then we'll resume our week. I'm getting a full seven days one way or another."

The following morning, Andrew and I ventured into the family dining room for breakfast as we'd received notice that King Nickoli, King

Cekaiden, and Prince Jakobe were set to arrive shortly. Henry and Aliyah were absent. Unlike us, they didn't have any pressing engagements.

I focused on my brother. "How are you liking your bond with Amarilla?"

"She keeps me amused," Joshua said with a soft smile.

"How so?" I asked.

"She's half terrified, half exhilarated by me," Joshua explained. "I also think her frivolity is a front to meet the expectations of her parents. There's something keen underneath the layers."

"Interesting," I said.

Andrew spoke over my head to Braidus. "How goes it with Brielle?"

"We've just barely reconnected," he answered, not seeming of a mind to discuss it.

"She is your true bonded," I said, wanting to see him happy. "Perhaps we should invite her to stay at the castle. From what little I heard of your conversation at the ball, it sounds like she doesn't have much in the way of family. She should be a part of ours."

"She is invested in the Healer's Guild," Braidus said. "I am not sure she would be willing to part with it."

I pleaded with my eyes. "Can I ask?"

"Fine," he said grudgingly. Despite no longer sharing a bond with him, I could see I still affected him enough to make it hard for him to say no to me. "We'll take a trip together tomorrow."

"Thank you." I leaned over and gave him a quick hug.

I met with King Nickoli, King Cekaiden, and Prince Jakobe in the study.

"I'm told congratulations are in order." King Cekaiden flicked his eyes at Andrew, then back to me. "You managed to make a choice after all."

"Yes." I smiled. "How is Calliope doing? Is pregnancy treating her well?"

"What do you know of it?" he asked, eyes suddenly sharp.

I smiled coyly. "Oh, very little. Is she hoping for a boy or a girl?"

"Come now, Isabelle," King Cekaiden entreated. "I do not like to dance around words."

"I can't tell much," I told him. "But I do know the child she carries with Timtric will possess her magic."

"You are sure?" he demanded.

I grinned. "Positive. The Gods can check as soon as the heart is formed. I personally blessed Calliope with a healthy pregnancy."

An exultant smile spread across King Cekaiden's lips. "This pleases me greatly."

"I thought it would," I said.

"Mila is expecting as well. I learned just before my departure," King Cekaiden said. "They have been good choices for my sons."

"Then you are doubly blessed," I said.

Talk turned to negotiations. Both kings and Prince Jakobe sought my allegiance should a need arise. We crafted lockets infused with my magic so they could communicate with me quickly. I reiterated my stance on keeping the peace and that I wouldn't kill unnecessarily. Overall, I thought everything went well. They left the following morning.

Early afternoon, Malsin, Andrew, Braidus, and I took a carriage to the Healer's Guild. Reading the anxiety on Braidus's face, I lightly patted his arm, wanting him to know he had my support. Stepping out, I gazed at the massive redbrick building. Green smoke wafted from an open window three levels above us.

Andrew stumbled, a curse escaping his lips. My grip on him tightened as I stopped him from falling. An arrow protruded from his back. "Andrew!" I cried.

"Let's get him inside," Malsin said, taking hold of Andrew's other side.

"I'll stay and see if I can find the culprit," Braidus said.

Together, Malsin and I helped Andrew inside. His face had turned deathly pale. Our arrival caused the healer at the front desk to drop his papers, which scattered across the table and onto the floor.

"Room three," the healer stammered.

"No time," Malsin answered. We helped Andrew to a chair resting against the wall and activated our green magic. "On the count of three." He put his hand on the shaft. "One, two, three." Andrew yelled in pain as

Malsin yanked it out. My insides constricted at the tear in his heart. *Heal,* I ordered Boomer. Green magic penetrated Andrew's body, repairing muscle and tissue. He shut his eyes and groaned as I mended him, the color coming back as I boosted his energy.

He tipped his head back and sighed. "Thank you, love."

Fear still pounding through my heart, I cupped his cheeks in my hands and kissed him fervently. In return, he grabbed my waist and pulled me onto him, responding to my kiss with enthusiasm. Malsin cleared his throat. Oops. My cheeks flushed as I pulled back. I'd forgotten where we were.

Andrew's blue eyes blazed with heat. "Mmm, maybe I should get shot more often."

I lightly slapped his shoulder. "No! Gods, you terrified me."

Andrew sobered. "I admit I was a little scared myself."

Braidus joined us with a scowl on his face. "I couldn't find the perpetrator."

Malsin studied the bloodied arrow. "There's a note attached." He held it out for Braidus to untie from the shaft.

Unfurling the paper, Braidus, read, "'Mages are a menace.'"

"Abominators," Malsin and Andrew growled together.

I cursed. "They don't know when to quit, do they?"

The men shook their heads. My hands curled into fists. How dare they try to kill my husband. I wondered if they'd change their tune if they knew how close to world destruction they had been a few days ago—that if it weren't for the mages, we'd all be dead. My determination lit a fire within me.

"Well, we'll see about that. I'll enlist the Gods' help. They'll be finished before they can say mage."

"Mmm, I'd like to see that," Andrew said, revenge in his eyes.

"Me too," Braidus and Malsin said simultaneously.

Andrew rose and tucked me into his side. We turned our attention to the man at the front desk, who'd been silently watching our interactions with jaw agape.

"Is Lady Brielle available?" Braidus asked.

"Brielle?" the man spluttered. "Of course. Right this way." His chair fell over in his haste to stand.

"Steady there," Malsin said to the nervous young man. To us, he said, "I'll leave you to it," and strode off.

We entered a room with light-green walls and sparse furniture. Brielle stood in front of a line of mothers and young children ranging from newborn to twelve. Judging by their patched, worn clothing, I suspected they had to be from one of the poorer districts.

"Crown Princes Andrew and Braidus Sorren and Crown Princess Isabelle Sorren to see you, Brielle," Nervous Man announced.

Surprise flitted across Brielle's face. The mothers eyed us with shock as they clutched their children to them. I doubted they'd ever come this close to royalty.

"What a surprise," Brielle said to us. Her eyes rested on Andrew with concern, no doubt noting the blood on the back of his shirt. "What happened?"

"Abominators," Andrew said.

"Can I help?" I gestured to the line of people. "I have more green magic than I know what to do with."

Brielle smiled. "We could always use more helpers."

"Then call on me anytime. I would love to be of assistance." I activated my magic.

Brielle reorganized the line, and I began seeing to the needs of women and children. Despite my initial hesitance at the fear in their eyes, I found joy in using my magic for a good cause. When the last family left, I turned to Brielle to voice an idea. "I'd like to come twice a month and offer my green magic to anyone who needs it, free of charge."

"You're going to put us healers out of business." Brielle grinned. "It is a novel plan. I'll highly endorse it." She assessed the three of us, her gaze lingering on Braidus. "So, what brings you here?"

"How would you feel about moving into the castle?" I asked.

She laughed. "You're joking, right?"

"Not at all," I answered. "I'm short on women friends."

"What makes you think we'll be friends?" she asked slowly.

"We share the same interests—healing, helping the less fortunate—and Braidus." I grinned at my former mage mate.

He chuckled.

Brielle laughed and said to Braidus, "I like her. She's not at all like those twittering snobs I've come to expect from the court."

Braidus flashed his signature smirk. "Isabelle is unique, to be sure. She captured my heart the moment I set my eyes on her."

"She snares hearts by the dozen whether she means to or not." Andrew wrapped his arms around me and placed a soft kiss on my cheek. His joy at getting me as his wife swelled through the bond.

I rolled my eyes despite being unable to keep a smile off my face. "We're not here to list my attributes. Happiness is at stake."

Brielle's eyes twinkled. "Oh, dear, this must be very grave."

I turned to Braidus. "Brielle is your equal. Ask her to court and then stay at the castle. Please."

"You don't think you're pushing it?" Braidus asked.

I shrugged. "It's revenge."

"For what?" Andrew and Braidus asked.

I lifted my chin. "For pushing me to choose between you two, then shoving me into a wedding."

"You were ready, love," Andrew said.

I nodded. "But it still hurts that I had to give Braidus up and that our bond is no more. I love him."

"Isabelle," Braidus sighed my name, no doubt struggling with the emotions my words brought up.

I rubbed my forehead, trying to stay calm. "What's done is done. I'm obviously not going to act on my feelings, and I trust Braidus to do the same. I am, however, grateful that my choice didn't leave him without another chance at true love. After everything I've seen and experienced in my life here, and in my short time as a Goddess, I think it's foolish not to jump at the chance of something wonderful." My gaze darted to Brielle and Braidus. "You two know you are true mage mates, predestined to be with each other. Forget the song and dance most people engage in before deciding to court. Joy is fleeting. Seize it while you can."

My heart expanded with the pride I felt from Andrew and the admiration I read on Braidus's face.

I saw respect in Brielle's demeanor. "Her passion is addictive," she said.

"Very," they said.

Braidus faced Brielle, his expression uncertain. "Do you think you could find it in your heart to love me again?"

Her features softened. Tentatively, she reached out a hand and smoothed the locks of Braidus's hair. "Oh, Braidus, I never stopped."

Within the week, Brielle moved into the castle. "It'll be a relief to be out from under Mr. Feder, my lecherous landlord." She made a face. "The threat of killing all pleasure to his loins with my magic has been the only thing saving me from his advances."

"You're under my protection now," Braidus said firmly. "No one would dare touch you."

Tears glistened in her eyes as she gazed adoringly at Braidus.

Unwilling to part with the Healer's Guild, Brielle took a carriage to work every morning and returned in time for the family dinner. Knowing she was Braidus's true bond, everyone welcomed her with open arms, though it was clear she struggled with becoming a part of my unconventional family.

"I've been the red-hair, mismatched-eyes pariah for so long," she confessed to me one night. "My noble upbringing made me too good for the lower classes, but my illegitimate status cast me from high society. I've spent a good number of years navigating a slew of bad romances. Do you know how many men ask me to court so they can have a caretaker at their disposal? Boys trying to avoid healer costs if they smolder at me. I'm not opposed to a free healing for a good cause, but I have to eat."

"Social status shouldn't mean so much," I told her. "I've been considered a noble my whole life, but I grew up in a small farming community. People should be judged for their deeds and not their birth or upbringing."

Brielle smiled. "Indeed."

Not long after, Brielle and Braidus decided to enact the bond—silver and gold threads melding with emerald and silver. Braidus worked closely with Malsin as he adjusted to the emotions of a different woman.

"Brielle is water to your fire," Braidus said to me. "She can be a force or a soothing calm when she desires."

"Sounds like she has better control over her emotions than I do," I answered.

He smiled. "She is very organized."

"You're saying I'm not?" I widened my eyes, pretending to be insulted.

Braidus gave me an honest answer. "Your appearance is, but your heart is messy. You feel everything deeply. It's both attractive and a curse."

I patted him on the shoulder. "Blame Haldren for meddling with me."

True to my word, I called upon the Gods for help concerning the Abominators. Haldren transported down to meet with me.

"Something has to be done!" I threw my hands up, exasperated. "Joshua is at his wits end trying to catch the sneaky rats. I literally had my soul ripped to save the world and keep my family, and now, when happiness is finally within my reach, these stupid Abominators try to kill my husband. I won't stand for it."

"Leave it to us," Haldren said, a dangerous glint in his eye. I didn't dare ask what he had in mind.

I woke the following morning to a heavy knock on my door. I hurriedly threw on a robe to answer it. Joshua stood in front of me, out of breath. "You need to see this."

After I roused Andrew out of bed, we dressed and met up with the rest of my family in the hall, then followed Joshua down to the front entry and outside. A hundred or so people sat on the ground, bound hand and foot with copper-hued rope, gags over their mouths so they couldn't talk. Each had been forced to hold a small sign that read "Abominator" and their rank in the operation.

We couldn't help but laugh. "Thank you, Gods," I said in appreciation.

Our family dinners grew in number with the addition of Aliyah, Brielle, and frequently Amarilla. Queen Averly beamed. "I'm getting so many daughters. This is wonderful."

Much to Joshua's chagrin, Amarilla's parents had demanded a wedding out of him during the Independence Day ball when they had only been acquainted a few minutes.

"I've never met anyone more desperate to claim a connection to royalty," Joshua later said. "They'd willingly send Amarilla into a cave of bears if it meant she'd claim a prize."

A bright flash and a scroll tied with red ribbon landed in my lap. I pulled the string and unrolled it.

"What is it?" Henry asked.

I scanned it. "It's the prophecy about me." I moved dishes out of the way and put it on the table. Above the words, I recognized Haldren's writing. *Fulfilled.* "It's been fulfilled."

"Read it out loud, please," King Brian asked.

**"Find a girl beautiful and fair,**
**Preordained to a fate not chosen.**
**At birth, a mark shall be imprinted.**
**A spiraled red sun,**
**a gift from the Gods as one.**
**Given powers beyond measure,**
**two will seek to make her heir.**
**Her allegiance to one will be the deciding destiny**
**in the struggle for power over the kingdom of Aberron.**
**Heed the warning now given:**
**without her presence in the fight,**
**both will lose to a mightier foe."**

"The first part is pretty obvious," Joshua said. "Preordained to a fate not chosen was your fate to be a goddess."

"Two will seek to make her heir," Braidus said, looking over my shoulder. "It could've meant me and Andrew or maybe something bigger."

"You and Andrew is a good thought, but what if it's the Aberron kingdom and Haldren?" I mused. "Haldren made me heir to his role as Goddess over Gods and the Aberron kingdom sought to marry me to a prince and become heir to the queen."

"You're allegiance to one will be the deciding destiny in the struggle for power over the kingdom of Aberron." Andrew looked at me. "Explain that one."

I kept my eyes on the paper. "I think the struggle of power is getting the illegitimate-child laws reversed and Braidus and Andrew becoming kings. If I had devoted myself to the Gods, I doubt I would have challenged Isaac to remove his curse on King Brian and Braidus and right the wrong. I would have completely ignored you like Isaac wanted."

Henry stood behind me, hands on my shoulders, as he read, "Without her presence in the fight, both will lose to a mightier foe."

"Isaac," we all said at once.

"And thus it is fulfilled," Braidus said.

I rolled it back up and tied the ribbon. "Fate conquered."

# EPILOGUE

*IFTY-SEVEN YEARS LATER*
Having officially become a Fate over Fates, I stood in a dark, cobblestone tunnel before the golden gates of the Realm of Souls, nerves swirling in my stomach. I took a breath and exhaled slowly, trying to calm myself. Andrew threaded his fingers through mine, his eyes caressing me with loving affection. Braidus enclosed my other hand in his and squeezed, offering silent encouragement. I offered him and Brielle, who stood on the other side of him, warm smiles. "Ready?"

"Ready," Andrew, Braidus, and Brielle echoed.

Pulling my hands free, I flicked my fingers at the gates, which swung open at my command. The four of us walked into the light and found ourselves standing in a white stone courtyard with a bright clear sky overhead and surrounded by pink, blossoming trees and flowerbeds bursting with color. Butterflies and bees flitted from one flower to the next. A flock of red birds sang sweetly in the branches above our heads. The beauty astounded me.

Ada, Cassius, Eli, and Emory, the four Fates now under us, greeted us with eager grins.

"Welcome to the Realm of Souls," Cassius said jovially. "We've prepared a present for you."

The four stepped off to the side, revealing a small gathering behind them.

"Oh!" My hand flew to my mouth as I gazed at my loved ones smiling at us. I saw my three sets of parents: Anne and Daniel, Nathan and Adel, and King Brian and Queen Averly. There was also Stefan, Malsin, and Falden—taken from us sooner than we expected. Additionally, there were a few others I hadn't known during my life in Aberron—a woman with blonde hair and hazel eyes whom I suspected to be Braidus's mother, Hannah, and another woman with raven hair and purple eyes, Braidus's first wife, Kiella. Beside Kiella stood a tall, auburn-haired man and a dark-haired woman. Both bore a resemblance to Brielle.

Tears of joy spilled down my cheeks, my heart bursting with joy. "Group hug!" Opening my arms wide, I barreled straight into my family, reunited at last.

## THE END

# Note to the Reader

I really appreciate the time you took to read Fate Conquered; I am thrilled you chose to add it to your home library. If you enjoyed reading this book, it would mean the world to me if you would do two things for me.

1. Share on social media or tell your friends about my books.

2. Leave an honest review by simply visiting my website:

www.ScribbledReads.com
click on the series,
click on the book you read, and
click the "Write a review" button,
or email me your review Tara@ScribbledReads.com

Thank you. Your reviews, and support help me to write more new worlds scribbled in ink!

# ABOUT THE AUTHOR

Tara Lytle is the talented author behind the captivating Fate Series, and enthralling Matching Series. She draws inspiration from her love of clean young adult fantasy and paranormal romance. With a steaming cup of hot chocolate, her Spotify playlist, and an open word document, she embarks on crafting worlds where love, adventure, and epic fantasy intertwine. Tara Lytle's passion for the genre fuels her creativity, resulting in two completed series in the last three years and more novels on the horizon. If you're seeking enchanting tales that transport you to new realms, her books are a delightful choice! Visit: www.ScribbledReads.com

# OTHER NOVELS BY AUTHOR TARA LYTLE

## THE FATE SERIES

FATE NOT CHOSEN
FATE CHALLENGED
FATE CONQUERED

## THE MATCHING SERIES

MATCHING FEATHERS
MATCHING FOXES
MATCHING FIRE

www.ingramcontent.com/pod-product-compliance
Lightning Source LLC
Chambersburg PA
CBHW061108310726
48974CB00002B/443